THE LEGACY

Also by Evelyn Anthony

ALBATROSS
THE ASSASSIN
THE AVENUE OF THE DEAD
THE COMPANY OF SAINTS
THE DEFECTOR
THE GRAVE OF TRUTH
THE HOUSE OF VANDEKAR
THE LEGEND
MALASPIGA EXIT
NO ENEMY BUT TIME
THE OCCUPYING POWER
THE PERSIAN RANDOM
THE POELLENBERG INHERITANCE
THE RENDEZVOUS
THE RETURN
THE SILVER FALCON
VOICES ON THE WIND
THE SCARLET THREAD
THE RELIC
THE DOLL'S HOUSE
EXPOSURE
BLOODSTONES

EVELYN ANTHONY

The LEGACY

BANTAM PRESS

LONDON · NEW YORK · TORONTO · SYDNEY · AUCKLAND

TRANSWORLD PUBLISHERS LTD
61–63 Uxbridge Road, London W5 5SA

TRANSWORLD PUBLISHERS (AUSTRALIA) PTY LTD
15–25 Helles Avenue, Moorebank, NSW 2170

TRANSWORLD PUBLISHERS (NZ) LTD
3 William Pickering Drive, Albany, Auckland

Published 1997 by Bantam Press
a division of Transworld Publishers Ltd

A catalogue record for this book is available
from the British Library.

ISBN 0593 03659X

Typeset in 11½/13pt Sabon by
Hewer Text Composition Services, Edinburgh.
Printed in Great Britain by
Mackays of Chatham PLC, Chatham, Kent.

To Caradoc King and to everyone at A. P. Watt. Friends and agents for over forty wonderful years.

I

Humfrey Stone had not gone to the funeral. He had got to know Richard Farrington very well in the six months before he died, but he didn't feel it was appropriate to go to the little Norman church. Personally he hated the idea of burial, but Farrington was old-fashioned; he had rejected cremation and chosen to be buried with his ancestors in the graveyard on the hill. Humfrey supposed that if you had as many ancestors as that, it made some kind of sense. He didn't like the house, but the library where he waited was the least intimidating of the public rooms. It had a bookish smell of leather and paper and a hint of mustiness. The armchairs were scuffed leather, deep and comfortable, and there were none of the Farringtons watching him from the walls; just books, and over the big open fireplace, a large, seventeenth-century map of the house and its parkland. The cartographer had enjoyed himself; he'd painted fish leaping out of the lake on the south-east, and oversized deer peering out of the Home Wood to the north.

Stone had first met Richard Farrington in his office. He wasn't typical of the firm's clients. Harvey & Stone dealt with the mega-rich, giant corporations, estates worth millions. Farrington had been taken on as a favour. One of the mega-rich was a friend of his, and he had gently tweaked Humfrey's uncle by the arm. Ruben Stone was a senior partner, and if he said, 'take a case', it was taken. Nobody argued with Ruben. Humfrey recalled that afternoon six months ago; the tall good-looking man in late middle age coming into his office, shaking hands, sitting down and saying with alarming directness, 'It's good of you to see me so quickly. Time, I'm afraid, is not on my side. I have only a few months to live.' An invitation to lunch followed. 'I want you to see RussMore,' Farrington said, 'then you'll understand why I'm doing this.'

Lincolnshire was flat uninspiring country, remote and secretive. Humfrey had never been to that part of England before. It didn't appeal to him. He liked the rolling hills and cosy villages of Sussex, with the hint of sea salt on the wind. The house was hidden in a dip, and it sprang on him as he rounded a sweep of drive. Red brick, gables, a slim tower crowned with a copper dome, windows that sparkled in the sunlight, and a great central window rising to the height of the first floor, glowing with stained glass. RussMore. The name hadn't prepared him for the size and grandeur of the house. Farrington had given him a pamphlet: *The history of RussMore and the Farringtons*. He'd glanced at it later. Built in 1568 by Roger Farrington, a rich London merchant who had married a Lincolnshire heiress . . . It was all very alien to Humfrey Stone. His past and a whole generation of his family had vanished in the gas chambers of Auschwitz.

There was a movement, and he turned. He'd forgotten he wasn't alone. A man with white-blond hair was putting a book back behind its wire grill.

'Found something interesting, Rolf?'

His voice was disapproving. He thought it unethical to pry into someone else's books or touch their property when they weren't there. The blonde man shrugged. He was younger than

Stone, taller, and with the ice-blue eyes of the far northern countries.

'Not really. I prefer documents to books. How long does it take to bury people in this country?'

Rolf Wallberg was one of Ruben Stone's protégés; a lawyer in Stockholm who was spending some months with a top London firm to gain experience of English law. Like most Scandinavians, he spoke perfect English and German and excellent French. He was clever, quick to learn and with a shrewd mind that he concealed behind a mocking attitude. He didn't pretend to like England or the English, and Humfrey Stone didn't like him. But again, nobody argued with Ruben Stone. He looked at his watch.

'They must have come back by now. I hope war hasn't broken out before they even know what's in the will.'

'If I was the son I'd fight,' Rolf remarked. 'It's the fault of these crazy English laws on inheritance. In Sweden all children are equal; there's no eldest son syndrome.'

Stone glanced at him. 'You've read the papers but you haven't met the Farringtons,' he said. 'I have, and I've read that son's letters to his father. Don't be too free with your judgements till this afternoon is over.' The Swede smiled. He knew he had riled Humfrey Stone. He'd got himself emotionally involved with personalities – a great mistake. 'It has the makings of good Scandinavian theatre. Hate and greed and passion over a woman and a house. A second wife . . . and a Swede. Ibsen couldn't have done better.'

Stone interrupted quickly. 'Someone's coming. You'd better sit over there.'

'So I can observe the drama,' Rolf said lightly. A long case clock began to chime three. Humfrey Stone liked clocks. It must be worth a fortune, like everything else in the house. He'd known families fall out over a chest of drawers; there was a lot to fight over here. War was the operative word for what was coming. The door opened and the housekeeper looked round.

'Mr Stone? Mrs Farrington says do you really want her to bring Lindy?'

'Just for the first part; it won't take long,' he said. 'Are the family coming? I do have an appointment in London at six o'clock.'

'They are on their way. She asked me to apologize for keeping you waiting.' The door closed. From his place in the background, Rolf Wallberg said sharply, 'Is the child necessary? She's only eleven!'

'It's in the will,' Stone said. 'There are things her father wanted her to hear.' There was a silence then. Stone pulled out a chair and placed it before the fireplace. He sat down, and as he did so, the door suddenly opened wide and Rolf saw Christina Farrington, holding her daughter by the hand.

The day of Richard Farrington's funeral was warm, a lovely midsummer afternoon, with a light breeze ruffling the tops of the oak trees lining the pathway from the house to the church. It had been the same time of year, almost to the day, twelve years ago, when Christina met him in the Hagaparken in Stockholm. Sitting very still in the musty gloom of the Norman church, waiting for her husband's coffin, the past and the present kept merging. Such a small decision, such a trivial impulse, to spend her free lunchtime in the park on a lovely day, instead of eating in a crowded café close to her office. And what consequences had flowed from it; completely changing her life, bringing her to a remote country church in Lincolnshire, a widow after twelve years of marriage. Hagaparken was crowded that day, couples strolled hand in hand, and most of the seats by the lake were full. She found a place and sat down, stretching in the warm sunshine. She had bought a bag of apples and she bit into one, tasting the crisp fruit and the clean juice. Swans sailed past, some waddled up out of the water, ungainly as beached galleons, hissing for titbits. She hadn't even noticed the man sitting on the seat beside her. Her mind was full of unhappy thoughts about another man, the one who had just left her a note at her office to say he was going to Finland and didn't know when he'd be back. She threw a piece of apple into the water, but the majestic bird rejected it.

'They are beautiful, aren't they? So long as they don't go

on dry land.' She turned in surprise; he'd spoken in English. And seeing him she knew that, of course, he was English. Blazer, tie, panama hat with a red and blue ribbon round it; no Swede would have dressed like that in the summer heat. The type wasn't unfamiliar, just quaint; she used to see them in London when she was studying there: remote, quaint, from another planet. He had warm brown eyes and he smiled at her. 'Out of their element, they're just ugly. But that's true of most things. Do you mind if I talk to you? I don't want to be a nuisance.'

'No, of course I don't. I love swans; as you say, so long as they stay on the water. I like birds anyway.'

'We have a lot of birds at home,' he said. 'Swans, ducks, some geese.'

'That must be nice,' Christina said. 'Do you live on a farm?' He shook his head; took off the panama and laid it on his knee. He had thick brown hair with a little grey in it. Again he smiled.

'No, not quite a farm. You're sure you don't mind chatting for a few minutes? I find Swedish people so open and friendly. It's my first visit and I know now why people call Stockholm the Venice of the north. It's really beautiful.'

'Thank you.' Christina decided she liked him. 'You're saying all the right things. Are you on holiday or business?'

'Not business, not really a holiday. I don't know what you'd call it. I came here on a cruise; one of those package trips that sail round the coasts of Scandinavia, stopping a day or two at the main cities. There was a lunch and guided tour of the Vasa Warship Museum arranged for today, so I decided to escape and explore the city on my own. I've got very bored with my fellow passengers.' Christina looked at him.

'Don't you like people?' Her directness surprised him.

'I like people I like, but not people for the sake of people. I'm enjoying this much more than eating smorgasbord with two large American ladies who never stop talking. I wanted my own company for a change.'

She shrugged. 'If you feel like that, why come on a package cruise?'

'I've been asking myself that question ever since it started.'

'If I wasn't enjoying it, I'd go home,' Christina said firmly. 'Holidays are supposed to be fun. But I suppose you'd lose your money; those cruises are very expensive.' She put the apple core into the bag and dropped it into a litter bin close by. He told her afterwards that London was treated like a rubbish tip. Swedes were proud of their city; nobody threw litter around.

'Where do you go for your holidays?' he asked.

'Skiing mostly, but I went to Spain last year with some friends. I'd been looking forward to it all winter.' She laughed. 'It was terrible! I got sick with the food and my boyfriend went off with one of the other girls . . . So I know how it feels. Next time I'll go to France. Do you know France?'

'Paris and the south: Cannes and Nice,' he said. 'We never travelled anywhere else.' We. She noticed it. 'You're married?' He should have resented the intrusive question, but there was a frank innocence about her that made him answer. 'I was – my wife is dead.'

'Oh, I'm sorry. A long time?' He shook his head.

'No, not long at all.' Christina felt embarrassed. Poor man; all alone. She blushed.

'I'm afraid I've asked too many questions, and now I've got to go; I have to get back to my office.' He stood up with her. He was very tall; he looked down at her even though she stood five feet nine without shoes. She noticed that he had a good body, lean and well proportioned. There were a lot of years between them, but he was attractive.

'And what do you do in your office?' he asked.

'I design textiles. There are four of us and we've set up our own company. I studied three years in London at Chelsea Art School. We're doing really well. I love it.'

'You look happy,' he said.

'Not really,' she said it simply. 'My man has just left me. Talking to you has helped; I forgot all about him.'

'He must be very stupid,' he said. 'Could I walk to your office with you? Would you mind?'

'No, but you'll have to come on the bus. It's about twenty minutes from here.'

He held out his hand. 'I'm Richard Farrington. And I like buses.'

She smiled. 'Hello, I'm Christina Nordohl.' They shook hands. It was so formal, so English. When they reached her office building she stopped and pointed out a small nameplate. 'There – Nordohl, Eleman, Design Consultants. That's us.'

'I'm impressed,' he said. 'Are you the senior partner?'

'No, that's my brother. He put up the money. He doesn't like me being late; so goodbye, and I hope the holiday gets better.'

'I doubt it,' he answered. 'Look, we don't sail until tomorrow. I've enjoyed meeting you so much. Would you have dinner with me tonight? Please say yes.'

There was no Jan to claim her that evening. 'Why not? Thank you – I finish work at six.'

'Do you like the Hotel Diplomat – it's supposed to be very good food?'

'I've never been there – too expensive. It sounds great.'

'I'll pick you up at six then.' He took off his hat to her, then walked away.

They had dinner that night in Stockholm and he never rejoined the cruise. When he did go back to England, she came with him as his wife.

It had been a strange courtship. Again, past and present overlapped in her mind, the solemn music in the church seemed to fade with its sad implications; a popular Swedish song hummed in her memory. Dinners, lunches, where they lingered too long and she had had to run back to her office. Trips to the countryside, long walks at weekends. And all the time they talked. Englishmen were supposed to be silent and reserved; Englishmen of his age and social class, at least. This one certainly wasn't. At dinner that first night, he had looked at her quite solemnly and said, 'As I told you, I'm a widower and I'm quite lonely. It's sweet of you to come out this evening; I'll try not to bore you to death.' And Christina had said simply, 'I don't think you could ever be boring. When did your wife die?'

'Three months ago.' He ordered champagne. 'If that suits you . . . ?'

'I love it; I only get to drink it when someone gets married . . . Was she ill for a long time?'

'She wasn't ill. At least I couldn't accept that drug addiction was an illness. She didn't have to take heroin – she chose to, in the first place. I can't see something like that in the same terms as someone getting cancer . . . You don't agree, I can see that.'

Christina shook her head. 'No, I don't, but then I've never had to cope with it. I'm sorry, I've no right to make judgements.'

He smiled briefly. 'Everybody else did. She'd come back from the latest clinic . . . there was always some new miracle cure on offer, and I really thought it might have worked. She was normal and well; I saw flashes of her old self.' He paused and half finished the glass of champagne.

'Don't go on,' she said quickly, 'it's upsetting you; I shouldn't have asked. Tell me about it another time.'

'No,' Richard Farrington said firmly, 'I want to tell you about it now. It's best to be honest. When I came home that evening, I knew at once. She had that look in her eye. I accused her and she denied it; she always denied it. Lying had become like breathing. I'd lived for twenty years without trust and, for a long time, without hope. We have two sons, you see, and I suppose I was going on for their sake. That night we had a row; I said I'd get a divorce and she could dope herself to death if she liked. I'd had enough. I meant it, Christina.' He had used her name for the first time. 'Alan and James were nearly grown up . . . I couldn't take any more. She got up, I can see her doing it, and poured herself half a glass of neat gin. She knew that it drove me crazy when she got drunk as well. "If you leave me," she said, "I'll make you sell the house."'

He paused. Christina didn't know what to say. She sipped her champagne; it tasted sour.

'I walked out,' he said. 'I was so angry, I wanted to hit her. I went upstairs and the next morning she was found in our swimming-pool. She'd gone for a swim, lost consciousness and drowned.' There was silence between them. Christina remembered that silence, remembered a couple passing their table, recognizing her and smiling. Suddenly he had said, 'I've wrecked the evening, haven't I? I don't know what the hell came over me to pour all that out to you. You poor thing, I'm so sorry. Would you like me to take you home?'

He looked so vulnerable suddenly that she reached over and held his hand. She had loved her father and brother, and she had no inhibitions about showing any man affection. He had looked down at their hands in surprise and, for a moment, gripped hers hard and then let go.

'Thank you for telling me, Richard.' She hadn't used his name before either. 'I don't want to go home. I'm hungry and I want dinner.'

He told her afterwards that he hadn't known whether to laugh or cry at that moment. 'You had this marvellous smile,' he said. 'Full of warmth. I'm sure that's when I fell in love with you . . .'

They hadn't talked about it again. Not until he asked her to marry him three weeks later. He had suggested they meet at Hagaparken, to celebrate that first meeting.

Christina had taken him home one weekend; her mother liked him; her brother was more wary. 'Look, if he's helping you to get over Jan, that's fine, but don't get too involved, Christa . . . You pick him up in the park, he takes you out a few times and you go to bed. OK, but don't fool yourself it's love . . .' But it was, and she knew it. It was very sexual between them, but it was more. They had a bond of tenderness which was quite new to her; they took care of each other in little ways. There had been three serious lovers in her life before Richard Farrington. Young men; lusty and self-centred, the first two, then the last one: sensitive, demanding and completely unreliable, Jan. Jan had made her miserable, while insisting that all he wanted in the world was to make her happy. She had told Richard about him with her usual honesty.

'He was a pig to me,' she said, 'an egotistical pig. We had just broken up when I met you. Thank God I went to eat apples in the park that day!'

They sat on a different bench; the original one was occupied by two Japanese tourists studying a map of the city.

'You look very happy,' she told him.

'I am,' he said. 'I'm always happy when I'm with you. And I've had a very good morning!' He did look happy, but also excited.

'What have you been doing?'

'Two things; let me tell you about the unimportant one first. I collect old manuscripts and I found a real treasure in a dealer's shop today. I just passed by and went in, and there it was, with a lot of quite inferior stuff. I couldn't believe my luck, darling.'

'What sort of manuscript was it?' she asked.

He grinned at her. 'Would you understand if I told you?'

She laughed. 'No, of course I wouldn't. Was it very expensive?'

'Why do you worry about me spending money? I've told you. I'm not poor.'

'Maybe, but I'm not rich and I have to earn what I spend. So what else did you do? What's the important thing, then?'

'Our picnic,' he announced. 'I wanted it to be special. After all, we've known each other three whole weeks. And because I know how much you like them, let's start with some apples.' He opened the bag; it came from Lundgren's, one of the best delicatessen stores in the Old City. 'If you look among the apples, you might find something else.'

'A present? I love presents.' She had scrabbled among the fruit like an excited child. She knew it was a ring by the box. 'Richard?' She had looked up at him, 'What have you been doing? You've been spending money again!' She opened the box.

'Oh, darling . . . It's lovely . . . Where did you find it?' It was an apple made of rubies set into a plain gold band. Then she had paused before trying it on. 'It's not a farewell present, is it?' It was only a few weeks since Jan had left her with only a brief note as a memento.

'No,' Richard Farrington had said gently. 'Unless you say

you won't marry me. Third finger left hand . . . that's the British custom.'

She had looked directly at him then and slowly fitted the ring on her finger. 'It's too big,' she said, 'but we can get it altered.'

They didn't go out to celebrate that night; they spent the evening in her flat. He had often said how much he liked it; simple furnishings, big windows, a light easy place to live.

'There are two big disadvantages, apart from me,' he said. Christina wriggled closer and nuzzled his neck. She wanted to make love; she felt voluptuous and light-headed with happiness.

'What could be bigger than you?' she whispered and giggled.

'Your new home. Darling, if you don't stop doing that, I won't show you the photograph.'

She sat up. 'Show me then.' He passed a Polaroid to her. She stared at it.

'Oh my God,' she said. 'You live there?'

'Yes, I live there. Is it a terrible shock to you?'

'It's nearly as big as Drottningholm,' which was the King of Sweden's palace. 'Richard, you really live there – it's not one of your silly jokes?'

'No, no joke. My family have lived there for more than four hundred years. Are you going to give back the ring?'

'Am I hell!' Christina had grabbed him round the neck and nipped his ear. 'So what's the second of your very big disadvantages?'

'My eldest son, Alan.' He moved her away from him. 'He loved his mother. He'll be very difficult with you, darling. He is very difficult, anyway. I should have mentioned this before but, to be honest, I haven't even thought about him; I've just been too happy.'

'I'll make friends with him,' she had promised. 'I'll do my best to make him like me.' Twelve years later he sat behind her in the church, and she could feel his hatred burning like a torch.

The music changed to the anthem, and they stood up and

turned as the coffin came up the nave. The girl holding her hand was as dark as Christina was fair; a tall slight child with her mother's bright-blue eyes. Tears were spilling down her cheeks.

'It's Daddy,' she whispered. 'Mum, I can't bear it . . .'

Christina slipped an arm around her shoulders. 'It's all right, darling. This isn't him any more. He's in God's hands; he's happy and watching over us.' She wasn't religious herself, but she had brought up her daughter in the Catholic faith. She was a Farrington, and they had stayed true to their Church for over four centuries. It gave Belinda comfort to believe that her father was in heaven. Christina only wished she could have believed it, too. They had been so close, the father and daughter. He had adored her as a baby, doted on her through childhood, and become her mentor and friend. And she had worshipped him. Christina had tried to persuade her not to come to the funeral, but to say goodbye to him lying peacefully in his bed at home, and so remember him, but Belinda had insisted that she wanted to be there, to be close to him up to the last moment. Christina put her arm around her as the service began. They had each other now and the memory of his love to strengthen them.

His son, Alan, had refused to join them in the pew. He and his wife sat immediately behind, bringing their animosity into public view. The younger son, James, was with them. He wasn't an enemy but a weak neutral, unable to withstand the powerful personality of his elder brother. There would be no help from him. He lived and worked in America and had only come to RussMore a dozen times in as many years. He had always seemed ill at ease and glad to get away. Duty visits, Richard used to call them bitterly.

'I wonder why he bothers . . .' There had been a lot of pain as well as happiness, and the author of it raised his voice loudly in the final hymn. The priest gave the blessing. The coffin was carried slowly down the aisle and out towards the graveyard. The church itself was Anglican, but there had been shared services between the two faiths for some years. Christina moved slowly forward with Belinda beside her. She gestured towards her stepsons. 'Alan, James . . .' They walked ahead of her without a word. She was surprised to see that James had been crying. For a moment Alan Farrington had stared her in the eye, and it conveyed as much insult as if he had filled his mouth and spat. Hatred, contempt and a horrible gleam of triumph; it was all in that charged look, before he swung away and strode on out of the church. At the graveside they stood well apart. Christina had a sudden sense of isolation. Nobody liked to intrude; she was left with her child and her enemies.

There was a whisper and she started; it was Alan's wife, Fay. 'How could you bring a child to a funeral like this . . . It's just ghoulish. Poor little thing!'

'Lindy wanted to come,' Christina said. 'She loved him. Which is more than any of you did.' She turned her back. Fay Farrington then stepped back beside her husband. She had struck her blow and she was satisfied; she hoped it had hurt. If anything could touch that calculating bitch . . . The way up to the house was a short walk between an avenue of massive oak trees. Mother and daughter went on alone. Tea was laid out for their friends and the representatives of the country organizations. Richard had been a magistrate and president of various associations and charities; they would be entertained and joined by the family after the will had been read.

'We'll go upstairs first, darling,' Christina said. 'You wash your poor face and we'll tidy ourselves; then we'll go down to the library.'

'Do I have to go, Mum? I hate Alan and he'll be there . . .'

'Daddy specially asked for you,' her mother said gently. 'He wanted you to know how much he loved you. It won't take more than a few minutes, and Alan won't be here for very long.' Belinda looked up at her mother.

'You hate him too, don't you? Daddy did.'

'Hating doesn't do any good. He'll be out of our lives soon and we can forget about him.'

Christina brushed her hair; she hadn't worn a hat and Richard had insisted she mustn't wear black. Her face looked pale and strained, with lines under the eyes. She had cried herself dry after he died; grief had left its mark on her. Her only concern now was for her daughter, and to get the ordeal over. She had made it sound simple. 'Alan won't be here long . . . He'll be out of our lives soon . . .' If only she could believe that.

Humfrey Stone stood up when she and Belinda came in; so did Rolf Wallberg. Stone went to meet her and shook hands. 'Hello, Mrs Farrington. Hello, Lindy. I'll try to get it over with as soon as possible – it's not complicated. You said Mr Wallberg could sit in; he's over there.'

'Yes, that's perfectly all right. You don't know my two stepsons.' Alan Farrington had followed her in, his wife Fay and his brother James close behind. He ignored Stone's outstretched hand. 'Who's this?' he demanded. 'Where's Paul Fairfax?'

Christina faced him. 'Your father decided to use a different firm of solicitors. This is Mr Stone of Harvey & Stone.'

Alan didn't even turn and look at Humfrey. Suspicion twisted his face. 'You mean he dumped our old family solicitors, the Fairfaxes, and went to some smart-assed shyster in London? What have you been playing at?'

'Alan,' his wife pulled his sleeve. 'Alan, wait . . . come and sit down.' He jerked away from her. Humfrey stepped between him and Christina.

'Mr Farrington, why don't you take your wife's advice? Otherwise I shall defer reading the will to another day. It's within my right, and if you are going to be abusive to my client, or to me, that's what I will do.'

Good for you, little Humfrey, Rolf conceded. He was a small slight man with a gentle manner, but he knew how to handle bullies. And he won, because Alan Farrington turned away and sat down; his wife and James taking chairs either side of him.

'Mrs Farrington,' Humfrey asked, 'do you want me to continue?' She had instinctively caught hold of her daughter's hand as her stepson confronted them.

'Yes,' Christina said firmly, 'we have guests waiting. Please get on with it, Mr Stone.'

'I won't worry you with the preliminaries; it's the usual: the last will and testament of Richard Rowley Farrington, dated 15 February 1995. Revoked all other wills etc. I'll read from the document now.' He cleared his throat and began. 'I leave all monies, shares and personal possessions, and everything not held in trust, to my beloved wife Christina Ingrid, who has given me perfect happiness throughout our marriage, and has cared for me in my last illness with absolute love and devotion. I cannot express what I owe to her. Her greatest gift among so many is my daughter, Belinda Mary. I have decided after much thought, and without any outside influence, to break with my family's long tradition and alter the Farrington trust, naming my daughter Belinda Mary as beneficiary. RussMore will, therefore, pass directly to her on my death, subject to the following provisions made for my said wife, Christina Ingrid.'

Rolf Wallberg had seen the explosion coming. He hadn't taken his eyes off Alan Farrington. Listening to the tributes paid to his stepmother, he had openly sneered. Now his dark face turned a dull red and he jumped to his feet.

'He can't do that! I'm his eldest son. RussMore can't be taken away from me! I know the terms of that trust – he couldn't break it, nobody ever has . . .'

Stone said coldly, 'He could and he did. He's left RussMore to his daughter with his wife as principal trustee and guardian. There's more; why don't you wait till the will's been read, Mr Farrington? You can make your objections later.'

For a moment Alan stayed on his feet. He spoke to Christina. 'You won't get away with this.' Then he sat down.

'I'll continue,' Humfrey said and cleared his throat again. 'My sons, Alan and James, were beneficiaries of their mother's will and were handsomely provided for. In addition, I made over to them monies and shares that my late wife Josephine left me, including items of furniture, pictures and silver that she brought to RussMore when we married. I have never received affection or support from my eldest son, who opposed my second marriage, and publicly accused me of neglecting his mother and contributing to her drug addiction and death. I therefore feel no obligation to provide for him. He is, in capital terms, much wealthier than I am. My second son, James, is living and working in the United States and doesn't intend to return to live in England. I therefore direct that Langley Farm and its four hundred acres should be sold and the proceeds used for his benefit under the terms of the trust.' Humfrey paused and spoke to James Farrington who was watching his elder brother; he looked embarrassed and uneasy. 'Mr Farrington, I may as well explain at this point that, under the terms of the new trust, the trustees would certainly release the capital sum to you, if you wish to make the funds transferable to the US. Now there are various bequests to members of the estate and household staff, and some charitable bequests as well. Do you all wish these read out? They're not so substantial that they need concern the family. Mrs Farrington?'

'Why ask her?' Alan said harshly. 'After all, she dictated the bloody will!' He pushed back his chair. He spoke to Humfrey Stone. His colour had faded now; his eyes burned like coals in the sallow skin. 'She made my father break the trust and cut me out of my family inheritance. He was an old man dying of cancer and she pressured him to get everything for her daughter and herself. But she's not going to get away with it. I'll fight this through to the House of Lords if I have to, but she's not cheating me out of RussMore.' He snapped at Humfrey Stone. 'I'll want a copy of that will and the trust deed sent to my solicitor, Hamilton Ross. I'm sure you'll have heard of *them*. Fay, let's go.' He looked over at his brother.

'Good on you, James. So you've been quietly arse-licking over the years behind my back. Clever, aren't you, Christina? Don't cut *him* out; divide and rule . . .' He went to the door and again he paused. He wasn't very tall or physically imposing, but he possessed a dynamic energy that crackled like an electric charge through the whole room.

'That little brat', he said softly to Christina, 'isn't going to get RussMore. I never believed she was my father's daughter and I'm going to prove it.' He went out, leaving the door open.

It was Wallberg who closed it. He had been sitting in the background, close enough to hear that last exchange and to see the child's bewildered face. Christina Farrington looked as if she had been punched in the heart. He said, in Swedish, 'Let me take your little girl out; don't worry, she wouldn't have understood.'

Christina looked at him; she'd hardly noticed the man in the chair behind her. She answered in Swedish, her voice uneven, 'Thank you . . . please take her outside . . . My God if I'd known he'd do something like that . . .'

Wallberg held out his hand to Belinda. 'Your mother says you'll show me the gardens. I'm Swedish, like her, and I've never been to an English house like this . . . would you mind?'

'Mum?' she asked her mother. She looked confused. She'd heard the words but they didn't seem real . . . Not her father's daughter.

'Lindy, you look after Mr Wallberg, then bring him in for tea. Go along darling.' Stone came up to her. And after him, looking awkward, James, her stepson.

'I don't know what to say,' Humfrey muttered. 'I've never known anyone to behave like that. It's unbalanced, disgraceful. What was that last exchange between you?'

'Nothing,' Christina answered. 'It doesn't matter. It's over and he's gone.' James was beside her then.

'I don't know what to say either,' he said. 'Except thank you. Father wasn't ever very close to me; I know I have you to thank for Langley Farm. It's a very generous legacy.'

'It was nothing to do with me,' she said. 'Nothing. I didn't even know he'd left it to you. All I knew was he wanted Lindy to have the house. I never even saw the will. I don't expect you to believe me.'

'If you say so, I do,' James insisted. She knew he would never have said that in Alan's hearing. Neutral at best, Richard had described him, weak at worst. *I could never look to him for support. You won't be able to either* . . .

She suddenly felt exhausted, and her eyes filled with tears. Stone said gently, 'You sit here quietly, Mrs Farrington. I'll bring you a cup of tea. That was dreadful for you, dreadful.' He was really shocked and angry.

'No, don't bother about tea. I must go and see people and thank them for coming. James, take Mr Stone into the drawing-room, will you? I'll come in a few minutes.' When they had gone, she went to the window and stood looking out, seeing nothing. If she gave in now, she'd never find the strength to go in and face their friends, to thank them for coming, listen to them offering sympathy and help, saying nice things about her husband. She opened the window, as if she could expel the hate and threat that hung in the air like a miasma. Green parkland, glorious trees in full summer leaf. The sounds of summer, bees, the scent from the massive magnolia that climbed the wall of that side of the house. So much beauty, tranquillity and certainty, enriched by its long history. It had become part of her now, as if she had been born to it, instead of coming as a stranger from a foreign country. She had learned new ways, new values, spoken and thought in a language that wasn't her own for so long it had shocked her to hear Swedish spoken. She loved RussMore; it would always be part of her memories of Richard and their life together. And of the child, Belinda, given the Farrington family names. Her father's treasure in his later years. She heard a noise behind her. It was James.

'I came to see if you were all right,' he said. 'People are asking for you.' *Neutral at best; weak at worst.* Stamped and labelled for ever by those words. He said simply, 'I heard what he said. I am so sorry. But he means it, Christa; he'll go to the wire, I know him. I wish I could do something to stop him, but I know he wouldn't listen. He thinks I sold out, so he'll never forgive me either.'

'You'll mind that, won't you?' she asked him. He shrugged. 'I suppose so. The elder brother syndrome dies hard. I always looked up to him. He stood his ground with Father, I never could; I admired that. I was shit-scared of him; shit-scared of Father too . . . I'm not a fighter, more like poor Mother. That's Alan's trouble, you know: he loved her; he couldn't accept it when she died, it turned him inside out.'

Christina said slowly, 'I wish I'd talked to you about it all before, James. We never had the chance.'

'Father wouldn't have liked it,' he said. 'He didn't think much of me and he was so possessive of you. I used to come over and see him, but I always felt he was glad to see me go.'

'He wasn't really,' she said. 'He was hurt because you didn't come more often or stay longer. What a miserable misunderstanding it's been. James, I'm so worried about Lindy.'

'You can pass it off,' he said. 'She'll forget it, if she even took it in.'

On their way to the drawing-room, Christina paused. She could hear a loud buzz of voices behind the door. 'Would you do me a favour?' she asked. 'Would you not go back to London? Stay the night here? There's so much I want to ask you. Would you do that?'

I could never rely on him; you won't be able to either. Richard's dismissal mocked her.

He hesitated. 'I have a dinner date, I can't easily put it off. I could come next week sometime . . .'

'Yes, of course,' she said. 'Just ring and invite yourself down.' Richard Farrington hadn't misjudged his son. She braced herself, opened the door and went in.

Rolf Wallberg had followed the child down to the lake. She had been strained and silent while they toured the rose garden, answering his questions with a few words. At the lake's edge they paused. Swans were sailing past, their heads held high in disdain of the humans who had come empty-handed.

'Do you like swans?'

She shook her head. 'No, they're so greedy. Daddy never let me feed them; he said they were dangerous. He said they can break your arm with one wing, they're so strong. I hate fierce things.'

'I hate fierce people,' he said. She looked up at him. 'Me too. My brother Alan's fierce. He hates Mummy and me; I don't know why.'

Rolf said quietly, 'Maybe he's jealous because your father loved you better than him.'

'Maybe,' she considered for a moment. 'But he's not at all nice, so why *should* Daddy love him?' Rolf smiled. The clarity of children's reasoning always amazed him.

'No reason at all. Shall we go back and find your Mother now?'

'All right,' she agreed. After a few minutes, she said suddenly, 'Is he really going to do awful things to Mummy and take RussMore away from us?' Rolf knew he had won her trust.

'No, not if Mr Stone can help it. And I'm going to help Mr Stone. So don't worry about it. We're on your side, Belinda.'

'I'm glad.' She reached up and held on to his hand. 'Mummy can't stand up to Alan by herself. I heard Daddy say that one day. He said she was too nice.'

'I'm sure she is,' he agreed, 'but I'm not, and nor is Mr Stone. Where do we go now?' They had come in by a side door. They faced a long stone passage, rows of boots and weatherproofs were ranged down one side, topped by an extraordinary variety of hats. Hats and coats for all the unpredictable English seasons, he thought. Mostly for mud and rain.

'Down here,' she said, leading him. A door opened into another passage, the walls covered in old faded photographs of dead men on horses, surrounded by packs of long-departed hounds. Extraordinary people, he mused. English ancestor worship, confined to the domestic regions, but then they tended to put their citations for bravery and their old school mementos in their lavatories. He had decided a long time ago that he would never understand the English, of any class.

The doors to the drawing-room were open, some people were already leaving. 'There's Mummy,' she said and hurried away from him. He stayed where he was, observing for a moment. She was talking to an older couple; he had retired military stamped all over him, from the neat moustache to the cropped grey hair and immaculately polished shoes. The wife was typical too. Dowdy, angular, with a hat like a flowerpot at an ugly angle on her head. He started towards them. Christina smiled as he came up; she looked pale and miserable in spite of the smile. He wasn't sorry for her; he wasn't concerned with people. He was interested but quite dispassionate. He had felt sorry for the child; he had a soft heart for children.

'Mr Wallberg, Colonel and Mrs Spannier; cousins of Richard's.'

'How do you do?' Said in unison and accompanied by a bone-crushing handshake from both.

Christina explained. 'Mr Wallberg is a lawyer from Sweden. He's working here with our solicitors in London.' The Colonel examined him. 'Really? Finding the law here very different, I expect.'

'Very different,' he agreed, 'but interesting.'

Jane Spannier turned to Christina. 'My dear, you've been wonderful the way you've coped. I just feel we could have done more to help, but our son Harry's coming home at the end of the month, thank God, and we've been getting one of the cottages ready for him. He's going into Peter's agricultural suppliers business and helping to manage the farm.'

'Jane, please, you couldn't do anything better than come today and support us. I'm so glad your boy's coming back, I know you've missed him.'

Peter Spannier snorted. 'Boy! He's thirty-five, but Jane thinks he's still a schoolboy. She's been running round like a broody hen getting the nest ready.' He smiled at his wife affectionately. She was born a Farrington, but she was the exact opposite of her cousin, Richard. Forthright, sensible, perhaps lacking a little imagination, he conceded privately, but dead straight and lion-hearted in her loyalty. They had been happily married for nearly forty years.

'I'll tell you what,' Jane said, 'when Harry comes home we'll invite ourselves to stay. I'd love him to meet you and Belinda, and see RussMore again. Would that be a good idea?'

Christina said, 'It'd be wonderful. Just call me when you want to come.'

'I will,' Jane promised. 'We'll get ourselves another cup of tea and a sandwich and then I'm afraid we'll have to be off. It's a hell of a drive home.'

She turned briefly to Wallberg. 'We live on the Norfolk coast,' she explained. 'Hope you enjoy your time in London. Come along, Peter. Goodbye, Christa dear. Look after yourself, and for heaven's sake, ring up if you feel like a chat.' She kissed her briskly on the cheek.

As they moved away, Christina said, 'They're very nice; they're not close relations, but they were very supportive when I was first married. Thank you for looking after Lindy; she told me she likes you.'

'She's a charming girl,' he answered, 'and very direct. She's frightened her half-brother is going to hurt you and take the house away, but I told her Mr Stone and I wouldn't let him.'

He has the coldest eyes, she thought; there wasn't a flicker of human warmth in them. 'I think she must have believed you. She's over there, eating cake and talking to some more cousins. She didn't mention that awful thing he said at the end. I don't know why I didn't slap him right across the face!' She flushed red as she said it. Not all softness and vulnerability. There was anger there, and a maternal instinct that could turn ferocious. 'For the same reason that I didn't punch him,' he said calmly. 'It would be playing his game, and we're not going to do that.'

'We?' she questioned.

'Yes. Humfrey didn't have time to tell you, but I shall be working with him on your affairs. I shall do my best for you; I promised your daughter, and I never break my promises to children.' He nodded, dismissing himself, and walked away, out of the door.

Humfrey Stone came up to her. 'I'll be going now, Mrs Farrington. Is someone staying with you tonight?'

'No, several people offered, but I said no. Lindy and I will be together; there's the housekeeper and her husband. We'll be fine. I'm actually so very tired.'

'I'm not surprised,' he nodded. 'It's been a terrible ordeal, quite disgraceful. I'll be in touch tomorrow and we can arrange a meeting in London. In the meantime, we do nothing.'

'Aren't you going to send Alan the documents?'

'No, let him ask for them; and I shall take my time. Give someone like that an inch and they'll grab a mile. It seems we're going to have a fight on our hands, but we'll fight it at our pace. Trust me.'

'I do,' she said, 'but tell me about Mr Wallberg; he says he's going to be working with you.' Humfrey noticed the slight frown and guessed that she and Wallberg were not compatible.

'It's Ruben's idea,' he explained. 'Rolf Wallberg is one of the best young legal brains in Stockholm, and not only there; he's worked in France and Germany and he's very highly recommended.' He smiled briefly. 'I'm quite glad he's not going to be permanent. He's far too sharp for my liking; we'd all have to watch our backs. But seriously, he'll be a real asset; he wouldn't have been assigned to work on your affairs otherwise.'

Christina accepted it. 'I'm sure you're right. So we wait for my stepson to make the next move, if he does decide to make one.'

Humfrey asked in his quiet voice, 'And do you think he won't?'

'No, I'm sure he will. Whatever his lawyers advise, he'll fight the will; he's never listened to anyone in his life.'

'That's my opinion, too,' Humfrey agreed. 'Well, goodbye, Mrs Farrington. I'm taking Rolf back with me. One of us will call you as soon as we hear anything. And don't worry, however much trouble he causes, he won't win. The trust and the will are unbreakable. Good night.' He shook hands and gave hers a friendly squeeze. He was a nice man, a man with genuine feeling in him. She hoped she would be dealing with him rather than Rolf Wallberg.

'You're doing ninety,' Fay Farrington protested. The grey Bentley gave no impression of speed. It devoured the motorway miles as silently as if it were on an air cushion. Alan Farrington didn't answer but he eased his speed. She was the only person he ever listened to and no-one in business, friendship or family circles knew what her secret was. But he did; he'd always known, from the first time he met her. It wasn't just that she was pretty, with light-brown hair and big grey eyes, a neat figure . . . there were countless girls with the same sexy equipment. But this one was different; she was on his side, as simple as that. Whatever he said or did or felt, was right in her eyes. It had made him love her, and it gave her a power over him that nobody else had ever had. With Fay he wasn't alone; he was at war with his father, but she was ready to fight with him. Over the years they had grown closer, more united. There were two small children; he was a doting father and his extravagant indulgence of his boys was balanced by a firm discipline from her. Fay glanced at the speedometer and relaxed. He had nine speeding points on his licence. The Bentley was a provocation to a number of traffic police; his rudeness and aggression always tipped the odds in favour of a prosecution.

'That bastard,' he said, staring at the road ahead.

'Which one? Your father or that wimp James?'

'Both of them,' he said. His mind was on James at that moment. 'Oiling round them. Pretending to side with us. What a little prick!'

Fay didn't answer. She had never liked James; she felt he was more overawed than loyal and she despised him for it. She laid a hand on Alan's knee. 'Don't let him worry you, darling, he's not worth it. He'll come crawling back to you, he always has.' Alan might forgive because he was in need of the family love he'd been denied, even from a brother he had dominated since they were children; she accepted that and understood it, but she wouldn't forget. Alan had been good to him, helping him to get the job with the US advertising agency through his own contacts. James had taken the favours and gone to his enemies behind their backs. 'What are you going to do about this will?' she asked.

'Fight it,' was the answer. The speed was creeping up again, indicating his hurt and anger.

'She's responsible,' Fay insisted. 'She was out to grab everything for herself and that little bitch. As for bringing her to the funeral – I said it was ghoulish! She didn't like it.'

'She married Dad for money,' – Alan slowed sharply at a roundabout – 'and she stuck it out, waiting for him to die, which he did, and a lot sooner than she expected. I bet she couldn't believe her luck when they diagnosed cancer. And did he have chemotherapy or try to fight it? Not fucking likely! She wanted him to come back to RussMore so she could get at him. He wouldn't have cut me out, Fay, however much he hated me. I know Dad, he loved all that family crap – four hundred years of history . . . he used to drive Mum and me up the wall talking about it. He wouldn't have broken the tradition if she hadn't worked on him as he was dying. Oh, for Christ's sake!' He cut across a car on the inside and was met by furious gestures from the other driver. Briefly he glanced in the driving mirror, lowered the window and stuck out two fingers. The car sped forward and eased into the fast lane.

'I never believed that kid was his. Just under nine months after they get married! It took him three years before he got my mother pregnant with me, and he was always at her, she told me, never left her alone. He wasn't that bloody fertile. That bitch conned him and I'm going to prove it.'

'How?' Fay demanded. She didn't argue, or try to convince him he was wrong. The girl Belinda had a look she recognized, and it was more than the dark Farrington skin and hair, it was movements, mannerisms of the hated old man. Alan didn't want to accept her as his sister; it hurt too much. Belinda was living proof of his father's callousness towards his dead wife; in his eyes it was a form of infidelity. She remembered him breaking down in tears when he told her about it soon after they met, using a weird old-fashioned phrase she'd never heard in her life.

'Not even cold in her grave . . . three months and he's fucking someone else!'

He had been so hurt, so vulnerable, and it aroused her to passionate love and bitter hatred in equal measure. Love for this tough strong man who sobbed in her arms that night, and hatred for the father who had brought him to such weakness through sheer pain. And she had a personal cause too: she didn't have a family background like the Farringtons. She came from sound decent people who had worked hard all their lives, brought up three children, educated them and set them on their way, and now lived in modest retirement in a South London suburb.

She would never forget the chill presence of Richard Farrington and his second wife at their small wedding. Christina's attempts to be friendly seemed condescending to Fay, aware of her mother's embarrassment and desire to please her son-in-law's grand family. A friend had said at the reception, 'Who's the old guy with the smell under his nose?' She had winced and turned quickly away. Then there was the ill-fated attempt to paper over the rift between father and son when they came for a weekend to RussMore. She was young and newly married, nervous for herself and protective of Alan. She had left the house in tears, after a high-octane row between Alan and his father; he had been grossly rude to his stepmother.

He was wrong to do it, and Fay had told him so, but in her heart she understood why, and didn't blame him. She would rather he'd pretended, but he wasn't capable of bending to any wind. She had hated Christina from that moment; hated her for trying to calm the old man down when she'd worked him up in the first place; hated her for playing the peacemaker. And then there was that child; spoilt and pampered, growing up in the world of privilege that was closed to her own boys. The rift had become so deep that they were hardly acknowledged and had never seen their father's family home.

'How are you going to prove a thing like that?' she asked again. 'It's impossible. Why not just go for undue influence – you've got a chance there.'

'I'm going for everything,' he said. They were in London now and the handsome car idled in traffic on their way to Chelsea. 'As for proving that cow cheated on my father.' At a red light he turned and looked at her. 'I've got something that could do just that. I didn't go down and stay in a bloody hotel the night before, like a stranger coming to my own father's funeral . . . I thought something like this might happen . . .' His resentment glowed.

He, himself, had left home after his father remarried. He had put some money into a small fast-food business, and by twenty-five he was a millionaire. The money he'd made provided them with every luxury: a fine house in Chelsea; a weekend cottage for sailing during the summer; a villa in the South of France. He liked to make a joke of his success at their big dinner parties. Fay provided the props and he basked in the spotlight, centre stage. 'I may make bucks out of junk food, but I make bloody sure I don't eat it myself!' And the guests always laughed because the food and wine was the best.

A manservant dealt with their luggage. He fell back into a deep sofa. 'Sweetheart, get me a Scotch, will you?' Fay didn't argue. She'd start protesting after the third drink and she usually won. All she had to say was, 'Do you want the boys to see you pissed?' and he stopped. His mother had been a drunk, as well as a druggie. There were photographs of her all over the house; old-fashioned soft-lens portraits of a beautiful woman, posing improbably against chiffon curtains or flower arrangements.

That was one area where Fay had no influence. Josephine Farrington was an icon. A tragic victim, driven to an early death by a heartless husband. It wasn't Fay's opinion of her at all, but she knew just how far she could go with Alan, and that was part of her strength.

She gave him the drink and poured a glass of wine for herself. 'Tell me,' she said, 'what do you mean you've got something that could upset the will?' He gulped down half the drink, and smiled. Hatred made it an ugly grimace.

'It's in my pocket,' he said. 'And after I've had a refill, I'll tell you about it.'

Rolf Wallberg thanked Humfrey Stone for driving him back to London. Stone went off to meet his client and Rolf took a cab to the Dorchester Hotel. He climbed to the first floor; he never used a lift if he could make use of the stairs. It was a simple aid to fitness, and physical training was part of his creed. The big plushy bar was two-thirds empty. He chose a seat by the wall, told the advancing waiter curtly that he was expecting someone, and would order when they arrived. She was on time; he was early, because punctuality was also part of his creed. She paused, saw him, smiled and came over. He got up, and greeted her with a token kiss on the cheek. She was an elegant woman in her thirties, sleek and expensively dressed. She smoothed her long golden blond hair, flicking it over a shoulder and said, 'How did it go today?' He didn't answer. The waiter was back; he gave Rolf a sullen look, thinking, Rude bastard, typical potato heads, the pair of them, jabbering away. He hated Germans; his family had come over from Italy after the war. Germans had machine-gunned their village and killed his mother's relatives.

'Two vodkas on the rocks,' Rolf said. He turned to the woman. 'As expected: they are at each other's throats. There'll be a fight and she won't win.'

She raised her eyebrows. 'That's a very dogmatic thing to say. How do you know?'

'Money,' he answered. 'I know the family's financial situation. There's a very big house, upkeep something like eighty thousand a year in maintenance, staff, outgoings. The let farms bring in a big income, but as they're tenanted, they're not realizable. Pictures, furniture, all valuable, but no one item would reach the magic million. And she'd have to pay heavy capital gains taxes if she did sell assets. To raise a really substantial sum, she'd have to strip the place, and she won't do that. If she sells the agricultural land, there isn't enough revenue to maintain the house – it's a catch twenty-two. I don't think she even realizes that yet.'

She smiled slightly. 'But you'll point it out to her.'

'I will. I'll also point out that her stepson is in a financial position to ruin her with litigation. Farrington Fast Foods have franchises and properties worth millions. He's one of the new rich, and he knows how to use money. She won't have a hope. I can't understand why the firm let the old man try to disinherit his son. Even if the will and the trust are unbreakable, there'll be nothing left after years of legal fighting, court appeals and lawyers' fees running into a fortune.'

'You sound almost sorry for her,' she remarked. She had dark eyes, an odd combination with the blond hair. They examined his coldly. 'Are you?'

'There's an eleven-year-old child in the middle of this mess,' he answered. 'I feel sorry for her.'

'A lot of children suffer in this world,' she remarked, 'we can't afford to be selective. So what happens next?' He accepted the rebuke. The fact that they had slept together on occasions did not alter their relationship; that had never been touched by sentiment.

'Alan Farrington opens the battle and we respond. Humfrey Stone has a big corporate case coming up and won't be able to give her the time, so I become Mrs Farrington's legal adviser. If she accepts me.'

She put down her drink. 'If? Why shouldn't she?'

He said coolly, 'Because she doesn't like me; I can tell. She's not fighting for herself; she's fighting for her daughter. I think she's honest and she has a mind of her own. Unless I can get her to trust me, she won't take my advice.'

'Then you'll just have to be charming,' she mocked him gently. 'You can be, I know. Charm her Rolf. Whatever it takes.'

'It may take a lot,' he said. 'Another drink? Are you free for dinner?'

'Yes, and I'm free for sex too. I've had a long and boring day; I think we could both do with some relaxation.' She laid a hand on his thigh and pressed hard. They looked at each other, sexually responsive, intimates who would never even be friends.

'Why waste time with dinner,' Rolf remarked. 'We can eat afterwards at my apartment. I'll get the bill.'

The waiter watched them go and swore crudely in Italian. The potato head hadn't left a tip.

2

James Farrington steeled himself to ring his elder brother. He had hesitated and put it off for three days; he had meant to telephone Christina too. The dinner date he'd used as an excuse was dull and unproductive; his friend ordered the most expensive dishes, drank everything on offer and refused to have sex with him afterwards. He felt sorry he hadn't cancelled and stayed at RussMore. But facing Alan frightened him. He played with the idea of just flying back to the States and doing nothing about either of them, but he couldn't face that either; he needed Alan's approval, even if he had to take a verbal beating first to get it. It was the pattern of his bullied childhood continuing on into their adult relationship – he had been afraid of his father and dominated by his brother. He never succeeded in pleasing either of them, but Alan, at least, paid him attention, and even helped him in a patronizing way, so long as he remained compliant and admiring. Any hint of independence and the support was withdrawn, accompanied by some crushing verbal assault that left him naked of self-respect. He was a very intelligent and sensitive man, and surprised his New York therapist by understanding his own problems so clearly. He couldn't fully relate to women; his mother had been an ineffectual shadow, drifting in and out of his life as he grew up, absorbed in her addictions and her bouts of treatment; her reactions to him unpredictable. An extravagant embrace, kisses, maudlin expressions of love, followed by angry rejection. He could never forget that phrase, often shouted and always so deeply wounding, *Oh, for God's sake go away, you little bore!*

He would creep away like a hurt animal. When she'd died he felt a guilty sense of relief, and also fear because she wasn't there to abuse him any more, so he turned to his elder brother for the mixture of brutality and security he needed. Alan was full of anger; unlike James he was his mother's favourite and, for such an overbearing boy, he loved her with uncritical devotion. It was the New York therapist who'd suggested he might have been in sexual competition with his own father. James had simply shrugged that suggestion aside; it was glib psychobabble and he didn't take it seriously; motives went far deeper than the simplistic theories of Freud. Alan had loved his mother because she was weak and it made him feel strong. He couldn't bear strength or determination in anyone because it challenged him. James understood that; their father never did. All he saw was a rebellious bitter-tongued adolescent, who accepted no point of view but his own. It was all very sad and, when the family broke apart, he felt more like an observer than a member of it. He didn't hate his stepmother, Christina. He thought she was a nice girl, rather naïve and bewildered by the situation with her husband and his elder son. He didn't see her in the role of money-grabbing tart – Alan's savage description; he felt his father, who was so much older and more sophisticated, had rather tricked her. He didn't dare say so, of course. He had made his career in the States and been glad to escape, but he kept in touch because he couldn't help it. He didn't want to be shut out, even though contact with his father always hurt.

Finally, four days before he was due to fly back, he telephoned Alan at his office. He knew better than to try Fay as a mediator; she despised him and he knew it.

'Who shall I say is calling?' Alan's secretary asked.

He was so successful now; a young industrial tiger, already on the prowl for other businesses to add to his restaurant chain. James admired that fearful energy.

'His brother, James,' he answered. There was a long pause while music trilled in his ear from the telephone system. He sometimes wondered why people had to have a maddening tinkle playing to assure them they hadn't been cut off.

Then, 'I'm putting you through, Mr Farrington.'

James swallowed with nerves. 'Alan? Hi . . . how are you?'

'Fine. What the hell do you want?'

'I'm leaving in a few days; I wanted to say goodbye. Any chance we could meet?'

'No chance,' was the answer. 'I'm surprised you're not down at RussMore, kissing her arse.'

'I didn't,' James protested. He knew the formula; he was going to submit to the tongue-lashing and then, when he'd grovelled, they'd make peace. 'I knew nothing about the will or Dad leaving me Langley. For God's sake, I made a duty visit once a year! He was getting old and I thought . . .'

'Yeah, yeah, you thought you might worm something out of him . . . and you did, didn't you! And that cow will release the money and think she's only got me to worry about because you've been bought off. You shit . . .'

'Alan, don't be like that. I'm your brother; I've always been on your side, you know that. She asked me to stay after the funeral and I said no. If you're going to fight the will, I'll do anything I can to help.'

'Once you've got the money,' his brother sneered. James said, 'Yes, of course, once I've got the money.' He must have become more assertive, he thought, to say that.

He heard a short laugh. 'Well, that's honest, anyway.' A pause, and Alan's voice was kinder. 'Look, you want to help me?'

'I said so,' James protested. He was suddenly worried, then

remembered he was leaving for New York and a promise was easy when he was 3,000 miles away.

'Fine,' his brother said, 'then go down and see her. Be nice; talk to her; find out what she's going to do, then tell me.'

As a child James had listened at doors, read any letter left lying around, pried and spied on everyone. Even if he was shut out, he had his secret knowledge of things he wasn't supposed to know.

'All right,' he agreed, 'no problem. I'll call today. She was disappointed when I said no; I'm sure she'll see me. I'll be in touch; maybe we can meet before I go.'

'Maybe,' Alan said and hung up.

Belinda had gone to stay with a friend; the family lived ten miles away. Both girls were pony mad and there was an older sister who liked teaching them; she was a serious Pony Club competitor, and she was Belinda's heroine.

Richard had refused to let her do more than hack around the park on a safe old pensioner. 'I won't have her growing up into a typical horsey English girl,' he'd insisted and then admitted to Christina that the real reason was fear for her safety. 'I had a first cousin,' he had told her. 'She was killed out hunting. She was twenty-two and lovely. Lindy's bold and brave – like you, darling, with your skiing. She'd take risks and I couldn't bear it.'

Christina hadn't argued. He'd suffered enough from one accidental death. Now she encouraged Belinda to go to her friends and stay as long as she liked. The child hadn't mentioned anything since the funeral, but she was subdued, and Christina was sure that she cried for her father in secret. There was so much to do in the days after Richard was buried: letters to be written, accounts to be settled, and always the threat of Alan hanging over her. Every phone call made her jump with nerves, expecting it to be from Humfrey Stone. But there were no calls and nothing came in the post, and the silence made her more uneasy.

Sometimes she found herself talking to Richard Farrington aloud. 'If only you could tell me what to expect . . . you knew him, you were able to cope. You always said I couldn't . . . I wish you hadn't protected me so much.' The dead do not answer. The Farringtons from the past looked down at her from the walls and gave no help. This was a battle she must fight alone, with an enemy she had never got to know. When the call came from her stepson, James, she said yes quickly. 'Please come down; stay the night.' She was actually looking forward to seeing him. He came in time for lunch, still awkward and vaguely uneasy, just as he was when Richard was alive. He presented a box of Harrods chocolates like a shy schoolboy.

'They're handmade,' he explained. 'I don't know if you like chocolates . . . I think they're rather good.'

'I love them,' Christina said. 'How sweet of you.' They sat out on the terrace overlooking the rose garden before lunch.

'Wonderful scent,' he remarked. 'That's one thing I miss in the States: England in summer . . .'

'Then why don't you come home? You could make Langley a lovely house. We're stuffed with furniture and pictures here; you could take anything you wanted. Why be an exile if you're not happy? Life's too short, James.'

'That's very generous of you,' he said. 'My father wouldn't have suggested that, or offered me anything. Funny isn't it . . . but you do.'

'You're wrong about that,' Christina said gently. 'He loved you, but he wasn't good at showing it. He felt you were influenced by Alan; he was a very proud man. I've always found this obsession with pride very difficult to understand; I'm not proud at all, when it comes to someone I love.'

James smiled briefly. 'No, I'm sure you're not. It's odd, you know, I keep thinking he'll walk through the door and come out and join us. I can't believe I'll never see him again. I suppose that's some kind of tribute, but I'm not sure.'

'I think it means you loved him,' she said. 'I can't believe it either. I find myself pouring out two drinks in the evening . . . some letters came this morning, and I didn't open them because they were addressed to him. Every time I open the library door I expect to see him.'

'We never went into the library when we were children,'

James remarked; 'that was the inner sanctum. Father was looking at his manuscripts and nobody was allowed to disturb him. Only Alan did, but then he would, because he resented being told not to come in. There'd be a shouting match and my mother would cringe and pretend not to hear. She called his collection, "Those dreary bits of paper"; it used to madden him. Perhaps that's why he was so defensive and secretive about it; after all, it was just a hobby. Did he show any of it to you, Christa?'

'No,' she looked surprised, 'he never mentioned any hobby. Oh I think he did once, when we first met; I didn't really take any notice. He did spend time in the library, but I just thought he loved browsing through his books. He never asked me to join him and I let him have his space; I felt that was very important, and for me, too.' She shook her head. 'He never talked about manuscripts. What kind were they?'

'I don't know,' James answered. 'I expect they'll turn up when everything's listed for probate. It's going to be a huge hassle, with so much stuff to go through, but I expect you'll manage. Knowing Father he won't have left anything to chance. Mind if I smoke, Christa?'

'Of course not.'

'What an easy person you are,' he remarked. 'People in the States are such bloody bores about cigarettes and pollution. This political correctness thing drives me ape; I long to say that women, blacks and gays are all inferior, but I don't have the nerve. I'm so brave in my imagination.' He inhaled with exaggerated relish.

'But you don't mean it, I hope?'

He grinned. 'Of course not. After all, I'm gay myself.' He studied her for a moment. There was a gleam of malice in the look. 'Surely you knew that?'

'Richard would never have admitted it,' she answered. 'I never thought about it. It's your life, and it's no-one else's business.'

'Father ignored it because he's just like Alan; if it's something they don't like, it isn't true. So simple, the Farrington philosophy. Didn't you realize how much alike they were?'

Christina said flatly, 'No, I didn't and I don't. Richard was gentle, loving and, above all, fair; your brother is a bully and a thug. Please don't try to make comparisons.' She felt herself blush with anger. He had shrewd eyes, they watched her and calculated. He had gone too far and he retreated quickly.

'I'm sorry, I'm sure Father was all those things to you, and to Belinda, of course.' He put out his cigarette. 'You're right about my brother; he's a bully and a thug, but there are explanations.'

'Then you can tell me about them after lunch,' she said. She walked past him through the French windows into the drawing-room. He closed the doors on to the terrace and followed her across the great hall into the dining-room.

She could be strong, he decided, and a lot tougher than she looked. Alan might not ride as rough shod as he hoped when he took on his hated stepmother. He might be very glad of any help that James could give him.

While Christina and James were lunching in the tranquillity of RussMore, Rolf Wallberg was called into Humfrey Stone's office. Humfrey pushed a file across to him.

'Farrington's solicitors,' he explained. 'Asking for copies of all the relevant documentation. Trust deeds, new executions altering the original settlement, minutes of meetings between Richard Farrington and ourselves . . . And, of course, the will. Cheeky letter from them too.' He frowned. The tone had been hostile and combative. Alan Farrington had chosen a firm that matched his style.

'But you expected this,' Rolf said. 'What's the problem?'

Humfrey looked up at him. 'The problem is', he said, 'I'm up to my eyeballs with the Ringwater Estate. I just haven't got the time to cope with all this. I was hoping Mr Ruben would handle some of it, but he's dumped the lot on me. Rolf, I'm going to ask you to take on this Farrington correspondence; deal with Mrs Farrington and keep it ticking over for the next few weeks. Can you handle that?'

Rolf didn't hesitate. 'Of course, but you'll need to explain the situation to your client, first. Clear it with her and I'll start right away.' Humfrey was still worried. He liked Christina and had fully intended to defend her interests himself, but Ruben Stone had decreed otherwise. 'You got on, didn't you?'

Rolf hid a smile. The fact that he asked meant he'd sensed they didn't like each other. Or rather that she didn't like him. 'We're both Swedes,' he assured him. 'We'll understand each other. My only interest is to win the case for her. Emphasize that when you talk. After all, it would do my reputation a lot of good internationally, if I won. This will be a high-profile action; it could go to the Court of Appeal.'

'It could go to the Lords!' Humfrey sighed. 'You'll be here for the next five years – no, seriously, the best course is to settle. We all know that there are no winners, only losers when it gets into court.'

Rolf raised his eyebrows in mockery. 'Aren't you forgetting the fees?'

Humfrey didn't rise. He worked hard and he earned a fortune, but he had always put his clients' interests above money. He doubted whether Rolf Wallberg could say the same. 'I'll put a call through to her.' He ended the meeting by reaching for his telephone. 'Get me Mrs Farrington, please, Joan . . . Thanks.' He hung up, waiting for the call to be put through. Maybe the Swede was a good choice; he was cold-hearted and ruthless in his outlook, and made no attempt to hide it. He might be just the man to fight Alan Farrington on his own terms.

Christina put the telephone down. Humfrey had been apologetic but reassuring. He would take up the case as soon as he had settled the more pressing legal problem that had surfaced unexpectedly, but Rolf Wallberg was a first-class professional, as competent as anyone in the firm, and he was very anxious to handle the case. 'He's ambitious and he'll fight for you, Mrs Farrington. He wants to win for himself and, though it isn't nice, it's a real plus when you're dealing with someone like your stepson. I have every confidence in him, and I'm always here in an emergency.'

James was out walking; lunch had been pleasant but strained. Both had put up barriers, and she wished, suddenly, that he would change his mind about staying and go back to London. Rolf Wallberg. She sat on the terrace in the sunshine and tried to feel confident. Humfrey said he was good, ambitious, out to win; she had judged that for herself. But he wasn't congenial; he was cold and remote, almost judgemental, as if he were watching the antics of another species. But he had been different with Belinda. Children had an instinct that Christina trusted. She'd spoken about him just before she went to sleep that night, when they had shared the same bed for comfort.

'Don't worry, Mum. I think that man will look after us.'

'What man, darling?' Christina had murmured.

Belinda had mumbled, 'The one with white hair. I showed him the garden . . .'

'Out of the mouths of babes . . .' The Biblical quotation came into her mind. Richard often talked of the great truths concealed within religious texts. 'Just because something's become a cliché, doesn't mean it isn't true,' he would say. She had never been able to share either the principle or the detail of his ancient Christian faith, and he had accepted that and never tried to convince her. 'One day, darling, maybe it'll come to you.' And he had kissed her fondly. He had been as fond as he was passionate; a lover and a friend. If it took a bastard like Wallberg to carry out his dying wishes, then who was she to cavil? She didn't have to like him or admire his attitude. If he wanted to win, then so did she.

'Hello,' James came up the steps from the garden. 'You look worried. Anything the matter?'

'Alan's solicitors have contacted Humfrey Stone,' she answered. 'He's going to contest the will.' James sat down opposite to her.

'Do they say on what grounds?'

'No, just asked for documentation and gave notice that they are preparing to challenge. James, why is he doing it like this? Couldn't he at least have behaved decently and talked to me first?'

'And would you have given up RussMore if he had?' She hadn't expected the question.

'No, I wouldn't, but we might have worked out some

compromise instead of having this fight and all the publicity and bad blood. You talked about explanations when I called him a bully and a thug . . . Well, I'd like to hear them!'

He lit a cigarette, taking time about lighting it and drawing the first deep breaths. 'That's why you asked me to stay after the funeral, isn't it? You wanted to know about all of us, not just Alan. My mother, father and us two sons. Am I right?'

'Yes,' she said. 'You are.'

'There's not much point if you get angry when I criticize him.'

'I'll try not to; so long as it's fair.' Fair – she was always using that word, but life wasn't fair, he hadn't found it so.

'Father never really talked about the family, did he? I mean, he didn't go into details? Just painted you a broad-brush sketch: Mummy was a drug addict, Alan was a thug, and as for me . . . what did he tell you about me, Christa? Can't be trusted, always takes the easy option. Something like that, I can see by your face. Oh, don't look embarrassed; he said it to me often enough.'

Christina said slowly, 'I can't imagine him ever being cruel.' He tapped cigarette ash onto the ground.

'I don't think he realized,' he said after a pause, 'because he was right. He just never looked for reasons, that's all. He didn't understand weakness, but then,' he grinned at her, 'he didn't like strength of character, either. Not when it challenged him. That's why I said he and Alan were alike, except that he was intellectual and Alan isn't. Father had an educated, cultured brain and Alan couldn't match it, so he went to the opposite extreme. He set out to be a lout, even when we were quite small. He picked his nose at the table, that kind of gesture; always two fingers up to Father. The more Father rejected him, the worse he got, and the more he turned to Mummy. Do you really want to hear all this? Neglected children, striving for acceptance, all that crap?'

'Only if it's going to help me understand what's happening. My family was so different. We were ordinary people; in England we'd be middle class. Doctors, accountants; my grandparents were farmers. There were rows between us, yes, but never like this; never all this bitterness and hate. If things went wrong, we came together to help.'

'It sounds ideal,' he said, and she looked up sharply. 'Don't you dare sneer, James.'

'I wasn't,' he protested, 'I'm just envious. It sounds so cosy and uncomplicated. I never knew where I was with either of my parents. Mummy was lovely at first; when I was very little, I remember her as happy and laughing and so pretty – then she changed. She liked London and parties and Father didn't, so she started going off without him. I suppose that's where she got hooked on heroin. I didn't realize anything was wrong for years; she was just unpredictable: sometimes sweet to me, other times an absolute bitch. I never knew what to expect. Alan could cope with her; she seemed to rely on him. When he went away to Harrow she wrote to him every day, and he wrote back. It was like a sort of conspiracy between them. My New York shrink says it was sexual collusion and that's what set him and Father at each other's throats.'

Christina interrupted. 'They would say that, wouldn't they? I don't believe it; that's the easy answer. When in doubt, blame it on sex.'

'That's what I said,' he agreed. 'It wasn't about sex, it was about power. Every conflict is about power; the use of it and the abuse of it. That's Alan's trouble; he's got to be number one; he's got to be the lead role. He couldn't do it with brain power, so he relied on brawn. And cunning; he's got plenty of that. He saw himself as the head of the family, but he couldn't be with Father still around, so he played protector to Mummy and she thrived on it. Funny how women will entrap their sons by pretending they're being ill-treated by their husbands.'

He paused and Christina said, 'But she didn't do that with you, and it wasn't true anyway; Richard did everything possible to help her.' He looked at her, and for a moment the bleak uncertain boy lurked behind the grown man.

'No, she used me like a football; it was more kicks than cuddles. I got on her nerves. I don't know whether it was true about father or not; she thought it was. Paying for a lot of expensive clinics doesn't stop you being cruel. I'm sure he hated her at the end.'

'Yes,' Christina said quietly, 'I think he did. He told me he'd lived with lies and without hope for fifteen years. Tell me, James, why do you like your brother?'

He smiled for the first time. 'I don't like him,' he said, 'but I love him and, in his way, I think he loves me. We're brothers and that makes a bond. God knows why. We've nothing in common but our childhood and this house and parents who hated each other. I felt so sorry for Mummy, but I despised her too. You see, Christa, I like strong people; she was so helpless, disgusting sometimes; that's why I turned off women. There'll always be a bond between me and Alan; I suppose we need each other.'

Christina hesitated. 'Is there any chance you could talk to him? I don't mean get him to drop the case, but try and defuse the anger. Maybe meet me, and at least discuss what's happened. You and I have talked for the first time today and it hasn't been difficult. Could you try?'

He shook his head. 'I could try but it wouldn't be any good, he's never listened to me in his life; he expects me to listen to him. That's the way it goes. I am hoping to see him before I fly back, but there's no guarantee. He's pissed off with me about Langley Farm; he feels I've been sleeping with the enemy.' He laughed; it was humourless and shrill.

'All right, all right, I'll try. You know something, I've just realized?' Without waiting for her answer he went on, 'This is the first time I've ever felt at home in this house. It's been so easy talking to you. Why don't I sack the shrink and just take Concorde twice a month and come to see you?' To her surprise he reached over and patted her hand. 'I could get to like you, Christa. It's just as well I'm going back to the States.'

After dinner they had coffee in the study. It was a small room, intimate by comparison with the Tudor public rooms. Christina had stripped off the dark patterned wallpaper and painted it a warm red. Richard had been so pleased with the effect he'd hung three of his best pictures there. A charming Reynolds portrait of an early Farrington bride, serene in her innocence, and soon to die in childbirth, the companion picture of her young husband; he had married three more times and produced eleven children. Over the fireplace there was a Tudor picture of a child; it was set off by a brilliant cerulean background. The round solemn face under an embroidered cap seemed to stare directly at them; it had a clear jewel-like translucence. One plump little hand rested on a skull. Richard had explained that it was a posthumous portrait, probably copied from one of the living child. The artist was unknown, but the quality was superb. She saw James looking at it.

'I know it's wonderful, but I hate that skull. Your father used to tease me about it. I said he'd come in one day and find that I'd painted it out!'

'Why don't you move it?' he suggested. 'If it makes you uncomfortable, hang it somewhere else; he won't know. I think it's gruesome.'

'This was his favourite room and I'm not going to change it,' she answered. 'Not immediately anyway.'

'I always thought he liked the library,' James remarked. 'He certainly spent a lot of time there. It used to irritate Mummy. I heard Alan say to her one day – he was about fifteen – "What's he do in there all day?" And she said, "He's studying comparative religions. That's what he said, whatever that means." And Alan said, "How boring! What a boring thing to do." And she giggled. After he married you he didn't bother; he didn't need to escape so much, I suppose. But you did say he liked to spend time in there.'

'Yes I did,' Christina agreed. 'Why, James?'

'Oh, nothing important. He's still a mystery to me, you know. I wonder about him; I wonder why he was so different with you that I don't recognize him when you talk.'

'He was happy,' she said gently. 'Happiness changes people. I know it changed me. Everything in my life changed when I came to England and started living here. He made me feel a part of it all, and I took on a new identity.' She smiled at him. 'I turned myself into an English lady. I've only been home a dozen times since I married. Once was when my mother died. My father and brother came here, but they weren't really comfortable;

I could see that. I'd changed and we hadn't the same things to talk about. I've promised to visit them in the Christmas holidays and take Lindy. She thinks Sweden is great and she can't wait to go and ski with her uncle. They got on very well and my father spent more time with her than with Richard and me.'

'She's an attractive child,' he said. 'And, of course, Father was besotted by her. I can't tell you how jealous I was when I used to visit and saw them together. Maybe if one of us had been a girl, he'd have liked us better.'

'James,' she said gently, 'don't, please. Don't go on hurting because he didn't love you; he did, I know he did.'

'You're too nice.' He said it lightly. 'And I'm not hurting, just curious and speculating, that's all. You look tired; don't let me keep you up. I'll have another cancer tube and then I'll go to bed.'

'Good night, then,' she said, 'I'll see you at breakfast.'

When she had gone he put out the newly lit cigarette, waited for a few minutes and then opened the study door and listened. The house was as silent as an old house can be. Timbers creaked and the structure made its own adjustments to the change in temperature, but there was no human voice or footfall, and the main lights had been turned out. Very quietly, James closed the study door and crossed the great hall to the library. He moved as softly as he had done throughout his childhood, when he was prowling through the house, looking for other people's secrets. Knowing what he wasn't supposed to know was his power fix. Listening at doors when his parents quarrelled or discussed their children, spying on the maids if they sneaked a boyfriend into the house . . . always spying and often stealing. Little things – a book, a holiday snapshot, loose change lying around. He compensated himself with little thefts, enjoying the discomfiture when the objects went missing. Now, light-footed and always listening, he opened the library door and slipped inside. He pressed the switch and flooded the room with subdued light. 'Now,' he murmured. 'Now let's see what you were really studying, dear Father.'

* * *

'Well,' Alan demanded, 'what did you find out?' He hadn't invited James to Chelsea; he felt his brother needed a little more humiliation to bring him to heel. 'I'll meet you at The Crown,' he said tersely when James telephoned him. 'We've got a party on at home tonight. See you there at six-thirty.' A party to which the out of favour were not invited. James swallowed the snub, as he had done all his life, and said he'd be at The Crown. He wasn't a pub man, unlike Alan, who loved drinking in them. He didn't feel easy in the noisy blokish atmosphere of London pubs; his brother, usually surrounded by cronies, was in his element. He arrived promptly and Alan was late. When he came, pushing through the crowd round the bar, he didn't apologize.

'How was the visit then?' he asked. 'Enjoy yourself?'

He was so full of anger, James thought. It burned in him, showing in his eyes, throbbing through the most casual remark. James was three inches taller and more powerfully built, but Alan frightened him.

'Not really,' he answered. 'She'd heard from her solicitors; she realizes that you're serious about contesting the will.'

'I'll bet she does. She ought to know I don't make threats I won't carry out. So what did she say, then?' He glared at James.

'She asked me to try and fix a meeting between you,' was the answer, 'so you could try and talk it out. She's not backing down, Alan, but she doesn't want to fight if there's another way.'

'I'll bet,' he said savagely. 'So she sent you along as peacemaker, did she? She doesn't know much about you, does she?'

'I'm just telling you what she said,' James answered. 'She spent most of the time asking questions about all of us; you, me, Father and Mummy.'

'For Christ's sake,' Alan hissed at him. 'Why did you go along with it? What did you tell her? You bloody fool! She was looking for dirt to dig up.'

'No,' James insisted, 'I don't think so. She said she was trying to understand why you and Father hated each other . . . where

I fitted in . . . what happened with Mummy. I know you hate her guts, Alan, but Father never told her anything. You know what he was like – he wasn't exactly communicative.'

'No,' Alan agreed, 'he never talked to me; he talked *at* me. If he'd sat down with Mum once, and tried to really talk to her, instead of pushing her into some fucking clinic and letting other people deal with the problem.' He stopped, lost in some bitter memory. James didn't contradict him. He had been his mother's confidant and favourite; he would never see anyone else's point of view. James had enough experience of the drug scene in New York to know that talking to addicts in rational terms is a waste of time. There was nothing Richard Farrington could have said or done to help his wife because she didn't want to help herself.

Alan dragged himself back to the present. 'So what did you tell her about our happy family? About me, for instance?'

'Nothing,' James lied, 'I talked about Father mostly. You remember how much time he spent locked up in the library? He didn't go there much any more after they got married. I know you'll hate to hear this, I know I hated it, but I think he was very happy with her, quite different to the way he was with Mummy. A doting father, too. I saw that for myself; he was all over that child.' He slipped the knife in, all innocence as he did so, knowing that every word made Alan writhe with jealous rage. The chances of hitting back were rare enough, but sometimes he risked it. Then he went on, covering up the wound, 'I've always wondered what the fascination was, why he spent so much time in there. Looking at papers, reading all that old stuff he collected. Religious, wasn't it? Studying world religions?'

'How the hell would I know,' his brother snapped. 'Probably a whole lot of pornography! Why?' His eyes glared suspiciously. 'Why the interest all of a sudden?'

James said, 'Well, it's all part of the estate, isn't it? His collection or whatever. And it goes to dear little half-sister Belinda, along with RussMore and everything else that should be yours. I'd be interested if I were you.'

Alan didn't answer. He understood James better than James

realized. He was playing games; with Christina and with him. He had always played games; it was his way of asserting himself. Alan had never bothered to look for the reason; he simply recognized a certain devious cunning in his brother and it made him wary. He would use James if he could, but he would never trust him. He swallowed his drink and said, 'So she wants a meeting, does she?'

James hid his surprise. 'That's what she asked me to ask you. If you could meet and talk it through.' He picked up Alan's empty glass. 'Can I get you another one?'

'No,' Alan snapped, 'and if you want to smoke, wait till I've gone. It's a filthy bloody habit!' James put the cigarettes away.

'What do you think – would it do any good if you did sit round a table? Might save a lot of trouble and a lot of money. Only the lawyers are going to get fat out of this, you know.'

'She *has* got to you, hasn't she?' Alan sneered. 'Since when have you minded about trouble? You'll revel in it, James, don't try and con me. And none of the shit will stick to you because you'll have the money from Langley Farm and you can sit in New York and watch the fun. I tell you what,' he leaned forward, 'I'll meet her; tell her that. But when I choose and where I choose. I'm off now; the party starts at eight. Call me before you go back.'

He got up and shouldered his way through the evening crowd of drinkers. James took out his cigarettes and lit one, then he bought himself a glass of wine. He didn't resent his brother's rudeness; being snubbed didn't diminish him because he was in control for once. He had something that could have helped Alan, but he had decided not to give it to him; even before they met. He would wait, and choose his moment to pull the strings and make the puppets dance.

'I'm sorry, Mrs Farrington, but Mr Stone is out of the office all day. I'll put you through to Mr Wallberg.'

He came on the line before Christina could protest. 'Mrs Farrington? How can I help?'

Christina hesitated. She had the letter in front of her.

Humfrey Stone was out all day, and there wasn't time to delay until he came back. 'I've had a letter from my stepson, Alan, asking me to meet him,' she said. 'Tomorrow, at his office in London. I wanted to let you know before I went.'

Rolf was thinking quickly. This move was unexpected. 'He's asked you for a meeting? I'm surprised. What is the tone of the letter?'

'I'll read it to you,' she answered. 'Dear Christina, James says you're willing to talk. Be at my office at five o'clock tomorrow. Alan.'

Rolf said, 'It's an ultimatum, not an invitation. Why did you initiate this, Mrs Farrington, without consulting us?'

'I don't have to explain myself to you, Mr Wallberg. This is just a courtesy to let you know I'm going.'

He interrupted quickly; her tone warned him she was about to ring off. 'Wait, wait, please, Mrs Farrington. I'm sorry if I sounded offhand but this is very serious. Please listen to me. Look, are you coming up to London tomorrow?'

'Yes,' Christina said firmly, 'I am. I've told you, I'm seeing my stepson.'

'All right,' Rolf agreed. 'Of course, it's your decision, but at least let us meet and discuss what you should say. Let me talk to you first, before you see him. I can drive down this afternoon if that's more convenient than meeting me in London. Please?'

'I don't see what all the panic is about,' Christina protested. Rolf began to relax; at least he'd persuaded her to talk to him.

'After all, the worst that can happen is he behaves like a pig and I walk out. But I have to try and avoid a lawsuit if I can.' Rolf saw the opportunity open and he did not hesitate.

'That is my own view exactly, and in this I differ from Humfrey. At all costs you should try and settle this business without going through a long legal fight.'

Christina hesitated. 'I'm surprised to hear you say that,' she said. 'I expected you to be much more aggressive than Humfrey. What worries you about this meeting?'

'Everything,' he said. 'Let me come down and explain. Five-thirty, would that be all right?'

But at five o'clock his secretary called to say he'd been delayed leaving and would be with her before seven. He was still in his office when the call was made; he had never meant to get there on time. He would be late, so late that she would have to ask him to stay for dinner. Trust had to be established and built into dependence, and this Swedish woman had all the independence and honesty of her race, and the courage that went with it. He knew the type, even though he didn't belong to it; it wouldn't be easy to fool her. But he had no scruples; scruples did not go with the job.

'Mummy, what time is Mr Wallberg coming?'

'Some time around seven,' Christina told her. Belinda was twisting up her hair into a long dark pony-tail, winding a coloured band to hold it in place. She would be striking rather than pretty as she developed; she had her father's academic gifts combined with a strong artistic talent. She drew and painted with real originality and, apart from her passion for ponies, which was a healthy pre-adolescent phase, she was a serious child with every promise of becoming a clever achieving young woman.

So far, and in spite of local boys she met at parties, she'd shown no particular interest in boyfriends. Compared with many eleven-year-olds, Belinda was still immature, and both her parents had been relieved that the problems of adolescence seemed in abeyance. Her interest in the lawyer surprised Christina. 'He'll have to stay to dinner, I'm afraid, coming this late,' she said. Belinda noticed the lack of enthusiasm.

'Don't you like him, Mum?'

'No, not much.' She had always been honest when asked a direct question and brought Belinda up to be the same.

'Why not? I think he's nice.'

'Lindy, you only met him once and he said all the right things, that's why you liked him.'

'He meant them,' was the reply. 'I know when people talk down to me and I hate it; he didn't. Can I have dinner with you, then?'

Christina smoothed out the long pony-tail of hair. 'Darling,' she said, 'he's coming on business; you can have supper in the study and watch telly. He may not even stay and, if he doesn't, we'll have it together.'

'I thought you'd like him,' she persisted. 'He's Swedish, too.' Christina didn't argue. There was a very stubborn streak in her child and she knew exactly where it came from; she would have put up the same objections herself to her own parents. Downstairs Richard's old terrier began to bark.

'I expect that's him, now,' she said. 'I'll go down. Come and say hello if you like, but don't stay long; I want to get this over with.'

He was waiting in the panelled drawing-room. He got up and came towards them, smiling. 'I'm so sorry, Mrs Farrington, I'm terribly late. I hope you got the message from my secretary?'

'Yes, I did,' she answered. 'Don't worry, it's quite all right. Lindy wanted to say hello to you.' He stooped slightly and shook hands with the child. It surprised Christina to see real warmth in his expression.

'Hello, Lindy. How are you? Enjoying your holiday?'

Belinda smiled up at him. 'Yes, I'm having a great time. I've been riding and staying with friends; they've got a super pony.' She gave a mischievous glance towards her mother. 'I'm trying to persuade Mum to buy me a decent pony so I can compete. We've got an old donkey who won't go faster than a trot!'

He laughed. 'I'm sure your mother will think about it,' he said. 'I'll try and talk her round.' He was naturally at ease with Belinda, but not with her. Guarded, calculating; she couldn't pin it down, but the effect was uncomfortable.

'Lindy, we've got to talk some business, so you go on and amuse yourself, will you?' she said. They waited in silence till Belinda had left them. Then she asked, 'What can I get you to drink? And do sit down.'

'Vodka on the rocks, please,' he said. 'But can't I get it for you?'

There was a tray of wines and spirits laid out on a fine walnut table. Richard had insisted that they had their pre-dinner drinks alone and talked about what they had done during the day. Not even the adored only child had been allowed to intrude on that private time. She had always prepared their drinks.

'No thanks, I'll do it.' She noticed with a jolt that he had taken Richard's chair. Not that he knew it, of course, but combined with his personality, it jarred on her. She poured vodka, added crushed ice and lemon and then a much smaller drink, filled with tonic, for herself. She sat opposite to him. 'It's good of you to come down,' she said.

'I felt it was really necessary. And again, I'm sorry I'm so late. I hope you're not going out this evening and that I haven't inconvenienced you?'

All this politeness, she thought; this modest approach – it didn't suit him. She wished he would stop and be himself, whatever that was. 'No, I wasn't doing anything. Lindy and I were just having a quiet supper together.'

He drank the vodka and said pleasantly, 'This is very good. Is it Stolichnaya?'

'Richard wouldn't touch anything else. I find it very strong. He always said I drowned everything.' She smiled slightly, not at Rolf, but at the memory of Richard's gentle teasing. 'Now, Mr Wallberg, why are you so worried about me seeing my stepson?'

He looked straight at her. 'Because I think it's some kind of a trap,' he said. 'You've given him an opening and he's taken it. Not because he wants a peaceful resolution, but because he sees it as weakness. Who else will be at this meeting? His lawyers? He didn't mention that, just gave you what sounded to me like a rude ultimatum. Can I ask you something? What gave you the idea of making personal contact? The letter mentioned James, your other stepson. Where does he figure in this?'

'He came down to see me,' she replied. 'I asked him to talk to Alan.' Rolf began to see the pattern. James had ingratiated himself with his brother by coming down to spy on her and report back, and she'd given him a weapon Alan could use against her.

Christina saw the hard expression and thought suddenly that he was as intimidating as Alan Farrington, yet he had said she should try for a settlement; that really surprised her. He caught her looking at him and knew that he was being examined. 'Mrs Farrington,' he said very quietly, 'you don't have to like me, but you do have to trust me. I'm your lawyer and I'm on your side, and I would feel a lot more comfortable if you called me Rolf. Please.' He saw her face flush.

'I'm sorry . . . I didn't mean to give an impression like that. I was just being po-faced.' She smiled at him awkwardly and said, 'Please excuse me.'

'Po-faced? I haven't heard that before.'

'I hadn't either till I came to live here. It's very English; very Fifties, I think. It means sour, disapproving. Boot-faced . . . they have such funny expressions.'

'They're a funny people altogether. We're open, easy to understand; they're not. I wonder how you managed to be happy; it's all so different from home.'

'Yes, but I've grown to love it,' she countered, 'and remember I had a wonderful husband. It took a little time to make friends; the English don't accept you until you've proved yourself, but when they do, they're the best friends in the world.'

She stopped, realizing they had lapsed into Swedish. For those few moments there had been a rapport between them. As if he sensed this, he spoke in English. 'That was nice,' he said, 'like being at home. But I musn't waste your time or forget why I'm here. What are you going to say to your stepson tomorrow?'

She hesitated, then she said, 'I'm going to tell him I understand why he feels so bitter and angry. I never knew what kind of an upbringing he and James had had, till James told me; I didn't know how much he suffered when his mother got into drugs and when she died. I'm going to tell him I'm not his enemy.' He nodded. 'But I'm not going to go against Richard's will; he can have everything that was left to me personally, but not RussMore.'

'Which is the only thing he wants,' Rolf countered. 'And do you really think he'll listen?'

She said quietly, 'I don't know, but I have to give him the chance. Both those sons had a traumatic childhood; it explains a lot about them.'

'A lot of people suffer trauma,' he said, 'it doesn't need to turn them into bullies; often the reverse. I wouldn't be too influenced by what James told you. Do you believe your husband was a bad father?'

'No,' she said quickly. 'No, I don't. He was a man of his generation and upbringing. He told me how miserable his life was; the anxiety; the hope that this cure or this psychiatrist would help her . . . the terrible disappointment when she went back on heroin. And she played Alan off against Richard, turning him against his father, making him take sides. She petted James one minute and rejected him the next; he was hopelessly confused.'

'Yes,' Rolf said. 'You know the saying? Show me an addict and I'll show you a manipulator and a liar; it's harsh but it's true. If you must see your stepson, let me come with you.'

Christina said, 'No, that would be provocative. I'm not starting off by being aggressive.'

Rolf could imagine the good intentions, the sympathetic approach, based on reason and discussion. He could predict Alan Farrington's reaction. She had a lot to learn about people, this Swedish country girl who had turned into an English lady. You fight force with greater force, otherwise you're dead.

He finished his vodka, leaned back in the chair and said, 'You realize he may have a tape running, recording everything you say, including this offer to give up your personal legacies? He may even be wired himself.'

Christina dismissed it. 'That's fantasy, not real life. People don't behave like that.'

'I've known it happen, several times. I can't persuade you not to go?'

'I'm afraid not.'

He paused. They had made progress; she was more relaxed, less cautious with him. He looked at his watch. 'I'm keeping you from your dinner,' he said. 'I should go. It's eight o'clock.'

Christina got up, she took his glass. 'We don't eat till eight-thirty, and of course you must stay. Perhaps we can talk about something else except this horrible business. Let me give you a refill.'

'Thank you, I'd like that. And we won't mention your stepson or the will. I think perhaps we can find lots of things to talk about.'

The dining-room was small and dark with heavy panelling. He noticed that the silver was beautiful, with the soft patina of age; the wine, too, was exceptional. He also noticed that she looked quite beautiful in the soft light from the pictures and candles. She had a fine bone structure that would age gracefully, and the clear Nordic blue eyes that were deeper than his own, and a full mouth that promised sensuality. No wonder Richard Farrington had fallen in love with her. She began by asking him about himself; more from politeness than real interest, he realized that, but it was a step forward. Brothers and sisters, she enquired. None, he told her. He was an orphan, adopted by a couple who lived in Gothenburg; good people but stern. Lutheran stern, he added, and Christina said, 'I know what you mean, but my family weren't like that, they were very liberal, very socially conscious. My father encouraged us to express ourselves, make our own decisions. We didn't worry about Church; truth was my father's God. The only time he ever punished us was if we lied.'

'You were lucky,' he remarked. 'I was beaten if I lied *or* told the truth. I learned early on it was better to say nothing. Maybe that's why I became a lawyer, so I could talk all the time. They were very proud of me; I was a success and they liked that, but I knew they weren't my real parents – they told me very early on. It made a difference, I think. I used to go and see them occasionally, but we weren't close. They're dead now.' She looked at him and her face softened.

'It sounds very bleak to me. And sad.' Easy to arouse her sympathy. He felt no scruple; what he'd told her was the truth. As adoptive parents went, he had drawn a very short straw.

'And what do you do when you're not being a lawyer? Are you married?' Christina asked him.

'No, and never have been,' he said, 'I don't like commitment. I have girlfriends, but I don't want more than that. I ski . . . show me a Scandinavian who doesn't, and for amusement, I collect old manuscripts.'

'How strange. So did Richard.' He lowered his eyelids, covering any sudden glitter of excitement.

'Did he? What a coincidence. There was no mention of a collection in his will. Perhaps it wasn't serious collecting?'

'I don't know,' she admitted. 'He used to go into the library and shut himself away sometimes, but I never thought about it. It was his hobby and I wouldn't have appreciated any of it anyway. You know, when we met in Stockholm, he told me he'd been to some dealer and got lucky. I can't remember what he bought, but he seemed very excited about it. James talked about this hobby of his, too. He said Richard was obsessed by his collection when they were children, and spent hours locked away in the library. It used to annoy them and their mother. He said something about the study of comparative religions.' She shrugged slightly. 'I'm afraid that sort of scholarship is way above my head.'

'The study of comparative religions through the Scriptures and the scrolls,' he remarked.

'I've heard of it; it's very esoteric. I'd no idea he was so intellectually gifted; Humfrey Stone described him as a nice old-fashioned English gentleman.'

'Which he was,' Christina said, 'with a wonderful sense of humour and a loving heart.'

He looked at her for a moment and then said, 'What a nice tribute. How many wives would say that of their husbands, I wonder? Not many.' He looked at his watch, pushed back his chair and said, 'If you'll excuse me for not having coffee, I should be going. It's a good two hours, even at this hour.'

Christina did what she would have done if they had been in Stockholm, and hospitality was a Farrington tradition. 'You've had too many drinks to drive and the police are very strict around here, you'd better stay the night. There's a room always ready for anyone who needs a bed. Richard never let guests drive home after dinner unless they didn't drink.'

Rolf smiled. 'Did he learn that from you?'

'No, he learned it from friends who'd lost their licences. Please stay.'

He hesitated; he didn't want to spend the night there; it was too seductive, too removed from the real world, and yet it was a major step towards gaining her confidence.

'All right, that's very kind, and perhaps you could show me your husband's manuscripts? I'd be so interested.'

'I would if I had any idea where to find them amongst all those books and folders in the library,' Christina said. 'If you come again we could look for them.' He had to be content with that.

3

He had gone when she came down to breakfast, and the housekeeper handed her a note: 'Thank you for dinner and a very pleasant evening. I'm in the office all day if you need me. Please call after the meeting. Rolf.'

Christina threw the note away. She had a busy morning and she planned to drive to London in time to keep the appointment and then come straight home to RussMore. Belinda had invited her friend over to spend the day and stay the night. She was a confident self-sufficient child; she had always been loved without being spoilt, and she had no doubts about herself, unlike Richard's two sons. Christina was glad to be occupied; it stopped her being nervous about confronting Alan. She meant to approach him reasonably, to try and defuse some of the rage and resentment which had devolved from his father onto her.

Above all, she told herself as she drove towards his Holborn office block, I'm not going to be intimidated. It was a tall glass-fronted building, with Farrington Fast Foods in heavy steel letters above the entrance. Alan's office was on the top floor. A secretary came to meet her; a smooth efficient young woman with an empty smile.

She knocked on the door of the inner office and Christina heard his voice call out, 'Come!'

'Mrs Farrington to see you,' and then she was walking in and they were face to face. He was standing, but he didn't move towards her. There was a huge window behind him with a view of sky and rooftops, and Christina noted a stream of cumulus cloud speeding past on a strong wind.

'Hello, Alan,' she said. He didn't answer for a moment; looking at her filled him with a surge of anger. He actually turned his head away.

'You wanted to see me,' he said abruptly. 'Sit down. I've a meeting at six-fifteen, so make it brief.'

Christina moved to a chair. She had felt the colour rise at his sheer rudeness, but she didn't falter. She didn't hurry; she settled herself, unbuttoned her jacket and faced him calmly.

'Why don't you sit down too? I didn't come for a row or a confrontation; and I'm not going to have either. I wanted to try and talk this through with you. Can't we discuss the situation like two rational people, instead of fighting?'

Alan glared at her. 'There's nothing to discuss,' he said. 'I'm contesting the will, and I'm going to win.'

She said quietly, 'I don't think so. Only the lawyers will win if we go to court. You can drag us all through the dirt if you want to, but your father had the best advice and he knew the trust and the will were unbreakable. I've come to make you an offer.' He smiled at her; it was a naked sneer.

'Oh, have you? Let's hear it then.'

Christina said, 'I'll give you everything your father left me, which wasn't in the trust: money, his personal portfolio, everything. I can't do more than that. I've nothing else to offer because RussMore is Belinda's.' She leaned towards him suddenly. 'Alan,' she said, 'I'm not your enemy; I'd like us to be friends. Why keep all this hatred going? Nothing can bring your mother back, or change the way you and Richard felt about each other; they're dead and it's over, and none of it was my fault. Believe me, now that I know more about it, I'm really sorry for James and for you.'

He leaned back in his chair, as if to distance himself. There was a pause; Christina couldn't read his expression because he refused to look at her. He picked up a folder, opened it, waited while he read something, and then he met her eye to eye. 'This', he said, making every word distinct, 'is the report on you from a firm of private investigators in Stockholm; it confirms what I always suspected. You were quite a slag, weren't you . . . lots of boyfriends. Let me see . . .' He riffled the pages. 'Here we are . . . a Jan Borg was knocking you up before you met my father, wasn't he? He'd only just dumped you when you picked the old man up in a park; and you were pregnant when you married him, weren't you? With Borg's child?'

Christina didn't realize how white she was; she went ashen pale when she was angry, and he misunderstood the signal. 'You clever bitch,' he went on. 'You conned the old fool, but you won't get away with it, I'll prove your bastard isn't a Farrington, and that fucks up the will and the trust. The trust says specifically that only a Farrington can inherit RussMore. So, you can stuff your offer; keep the money, you're going to need it; I'm going to take everything else.'

She got up, walked up to the desk and said, 'Before your father died, he said to me that you had bad blood, inherited from your mother. I didn't know what he meant, but I do now. You would injure a child – Belinda is *his* daughter. I will fight you to the end of the line. You will never, ever have that house, whatever it takes to stop you.'

Then she turned away and walked out of the office, leaving the door wide open. When she was in her car and tried to switch on the ignition, she was shaking with anger so much that, for a minute, she could not turn the car key. Suddenly, without thinking, she lapsed into Swedish. She had forgotten what she had become; she was Christina Nordohl again, and she called him a string of names in her own language. She had felt sorry for him. She had worked up a sense of guilt about what Richard had done, imagining the rebellious, misunderstood boy seeing his mother sink into drugs and die a fuddled death by drowning. She had been genuinely sorry for him, and ready to give up her personal independence to make up for it all. 'Oh,' she spoke the words out loud, amazing a driver parked alongside at a red light, who couldn't see anyone else in the car. 'Oh, you damned bloody fool.' English and Swedish were mixed up. 'You thick-headed idiot. To be sorry for that pig, that filthy bullying pig.' She was hooted into action by the car behind, and she drove on after the lights had changed, so churned up with anger that she went too fast and had to brake too hard. Now there was something else besides outrage. Fear began to creep into the turmoil of emotion, cold fear, cooling the heat of temper. He'd got a dossier on her private life before she married. The insult spat at her, *You were quite a slag . . . Lots of boyfriends*. He had made the teenage love affairs and the brief involvements of her twenties into something dirty and shameful. *I'll prove your bastard isn't a Farrington.*

It could destroy Belinda. Christina said, 'Oh my God,' in English. 'What am I going to do?' She signalled, pulled into the kerb and stopped the car. She couldn't go back to RussMore without talking to someone. Belinda and her friend would be there. 'What happened with Alan, Mum?' asked almost as an afterthought. Talk about ponies and competitions.

Your bastard isn't a Farrington.

Christina dialled the number on her car phone. 'Mr Wallberg, please.' A pause. 'I'm sorry, he left the office about twenty minutes ago. I'll put you through to his secretary. May I ask who's calling?'

'Mrs Farrington. Look, it doesn't matter.' But she was put through anyway.

'He left a number where you can reach him,' the secretary said. 'He was expecting you to call. He's at the Lancaster Hotel. Can I get him to call you?'

'No,' Christina decided, 'I'll call him. He should be there by now. Give me the number.'

'Alan?' Fay shouted down to him, hearing the front door bang. 'Alan?'

'Yeah,' he shouted back, irritated that she was upstairs. 'I'm home, for Christ's sake. Who d'you think it was?'

'I'm coming,' Fay called back. She frowned, hearing the bad-tempered answer. It hadn't gone well; he was upset. That bitch, she fumed, closing the nursery door on the children with an abrupt 'You just be quiet, I'm going to talk to Daddy.'

He was in what she called his den – a term that would have made her dead father-in-law cringe – and he was already downing a very dark whiskey.

'What happened, darling?' She came in and put her arm round his shoulders.

'She started by saying how sorry she was for me,' he said. 'All sugary sweet, "I want to be friends," that kind of crap. I nearly chucked up.'

'You mean she backed down?' Fay said slowly.

'Like fuck,' he snarled. 'She went into a real act. "I'll give you everything your father left me . . . money, shares . . . but RussMore belongs to Belinda."' He mimicked the Swedish accent. Half the whiskey went down, but Fay didn't comment.

'So?' she prompted. 'You told her what to do with it?'

'Yeah, I told her. I told her about the dossier; I told her we knew about all the men she'd shacked up with. Then I played my ace: Mr Jan Borg. Just out of bed with him and in with Dad. She had one up the spout when she married him. I wish you'd seen her face; that got to her.' He moved, easing away from her comforting arm. She took the empty glass.

'I'll get that,' she said quickly. 'All right,' Alan muttered, 'but I want a decent drink, none of your cat's pee.'

'Here,' she said, handing him the drink, 'and stop taking it out on me, will you. I'm on your side, remember?'

Alan looked up at her and shook his head. 'Sorry, sorry,' he said. 'I didn't mean it. She just got right up my nose, darling. Right up it. All that sympathy and understanding shit. But it didn't last; I told her I'd prove that kid was a bastard and she dropped the act bloody quick.'

'Alan?' Fay stared at him. 'Alan, you didn't mention what

you did . . . before the funeral?' She was horrified that his temper might have betrayed him.

'No, of course I didn't,' he snapped. 'What sort of a fool do you think I am? Of course I didn't say *that*! That's the trump; the ace in the hole. Right at the door of the bloody court!' He tasted the drink.

'She didn't back off then,' Fay prompted again. He should have been triumphant, crowing, but he wasn't and she couldn't understand why.

'No,' he answered emphatically. 'No, she didn't. She said she'd fight me all the way; after she'd taken a dirty swipe at my mother, saying it came from Dad, of course. It was just as well I had the desk between us or I might just have hit her.'

Fay said quietly, 'Thank God you didn't.' So that was it: his mother. She had dug into a nerve when she attacked the sacred icon of Josephine Farrington; he had no defence against that. Fay knew him so well; she recognized the terrible unhealed wounds behind the hectoring and the bluster. She was more maternal towards him than towards her own small children.

'I hate that woman,' she said softly. 'I think I hate her more than you do. Never mind what she said, she'll lose and she'll be dragged through the dirt in public, with her bloody daughter. Because,' she came to the chair and, bending, kissed him. 'Because I have a brilliant clever husband. No-one would have thought of doing what you did; I'm proud of you. Now come up and say good night to the kids; they won't go to sleep till they've seen you.'

She took the glass of whiskey out of his hand; he didn't protest. 'You can finish that when you come down. I don't want you smelling of Scotch when you kiss them.'

They went upstairs hand in hand.

The elegant blonde smiled at Rolf Wallberg. She never went to his office; when she called a meeting unexpectedly he had to go to the Lancaster. Not without protest. 'I'm expecting a call from Mrs Farrington.' The answer was swift, delivered with the mixture of authority and smoothness that was her trade mark.

'So leave this number. I have to see you, I'm flying home on the nine o'clock.'

She attracted attention wherever she went. The gleaming blond hair, the perfect make-up, above all the model figure, with the bonus of a generous bust. Rolf noticed the scrutiny of other men as they sat together. It amused him; he found her a sexually satisfying machine, programmed to please herself and her partner. She was the most unfeminine woman he had ever known.

'Well, you're making some progress,' she conceded. 'It's taking time. One thing, Rolf; one question bothers me. Why didn't you search the library when you had the chance?' The suspicion was there, lurking in the very dark eyes. She didn't trust him, but then trust wasn't part of her job, suspicion was.

'If you saw the library,' he said, 'you wouldn't ask the question. I'd say there were around two thousand books in the place. Drawer upon drawer of catalogues, references, indexing and cross-indexing. It's not a library for show, Irma; it's for real. I've suggested we look together and she agreed.' He checked his watch. It was well past six, and Christina had not called. Normally he never used the name Irma because she didn't like it. Doing so was a measure of his irritation at this last-minute summons, and the inquisition that followed. He looked at her and let his feelings show.

'If you think anyone else can do the job faster, then get them and I'll pull out.'

She said, 'If I thought that, I would. I have to report back, you know. This is costing money, resources and time. Some people think they could be better employed on our other problems. After all, you do have a personal motivation.'

'I do,' he agreed, 'and I'm quite ready to see it through without back-up. Take that message home with you.'

Suddenly she relaxed; she picked up the glass and swirled the ice-cubes round the vodka, before taking a delicate swallow.

'Cool it,' she advised, 'I'll forget you said that. And I think I see someone coming over; I'd say this is your telephone call.'

He stood up; she was right, a Mrs Farrington was on the line. 'I'll take it in the booth,' he said.

'I'll wait here,' the woman promised. 'Don't be too long; I have to be at Heathrow by seven-thirty.'

'Rolf?' Christina said. 'Sorry to disturb you.'

'You're not,' he interrupted quickly, 'I've been waiting for your call. What happened? You sound upset.'

'I am. You were right, I shouldn't have gone. I just need to talk to someone before I go home. Are you busy or can you spare a few minutes?'

'Where are you?'

'In my car. I'm parked up by the Guildhall.'

'Give me the name of the street, I'll come straight there.'

'No, please, you don't have to do that.'

'I want to,' he insisted. 'Where are you parked?'

'Coleman Street,' she answered, and was surprised at the sense of relief that he was coming.

'I'll catch a cab,' he promised. 'Give me fifteen minutes. And don't worry, I'll take you for a drink somewhere and we can talk it through.'

He went back to the bar. She had finished her drink; he didn't waste time. 'I have to go,' he said. 'I'm meeting her. Have a good flight. Pay the bill, will you?' Then he was on his way out.

They found a wine bar near the Guildhall. It was small and noisy, crowded with City workers stopping off for a drink on their way home. Rolf looked round, frowning.

'This is hopeless,' he said. 'We can't talk here . . . there's no table free.'

'Yes, there is,' Christina interrupted. 'Look, over there, they're just going.'

He didn't waste time; he elbowed his way to the table before anyone else could get there. Christina sat down.

'What can I get you?'

'Red wine,' she said. She hadn't noticed the way he moved until then. Nothing deflected him, and however dense the groups, people seemed to give way. He was back very quickly with two glasses.

'Now,' he said, 'tell me.'

She looked stressed and pale; it was her own fault, he decided. She had been determined to try sweet reason with someone who would only interpret it as weakness. But Alan Farrington must have hit her hard. Christina drank some of the wine and grimaced; it was raw sour stuff, gulped down by the undiscerning.

'He was so vile to me,' she said. 'Apart from what he threatened, it was the way he did it, the way he spoke to me. I've never felt so degraded.'

'You've never been hated before, that's why; it's a very unpleasant experience. Don't be surprised that it's upset you. But at least you've learned not to try and deal with him hands on,' he said.

She looked up at him and said quietly, 'You were right. I'm sorry I didn't take your advice; I won't make that mistake again. I'm sorry I got hysterical and interrupted your evening, I just need to talk to someone before I go home.'

'You didn't interrupt anything,' he said, 'just a business appointment with a client; a demanding and difficult client. They're not all as thoughtful as you are. We really need to talk this through. Can I ask you one question? A difficult question?'

Christina hesitated. 'I don't think so. I'm sure I know what you're going to ask me and I'm not able to answer it. Not here and now.'

Rolf nodded. 'I understand. Well then, this is much easier. Are you going to fight your stepson, or give way to blackmail because you want to protect Belinda?'

She answered him, just as he had hoped. 'I will never give way. I think my husband would rise from his grave if that man got his hands on RussMore. He can throw all the mud in the world at me, but I'm not backing off. He wants a fight, Rolf, and I'll give him one.'

He smiled at her. 'Good, that's what I expected. He may be a clever businessman, but what he did today proves he's a fool. You're not a woman who responds to bullying. Now, if he'd been reasonable, even pleasant, I would have been really worried. I think we should go and have dinner somewhere quiet where we can have a proper discussion. Why don't you stay in London? Or, if you prefer, I can drive back to RussMore with you; whichever you like.'

She felt drained of energy. 'Can't we have a meeting later this week? Is it so urgent?' He wasn't going to let the relationship cool over the next few days. He had progressed further and faster than he had dared to hope.

'I think it's very urgent,' he persisted. 'Farrington will be meeting his lawyers tomorrow morning, be sure of that, so we can't delay. We have to plan our moves ahead and book a first class QC. There's a lot to be discussed. I want to be able to put everything in place and then go direct to Ruben Stone for his approval. I think we should talk tonight, while it's all still fresh in your mind.'

Part of her wanted to refuse, to resist what on instinct she felt was his manipulation, but there was a temptation to let him take control. For twelve years there had been a man to protect and defend her; she needed something more than her own resolve, and the trusting love of an eleven-year-old child.

'I hate to pressure you,' he said, 'after what you've been through today, but I think you're a strong lady. Why don't you stay in London tonight?' He knew that the Farringtons had a small service flat in Chelsea. He knew every asset that Christine possessed, and its value down to the last pound. He had all the arguments ready and the figures to back them. 'We could have dinner and you wouldn't have to drive all that way at night. Your staff can look after Belinda.'

Suddenly it seemed very persuasive, and she was tired; dinner and a positive plan of action, followed by a night in the flat. 'That's no problem,' she said. 'I can just call and tell them I'll be back tomorrow.'

'Good.' He smiled again. 'Then let's get out of here.' Briefly, as they pushed their way to the door, he touched her arm. When they reached the car, he said, 'I'll drive. You tell me where to go.' She gave him the keys and got in beside him.

'There's a bistro in the King's Road,' she said. 'Richard and I often went there. It's quiet and we can talk. He hated noisy restaurants.'

'So do I,' he agreed, 'I like to talk as well as eat.'

They were early by London restaurant standards and they settled into a small cubicle, facing one another. He ordered a vodka for himself and wine for her. It was a very good bottle, she noticed, glad to get the vinegar sharpness out of her mouth after the wine bar.

'I'm not very hungry,' Christina admitted.

'You should eat; food calms the nerves. It's better than drinking.'

'You know,' she said suddenly, 'coming here brings Richard back. It makes me think of the happy times we had, all the fun. This whole thing's like a nightmare: fighting his son for the house . . . I wish to God he'd never changed anything. Belinda and I would have been happy living somewhere else.'

'I thought you said you were going to stand up to your stepson,' he reminded her. He leaned forward, facing her closely. 'This isn't the time for nostalgia. You were happily married, but that's in the past. What matters now is the future and to do what your husband wanted, so let's not be sentimental, Mrs Farrington. Let's talk about money.' It was brutal and it startled her.

'Money?'

'Yes, money. A lot of money to buy the kind of legal representation that you're going to need. Harvey & Stone are top of the league; our fees alone will run into tens of thousands. As for the best QC in the field . . .' he shrugged, 'and the time factor – maybe two years before we even get to court. You could be looking at a cost of, oh, three hundred thousand pounds.' Christina actually gasped.

'But that's impossible, I couldn't afford anything like that. I'd have to sell the shares Richard left me, I don't have valuable possessions; the family things are entailed for Belinda.' She was really frightened and she wasn't thinking clearly. He pressed on.

'I am looking at the worst scenario,' he said. 'It might reach the courts earlier. But then if Alan Farrington knows what he's doing, and he'll get the best advice, be sure of that, he could drag it on and on, until you've literally sold everything and run out of money. If he was my client, that's what I'd tell him to do.' He waited, before adding, 'Then again, he may realize he's unlikely to win and withdraw, but I don't think that's his style.'

'He's very rich,' she said slowly. 'He could go on bleeding us till we had to start selling off the land. In the end there would be nothing left but what the trust owns: RussMore and the contents and a couple of tenanted farms.'

He poured a glass of wine for her. He refused to feel sorry for what he was doing. He ignored the visible signs of stress, the anxiety in her eyes as she looked at him. Instead he said gently, 'In the end RussMore would have to be sold, and he'd buy it.'

Christina put down the glass untouched and said. 'Is this why you were advising me to settle in the beginning?' He nodded.

'I foresaw what could happen,' he said.

'And now you're encouraging me to fight?'

'Yes,' he agreed. 'Yes, I am.'

'Why? How could you?'

He smiled; it was an odd smile, without warmth. 'Because I know something now that I didn't know then. I've given you one scenario – the worst one – now I'll give you the alternative.'

Suddenly he saw her flush with anger. 'Will you stop playing bloody games with me!' she said fiercely. 'You frighten the hell out of me and then you say there's an alternative . . .'

'You needn't worry about money.' He spoke calmly, unmoved by her anger. 'All you have to do is find the document your husband bought from that dealer in Stockholm, and you'll be rich enough to break Alan Farrington.'

She hardly slept that night. The more she went over the story he had told her, the more gaps appeared in it. Richard had stumbled on a priceless manuscript by making a casual visit to a dealer in rare books and early documents in Stockholm. Rolf Wallberg had glossed over the details, and she had been too surprised by the revelation to press him. It was part of the Song of Solomon, and centuries old. That meant nothing to Christina; she had a vague idea that it was connected with the Jews and the Old Testament, but that was all. He kept emphasizing the value, using the word priceless several times. Christina could name her price in the antiquarian world for such a treasure. Her problems would be over; she could outwait and outspend Alan Farrington until he, and not she, was forced to back off. Wallberg had seemed so excited; he was full of energy and enthusiasm. 'We're going to win,' he insisted, and then she had stopped him with a single question.

'How do you know about it? Why didn't you say anything before?'

The answer had been evasive, glib. 'I had to be sure; I didn't want to raise your hopes. I contacted the dealer and he remembered what he'd sold your husband; then I knew I was right. All we have to do is go through your husband's collection and find it!'

His confidence infected her. 'I can't believe it,' she said. 'Richard was comfortable but not really rich, and he stumbled on a fortune by accident . . .' Wallberg had smiled at her, the icy blue eyes almost warm.

'I'd say he found two treasures: the document and a wonderful wife! Now, when can we start to look? Tomorrow?'

'No,' she had said, remembering. 'No, not tomorrow. Richard's cousins are coming to stay. Their son's over from South Africa. You met them, I think, Peter and Jane Spannier.'

He said quickly, 'Put them off, this is more important.' The ruthlessness jarred on her.

'I can't,' she said, 'I'm fond of them and it's been arranged for weeks. I'll call you. You'll have to help me, I wouldn't know what to look for.'

He hadn't argued, but he became a little distant as if she had annoyed him. 'Of course, I forgot you have social obligations.'

'They're family,' she corrected, 'not social, and they were very good to me when I came to England.'

'I'm sorry,' he apologized. 'I never had a family, just the people who adopted me. I didn't mean to pressure you, I just got excited, because now I know we can win. I like to win.'

'So do I,' she answered, 'and I'm so very grateful to you, don't misunderstand. If you've discovered this, this manuscript, then I owe you everything.'

He saw her to the front entrance of the flat. He held out his hand and she took it. 'The trouble is, Mrs Farrington, you are a very nice woman, and I'm not a nice man. Maybe I can learn from you. Call me very soon, please.'

'I will,' Christina said. 'Good night, Rolf.'

When she was alone, the questions started coming, and there were hardly any answers. How had he known Richard had found something so rare and so valuable when no-one else did? How had he known which dealer and what to ask him? All he had been told, quite casually, as part of her conversation with her stepson, James, was that Richard Farrington collected ancient religious documents. Christina woke with the questions clamouring but unanswered. She made coffee and watched the sun rise above the Chelsea rooftops.

He had shown her a solution to the problem that had seemed insurmountable only a few hours before. Her stepson's face floated before her inner eye, twisted with hatred. *I'll prove your bastard isn't a Farrington.* He could ruin her; force either the sale of RussMore or the breaking of the trust in his favour. As the trustee and Belinda's guardian under its terms, she had the power to do that, so why should she probe into the mouth of this gift horse Rolf Wallberg had given her? Why did she feel uneasy instead of exhilarated and relieved? Because she didn't trust him and the man himself was at the core of her disquiet. He had avoided answering questions, but there were questions she had to ask herself. Did her instincts matter? If they were right, and there was something doubtful about this treasure Richard had found, should she enquire too closely? Her first obligation was to Belinda, to safeguard her future and pass on RussMore as Richard Farrington wanted.

She sat on the edge of the bed, watching the rosy dawn light change to early sunshine. Find it first, she decided, then see if Wallberg's assessment of its value was right. And that raised another question: He was a lawyer, not an antiquarian; how did he know the document was worth so much? There was no answer to that either.

She finished her coffee, locked up the flat and drove home. Before she reached RussMore, she had decided to confide in the Spanniers.

'You'll like Christina,' Jane Spannier insisted. 'It wasn't easy marrying Richard so soon after all that ghastly business with the first wife. Personally I couldn't stand her.' Harry Spannier watched the Lincolnshire countryside speed by as his mother drove and talked in her vigorous way; his father dozed in the passenger seat. The more she assured him that he would love RussMore and like Christina Farrington, the less convinced he became. He had been living and working in Johannesburg for the last fifteen years, been married and divorced over a year ago, but she still talked to him as if he were a boy and she knew his reactions better than he did himself. He knew she had disliked Josephine Farrington because she never hesitated to say so; she had no time for weakness, or illness, unless it was terminal, and even then his mother felt it should be endured without fuss. He had memories of a beautiful woman, with two sons younger than himself; one was a lout, the other a diffident boy with a reputation for stealing at his prep school. He had never been friends with them, although they were his cousins. RussMore was a very big, rather dark house, where he went to children's parties and a teenage dance at Christmas. He couldn't see why he should suddenly like it when he never had before.

'Of course,' his mother was saying, 'the poor girl's having a dreadful time with Alan. I heard from Sheila, who was told by friends in London, that he's going to contest the will!'

Harry roused himself to ask, 'Who's Sheila, Ma?'

'Sheila Duffield, cousin Philip's widow. She married old Tony Duffield a few years ago. He's nice but terribly dull, but Sheila loves being Lady Duffield, so she doesn't mind being bored to death.'

Harry laughed. 'I'll bet you told her so too.'

She was robust in her opinions and always free to give them. She maddened him at times, even after such a long absence and such a very different lifestyle, but he loved her, and admired her too. He'd had his fill of slyness and deceit, all five unhappy years of it, until he'd finally caught his wife in bed with his business partner when he came back early from a trip. Even then she'd tried to lie her way out of it. He'd punched lover boy, knocking out a few expensively capped teeth, and thrown her naked out of the bedroom, locking the door. The scandal had gone through Johannesburg like a bush fire. His wife came from a well-established South African family with strong Afrikaans connections, and his behaviour was criticized by a social group that condoned adultery but not publicity; he hadn't coped like a gentleman. His partner threatened to sue for assault. Harry had offered to knock the rest of his teeth out to make it worthwhile, sold his share of the export business and moved to the Cape to start again, but it hadn't worked. The transition to black majority rule had been a miracle; it promised a great future, but Harry Spannier suddenly felt homesick for the England he had left. He sold up and accepted his father's offer to come home and run their family business and the small farm.

So his cousin was contesting his father's will. 'Is he going to win?' he asked.

'What, darling, win what?' His mother had begun thinking of something else by the time he asked. 'Alan,' he reminded her, 'will he overturn the will? Whatever it is.'

'God knows,' Jane Spannier answered. 'He's got tons of money. I don't think there's an awful lot besides RussMore and the land, and that's all tied up. We can ask Christina; we'll be there soon. She's done wonders with that house; it used to be so gloomy.'

'So I remember. I'm surprised Richard let her touch anything; he was so possessive about it all.'

'Oh he doted on Christina,' she said briskly. 'Couldn't say

no to anything. And, of course, he adored the child; amazingly, she's not spoilt. Here we are; I can see the lodge gates through the trees, just ahead of us. It's lovely at this time of year, and the food's marvellous.'

His father had opened his eyes. He turned to his son and grinned. 'So's the wine,' he said. 'Dick kept a bloody good cellar.'

Harry grinned back. 'Then I *will* enjoy myself,' he said.

'If I were you', Fay said, 'I'd be careful what you say to him.' Alan Farrington had his smallest son on his knee. He looked at his wife over the child's head and said, 'He's my brother, and I've asked him to lunch before he goes back to the States, so why make a production out of it?'

Fay didn't retreat. 'Because I don't trust him. All right, he went down and saw her, and as a result you had the meeting, but so what? He's still got a nice big farm worth a small fortune and you've got nothing. One of our boys should have had Langley. But they weren't even mentioned in that will; not a word about them, as if they didn't exist!'

Alan knew how much their sons' exclusion riled her; she had always resented the way their grandfather had ignored them, and he shared her feelings. 'Darling, I know all that, but my bloody father hated me; he wouldn't leave anything to my children. You can't blame that on James, and whatever you say, he did help. The fact that that bitch offered to give Dad's legacy back is a sign of a weak case. My lawyers have the tape recording. Come on, be nice to him.'

'All right,' she agreed, but she didn't want to be nice to James; she didn't trust him.

'There's James now,' Alan said. 'Timmy, down you get. Go and call Robert.' He brushed the little boy's hair back; he loved his two sons. He often told himself that he was getting RussMore back for Timmy, the eldest, as much as for himself.

James came in as the child ran out. He smiled and said, 'Hello, Timmy,' but the child ignored him and ran off to find his brother. James kept the smile on his lips, but his eyes were hooded to hide the apprehension. He knew how much his sister-in-law disliked him, but he didn't care; it was Alan's reception that mattered and that might depend upon his mood.

'Hi,' Alan said, and James relaxed. He was friendly, even pleased to see him. Immediately James felt warm towards his brother; carrot and stick as his therapist described their relationship. James agreed with that; he knew it would never change.

Alan poured him a gin and tonic. The children came in and were encouraged by their father to kiss their uncle. They were nice children, James conceded, although children didn't appeal to him. Good-looking, with their father's dark hair and eyes, and with nice manners. He had brought each of them a book. He hadn't known what to buy, so he had resorted to his own childhood favourites and gave *The Wind in the Willows* to Timmy and *The Adventures of Peter Rabbit* to the four-year-old Robert. Both were expensively bound, from a specialist bookshop in Hill Street. He was duly thanked, given another prompted kiss, and then the boys were collected by their young nanny and taken off for lunch.

James was flying early next morning and was looking forward to going home; he thought of America as home, in spite of the brief pang of nostalgia when he was at RussMore. That life was not for him . . . He had friends and a lifestyle in New York that suited him. The remembered scents of an English rose garden were irrelevant to the man he had become. He would set about selling Langley and remitting the proceeds; there was a fine apartment on East 25th that could be bought with the money. He talked business to Alan during lunch – the progress of his own company and the future expansion of Alan's restaurant chain. Fay said very little; her interests were domestic so she didn't even try to join in, and James enjoyed excluding her. Then, when they were having coffee, he couldn't contain his curiosity any longer.

'Any developments with our dear stepmother?' Alan had described the meeting over the telephone; it had made James cringe. Brutal, insulting . . . he had felt sorry for Christina. He knew what it meant to suffer Alan's verbal assaults. He even regretted setting the meeting up, but the regret disappeared when he was thanked and asked to lunch. Alan ignored Fay's warning look; he'd eaten well and drunk a lot of wine, and he felt expansive, almost paternal to his younger brother. Alcohol could ignite aggression or make him sentimental, but now he was in a kindly mood.

'I took the tape along to my lawyers; they said it would be very useful.'

Fay tried to interrupt. 'Why don't we have coffee in the garden? Then James can see the children?'

James, longing for a cigarette, was tempted to agree, but he wanted to hear Alan's news. He recognized the diversion and said pleasantly, 'Oh, I'm happy staying here. So go on, Alan. What else did they have to say?'

'Their advice was to drag it out,' Alan said. 'Delaying tactics. Run her into debt with lawyers' fees, and if we lose the first round, go for an appeal. Be prepared for a three-year fight, at the end of which, she'd be forced to give in or sell up.'

James pulled a face. 'But what about the cost to you?'

Alan grinned. 'That's what I said. Why should I shell out money when it isn't necessary? I turned the idea down flat, and told them to get on and go for it! Book the best Queen's Counsel and try to get an early date for a hearing. They weren't pleased.' He laughed. 'They gave me a lot of arguments. Tried to say I don't have a very strong case. Dad was very ill, but he wasn't that old when he died, so undue influence is going to be tricky to prove . . . Married for twelve years, all that down-beat crap, trying to make me see it their way; I just said I'd do it my way. I know I'll win, even if they don't.'

'And you're really confident?' James asked him. The look in his brother's eyes gave him a curious thrill, part fear, part admiration.

'I'm confident,' was the answer. 'I can't lose, James. She tricked Dad into accepting her lover's child. I told her to her face and I can prove it.'

'How?' James stared at him. 'How can you prove it?'

'Alan,' Fay said, her voice very sharp. 'Alan, are we going

to see the boys again before James goes or not? They're going out for tea!'

'Yes, all right. Come on, let's go into the garden. You can have one of your filthy cigarettes outside.' The moment had come and gone. He wasn't going to tell James anything more; he had been boasting, enjoying himself, Fay need not have worried.

As they went through into the charming patio garden he whispered to her, 'I'm not pissed, and I wasn't going to tell him.' He slapped her lightly on the bottom. 'Now, let's talk about something else,' he announced. 'Darling, call the boys.'

James left soon afterwards without learning any more. He had his sister-in-law to thank for that, and he wouldn't forget it.

Rolf Wallberg's secretary buzzed him. 'Mr Stone's free, he'd like to see you in his office.'

'Thanks, Judy, I'll go right up now.'

He had only met the senior partner of Harvey & Stone twice since he had arrived from Stockholm. He had been expecting the summons at this stage. Ruben Stone's office was on the top floor of the building in Chancery Lane. It was a big room furnished with fine antiques and early-eighteenth-century racing pictures. The desk was suited to the man: large, imposing, richly carved, the finest quality. Ruben got up and came to greet him.

'My boy,' he said, 'how are you? Enjoying your work with us?' He didn't pause for an answer. 'I hope so, I hope so. Sit down, let's talk for a while. I have a client coming in fifteen minutes, but they're always late; they think it makes them important to keep other people waiting.' He gave a low throaty laugh. He had deep brown eyes, full of humour, and a charming manner that inspired confidences. He was the shrewdest solicitor in London and anyone taken into the firm was the cream of the young professionals. Rolf sat down; he refused a cigar and waited quietly while Ruben lit his own. 'My doctor says I should give up,' he remarked, 'but I don't listen to him. I smoke in moderation, I drink in moderation and I work hard – the recipe for a long life.

Now tell me, how are you getting on with the Farrington estate?'

He would know all the progress made already, but Rolf was expected to state his own case.

'Better than I expected,' he answered. 'Much better. I've convinced Mrs Farrington that she must fight her stepson's claim.'

Ruben puffed on his cigar. 'And she's agreed?'

'Yes, I am going down to see her soon to work out the financial arrangement. I believe I've given her confidence that she can afford the costs.'

'Good,' Ruben said thoughtfully, 'and she knows what they're likely to be? I wouldn't want to mislead her; she's a very nice lady and I liked her husband. Beautiful house, so Humfrey tells me. Have you reported to him yet?'

'No,' Rolf said, 'I am dealing with her myself; she seems quite happy with that. I will let him know the direction we're taking in due course, but he's very tied up right now.'

'He is, he is.' Ruben nodded. He looked into the chill blue eyes and smiled. 'You're doing well; it's not an easy case,' he remarked. 'I hope the experience will be useful to you when you leave us. And one more thing; leaving the professional aspect out of it, I've seldom come across a nastier shit than Mr Alan Farrington.'

Rolf looked up. 'You've met him?'

'Oh yes. He was at a charity dinner with his wife. Pretty girl.' He paused, tapped ash off his cigar before continuing. 'He made some very unpleasant racist remarks – I think he'd been drinking. My son was there too; I persuaded him not to make an issue of it, but he got very angry. We lost a lot of relatives in the last war; some were lucky enough to get to Sweden. It was very galling for the Germans to have them so close but out of reach. My son was very interested when I told him we were acting against Farrington for his stepmother. It's such a pity he decided to become an architect instead of coming into the firm. Yes, as I said, the man is a nasty shit, and if I wasn't head of a profit-making firm, I would defend Mrs Farrington for nothing.' He looked at his watch. It was a beautifully understated Cartier tank watch. 'They're late, my clients, just as I expected. What do you think of my new picture? Over there by the cabinet.'

Rolf twisted round and then got up to have a clear view.

'It's very fine. You like horse-racing?'

Ruben laughed. 'Yes, but only on canvas. That's a Ben Marshall; lovely quality. Came up for auction three months ago. It's been cleaned and reframed and it looks very well there; much cheaper and lasts longer than the real thing. Racing is one way of losing money; the next best thing is to make a bonfire of it. Now, my dear boy, I must let you go back to your office; I have some notes to study before my client *does* arrive. You're doing good work, and don't forget, I'm here if you ever need advice. And also don't forget to keep my nephew, Humfrey, in the general picture; he's a sensitive boy and I wouldn't like him to feel hurt.'

'I won't forget,' Rolf promised. 'Thank you, Mr Stone, and congratulations on the picture. It looks very good, even though I don't know anything about English paintings. If it was a Swedish landscape, I might have an opinion.'

He went down to his office to find a note on his desk; Mrs Farrington had called to ask if he could go down to RussMore on Saturday. He gave a deep sigh of satisfaction. Yes, indeed he could, and stay until he found what he had come to England to discover. He got his secretary to ring back and accept.

Christina had arranged a small dinner party for the Spanniers. She rang round their local friends and one couple had a daughter staying, so she included her for Harry Spannier. Because of Richard's age, their friends tended to be older than she was, and she hoped the Spanniers' son would enjoy himself. She was disconcerted to find that Harry Spannier spent the entire evening staring at her and hardly talked to his date. He wasn't what she had expected when he walked into the hall with his parents; she had imagined someone tall and bronzed from the South African sun. He was certainly tanned, but he was slightly built, no taller than she was, with a thin fine-featured face and deep-set dark eyes that reminded her suddenly of Richard. Jane embraced her, pronounced her tired-looking, which Peter promptly contradicted, saying she was looking super as always, and then they introduced Harry.

'I'm so glad to meet you,' Christina said. 'How does it feel to be home?' His answer was unconventional.

'I've no idea yet. It doesn't feel like home, but I'll get used to it. I'm glad to meet you too.' He had looked round the study and said, 'What an improvement – I remember this as a ghastly coal-hole of a room, you've made it bright and cheerful.'

Jane had said briskly, 'Take no notice of him, Christa. He speaks his mind, like me, I'm afraid. Typical Farrington.'

She gazed at him fondly. He gazed back and grinned. Then he had said to Christina, 'Not typical at all. They're a very secretive devious lot. My mother is some kind of throw-back.'

She was suddenly glad they had come; this rather odd man sparked his parents off, and she felt she would enjoy herself. Jane was enthusiastic about the friends coming to dinner. She knew them all and gave a candid opinion on the faults and virtues of everyone in turn. Once or twice Christina caught Harry Spannier's eye and he shook his head in mock exasperation.

'We'll dress up tonight,' Christina told them, 'to celebrate you coming and Harry being back. It'll do me good, so I hope you don't mind. I want it to be a proper party for you.'

'You're sweet,' Jane said and meant it. 'I brought Peter's old velvet jacket and I packed something for you, Harry; I hope it fits.'

'It should,' he said, 'I haven't exactly put on weight; lost a lot of it, in fact.' He spoke to Christina. 'There's nothing like a really messy divorce to get the kilos off.'

Jane had mentioned a broken marriage, but she hadn't gone into details. She said quietly, 'I'm sure. Let's have a drink before we go up and change.' He had stepped forward. 'I'll fix the drinks,' he said, 'just point me in the right direction.'

'Over there, by the window,' Christina had told him. 'It's all laid out. I'll have a very weak vodka and lots of tonic.'

'And Ma and Pop will have two *not* very weak whiskies. And I'll have a stiff pink gin, Jo'burg measure. Three fingers gin, two ice-cubes and wave the pink over the glass.' He came back with the drinks and went up to her. 'Cheers!' he said. 'Nice to be here.'

The party was a success. Christina sat at the head of the table; even Peter Spannier, whose ultimate judgement of a woman's looks was confined to 'super', like an enthusiastic schoolboy, managed to mutter to his wife, 'My God, doesn't Christa look good. Can't believe she'll be a widow for long!'

'She'll have to be careful,' Jane retorted. 'Lots of local men will have their eye on her, but they won't be thinking of marriage. There's hardly anyone round here who's single unless they're queer. That Copford girl is nice, but Harry's not made any effort with her; hardly said a word to her during dinner.'

Peter Spannier had noticed. He had also noticed that his son hadn't taken his eyes off Christina from the moment they met, but he knew his wife's tactless tongue, so he didn't say anything. As soon as coffee was over, Harry cornered her; the elderly retired naval captain gave place and moved on.

'You know,' he said, 'I've forgotten how civilized English parties can be. I remember thinking they were dull beyond description, but I've really enjoyed myself tonight, and you look wonderful in that black dress.'

'Thank you,' Christina answered, 'but surely life in Johannesburg was just as civilized, rather grander than the way we live now.'

'Oh, it was,' he said. 'If you had plenty of money you lived like a king. My wife was quite rich, so we had all the trimmings: lots of servants, big house, swimming-pool. I'm just sour about the whole thing, don't take any notice.'

'I won't,' she promised. 'Who would you like to talk to?'

He looked at her. 'You,' he said. 'I hear you're having trouble with Alan. Ma said he was taking you to court over Richard's will. Is that true?' She turned away from him.

'Yes, it is, but I don't want to spoil a happy evening talking about it. Come over and talk to Mrs Francis. She's just come back from a trip to St Petersburg.'

'All right, if I must,' he said. 'I'm sorry, I didn't mean to put my big foot in it. I'll give the tour of the Hermitage half an hour and then I'm coming back to talk to you.' He went over to where Mrs Francis was sitting and asked her, in a loud voice, to tell him all about her trip to Russia.

When the guests were leaving, he joined Christina in the hall. He helped some of the ladies with their coats – Mrs Francis gave him a warm smile. 'I have enjoyed meeting you,' she said. 'What a pity you're going to live in Norfolk!'

'Isn't it?' he agreed. She was recently divorced, mid-forties and hungry for male attention.

To Christina's embarrassment, he looked across at her and winked. She said softly to Jane, 'Was he always like this?'

'Worse,' his mother said. 'Believe it or not, he's mellowed. He used to be a nightmare if he didn't like somebody, but he certainly likes you. Be nice to him, dear, he's still very hurt; don't be put off by the bravado, he adored that wretched wife. I could kill her for what she's done to him. Peter, bedtime.'

'Don't bully me,' her husband retorted. 'Christina, I'd like a nightcap, if you don't mind.'

'I'll have one with you,' she said. 'Then we can all go to bed. Jane?'

'I'd better, otherwise he'll just drink brandy and go to sleep in the chair. Harry, are you joining us or do you want to opt out?'

He shrugged. 'I was hoping to be alone with the beautiful lady, but you've buggered it up, Pop, as usual. I'll have a drink if one's on offer.'

The evenings were cooler and there was a fire in the study. The big drawing-room was daunting without a crowd of people. Harry Spannier stopped before the Tudor portrait above the fireplace.

'What a strange picture! I don't remember that being in here.'

'It wasn't,' Christina explained. 'It was in the hall, and when I redecorated the room, Richard moved it in. He loved it. It's supposed to be a Farrington but there's no name.'

'I don't fancy the skull bit,' he said.

'Oh, God,' Jane interrupted, 'nor do I, but I never liked to say anything. Dick was very touchy about criticism.'

'James said the same thing,' Christina said. 'He suggested I moved it somewhere else, but I said no.'

'Speaking of James,' Jane Spannier said, 'I hear you're having trouble with Alan.' Christina hesitated. She had made up her mind to confide in them and ask their advice. She wasn't sure that one o'clock in the morning was the right time to do it, but why not, she decided. It might be easier than calling a conference in cold blood.

'He's contesting the will,' she said, 'and the terms of the new trust, leaving RussMore to Belinda. Actually I'm very glad you're all here, because I need your help. Harry, if you'll give everyone a refill, please, I'll tell you all about it.'

4

'It seems to me you'd better get this Swedish fellow down here and find this manuscript, or whatever, as quickly as possible.' Peter Spannier gave his verdict after a pause. It hadn't taken long to explain the bare facts: Alan's contesting of the will and the validity of the new trust; Rolf Wallberg's scenario of how the case would go; her inability to fund a long drawn-out legal battle and then the discovery of a priceless asset which could change everything.

Jane agreed vigorously. 'Get on with it, Christa, put the stuff up for sale and get the money behind you. I think Alan's behaviour is absolutely disgraceful! I shall write and tell him so.'

'Don't waste the stamp,' her husband interposed. 'He never cared what anyone thought of him. You couldn't penetrate that thick hide whatever you said.'

'You've been so good, letting me burden you with all this,' Christina said. 'It's been a great help just to talk to someone.

It's not something I'd discuss with friends, Richard wouldn't have wanted that. It's a family matter.' She got up. 'It's late and I've kept you all up.'

The elder Spanniers kissed her good night; she held the study door open for Harry but he closed it.

'There's a lot you didn't tell them,' he said quietly. 'Why don't you tell me?'

'Because I want to go to bed.'

'Christina, I'm family and I'm not as stupid as I look. You're in trouble, and I want to help. You never said on what grounds Alan was disputing the will. Breaking a family trust drawn up by experts like Harvey & Stone is bloody near impossible. What's he got over you?'

Christina opened the door and looked at him. 'Harry, will you please go? I want to turn out the lights.' He didn't move and, for a moment, she thought he might bar her way.

'All right,' he conceded, 'but I like you and I know you need a friend; I'd like it to be me. Doesn't it strike you as a bit odd that your Mr Wallberg knows more about ancient manuscripts than he does about the laws of inheritance? You can't sell anything out of the estate until this mess has been cleared up. Good night – see you in the morning.'

'Wait,' Christina caught hold of his sleeve, 'what do you mean . . . I can't sell anything?'

'Let's talk about it in the morning, shall we?' He put a hand on her shoulder and kissed her lightly on the cheek, then he left.

He wasn't at breakfast.

'Where's Harry? I've got to talk to him,' she demanded.

Jane heaped marmalade on her toast. 'Gone for a walk. Why, Christa, what's he done? I noticed he stayed behind when we went up last night.'

'He said something that made me so worried I couldn't sleep. Jane, is it true that you can't sell anything if a will is under dispute?'

'God knows, I've never had the problem,' was the answer. 'I'll ask Peter when he comes down. Sorry he's late by the way. Maybe it's to do with probate being granted. Is that what Harry said?'

'Yes, I think so. Jane, can't you stay until after Saturday? I've got Wallberg coming down to help look for this manuscript.'

'My dear, I wish we could. But Friday's pay-day for the men, and I've got a parish council meeting in the afternoon. We really must get back on Friday morning, early as possible. I'll ring you Saturday evening to see how you've got on, and don't worry, it'll sort itself out.' Poor thing, she thought kindly; she looks so anxious. It must be awful not having anyone to confide in. She decided to change the subject. 'What's the plan for today, then?'

'We're going over to Longstanton for lunch.' Christina thrust her problems aside. 'Then the Heatons have asked us for drinks this evening. I didn't plan anything for dinner, so Belinda could join us. Just a quiet evening, with telly afterwards, if there's anything to watch.'

'Lovely,' Jane enthused. 'How is the child? Getting to grips with life? So difficult losing a parent. When does she go back to school?'

'September; she's looking forward to it. I think she's coped very well; she's a brave little thing, very like Richard in so many ways.'

'She's not the only one who's brave,' Jane retorted. 'There's Harry, I can see him coming along the path out there; go and make him explain himself.'

Christina watched him through the window. He was walking briskly, but she felt he was far from his surroundings. She said slowly, 'Jane, do you mind if I say something? He's odd, isn't he? I mean he's not at all average.'

'No, he certainly isn't, but if he likes you, he's the best friend you could ever have. He's got a very good heart. Go and find him.'

She went out into the garden and hurried to catch up with him. He didn't seem to hear her when she called out. 'Harry!' He went on walking, head slightly bent, deep in private thought. Finally she reached him and he stopped, turned and then he smiled at her.

'Hello, there.'

'Don't you want breakfast?'

'No thanks. I've been inspecting the grounds. I'd love to come over one day and go around the whole estate. I'm taking on Dad's farm as well as the business, and I could learn a lot from the ways things are done here. Could I do that?'

'Yes, of course, any time you like. I'll get Bob Thorn to go round with you; he's our estate manager. I saw you through the window; you looked rather miserable.' They were walking side by side, his pace slowed down to match hers.

'I'm not miserable,' he said slowly. 'Not as miserable as I was. I'm just bloody angry about the way my life's turned out. I never meant to come back to England; I loved living in South Africa. I've got a younger brother who's married and farming forty miles away from home, and he expected to take everything on when Dad gave up or died; he's not best pleased with me for coming back.'

'Why did you? Couldn't you find someone else and start again? Divorce isn't the end of the world; it's so common these days.'

'Too common,' he said shortly. 'People break up for nothing. I found my wife on top of my business partner at three o'clock in the afternoon when she thought I was a couple of hundred miles away. To me, that wasn't nothing, so I booted her out and sent him along to the dentist for some new front teeth. I decided to cut my losses and come back to England. Ma was thrilled.' He smiled, thinking of his mother. 'She always found excuses for me. I was a difficult little bugger as a teenager. Then, when I started to behave like a human being, I went to the other side of the world, never mind how they felt about it. Then I come back, and they kill the fatted calf. I'm lucky, I've got great parents. Did you think about what I said last night?'

'About not being able to sell anything – I couldn't sleep till four in the morning,' she protested.

'Sorry about that,' Harry apologized, 'but I think I'm right. Ask your Swedish chum. Ask him how he knew Richard had such a valuable manuscript when nobody else did, and how he knew which dealer he bought it from. I didn't sleep much either because I kept thinking up questions I'd like to ask him.'

Christina said slowly, 'I've thought of them too, Harry, but

I'm not going to do anything until we've found the manuscript. He's coming here on Saturday to help me.'

'I'd offer,' he said, 'but I wouldn't know what I was supposed to be looking for. Will you let me know what happens?'

'Yes,' she said, 'I will. I'd like to take you up on that offer you made me last night; I do need a friend and I'd like it to be you.'

It had started to rain as Rolf approached Lincoln. The great cathedral glowered down from its hilltop, sinister in the dull light and driving rainstorm. He wasn't excited – he wouldn't allow the adrenalin to flow – he was icy calm. It had all gone so smoothly; faster than he had hoped. Everything had gone his way: the family feud, the disputed will, all the hatreds and hang-ups of these strangers were working towards his goal.

No, he thought, there is no place for excitement. That will come later, when I have it in my hands. Slowly the rain-swollen clouds moved away across the Lincolnshire skies, leaving them washed and clear blue in the pale sunlight. The landscape stretched ahead of him, flat and featureless. He saw the rooftops and the green copper dome of RussMore above a thick belt of trees, and began to slow down.

He knew what he had to do. He wouldn't allow a flicker of compunction or regret.

She was a lovely woman and he was attracted to her, but without passion, without feelings. He had no scruples; he had killed them a long time ago. If she went back to Sweden in the end, it might be the best thing for her, but it wasn't his concern. As he drove up the long drive, the great house rose like a distant jewel. He hated it and everything it represented. People blessed with a family, while he had none, savaging each other like greedy animals, and all for the possession of this out-dated irrelevant pile of bricks and stone. She was a fool to want to stay in it, playing the guardian for something that had no real connection with her, for the sake of a child who would be better off without it, and to satisfy a dead man's spite against a son he hated. He braked too quickly, the skidding wheels kicking up gravel. She was watching for him because she opened the door herself and came down the steps to meet him.

'Rolf, hello, it's good of you to come.' She looked young, very slim and neat in jeans and a shirt, her blond hair tied back. She looked like a girl in her twenties instead of a widow of thirty-three. Her hand felt cool; he held it for a second too long and then let go.

'How are you? How did the relations enjoy their visit?'

Christina was surprised he remembered. 'Very much. I wanted them to stay over and be here to see you, but they couldn't.'

He hid his flash of alarm. 'What a pity. But do they know what we have to find?'

'Not really, no more than I do. Their son had some queries, but I'll mention them later. Would you mind if we started right away? I just want to get on with it.'

'So do I,' he agreed.

They walked into the house together. It smelled fusty and cold. Swedes love the sun, he thought suddenly, and I shall live in the sun one day. He remembered the library and his first sight of the Farringtons, all waiting for Richard Farrington's will to be read. Humfrey Stone looking solemn and a little pompous; the eldest son and his wife, radiating hostility; the younger one with the sly diffidence that invited Rolf's contempt – he smelled weakness and he hated it – and Christina sitting with her daughter, looking so pale and drained after the funeral, and so beautiful. He crushed the memory. 'Well,' he said. 'Where shall we begin?'

Christina said simply, 'I don't know. I leave it to you.'

'Let's start with the cabinets,' he said. 'These, on the left. They should contain portfolios.' He was right. The sliding trays behind the cupboard doors were packed with folders containing old household accounts; land deeds; correspondence going back for generations; architects' plans, dated in the 1700s, when a Farrington decided to extend the rear of the house, making an extra wing. There were leather-bound folders, tied with faded tape, containing prints and original drawings, with remarks written by hands long dead. In the first cupboard, the second and then the third, they had found nothing but family records and trivia from the last 200 years, and there was a mass to be sifted through and fifteen more cupboards to be explored.

They were sitting on the floor, grimy-handed from the dust of the undisturbed past. Christina said, 'There's nothing here, nothing of Richard's collection; this is family archive stuff.'

'We'll just have to go through it all,' he responded. 'You start with that cupboard and I'll begin on the other side. We'll work our way round the room that way. Don't worry, we'll find it.'

But after more than three hours, they had found nothing.

'It's nearly one o'clock,' Christina said. 'We've been looking since nine. Don't you want something to eat?' They had emptied every cupboard and sifted through all the trays.

Rolf shook his head. 'No,' he said, 'unless we have a sandwich and keep going.'

'I'll get some made,' she agreed. 'And a drink.'

'Coffee,' he advised. 'We need to concentrate in case we miss something. Your husband may have hidden his treasures among other things. Some collectors do that.'

'Why should he?' she asked. 'Nobody knew what he had. He wasn't secretive.'

He said, 'I'm afraid we have to start looking through the books.'

'There must be thousands of books in here,' she protested.

'Then we'll just have to go through them all,' he answered.

Christina paused by the door. She had brushed a hand across her face and left a smear of dirt. Seeing her, he smiled suddenly. 'When you get the sandwiches', he said, and his tone was gentler than it had been, 'you'd better wash your face; you've got a dirty mark on your forehead.'

They ate sandwiches and drank coffee, crouching on the library floor. Rolf had been thinking. 'While you were gone,' he said, 'I made a quick examination of the first bookcase. Everything is in categories. There's half a wall devoted to fiction, all in alphabetical order. Some of the books are extremely rare – first editions; there could be a lot of value, but not enough. I think we can try something. Let's look under R for religions. It's quite possible that there's a folder placed between the books. The only way to find out is to take them all down.' He drained his cup of coffee. Then he looked at her and said, 'If I'm bullying you, Mrs Farrington, you must say so. When I'm working I'm not very considerate to other people, that's what I'm told.'

'I don't suppose you are,' she answered, 'but if I objected, I promise you I'd say so. And if I had a dirty mark on my face, you've got a filthy blob on the end of your nose!' They both laughed at the absurdity and Christina said, 'I think you can call me Christa, don't you? Everybody else does.'

He wished she hadn't said that, but he smiled back and said smoothly, 'Thank you, Christa. Now, let's start on the books.' He found them in the second row: four folders bound in green morocco leather, with the title, *Comparative Religions*, and the legend, *Collection of R. W. Farrington*, underneath. Wallberg pulled them out. Christina was busy with the books on the lower shelves.

'There's a whole shelf on Islam,' she said. 'It wouldn't be in among these, would it?'

For a moment, he hesitated. 'No,' he said, 'but I think it might be in these.' He stepped down off the library steps and she straightened up and hurried to see what he was holding.

'How stupid of me,' he exclaimed. 'Why didn't I start with this? *Comparative Religions. Collection of R. W. Farrington.*' He said in a low voice, 'You're right, he wasn't secretive. He wasn't hiding anything. It must be in one of these.'

Each folder was stamped in gold on the front cover. Buddhism, Christianity, Hinduism, Judaism. Rolf Wallberg opened the last of them, discarding the others. Each piece was protected by a sheet of acid-free paper, enclosed in a thin transparent plastic. And there was a brief scholarly description of the contents in Richard Farrington's careful handwriting, together with the time, date and place of purchase. The fragments meant nothing to Christina; some were badly damaged, others truncated pieces of old parchment, the ancient language varied. There were Greek translations and

Hebraic texts. His notes were too esoteric to interest anyone but a classical scholar. Some he was pleased with, others were a source of frustration because they were incomplete; a number of them were described as good late copies of lost originals.

Unable to bear the suspense, Christina interrupted his slow search. 'For heaven's sake, what are you looking for?' He turned over and she heard a sharp hiss as he caught his breath. Richard Farrington's neat handwriting was headed by capitals and double underlined. 'The Jewel in my Crown. Stockholm, 1983. Bought for the incredible sum of twenty thousand Kronen.' He turned and looked at her.

'This,' he said. 'This is what we're looking for. Open the pages. It belongs to you.'

Christina took the heavy folder and separated the cellophane slip, turning it carefully. There was nothing but another sheet of protective paper, with her husband's writing on it. 'The best-known piece of Old Testament writing in the history of Judea: the Song of Solomon. A copy of the original dating from the twelfth century AD. Sephardic origin, originally kept in a scroll, which would account for its excellent unbelievable condition; it's been perfectly conserved over the centuries with hardly any loss of text. I found it hidden in a pile of rubbish in an antiquarian bookshop in Stockholm, where I called in by chance, on the day I asked my darling wife to marry me. Of all the treasures in the ancient world, it is the most appropriate. In the words of the twenty-third Psalm, "my cup runneth over". I shall never collect again. I've found perfection.'

Christina turned the page, then the pages after it – they were blank. The rest of the folder was empty.

'There's nothing here,' she whispered to him. 'Nothing . . . it's gone.'

Rolf was staring at the two sheets of paper, guarding a vacuum. He seemed unable to speak. 'I don't believe it,' he said at last. 'I won't believe it. Give it to me . . . It's been misplaced. I must have missed it!'

But the slow and painful search from beginning to end yielded nothing. He began to look through the other volumes; he seemed possessed. He slammed the last of them shut. His face was bloodless; his eyes dilated as if he were in shock. 'It's gone,' he said slowly. She was startled when he seized her arm, gripping it fiercely. 'It's been stolen! Who's had access to this room since he died?'

She pulled her arm away from him.

'Only the cleaners and the housekeeper. I haven't come in here since the funeral. How could it have been stolen? Nobody even knew it existed . . . and what is it? Solomon's relic?' She saw his hands clench into fists.

'Not a relic,' he said harshly. 'The Song of Solomon. The earliest known copy of the most famous Book in the Old Testament. Christina,' he caught her by the shoulders. 'Christina, who could have sneaked in here and taken it? Think! Who's been here? Who knows the house?' Then, before she could say it, he answered himself. 'Your stepson, James, came here; he stayed the night. He told you about his father's hobby, didn't he? Collecting religious manuscripts. You told me, remember?'

'Yes,' she said. 'Yes, he did. Rolf, let go, you're hurting me.' His grip slackened, but he kept his hold on her.

'He's stolen something worth a million, maybe more . . . He tricked you, Christa. So much for your kind heart, making excuses for him. By doing this he's given RussMore to his brother Alan, but he's not going to get away with it.' He had turned her to face him. She felt a spasm of alarm. Something in his expression, in his eyes. He said in a soft voice, infinitely menacing because it was almost a whisper, 'I'm going to get it back for you. For both of us.'

They were so close, their bodies nearly touching, that he had only to bend his head. It was a lightning flash of sheer sexuality as his mouth closed over hers; in horror, Christina felt desire rising in her to meet it. She couldn't struggle or resist him and she didn't want to. She opened her mouth to the insistence of his kiss and everything blurred. Suddenly he stopped and let go of her. On a blind impulse, directed more at herself than him, Christina slapped his face. He didn't even blink.

He said, 'I'm sorry. I deserved that.'

'You'd better go,' she said, and her voice trembled. 'I've made a fool of myself. Please, just go.'

Facing her with a strange calm. 'I've wanted you from the first moment I saw you walk into this room. Don't blame yourself. You're a young and lovely woman; you're not meant to be alone. I shouldn't have touched you, but you weren't unwilling. I promise you, it won't happen again.'

'It shouldn't have happened at all,' she said. 'He's not three months dead. How could I? I don't even like you.'

He smiled. 'You don't have to like someone to want them.'

'Oh,' she said, 'I didn't mean that; it was cruel and it isn't even true. I'm just so angry with myself.' He followed her out of the library, across the hall and into the garden.

She said, 'I can't even think straight.' He walked beside her, careful not to brush against her accidentally. He had so nearly ruined everything for that one mad moment. He had told her many lies and he would tell her many more, but that had been the truth; he had wanted her from the first moment. *I don't even like you.* He wasn't wounded by that. He thought of James in a black anger. He had stolen the manuscript, not out of knowledge or scholarship, more likely out of mischief, an attempt to win his brother's favour. Between them they were capable of destroying it, certainly, Alan Farrington was. Anything his father valued so much, he'd throw into the fire.

They turned down towards the herbaceous border; it ran for a hundred yards to the edge of a water garden, backed by a tall red-brick wall of the same great age as the house. It was full of rich summer colour, but neither of them saw it. Christina felt dazed and shocked; shocked by the loss of the manuscript, dazed by the dreadful moment of surrender to sexual need. They came to the end of the walk; ahead of them the water garden was cool and shaded, filled with moisture-loving plants, the giant gunnera reaching huge flat leaves to the overhanging willow trees.

Slowly Christina turned and faced him. 'What are you going to do? How are you going to get it back?'

'I shall go to New York,' he answered. 'I shall see James Farrington and tell him he'll be arrested for theft if he doesn't return your property.'

Christina remembered then. 'But it isn't my property. I can't sell anything till the will is proved and probate granted. Why did you tell me I could?'

He had the answer ready. It had always been ready. 'Because nobody knows it exists. I have contacts; I could sell it for you privately.'

'And break the law?' she countered.

'I want to help you; I want to win this case. I wouldn't have hesitated; I won't hesitate. Christina you can't afford scruples. How many does Alan have? You'll lose the house and Belinda's inheritance. What would Richard tell you to do? What would he have done?'

Christina answered without hesitating. 'He'd give me the same advice as you. He had a ruthless side to him; I never experienced it, but I knew it was there. He once said to me, after a row with Alan, "I'd burn this place down before I'd let him have it." But he's dead and I have to make the decision. I'm not him; I have to do what seems right to me.'

Rolf knew he would lose if he argued. She had strength and that clear moral certainty he found so disconcerting. 'You're right,' he said, 'but, at least, let me get back what belongs to you and to Belinda. What you do with it afterwards is your decision, just as you say. Then if you want my help, I'll give it.'

She had started walking again. 'You're not telling me the truth. How did you know about all this? You knew Richard had this manuscript long before I ever mentioned anything. You knew where he bought it and when.'

'I haven't lied to you,' he said. 'Stop walking away and look at me. Face someone when you accuse them of lying. Don't you know you can tell by their eyes?'

'No,' she said, but she did stand still. 'I've never believed that. If you haven't lied, you've kept things back. You haven't been honest with me from the beginning.'

'No I haven't,' Rolf Wallberg answered. 'Is there anywhere

we can sit down? If you want the truth it will take time.' A few spots of rain began to fall.

'We'd better get back to the house, then,' she said.

Harry Spannier put his head round the kitchen door. His mother was peeling vegetables.

'Ma, has Christa rung?'

'Not yet, I expect the lawyer's still with her. That library could take days to search through; if there's anything to find. Let's hope so, for her sake. The more I think of that wretched Alan, the more furious I feel.'

He said, 'I don't like the sound of it at all. The Swede sounds a very dodgy bet to me.'

Jane started slicing cabbage. 'You've taken quite a fancy to her, haven't you?'

'She's attractive and she's a rich widow. Why shouldn't I?' He was teasing and she knew it.

'That's not the reason,' his mother retorted. 'I know you, darling. Just don't get in too deep. There's a bag of new potatoes in the pantry, get them for me, will you? Thanks. Where's your father?'

'Watching cricket on the telly. Not very happy – the West Indies are two hundred and fifty-eight for four! You don't want any help, do you?'

'Since when did you peel anything except an apple?' she laughed. 'No thanks, darling. Go and keep Pa company. I'll join you as soon as I've finished this. We'll have a drink and then we can ring Christa.'

'I'll give it till eight,' Harry said. 'If she hasn't called, I'll ring her.'

But the time went by and the Spanniers settled down to drinks before dinner and there was no telephone call from Christina.

'How old are you, Christa?' He knew, of course, but he wanted to set the scene.

'Thirty-three. Why?'

'Because what I'm going to tell you happened twenty years

before you were born; before I was born, too. But for me, it doesn't make it any less real. You were right when you said I knew your husband had a priceless manuscript; I knew where he bought it and when, but only recently. It's not the first work of art we've tracked down, but it's certainly the rarest and one of the most valuable.'

Christina said, 'Who's we?'

'My firm,' the answer came easily. 'We've been working on the legal aspects of recovering property for a number of clients for almost five years. We've employed investigators, sent enquiries out all over Europe, and we've been successful in a number of cases. It's taken a lot of patience because there were so few sources to work on. The original owners were all dead, you understand. The claimants were distant relatives, some living in America. Considering how few families were involved in the beginning, it's surprising how many claimants there are . . .'

She frowned. 'You're not being very clear,' she remarked. 'Are you saying that this manuscript was stolen? But Richard bought it in good faith.'

'Of course he did,' Rolf agreed. 'So did other people who were offered Impressionist paintings and Old Masters and some very fine jewellery; they all bought in good faith. We traced a Renoir and two Matisses to private owners in places as far apart as Helsinki and Greece. Having found them, it was my specific job to pursue the question of ownership; in many cases the threat of legal proceedings was enough. We recovered the property; the items were always sold and the money distributed to the claimants. I remember there was one exception: a man wanted his great-aunt's jewellery to give to his wife. You're looking confused, I'm sorry, I know it all so well I forget to explain it properly.' He seemed very detached from what he was describing. 'You know about the Holocaust, of course. Nobody could avoid it; the Jews make sure of that!'

Christina's reaction was angry. 'And so they should! People must never forget a horror like that!'

He allowed himself a thin smile. 'Not everyone agrees with you.' She didn't like his tone. She hated that last comment.

'Don't you?'

'I'm neutral, Christina, like Sweden. We stood aside while Europe tore itself to pieces, and we were right; because of that neutrality, we were able to help the Allies more than if we had been occupied. It's a point of view and I think it makes sense, but we are both too young to have any idea of the choices involved, or the consequences if they were the wrong ones. I am sure you will have guessed that the owners of the works of art were Jews; wealthy German Jews who had, so far, succeeded in buying immunity from the extermination camps.' He actually leaned back in his chair, one leg crossed over the other, the foot idly swinging. 'Germans are human beings too. Even the SS had corrupt officers who could be tempted by a bribe. The poor went on the trains and into the gas chambers.'

She challenged him, as he had expected. 'You're saying the rich didn't? There were no Jews left in Germany.'

'At the end, no,' he agreed. 'I'm saying that the rich Jews, some of them, lasted longer than the poor ones. A very few of them managed to get out of Germany, into Sweden for example, but not many. Towards the end, when the war was going against Hitler, they were all taken. You think I'm anti-Jewish, don't you?' He shot the question at her.

'You're sounding like it,' she said. 'I know there are people at home who have those views, but don't try and express them in this house.'

'I won't,' he said smoothly, 'because I'm not one of those people. I'm working to recover Jewish property. Richard's manuscript was on my list. Does that answer your questions?'

'No,' Christina answered. 'No, it doesn't. You haven't really explained anything. How was it stolen? And if it was, you should be claiming it back from the estate instead of telling me to sell it!'

'The clients want it sold,' he countered. 'They want the money. I've arranged deals like this in other cases; they take half, you take half. There's no legal wrangling and everyone is happy. I felt I could satisfy all the criteria if I did it that way, and help you fight Alan and win.' He leaned towards her. 'I want that, Christina. I've done deals before, but this is important to me. I admire your courage and your honesty, just as much as I want to make love to you. But we won't talk about that.'

She said quickly, 'No, we won't. What happened to the people who owned all these things? What happened to the ones who owned the document?'

He didn't answer at once. He sat there with the dying summer light behind his white-blond head, giving it a silver halo. His face was in shadow. 'They were all murdered,' he said, 'all but two: a girl and a five-month-old baby. Those Jews thought they had a friend, someone they knew from the good days before the Nazis, someone they trusted.'

Christina shivered. 'And he betrayed them? How horrible . . .'

He sounded quite unmoved. 'It happened many times. Money or goods in exchange for exemption from deportation. Often they were arrested as soon as they got home. But this was different; this was based on friendship, and trust, as I said. Shall I tell you about it? It may help you to get rid of Richard's "Jewel" when you know its history.'

Christina didn't hesitate. 'Yes, tell me. I want to know.'

He heaved himself out of the chair; his body uncoiling like that of a powerful animal. She had felt the power of his physical strength when he held her in the library. He said slowly, 'I'll find it easier to tell you what happened if I tell it as a story. It's a story I've pieced together from other people's memories, recollections, bits of conversations. But first I'll get you a drink. I think you're going to need it.'

5

'Klaus Himmelsbach was such a charming man, and handsome too. His women clients liked him, appreciated his good manners and subtle flattery, and the men found him amusing and amenable to bargaining. The firm had been established in Hamburg for over eighty years. The name, Himmelsbach Galleries, was a guarantee of authentic antiques and works of art in northern Germany. They sold everything from furniture to Fabergé trinkets. Klaus Himmelsbach specialized in gold boxes and miniatures; his father, Frederik, dealt in the best eighteenth-century German furniture, with a few flamboyant Italian pieces for those who liked to make a show. Klaus had expanded the range to include Fabergé's exquisite toys and artefacts which came from post-Imperial Russia via the refugees. Many had escaped with only what they could cram into their pockets. He bought cheaply from those desperate to sell, and sold expensively to rich Germans with an eye for beauty. He had his own clientele; he cultivated women because they introduced their husbands. He was a social figure in Hamburg after the Great War. It was a period of ruin and inflation that left the ordinary Germans destitute, but fortunes were made by men with vision and business acumen, who invested in assets rather than bonds and paper money that became worthless in a matter of days. He had a group of Jewish customers who bought and sold through him and whose families had dealt with his father and grandfather; he and his wife were even invited into their homes. They would all sit and moan about the terrible state of the country, with the crazy inflation, the unrest among the working classes and, above all, the rise of the Communists. There were riots, street fighting between rival political gangs, virtual anarchy. The old Chancellor Hindenburg, visibly senile, was unable to stabilize the country.

'Nobody wanted the Communists. Tales of horror spread from the tsarist refugees: murder, property and possessions seized, wholesale arrests of the wealthy classes, executions. Communism was the worst of the options open to Germany at the time, and nobody inveighed against them more stridently than the rich professional classes. Klaus Himmelsbach donated money to the National Socialists; they seemed the only alternative to the Bolshevik terror threatening them from Russia. When the racial attacks and the vicious anti-Jewish propaganda became official policy, after Hitler assumed power, Himmelsbach reassured his Jewish clients. He no longer described them as 'friends' in public. He advised them who would help; useful contacts with business undertakings – discreetly, of course; he emphasized discretion. Later, when the war began and Jews were being moved out of German cities into so-called work and rehabilitation centres in the east, Klaus advised them who to bribe. Klaus was the intermediary. He took nothing for himself; he refused presents, even from the dwindling few who had anything left to give. There were at least a dozen local Jewish families who had been regular clients in the early Thirties. By 1944, there were only four families left. The Steinbergs, whose clothing factories had long been taken over without compensation, all of them now lived in a tiny flat on the outskirts of Hamburg. The Brauners, rich shipping magnates, now reduced to poverty, moving from one hiding place to another to escape the mass arrests of local Jews. Frau Rabinowitz and her three surviving grandchildren, sheltering with Aryan German friends; the rest of her family had been seized and deported. And, lastly, the Rubensteins, a family of respected doctors and lawyers with inherited money, who had all been driven out of practice, and kept their lives by heavy bribes of cash and valuables. But the end was coming; Himmelsbach could see it. The end for the last of the Jews of Hamburg and their families, and the end for Germany, for the war was lost. Millions of German soldiers had been killed in Russia; Germany's chance of victory in Europe died with them. Klaus was a student of history; it was part of his training in art.

'As with Napoleon, so with Hitler. Now Germans waited for the Allies to invade. Klaus Himmelsbach and his wife and young children had spent nights in the foetid air-raid shelters while the city and the port were bombed. He had seen the fires and devastation. It was a portent of the future, a future too terrible to be contemplated, for the Russians would be coming from the east.

'One night, free from the howling of the sirens and the crash of bombs and anti-aircraft fire, his wife heard a knock on the kitchen door. Dousing the light, she opened the door, fearing it might be one of the bullying street wardens complaining that the blackout was not effective. She lived in fear of them; too many complaints and they would be arrested. But the woman standing on the step in the darkness was small and shrouded in a coat, the collar pulled up to hide her face.

'"Frau Himmelsbach?"'

'Leni Himmelsbach gasped. She thought she recognized the voice. "Frau Steinberg? Is that you . . . Oh my God . . ."

'"I'm sorry to come." Her voice was so low she could hardly hear it. "My husband sent me. He's sick with a bad cough. Can I speak to Herr Himmelsbach, please?"

'Leni hesitated. She had been friendly with Ruth Steinberg long ago and quite liked her. They had been such good clients;

very hospitable, very lavish when they entertained. She knew Klaus had not been in contact with them for a long time. "Please?" She wasn't immune to pity. If Klaus didn't want to see her, he would know what to do.

'"Wait there," she said. "Don't knock again, he'll come." She closed the door and went to find her husband.

'Leni waited upstairs for him for a long time. She prayed the sirens wouldn't go. If that woman was caught on the street, she'd tell the police where she had been; they would beat it out of her. She sat trying to sew and shivered with cold and fear. She began to hate Ruth Steinberg for coming. When Klaus came in, he was carrying something rolled up under his arm.

'"Has she gone? Did you get rid of her?"

'"Yes, she has gone home."

'"What did she want? She'd no right to come here and compromise us." He didn't respond to that. He came and sat down and placed the roll on the table. He unrolled it slowly and held it in place with both hands. Leni leaned over his shoulder. It was a canvas, cut from the frame. A landscape in soft dreamlike colours with an ethereal white-clad figure, so delicate it seemed blown by a hidden breeze, one hand catching the brim of a hat.

'"Oh," she said. "It's lovely. What is it? Did she give it to you?"

'It amazed him that after so many years in close contact with his business, she remained so blindly ignorant. He said patiently, "It's a Renoir. She tried to give it to me, but I wouldn't take it."

'She stared at him. "Oh, why not? It's worth a lot of money! It's no use to them. What did she want?"

'He rolled up the canvas very carefully and knotted a piece of dirty string around it. "She asked me to help the family to get out of Germany," he said. "They've heard about the new edict. The Führer says all Jews everywhere in the Reich must be taken east. There'll be house to house searches soon; no-one will escape. She begged me to help and offered me the Renoir; they've nothing else left, except some jewellery. She said they could sell it if they got away to Sweden."

'"Why Sweden?" she asked.

'He showed a rare flash of temper. "Don't be stupid! Sweden's neutral. Where else could they go? Why don't you stop asking stupid questions and make me some coffee?" He scowled at her.

'The coffee was a disgusting blend of acorns and some substitute, but at least it got rid of her and gave him time to think . . . He untied the string and examined the canvas again. He got up and searched in a drawer for some tissue-paper which Leni used as a lining. He spread it carefully over the painting before he gently rolled it up, retied it and put it away. It was the end for the Steinbergs; the end for the Jews of Germany, but the end for the Himmelsbachs too. Now the two were fused in a common destruction; theirs less immediate, but no less inevitable. He had made Ruth Steinberg sit down, given her a glass of water, calmed her nervous protest that she must go, she mustn't endanger them. He wouldn't accept the Renoir. They had been his friends, and their parents had bought from his father before they bought from him. He would think of some way to help if he could, and then he had asked if there were other Jewish families, people they knew who would risk an attempt at escape rather than wait to be rounded up. She said simply, "Yes," she knew of two more: an old lady with three little grandchildren, ready to try anything to save them from disappearing like their parents and elder brothers. Frau Rabinowitz, did he know of her? He knew of her; they had been very rich industrialists, but not clients.

'"The Brauners – Hilda and Benjamin, his parents, and their two children?"

'"Ah, yes," he said, "I didn't know there were any of them left." He sounded sad. "They came to us for everything. I started their Fabergé collection. How are they?"

'"Desperate, like us," was the answer. And sitting at the kitchen table, watching her drink the water and gaze at him with haggard eyes, he had said gently, "But how will people like the Brauners live, if they get to Sweden? Elderly relatives, young children . . ."

'"They will have saved something," Ruth Steinberg answered.

"We all did. Jews have always kept something back, against the pogroms or the tax collectors. It's in our blood to be ready to run. We'll all be able to pay for our lives."

'And he had reached over and taken the cold thin hand in his and said, "You will never pay me. I'll find a way to get you and your friends out and you will take your treasures with you. Come back in three days at the same time, or the next day if there's an air raid, and I'll try and have some news by then?" She had seized his hand and kissed it.

'"God will reward you. Keep the painting till I come. If I'm picked up on my way home, I don't want *them* to get it. I'll come back in three days."

'His wife came back with the coffee, disturbing his thoughts. "I've put some schnapps in, it'll help it taste better." She didn't like him to be angry. He smiled at her.

'"Thank you, Leni." She glanced round.

'"What have you done with the painting? I wanted to have another look. It must be very valuable." A whine crept into her voice. "Couldn't you keep it? After all, she offered, didn't she . . .?"

'"Yes," he answered, "I could keep it, but what would the Russians give me for it, do you think? A good fair price?"

'The sarcasm passed her by; she stared at him. "The Russians! Oh my God . . . don't even mention that. They won't get here. They can't . . . the Führer says every German will fight to the death! I won't sleep if you talk about the Russians." He saw her wide blue eyes fill with tears. Such a silly woman, born, as he once said to his father, with big tits and no brain.

'His father had laughed and said, "Isn't that the best recommendation for a wife? Never marry a clever woman, they're troublesome."

'"I shouldn't have worried you," he said kindly. "You're right, they won't invade Germany, I was just being defeatist. No air raid so far tonight. Why don't you go to bed and I'll follow soon." He gave her a playful slap on the bottom. At forty-nine and after five children, she still had a good figure. "Don't dream about Russians raping you," he said, "it'll only be me!"

'Then he sat back and began to think, carefully and in great detail, as he had done all his life before he risked his capital and went into the market to buy.'

'Albrecht Hoffman had lost his leg below the knee on the Russian front. He had served with the SS panzer division that fought at Smolensk. He was in his late thirties, but he looked much older. The leg was amputated because of frostbite; he'd lain in the bitter cold, shot through the lung, freezing to death, before they could stretcher him back to a field hospital. His suffering showed in the deeply lined face and remorseless hatred in his distorted mind. He blamed the Jews for the war which had left him a cripple. He had a civilian posting with the port security at Hamburg; the SS looked after their own. His wife and only child had been killed by Allied bombing while he was in hospital.

'He had found a group of Jews trying to escape by fishing boat; the captain had accepted their money and then betrayed them to the authorities. They were carrying jewellery and gold trinkets; these were forfeited. Hoffman managed to hide a little box with a monogram in diamonds for himself. He personally supervised the weeping badly beaten Jews onto the next cattle trucks bound for Auschwitz.

'He didn't know what to do with the gold box, or how to get it valued. He was well educated and clever; he had been an accountant until he joined the SS. He asked permission to see the files at the Gestapo headquarters in the city and it was given readily; he was a war hero who'd also lost his family. All professions and trades were listed, with the names of the principals, their police records if any, their reliability and Party affiliations. Klaus Himmelsbach had a high rating; he had personal contacts in the SS and the Nazi Party officials in the city, he donated generously to the Welfare Fund, and he had provided useful liaison with the wealthy Jewish community. Hoffman knew what that really meant. He went to the Himmelsbach Galleries and asked to see Herr Himmelsbach. The little box was an eighteenth-century presentation box, given by the Elector of Hanover. Klaus knew where he had got it, because he had sold several such boxes to a collector as a hedge against inflation during the old Chancellorship. He gave him a handsome price and it was worth it. Hoffman had sold goods that belonged to the State, confiscated from Jews; from now on he was in Klaus's pocket.

'They met at a dock-side café the day after Ruth Steinberg's visit; Klaus never went to his office. The effect of the air raids was all round them: shattered buildings, rubble, gangs working to repair the dock facilities, a smell of smoke and oil that caught in the throat and stung the eyes.

'"Albrecht," he said quietly, "how long can we survive this?"

'Hoffman stirred his coffee. There was no sugar; rations were small and getting smaller. "Not long," he answered. "We'll be invaded soon, then the Russians will come. I won't stay alive to see them come to my city; I know what they can do."

'"Killing yourself won't help anybody," Klaus remarked. "You've done your duty for the Fatherland; no man could give more. You should be thinking positively; you have a life to live, you deserve it."

'Hoffman's face twisted. "What kind of life? A slave under the Russians. They killed our wounded . . . Better to put a bullet in my head."

'"Better to live in Sweden with a nice bank account," Klaus said. "That's what I plan to do. I'm not waiting with my wife and children for the Russians, and I'm not escaping to live in poverty. Albrecht, we can help each other, we can both have a future. But there is a price."

'Hoffman didn't answer. His stump itched and he couldn't scratch it. He shifted uncomfortably on the hard chair, scrabbling uselessly at his trouser leg.

'"Tell me about it," he said.'

'There were two nights of ferocious air attacks. Klaus and Leni spent them in the communal shelter with their children. Sleepless, nerve-wracked, the people emerged each morning to deal with the fires, the wreckage and the casualties. On the third night there was a lull and Ruth came to the kitchen door.

She was not alone; there was another woman with her. Women attracted less attention than men, and both wore coats without the yellow star. If they had been caught, the penalty for defying that humiliating law would have been a systematic beating at the police station, just for good measure.

'Klaus sent Leni upstairs. He asked Ruth to sit down, and waited for her to introduce her companion. In the electric light he noted that she was a beautiful young woman, so blonde and blue-eyed she could easily have passed for an Aryan German. She looked ill and underfed and she said nothing.

'"This is my friend's daughter," Ruth explained, "Hester Rubenstein. I've brought her along to see you. Have you any news?"

'"Sit down, please," Klaus invited them. "I have some wine saved to offer you. What terrible raids these last two nights? We had bombs very close here." Jews couldn't risk the shelters; they stayed hidden above ground. He poured two small glasses of hock. Hester Rubenstein shook her head.

'"Thank you, no. I'm feeding a baby and wine might upset him."

'A baby; that must account for the poor girl's drawn exhausted look. He said kindly, "I wish I had something else to offer . . . but I have news, good news. I have arranged a ship."

'He heard Ruth Steinberg catch her breath, and saw the look she gave the girl.

'"A ship? To take us away?" He nodded. "Yes, It's been very difficult to arrange. I had to find someone I could trust." The women were gazing at him; he was their saviour. He saw the blonde girl blink back a rush of tears.

'"I have a friend in customs," he went on, "from the days when I shipped goods abroad. He introduced me to a Swedish ship's captain. It's a trawler, not very big, but he's agreed to take passengers across to Sweden; for a price, I'm afraid, a high price."

'Ruth interrupted. "I told you, we can pay. Anything. How much does he want?"

'Klaus explained slowly. "Not in money. He doesn't want Deutschmarks; he says they'll be worthless when we lose the war. He wants something he can sell. Ruth, you offered me your lovely painting, and I offered it to him; that's the price. He can take twelve people for that. It will be very cramped and a rough sea crossing, but you'll be safe at the end."

' "Twelve?" Ruth repeated. "But we're nineteen with Hester's husband and his parents . . ."

'Klaus said sadly, "No more than twelve; even so you'll be lying on top of each other. He won't take one more; I asked. You'll have to decide who stays behind. Thank God it's not my choice."

'Ruth stood up. "Leave that to us," she said. "How can we ever thank you, Herr Himmelsbach? You've saved all our lives. Hester has a little boy, five months old. She must go. No," she turned to the girl, forbidding protest. "No, your son has to live his life, and he must have his mother. How do we get to the boat? When do we leave?"

' "My friend in customs has helped with that. He is a good man; he hates what's being done to our Jewish people. He has an official van that is under repair at this time, so it's off the roster, but it will be ready sooner than expected; he's going to see to that himself. It can collect you and bring you to the pick-up point on the coast. The trawler will anchor close in to shore and they'll send a boat for you. Bring all your goods, but nothing too bulky. Cut pictures out of their frames – roll them, as you did," he said to Ruth. "Put other valuables in your luggage – remember that space is vital. Wear thick clothes; it'll be very cold on the journey, and don't bring food; he'll share some rations with you." He looked at them and said, "Get all the families together in one place."

' "They can come to us," Ruth Steinberg said. "They can hide with us. But when? How long?"

' "You'll sail on Friday," Klaus told her. "The van will park outside your house at one o'clock in the morning, for five minutes, no more. You must all be ready; no delays or he won't wait. The driver is risking his life to help you."

' "God will reward him," Ruth said fervently. "And you."

'Hester Rubenstein said nothing. Klaus smiled more warmly, but with a hint of modesty. It had won him many clients and clinched some good deals in the past.

'"My reward will be to know you're all safe in Sweden," he said. He couldn't help looking at the blonde girl, with feeding and care she would be a startling beauty, and he had always appreciated beauty in objects and in people. "You had better go now. I'll give my friend the address. For God's sake, don't get picked up." He saw them disappear down the backstreet in the darkness. For a moment he shuddered. It was cold outside with a night mist and the two figures looked like ghosts.'

'The families assembled over the next three days. They came singly and in couples, moving by night, watching in terror for the wardens who patrolled the streets. They braved two more air raids. The seventy-five-year-old Heime Brauner collapsed with a heart attack; they left him dead in a doorway. Each carried a bag of clothes, what little food they had to last till Friday, and the treasures hoarded against just such an eventuality. The Brauners had some jewellery and what was left from their Fabergé objects and some gold coins; the Steinbergs had a Matisse and a Raoul Dufy, rolled up and wrapped in paper. The last adult survivor of the Rabinowitz family was seventy-nine years old; her grandchildren – two boys and a girl – were eleven, nine and six years old. Their parents and all other relatives had been deported east. Frau Rabinowitz had three exquisite gold boxes, one encrusted with diamonds. They would fetch enough for her and the children to live on till the war was over. She had distant relatives in America who would take the children.'

'Hester Rubenstein's parents-in-law brought more jewellery – loose stones prized out of their settings and stored in a leather pouch – and in their luggage was a treasure that would never be bartered for their lives. Its survival was as important to the Rubensteins as their own children. They had been guarding it for centuries, ever since a Sephardic Jew on a rare excursion into Eastern Europe, had entrusted it to their ancestors as he lay dying. The Rubensteins were Ashkenazi Jews, inferior in purity of race and belief to the Sephardi, but it was the lesser of two evils to pass on the ancient treasure to them, rather than risk it falling into Gentile hands. It was hidden in a leather scroll, and for hundreds of years, no Rubenstein had unrolled and exposed it to the light; father had passed it to son and told him what was inside. When the family escaped to Sweden, they would take the scroll with them.

'The group was excited and nervous. Even the children, so long used to living in terrified silence with their German protectors, made a little noise and quarrelled. They had parted from their Aryan friends with tears. Frau Rabinowitz reminded her grandchildren every day that there were good brave Germans, risking their own lives to save Jews. But one heart-breaking problem remained: there were eighteen people and only twelve places. The elders made the choice on Thursday night. Ruth's husband refused to go. His parents were old and in poor health, and he must take care of them; he would try to escapc separately. Frau Rabinowitz was not discussed; her grandchildren guaranteed her a place. Hester's parents-in-law stepped down for her, the baby and their son. That left four more places. Heime Brauner's widow stood up and said simply that, without her husband, she had no wish to start a new life in a strange country. God would protect her; she would stay behind, and live on through her children, Hilda and Benjamin, and their two children. The hours before 1 a.m. on Friday were spent in prayers. It was a bright moonlit night, with every star in the sky glittering like diamonds. Hester's husband embraced his parents and wept; his father held the baby in his arms and blessed him. His last words to his son, Jacob Rubenstein, were, "Take care of the boy and remember what you carry with you. Pass it on to him when the time comes. Go and live your life and be happy."'

'At exactly one in the morning, Albrecht Hoffman stopped the van outside the back entrance of the house. He opened the rear doors and the first of the Jews came out. He didn't speak, but only made an impatient gesture for them to climb inside. Watching them, he felt a cold rage; they thought they were escaping, carrying their money and their loot.

'The baby in a woman's arms made a whimpering noise and she stifled it with her hand. He wanted to curse the old ones for their slowness. In the old days he would have speeded them on with blows or a kick. He closed the door on them and bolted it shut, then he began the drive through the night to the coastal spot of Büsum where the Swedish trawler would be anchored offshore.'

'The boat rocked in a gentle swell. The captain surveyed the bright night sky and cursed. He was fifty years old, toughened by years of brutal dangerous work. He had smuggled goods over the years, and occasionally people, so long as they could pay. He believed that laws were made to be broken by men clever and ruthless enough to get away with it. For the last two years he had been spotting for German U-boats. The victims had never once come into his mind. Money was his love, his sole motivation; he would do anything for money. He had hand-picked his crew from the scum of the seaport: ex-criminals, drifters, ready to do anything if the reward was big enough. He had worked for Albrecht Hoffman before and he knew what was expected. He didn't like the bright sky; British planes might ignore the Swedish colours painted on his upper deck. He cursed again, and scanned the shore through night glasses. Then he saw the van's sidelights, coming along the coast road, pulling in and driving slowly down the track leading to the beach.

'He shouted an order. "They're here. Make the boat ready!" It would take two trips. They were huddled on the beach now, muffled indeterminate figures. Five smaller ones. He cursed again. "Children, shit! Never mind." The boat was lowered; it chugged across the slight swell, heading for the beach. His first mate was a big morose Swede, who had served a long prison sentence for killing a man in a fight; the crew were in awe of him because of his size and reputation. The Captain said, without turning, "Get the hatches off the hold." The first mate gave the order as, below them, the little boat was coming alongside.

'A rope ladder was thrown over the side. "Help them," the first mate ordered, and two men steadied the ladder and reached down to heave the passengers on board. When they were on deck, the boat returned for the others waiting on the beach. They stood uncertainly, looking around them; there was an atmosphere of unease; one of the children – the six-year-old Rabinowitz child – burst into tears.

'"Welcome aboard," the captain said in thick German. "You'll have to go below. It stinks of fish, but you'll have to put up with it. And there's not much room, so leave your baggage up on deck and we'll stow it where we can. Hurry along now." The crew were helping them climb down into the hold; the stench was nauseating – fish and bilge-water. Water gleamed in the moonlight, slopping about on the floor of the hold. Benjamin Brauner protested. "My wife can't go down there . . . it's filthy!"

'"Better than a cattle truck," the captain said.

'Hilda Brauner said quickly, "He's right. What does it matter if it's dirty . . . smells can be washed away. Come on, don't make a fuss . . ."

'Obediently they disappeared into the hold. The boat returned from its second trip. It was the youngest crew member who helped Hester Rubenstein climb up the ladder by going down and taking the baby out of her arms. He handed her up over the side. Her pale face was visible in the brightness; her shawl had fallen back and her hair was like silver. He stared at her. She held out her arms for the baby. "Thank you," she said. "Thank you for saving us." He had been in trouble since he'd run away to sea at sixteen. He hated authority, that was the cause of his brushes with the police, and his dismissal from one ship after another. He'd lived like a dock rat, thieving and earning money without asking questions, but he had never seen anything like that girl, with her face like a pearl in the soft light, her long hair come loose and waving gently in the night breeze.

'"Down in the hold," the first mate said. "Hurry it up!"

'The young crewman held her back. "She can't go down there . . . she's got a kid!"

'The big man stared at him. "I've got eyes," he said, "I can see. She goes down with the others." He swung away as the captain shouted for him. Hester Rubenstein started to follow the last of the Brauners.

' "No," the crewman said in Swedish. "No, you don't go there, you come with me." He spoke in Swedish and she didn't understand. He caught her by the arm and hurried her aft, skirting the hold. When she resisted, he pulled her after him. They weren't noticed; the crew were busy preparing to close the hold and batten down the hatches.

'He didn't take her to the crew's quarters, instead they climbed down the ladder below the main deck. She refused to go any further, but stopped, hugging the baby with both arms, staring at him in terror and confusion.

' "Where are you taking me? I want to go to my husband. Let me go!" Her voice was rising to a scream. If she was heard, he'd get into trouble for disobeying the first mate's order; he couldn't let that happen.

He grabbed her and held her mouth shut with one hand. He put his face close and said in a whisper, speaking a bastard German picked up from other seamen, "You want your kid to die? You make a noise and you both die . . . you understand me. You keep quiet, you stay quiet. You don't move, see, you don't let the kid cry."

'He looked round; there was a cramped little storeroom, not much bigger than a cupboard. He reached out and opened the door. It was dark and smelled of oil and tarred rope. The light in the passage showed that there was just enough room for her if she crouched down. He pushed her inside, freeing her mouth. "Stay quiet," he repeated. "I'll get you later, you understand?"

' "My husband," she moaned. "Where's my husband?"

' "He's with the others," he said. "He'll be all right. Safer for you here. Safer for the kid." He put a finger to his lips to make sure she understood, then he closed the door. He didn't know why he'd done it. He didn't understand what it was about her in those few seconds when she came aboard and held out her arms for her child that made him save her life. He'd just given way to the impulse. The first mate would beat him to a pulp if he found out. There was a bolt on the door, and he shot it quietly into its socket. Now she couldn't get out. He went back up on deck.

'Down in the darkness and the stink of the hold, Jacob Rubenstein was calling his wife's name. He couldn't see and he couldn't find her; he stumbled over others; they cried out.

'"Hester? Hester?" The Rabinowitz children were screaming because they were frightened, some of the other women began to sob, and Ruth Steinberg, overcome by the fumes and the smell, crouched in the two inches of slimy sea water, retching. One of the men managed to climb up and bang his fists on the hatch.

'"Let us out! Open this, let us out . . . We can't breathe down here!" The boat suddenly dropped into a wave trough and he was thrown off the ladder. He fell backwards, striking his head. Up on deck, the captain heard the cries and the screams of the children. They were well away from the coast, heading for the open sea. There was wind coming up and the swell was getting heavier. It wouldn't do to delay too long; his men couldn't manhandle the Jews in heavy weather. He gave it until land was out of sight and there was nothing but the dark waste of the North Sea, white-foamed waves breaking the surface. He looked at his watch; they'd been out nearly two hours. The disturbance in the hold had stopped; he guessed they were prostrate with the ship's motion. He gave the order to stop engines and drop anchor. He had the crew summoned on deck with a man at the wheel to keep her steady in the swell. He chose Johansen, the crewman who had sneaked back up on deck from the storeroom.

'"Johansen, take the wheel. Open the hatches and get ready. Stand by!"

'They came willingly, desperate for fresh air and release from their vile heaving prison below, and as they climbed over onto the deck, they were seized. Those who resisted, like Jacob Rubenstein and the younger Brauners, were clubbed before being thrown over the side. The women were grabbed like sacks and flung over the rail. The children, screaming and clinging to their grandmother, presented no problem; the old woman went overboard and they fell with her. It was done in less than fifteen minutes, then there was a silence. The crew stood and stared at the heads bobbing in the water and listened to their cries. The sea temperature would kill most of them before they had time to drown. The captain gave the order.

'"Start engines." The pulse began to thud beneath their feet and the boat drew away, leaving a wake behind. The captain did not even look to see if anyone was still above the surface. He gave another order to the first mate. Men went below to swab what human refuse had been left in the hold and the baggage brought aboard was locked in his cabin, safe from thieving curiosity. He didn't intend to steal anything himself; he knew Albrecht Hoffman and the SS had a long arm. He would get his price and the crew would get theirs.

'Hester had heard the noise; it was muffled by the deck above and the closed door, but she heard shouts and shrill screams. Something terrible was happening. She held the baby tight. He started to cry and she fumbled, giving him her breast to quieten him. Nobody heard his hungry wailing among the other human voices crying out. Then it was quiet. The engines had stopped before the shouting began, and now they started up again. She didn't realize that she was shaking as if she had a high fever. She fought down hysteria by trying to squeeze some milk from her almost empty breast to feed her son. The jumbled German words echoed in rhythm with the beat of the engine.

'"You make a noise and the kid dies . . . stay quiet . . . the kid dies." She crooned a whispered song to him, and in the dark airless place, she lapsed into sleep at last. The sleep was her refuge from insanity. In the morning, when they were docked in Gothenburg, the man who had saved their lives opened the door and brought her up on deck. He had volunteered to stay aboard as watch; the rest had gone. The captain's cabin had been emptied and the bags and bundles taken in a cab to a boarding-house; it would be collected by Albrecht Hoffman. Hester didn't speak; she followed him in silence, hushing the baby, as they left the ship.

'"Money?" he asked her in his poor German. "You have money?"

She shook her head. Then she held out her wrist; she was wearing a gold watch. He took it off. "We'll get money for this," he said. "I'll buy food for you." He looked at her in the pale daylight; her face gaunt, her blue eyes huge and empty. He said simply, "I'll take you home to my mother. I'll be good to you." He had never said such a thing to any woman before. They took a tram to the city centre, where he sold the watch to a jeweller, who gave him a fair price on account of the silent exhausted girl carrying a sleeping baby in her arms. Then on to the railway station; Johansen bought tickets and some food for the journey, and they caught a train. She still hadn't spoken. He pressed food on her; she ate a little and then she said, "What happened to my husband? What happened to the others?" He shifted on the hard seat. The train was half empty; the only other person in their carriage was an old peasant woman, asleep and snoring in the corner.

'He said, at last, "They're dead; they went overboard. I hid you because I knew the orders. What's your name? Mine's Hendrik Johansen." She didn't answer; her stare became wider, more vacant. It worried him. He asked again, jostling her with his elbow. "Your name? What's your name?"

'Hester said, very slowly, "I don't know, I don't remember."'

There was a knock on the study door. Christina didn't hear the first time. There was a second louder knock. It was the housekeeper.

'Sorry to disturb you, Mrs Farrington. There's a Mr Harry Spannier on the telephone. Shall I put him through?'

Christina shook her head. 'Tell him I'll call him back.'

'I know you didn't want to be disturbed,' the housekeeper went on. She couldn't ignore the atmosphere in the room; she had worked there for nine years and never felt anything like it. 'But I have some soup and a cold supper prepared for you and Mr Wallberg. Belinda's had hers; she's watching telly.'

'Thank you. We'll have it later. I'll call on the house phone.'

The housekeeper looked quickly at the lawyer. His face was like a stone carving, as she described it to her husband later. 'Grim looking. And she looked like she'd been given some really bad news. Shocked, that's what she was. I expect it's something to do with that horrible Alan.'

Alan Farrington was part of the staff's demonology. If he got the house, he'd sack the lot of them.

'I'll bet it is,' he had agreed. 'Not to worry, dear. Nothing we can do about it.' He was a philosophical man by nature. He wanted to watch his favourite quiz programme and not waste time worrying about what they couldn't alter.

When they were alone, Christina got up; the room felt cold, perhaps because the fire was low or because she herself felt chilled by the horror of what she had been told. She put some logs on and poked at them till they began to burn.

'Rolf? Aren't you going to finish it? What happened to the girl, Hester, and the baby?'

He said in a flat unmoved voice, 'Johansen took her home to his family; she never remembered her name. The boy was a year old when she went into the garden shed and drank a bottle of carbolic disinfectant. There was an inquest and an autopsy and they found that she was three months pregnant by the Swede. He had been good to her in his way, but I suppose that was too much for her. Maybe she remembered. No-one will ever know. He went back to sea and his mother had the boy adopted. The point of this story is that the scroll was part of the loot stolen by Himmelsbach and Hoffman. When all the stuff was sorted and stored, they found the scroll and opened it, but nobody knew what this Hebrew document meant. They were looking for pictures, gold, valuables. Jews would say that the Lord God protected it, because it wasn't destroyed. In fact, when Hoffman and Himmelsbach divided everything up after the war, Hoffman put it among some drawings Himmelsbach didn't want and sold them. So, many years later, your husband found it in the dealers in Stockholm. If I believed in a God, I'd say there was some kind of Providence at work.' He gave a mirthless little smile. 'But I don't believe, so I put it down to chance. I suppose you're going to ask me how I know all this?' He got up and stretched a little. 'As everyone was dead, including Hester Rubenstein, and the baby was adopted, how did I find out what happened?'

'Yes,' Christina agreed slowly, 'I was going to ask that.'

'I said everyone was dead, which is true of everyone who went on that boat, but Hester's parents-in-law stayed behind in Germany; and the father survived. His wife died that winter and he stayed hidden until after the war. Then he went to Sweden to find his son and daughter-in-law and the baby. He started searching, investigating but nobody knew anything. They'd never reached Sweden. The family and the scroll had vanished, along with all the other Jews who set out on that journey. All he had to link up with them was Himmelsbach, but he had disappeared too. When Rubenstein traced him to Sweden, it was already too late; he was dead. So, in the end, the old man asked for help from other sources. What they were is too complicated and doesn't really matter, but, because of the importance of the scroll, certain people became interested, and so my firm became involved. The practice of taking refugees out of Germany in order to rob and kill them was not unknown; it looked like just such a case. So we started from there; we had a date to help us, and we had old Rubenstein's clear recollection of what had happened and the deal that was made. Swedish criminal records led us to the sailor who saved Hester's life; he was an old alcoholic, living by begging at the dock side, but he remembered the beautiful Jewish girl as if it had happened yesterday. He cried as he talked about her.'

Christina looked at him. 'You said you were adopted? Are you that child?' He smiled then and shook his head.

'How neat it would be to say yes, but that sort of thing only happens in novels. No, I'm not the boy; I couldn't be because of the age difference. I tried to find him, but he'd died of appendicitis when he was six. The adoptive parents were poor farmers, living miles from a doctor, let alone a hospital. Yes, I was adopted, but that's the only similarity. I'm not a Jew, Christa. You don't have to be Jewish to want to right such a terrible wrong. That's why I took the case, why I was so anxious to find the manuscript and restore it to the Rubensteins' surviving relatives. Hester's father-in-law is dead now; they are poor people and not Orthodox, living in France. They would be happy to sell it, and I could have helped you at the same time. Can you understand this?'

'Yes,' she said. 'Yes, I can. What I don't see is how I could take any money for it. I'd better call Harry Spannier, then we should have supper. Help yourself to a drink, I won't be long.'

She went out of the room to telephone. He noticed that.

'Well,' Jane Spannier demanded. 'What's the news? Did they find anything?'

Harry said, 'Apparently it was a copy of the Song of Solomon, hundreds of years old. It must be priceless. But it's gone! Christa said it's been stolen!'

His parents stared at him. 'Gone?' Peter Spannier questioned. 'How could it have gone? Who could have taken it?'

'James. He's the only one who's been down there since Richard's funeral, and Christa thinks he must have pinched it then. She says this Swede is going over to New York to get it back. She said the whole story is too horrible . . . she sounded pretty upset. I'm driving down to see her tomorrow.' Jane and Peter exchanged glances.

'Shouldn't I come with you?' his father suggested.

'Not unless you want to come to Sweden,' Harry answered. 'This whole business stinks as far as I can see, especially Wallberg; he needs checking out. While Wallberg's in New York, Christa should go back to Stockholm and ask a few questions. I'm not busy, so I can go with her.'

'And she's agreed?' Jane queried.

'No, I haven't told her yet; but she will. Now, Mum, I'll help you with dinner. I'm very house-trained, you'll be surprised.'

'I'm sure,' his mother retorted, 'and that's not the only thing about you that'll surprise me, I can see . . . you can set the table.

And Peter, not another gin and tonic, darling, please . . . I'll be ready in ten minutes.'

'Good,' he said cheerfully. 'Just time for me to put one down, dear.'

'He's impossible,' Jane murmured as she went out with Harry.

'He doesn't like being nagged,' was the answer. 'I don't know why you bother, Mum.'

'Habit,' she retorted. 'He expects it, and rather enjoys doing the opposite, like you. So I'm not going to repeat myself and tell you to be careful and not get too involved with Christina, because I know you won't take a damned bit of notice!'

Rolf Wallberg watched her; she hardly ate anything. He was very hungry. 'I've shocked you, haven't I? I shouldn't have been so graphic,' he said at last.

'I keep seeing them', she said slowly, 'being thrown into the sea. Richard would have been horrified if he'd known.'

Would he, Rolf wondered; he wasn't convinced of English scruples. They'd plundered half the world without a qualm of conscience, just as Richard had cheated the unsuspecting dealer, Poulson. But he didn't say anything to contradict her. He finished his food, gulped a glass of wine and said, 'I'd better go. I won't stay the night this time. It's better for both of us if I start early tomorrow. I'll get a flight to New York, and pay a friendly visit to your stepson.'

'Supposing he denies it? He's always lied; he couldn't help himself. You can't force him.' He came over to her and, for a moment, he laid his hand on her shoulder. She stiffened, but the same flicker of response was there. She repeated herself. 'You can't force him to give it back.'

'I can try.' There was a brief pressure of his hand, then, without saying goodbye, he left her.

'Mum?' She hadn't heard Belinda come in. 'Mum, has he gone?'

'Yes, he had to go back to London.' Belinda looked closely at her mother. 'You looked worried . . . wasn't he able to help?'

Christina had explained briefly that they were searching for something valuable they could sell to help fight the court case with Alan. She put an arm round her mother. 'Don't worry,' she said, 'you'll find it. We can look tomorrow.'

Christina held her close. 'It isn't here, darling, but Mr Wallberg thinks he knows where it is. He says he'll get it back for us.'

Belinda said happily, 'Then if he says it, he will. Come on, there's one of those films you like on telly, that's why I came to fetch you. I thought he might like to watch it too. It's a shame he's gone.' The film was a riotous Steve Martin comedy, which Belinda had seen several times. Sitting with her daughter, Christina wondered what it was about that cold unfathomable man that so attracted her child. Was it some sense of budding sexuality, an innocent recognition of the magnetic force that had shaken her so badly and made her afraid of herself . . . She had never experienced such an impact with Richard or Jan or any of her boyfriends. That one kiss had been a lightning bolt of sexual fusion between them, and it was Wallberg, not her, who had pulled back. And then he had steeped her in horror, sparing nothing in his description of that mass murder of the innocent. *You can't force him*. They were her words. *I can try*. And that hot-hand contact that burned through to her skin. She remembered, with a sense of overwhelming relief, that Harry Spannier was coming the next day. Suddenly it made her feel safe.

James Farrington called his brother from his office. He was prone to little meannesses, like charging his personal calls to his employers. It was early morning, New York time; he knew Alan would be in his office after the mid-morning conference. There'd been no word from his brother and James was uneasy; they always kept in contact, though it was more on his side than Alan's. Alan usually expected him to make the running; it was part of the power game. James had played it so long it didn't occur to him to see their relationship as one-sided; he knew it was and that it wasn't going to change. But he'd made three unsuccessful calls to the Chelsea house, leaving messages, and his brother hadn't rung back, so he put the call through to his Holborn office. Alan's voice came on the other line after a pause. 'Hi.'

'Hi,' James responded. The American-style greeting sounded so bogus from someone like Alan who hated Americans and sneered at foreigners.

'I've left messages for you,' James complained. 'I just wondered how things were going . . .'

'They're going fine, if you mean the case,' was the answer. 'We've briefed Cunningham to act for us and he's hopeful of an early hearing. Her side are toughing it out, but then they would. How are things with you?'

'Busy,' James said. 'We've just landed a big contract for a design centre and industrial complex in Florida. I'm flying out to finalize it at the end of the week. It's a very good deal – mega bucks!' He gave a little chuckle. Alan wasn't interested in his younger brother's success, and he brushed the news aside.

'We're making a bid for the Bambio Burger chain,' he said briskly. 'There's been a lot of press coverage: photographs, articles in the financial papers, that sort of crap. I reckon we'll win, then I might consider going public. Our brokers reckon we'll be a sell-out on the market if we do.'

That capped anything James might have achieved in Florida. 'Great! Great stuff,' he acknowledged. 'You won't be needing money then?'

There was a snort of derision down the line. 'Money? I'll be printing the stuff; why the hell should I need money?'

'Oh, fighting the case and paying all the legal fees,' James murmured. 'Cunningham's one of the best QCs at the Bar; and the most expensive.' He let the comment die away. He could sense Alan's irritation even 3,000 miles away. He'd played with the idea for weeks, teasing it backwards and forwards. Father's old Jewish document was back in his apartment in the wall safe. He'd been so pleased with his find he'd given up collecting. James couldn't make any sense of the script and he had hesitated to show it to anyone in the antiquarian trade. He wasn't sure why, but he had simply kept what he'd stolen as he'd kept things all his life: talismans against not being loved or noticed, proof that he was clever enough to cheat the superior people that made up his family. Offering it to help Alan was a fantasy he indulged in; putting his brother in his debt.

I've got something that may be worth a lot of money. If you like I'll let you have it. He loved the day-dream: being in control. But Alan didn't need money. If he'd mentioned it, Alan would have dismissed it, making fun of the offer. 'Who's Christa's lawyer?' he asked.

'They haven't said,' Alan answered. 'They weren't expecting us to push ahead so fast. Why don't you come over, James, and see the fun? I can't wait to see that cow get her comeuppance!'

'Well,' James said, 'it's great that you're so confident.'

'You can believe it,' Alan said. 'I can't lose. I hold all the cards and I'm going to play them. I'll be in RussMore by Christmas!'

James knew that was an exaggeration; the case couldn't be heard and concluded in such a short time. But it was typical of Alan to put such a date on it; it heightened the drama.

'Well, let me know and I might just do that,' he agreed. Then, dutifully, 'How're Fay and the boys?'

'They're fine. Robert's got measles, poor little sod. I've got to go, there's another call on hold. Keep in touch.' The line cleared.

James thought of Fay nursing her measles-ridden child and hoped that, by some miracle, she had escaped it when she was a child herself. He relished the thought of her feverish and covered in spots. 'Bitch,' he muttered. She'd neglected to give his messages to Alan. He preferred to think that, rather than admit he'd simply been ignored.

Alan was going to win the case, force his stepmother and half-sister out of RussMore and triumph over his hated father at the end. What a scenario! James was an avid theatre buff, and he had friends who shared his enthusiasm. The Farringtons were the stuff of any bloodthirsty Jacobean drama. The thought made him smile; all that was lacking was murder. He was going to a new play that night with an old lover who was now a good friend. None of his relationships lasted, but he stayed on friendly terms whenever possible. A lot of women liked him; he was intelligent, artistic and an amusing companion; he moved in a wide social circle of the literary and artistic in New York. He had made a new life for himself, where he was valued and his qualities appreciated, but still the umbilical cord pulled him; he had never escaped his family. He decided that he must take his father's treasured piece of Hebraic history to someone who knew what it was and how much it was worth. His ex-lover had contacts in the big auction houses; maybe Christie's or Sotheby's would be the people to approach.

He took the subway back to his apartment, reading the new copy of the *Arts Review* which was sent to him from England every month. He didn't notice the man on the subway who had followed him from his office, nor did he notice him leave the train and follow him for a block and a half to his apartment building, or come up behind him as he opened the main door with his security card. He noticed nothing till the knife touched his throat and a voice said, very softly, behind him, 'Just keep going. Make a noise and you're dead.'

'What do you want?' James asked. He was trying to keep calm; he knew a number of people who had been mugged in the street or in their homes. Never show aggression and try not to panic; stay cool, give them what they want; never, ever look at their faces, then you can't identify them; that was the way to cope. James had his back to the man. He'd gone up in the lift with him, walked the few yards down the hallway to his front door, opened it, gone inside, and never once turned his head. There was no answer. His skin crawled with fear. Maybe it wasn't a thief, maybe it was some nut with a grudge against gays; there had been two horrific murders in the last three months, both victims were mutilated before death.

James tried again. 'I'll give you my wallet. My watch . . . it's a Rolex . . .'

'Go sit in the chair over there,' the voice hissed at him, only inches away. The blade touched his neck. 'Don't turn around.' James felt bile rise up into his mouth. The two dead men had been bound to chairs.

'Move it.'

He was given a slight push in the small of his back. James made it to the chair. He sat down and started to shake, and because he was so terrified, he found his courage. He was a big man, physically strong and fit, better to defend himself and die of stab wounds than be slowly cut to pieces by a sadistic maniac. His shoulder muscles tensed; he was just about to launch himself at his attacker when the voice said, 'The wallet, and the Rolex. Slowly, don't make any sudden move.' The sex killer hadn't robbed his victims. James brought out his wallet, held it over his shoulder, and felt it grabbed out of his hand. He took off his watch; that was taken too.

'What else you got in here? You got jewellery? Where d'you keep your cash?'

The edge of the blade pressed against the artery in the side of his neck. 'There's a wall safe,' James said quickly. 'There's about ten thousand dollars, my cuff-links. I'll give you the combination.'

'You open it for me,' the voice said. 'You do like I tell you and maybe you'll get lucky and I won't cut your throat.'

The wall safe was behind a convex mirror. Glad to be out of the chair, James eased himself up and walked across to the glass and lifted it off the wall. There was a steel door with a dial set in the middle. The safe was alarmed. James reached up and pressed a screw on the left of the safe door; that switched it off.

'Open it!'

He turned the knob, completed the combination and pulled the door open. An inner light came on.

'Take everything out and drop it on the floor.'

The money came first. Five rolls of $2,000; James kept a month's cash in the safe. Cashpoints were a target for muggers, even in daylight. The three boxes of cuff-links dropped one by one: two from Tiffany's, gifts from a boyfriend; and the old-fashioned pair his father had given him when he was twenty-one.

'That's all there is,' he mumbled. 'The papers are just personal stuff: my will, deeds to the apartment.'

'Everything on the floor! Don't mess with me.' James scooped everything out with both hands.

'Close it. Stand facing the wall, hands above your head. You turn round, you're dead meat.' He did as he was told. The man was bending, picking up the money. It was his chance to put up a fight, but he didn't take it. This was a robbery; if you didn't make trouble, you didn't get hurt.

The blow that felled him was a classic karate chop, designed to immobilize but not to kill. He staggered and then dropped in a slow fall, buckling at the knees; he was unconscious before he hit the floor.

The man who had knocked him out had stuffed the money into his pocket, almost casually. He threw the boxes on the table and began to look through the papers. He found what he wanted in a plain brown envelope, the will and the deeds he kicked aside. Carefully he placed the envelope inside his jacket, then he opened the leather boxes, took out the cuff-links and dropped them into his pocket with the money and the Rolex. He bent and checked the pulse in James's neck; it was steady. He'd come round in a few minutes. He walked over to the telephone and ripped it out of its socket, then he let himself out of the apartment. He went down in the elevator, saw two people in the hall and walked past them to the entrance and the front door. They didn't see anything they thought unusual, as they told the police afterwards; there was just a man wearing a smart business suit, with a snap-brim hat and dark glasses.

The two NYPD detectives were bored; they'd heard similar stories so often they could have written the script. They took down the details, interviewed the husband and wife who had seen a stranger leaving at around that time, and privately decided that Farrington had brought a pick-up to his apartment and got mugged instead. $10,000, a Rolex, a wallet with fifty inside and his credit cards, and three pairs of gold cuff-links.

There was some crap about a missing envelope but the guy couldn't even tell them what was in it. Some old document he'd gotten from his father . . . Their attention span cut out as

James was talking. They made reassuring noises about putting the details on computer, along with a thousand other incidents of the same sort that day. They were partners and good friends; they went for a beer on their way home after their shift was over and talked over the day's action. Neither bothered with the robbery; the guy hadn't even been hurt, just knocked cold for a few minutes. Big deal.

'I can't think why I let you talk me into this,' Christina protested.

'Because you wanted to get away,' Harry Spannier retorted. 'And Belinda liked the idea too, didn't you?' He grinned at the child and she laughed. 'Oh, I think it's great. I know we're going at Christmas, but this will be fun too!'

The lights flashed above them, 'Fasten Seat-belts.' The aircraft began to taxi, gathering speed and finally lifting off smoothly into the steep climb over London. The stewardess came along the aisle, pushing a trolley with soft drinks and duty-free, then the captain's voice came over the intercom.

'Good morning, ladies and gentlemen. This is Captain Lindsen speaking. Welcome to our Scandinavian Airways flight to Stockholm. We will be cruising at around thirty thousand feet, the weather outlook is fair and the flight time is approximately two hours and twenty-five minutes. The cabin crew will be happy to serve you drinks and a light snack. Thank you.'

Stockholm. Christina looked out of the window; cloud was banked beneath them, brilliant blue skies around them. Harry was right; she'd let him persuade her to fly to Sweden, taking Belinda with them. Cleverly, he had enlisted the child's support.

'Oh, please, Mum, I'll be starting school in ten days – can't we go? I'd love to see Grandpa and Uncle Sven. Please, Mum?'

'But why,' she had demanded when it was suggested. 'What would be the point?'

He hadn't minced words. 'I think we should check up on your Mr Wallberg, for a start. Everything you know about him is at second-hand.'

'But he's with Harvey & Stone,' she had protested. 'You're not going to tell me I can't trust them!'

'No,' was the reply, 'but the story's too glib, Christa. Here's a noble Swede, with just a touch of anti-Semitism about him – you noticed that – going on a crusade to restore property stolen fifty years ago to a lot of vague descendants who want the money, including, of course, this apparently priceless Hebrew document Richard picked up by accident. I say we do a bit of checking, that's all. What do you lose? A break from here and worrying about what that shit Alan is going to do next, a holiday for Belinda before she goes to a new school, and a chance to show me around your home town while we snoop. I'll call the airline and find out about planes.'

She had given way too easily, because, of course, he was right about her reasons too: she did want to get away. She wanted to stop thinking about Rolf Wallberg and what might have happened. Harry was safe; he was family and he was a friend. He had won Belinda over very easily; she wasn't fascinated by him, as she was with Rolf, but she accepted him as a cheerful, slightly unpredictable cousin who proposed they should do fun things on the spur of the moment.

A call to her brother got them a couple of rooms at the Emburg Hotel – 'not too up-market for me,' Harry had shouted, 'I'm the poor relation' – and a return call fixed it for Belinda to stay with her grandfather at Yurgen. He'd take her sailing, so she'd have a good time while Christina and Harry were in Stockholm; they were invited to come up and join in when they'd had enough of the city. So there they were, cruising high in the cloudless skies above the North Sea, and she didn't really know what they were supposed to be doing. Checking, Harry kept saying. Checking on the noble Swede, as he had taken to calling Wallberg whenever his name was mentioned. It made him sound ridiculous; that, she suspected, was Harry's intention. The day after he'd left her so abruptly she'd had a call from Humfrey Stone; he was reassuring. Rolf Wallberg had been called to New York for a brief trip, and he, Humfrey, would be available for her till Wallberg came back. Which, she realized afterwards, meant that Rolf hadn't told

Humfrey the truth: she was the reason for his trip; she was the client. But then how could he tell them? He was ready to break the law by helping her sell the document, so, of course, he had to lie.

For a moment she was tempted to call James direct and warn him Rolf was on his way, persuade him to give back what he had stolen, but she resisted. There was no reason to be afraid for James; all Rolf could do would be to threaten. James didn't need her protection.

It's just as well I'm going back, Christa. I could get to like you . . . James had come to RussMore and betrayed her trust; she owed him nothing. They were making their descent. Seat-belts fastened, Belinda craned to see out of the window as they broke through the light cloud and came into view of the islands linking together to form one of the most beautiful cities in northern Europe.

Home. She hadn't thought of it in those terms for nearly ten years. Harry nudged her. 'Want a hand to hold? I hate landing.' Belinda heard him.

'I love it,' she said. 'It's so exciting seeing the ground coming up so fast.' He grimaced.

'I hate kids,' he said; 'they've no nerves. Bump! There we are, safe on Swedish soil. Thank God!'

'You're not scared,' Belinda giggled. 'You just want to hold Mum's hand!' She thought it terribly funny.

Harry ignored her, and said seriously to Christina, 'I particularly hate eleven-year-old girls . . . because she's right, of course.'

Her brother was meeting them. Christina thought how much older he looked; they hadn't seen each other for three years. He'd sent messages and flowers, but he hadn't come to Richard's funeral. She'd been hurt, but accepted the excuse: his girlfriend was pregnant and the birth was scheduled by Caesarean for the same day. It was their second child; neither had ever mentioned marriage. Richard had been disapproving, and she realized that she'd been influenced by his opinion. But he was there now, waving at the head of the crowd in Arrivals, and she waved back.

He was a big man, fair-haired and blue-eyed, but the resemblance ended there. He had a round face with a broad brow and a nose flattened in a skiing accident when he'd slid into a tree. He was clever and hard-working and had built up the business they'd worked in together. Now there were Nordohl design centres in Stockholm and Gothenburg with a strong wholesale market. He embraced her, shook hands with Harry, who was introduced as Richard's cousin, and hefted Belinda into the air for a bearish hug. 'You've grown so tall! You were a little girl when I saw you in England. Christa, why didn't you bring her over before? Give me a kiss.'

'Why didn't you and Gerta come to us?' she couldn't help saying. Invitations had been issued and avoided, because he and Gerta didn't feel comfortable at RussMore. He didn't pay attention, but went on playing the fool with his niece, who was giggling with pleasure.

Harry noticed and took Christina's arm. 'I thought only Farringtons had family rows. Come on.'

They left their bags at the Emburg; it was a pleasant second rank hotel in the Old Town. They all lunched together, and then Sven Nordohl was going to drive Belinda up to her grandfather at Yurgen. It was a friendly meal, but there was a distance between brother and sister; she'd done more than just move to England and adopt English ways, Harry realized; she'd broken her own family ties in the process.

'Well,' Sven Nordohl said, 'you didn't really say why you've come over. Holiday?' There was a question within the question: What was Christina doing with this "cousin" of her late husband's. She understood and flushed with resentment; Sven's morals were his own business. Her attitude had changed.

She said flatly, 'I'm not happy about the lawyer who's advising me on Richard's will. He's a Swede, acting with our London solicitors, so I've come over to find out more about him. Also, Richard bought something when he was over here; apparently it's very valuable. I don't know if I told you but my stepson, Alan, is taking me to court, because Richard left RussMore to Belinda.'

'No, you didn't tell me, but then we don't communicate

much, do we? And I'm not surprised he's going to court; you're not allowed to treat your children unequally in Europe, you'll have to change all that in time.' Belinda looked up; she was eating a very rich chocolate cake and there were dark little crumbs around her mouth.

'Alan's horrible,' she said. 'Horrible to Mum; horrible to everyone.'

'I don't think we need go on about the rights and wrongs of English inheritance after that,' Harry said cheerfully. 'Wipe your mouth, Belinda, you've got chocolate all over your chin. Actually,' he addressed himself to the discomfited Sven, 'you could be a help in all this. Where would we go to buy antique books, documents, that sort of thing? Is there a street where the dealers have their shops? There is in London.'

'Yes, it's not too far from the Emburg,' was the answer. 'A couple of streets away. Most of the antiques are in the Old Town anyway because of the tourists. They're very expensive.'

Harry grinned in his disarming way. 'We're not aiming to buy, just to ask a few questions. And where would I find a list of lawyers? Top of the range firms?'

'There'll be a directory,' Sven Nordohl answered. 'The Emburg'll have one. I think,' he glanced at his watch, 'I think we should be setting off; it's a long drive.' He smiled at Belinda. 'Your grandpa's so excited you're coming. He's got a lot of nice things fixed up for you to do.'

Belinda nodded. 'I'm excited too.' She looked at Christina with the direct gaze of uninhibited childhood, then she turned to her uncle. 'My brother Alan *is* horrible,' she said, 'and I don't want him to live at RussMore.'

Sven insisted on paying the bill. As he did so, Harry murmured to Christina, 'She's certainly her mother's daughter; doesn't mince her words.'

Goodbyes were said, and as they hugged, Christina whispered to Belinda, 'Darling, have a lovely time, and give Grandpa my love. I'll call you tomorrow. And be good, won't you?'

'I will, Mum. You have a nice time too, won't you?' Then the car drove off, with the child waving to them out of the window.

'He's chippy, isn't he?' Harry remarked. 'Nice man, but chippy with you.'

'He thinks I've turned into a snob, that's why. Grand houses and English upper-class ways don't go down well with Swedish people; we pride ourselves on being democratic and fair. Sven thinks, in some way, I sold out by marrying Richard. If he feels like that, I can't help it.'

'Your father, too?' Harry asked.

'No, not Papa. He's the least judgemental person in the world; he thinks everyone has a right to live their lives and believe what they want, so long as they don't hurt others. Sven has a lot of prejudices, though he'd never admit to them. Harry, I don't mind, I've been away too long to let it get to me. Maybe he's right; I have changed, and he doesn't recognize me any more.' She smiled. 'I couldn't help being proud of Belinda, the way she spoke up. I suppose it was rude, but I loved her for it. It's funny, if ever I've thought of giving in to Alan, she does something to make me tough it out.'

They were in the street, walking in the direction of their hotel. As they crossed the road, Harry slipped his arm through hers and kept it there.

'Let's start with the place Richard bought that document,' she said. 'I want to get on with things; that's why we've come, after all.'

It was a narrow cobbled street, with picturesque overhanging houses, and there were shops everywhere. Shops selling furniture, ceramics, antique glass and several dealers in rare books, but none by the name of Poulson. 'Let's go left,' Harry suggested.

Remembering, Christina shook her head. 'That's nothing but gift shops and tourist tat. There used to be a street somewhere towards the right where there were more shops, not such expensive ones . . . Let's try there.' But time had changed it; there were only three moderate dealers offering Swedish glass and ceramics of doubtful value, and a lot of cafés.

'Back to where we started,' he suggested. 'Maybe the name's changed? After all, it is twelve years ago. We can go in and ask.'

The first bookseller was unable to help. He had been established for a year, moving premises from Gothenburg, and he was more interested in trying to sell them some eighteenth-century maps than helping with information. Three doors down the proprietor was a woman. The shop was discreetly lit, with the distinctive smell of old leather. Harry noticed there was a cubicle with special lighting where a buyer could examine at leisure.

'May I help you?' She spoke in English. Christina answered.

'We are looking for a shop called Poulson,' she explained. 'We've been up and down the street but we can't find it, perhaps it's changed its name. Would you know about it?'

She was in her mid-forties, dowdy, scholarly, as befitted her calling, but with shrewd eyes. She said, 'Everybody knows about it. Poulson's was closed two years ago when the owner was murdered.'

She made them coffee and they sat in her inner office, leaving the door open so she could see if a customer came in. She was attentive when Christina explained that they were trying to trace the dealer who had sold an ancient Hebrew document to her husband; if the lady was interested in antiquities, she might well end up being a client. Nice to think of a Swedish girl getting on so well in the world. Her clothes and accessories told her there was money, and the Englishman with her was no gawping tourist; she sold to people like this couple. She made herself very helpful, and she noticed that the woman looked shocked when she said Poulson was murdered.

'He was from Denmark, originally,' she told them. 'Been here for years. We all knew him well. He was good, but sometimes careless. My husband bought a beautiful Gothenburg Bible from him at half its worth and sold it at a big profit. Poulson didn't hold a grudge; he took life easily. That's what made the murder so horrible.' She had leaned forward a little, enjoying her role as storyteller. 'It was a robbery, so the police said, but they weren't just ordinary thieves. The poor old man was tortured before they killed him. Can you imagine anyone doing that? Seventy years old and he'd been tied up and tortured. They'd broken his fingers, one by one. God knows why. The shop was turned upside down, but the stock records showed nothing was missing; that's the extraordinary thing. Some of us wondered if he'd been dealing in stolen goods. They never found the brutes who did it. You can understand why the place stayed empty for so long. Then that young man moved here from Gothenburg and opened it up again.'

'But we asked him,' Christina protested; 'he said he'd never heard of Poulson.'

'Well, he would, wouldn't he? It's not a selling gimmick, is it? Not that he tells the truth about some of his goods either.'

Harry spoke then. 'And this happened when – two years ago?'

She nodded. 'About that. I was away visiting my daughter at the time, but my husband was here; he noticed the shop was closed up without any lights on. After two days he called the police, and they broke in and found the poor man. I'm afraid that's all I can tell you.'

Christina said slowly, 'And no-one knew what they were looking for? Or if they found it?'

The dealer shrugged. 'The police said they'd questioned him for hours before they killed him. He didn't have a fine stock, just one or two things. He wouldn't have stood all that pain if he could have helped it. I just don't know; it's a mystery. It'll never be solved, I'm afraid.'

In the street outside Harry took her arm again. 'Before we jump to any conclusions, let's go back to the Emburg and look up some lawyers.'

'It's not like you', Christina said slowly, 'to be so cautious. What a horrible coincidence!'

'Very nasty,' he agreed, 'if it was a coincidence. Which I don't think you believe and I don't either but, as I said, we won't jump to conclusions. Now, which way do we go? I'm lost.'

'What a nice apartment,' Rolf Wallberg remarked.

James Farrington said, 'Thanks. Actually I'm going to sell it and move somewhere more secure. Two days ago I was robbed in here at knifepoint! The bastard hasn't been caught and he could come back some time. It doesn't make for sound sleep.'

'How unpleasant,' Rolf said coldly. 'But you weren't hurt; that was lucky anyway. This is such a violent city.' He took a seat without waiting to be asked.

James said awkwardly, 'You wanted to see me on Christa's behalf. I'm not sure what I can do to help but, of course, I'll try. Can I get you a drink?'

'No,' Rolf answered, 'this is not a social call, Mr Farrington. I've come for Mrs Farrington's property: the document you stole from your father's collection.' He saw the colour creep into James's face. He had looked pallid and strained, still slightly shocked from his ordeal two days ago; now he went scarlet and then white at the lips.

'Please don't waste time denying it,' Rolf went on. 'You stole it and, so long as you give it back, Mrs Farrington will not take any action, or tell anyone what a thief you are. So where is it?'

James didn't answer. He went and poured himself a very dark Scotch and sat down, his shoulders slumped in despair. Too easily cowed, Rolf decided; he'd played this part many times before. He drank some of the whiskey. 'I don't know what you're talking about,' he said in a voice that didn't invite belief. 'I never stole anything.'

Rolf stood up and moved a step towards him. 'Your stepmother is a kind forgiving lady. I'm not kind and I don't like people fooling with me. Where is it?'

James said loudly, because he was aware of a real menace about the man, 'Are you threatening me?'

'Yes,' was the answer, very quietly spoken. 'Yes, I'm threatening you. I shall beat the lying shit out of you, Mr Farrington, and you won't dare to complain because you can't explain why I did it. You have two minutes.'

James put down his glass. His nerves were already undermined, now they disintegrated. He had lied in self-protection since he was a child, evading punishment, but lying wouldn't help him now. 'I didn't steal it,' he protested, 'I was just curious.

Father was so secretive, shutting himself away for hours when we were children. I wanted to see what he had hidden there, so I borrowed it for a while. I would have given it back.'

'I'm sure.' The smile was unpleasant. 'Out of interest, how did you know where to look?'

'I knew my father's love of categories. Everything in the library was filed in alphabetical order.'

'So now you know what it is,' Rolf said, 'you can just return it, can't you?'

'No,' James said, 'I can't; it was stolen by the man who robbed me. He took the envelope out of the safe, and some money and my cuff-links. I reported the theft to the police; it's on their records. You can check if you don't believe me.' Rolf turned and sat down again.

'Did you show it to anyone? Did you find out what you'd taken?'

'I was going to,' James admitted. He slipped in a lie because he couldn't resist it. 'I thought it might be valuable and I could tell Christa, but I never got round to it. It looked like a lot of Arabic to me. Do you know what it was? Why is it so important, that you come all the way to New York and behave like some thug to get it back?'

Rolf Wallberg fixed him with a cold stare. 'Because it is worth a million dollars or more. It's a priceless piece of Jewish history, and only your father realized what it was. I couldn't let you give it to your brother, Alan, could I? And you would have done in the end, wouldn't you? Just to show him how clever you are . . . put him in your debt. So I had to come and persuade you to return it, but it's gone, hasn't it, Mr Farrington? Your thief probably tossed it in the garbage when he saw it wasn't money, so now nobody benefits. What a pity.' He stood up, startling James. James got to his feet too; he felt less threatened standing.

'Does Christa know you're like this?' he asked. 'What would she say if I told her you were going to use violence? I don't think she'd like it.'

'I don't think so either,' Rolf agreed, 'but you wouldn't gain anything and you'd make an enemy of me. I'm a bad enemy, Mr Farrington, and I'm not pleased with what you've done. You've lost my client a fortune, and I don't like you for that.' He shrugged. 'But there's nothing I can do, and nothing you can do either. I hope you find a safer place to live. I'll let myself out.'

He moved very quickly and James heard the apartment door close. He swallowed the rest of the whiskey, and when he set the glass down, his hand shook. Very softly, as if he could be overheard, he whispered, 'Jesus Christ, what kind of lawyer *is* that guy . . .?' He couldn't answer his own question.

Harry Spannier made the calls. 'Could I speak with Mr Rolf Wallberg?'

'I'm sorry, but there's no-one of that name in our office.'

Christina protested. 'But this is crazy. Harvey Stone told me Rolf was one of the best-known lawyers in Sweden with an international reputation. Surely they'd have heard of him!'

'Not necessarily,' Harry contradicted, 'that was a switch-board operator and that was only one firm; next time I'll ask to speak to one of the clerks. Even if he's not with them, they'll know of him.' He swore at his own stupidity. 'Hell's teeth, why didn't I think of that before? Bloody bad detective I'd make . . . More like Inspector Clouseau than Sherlock Holmes. Did you see *The Pink Panther*?'

No, Christina could have screamed with impatience; he often made remarks that had no relevance to anything. 'No, look – let me try.' She took the telephone out of his hand. 'Get me the next number and the name of the firm. What . . . they're the biggest lawyers in Stockholm. They must know him. Hello? Good afternoon. I wonder if I could speak with Mr Helstrom? Oh, he is . . . yes, his secretary would be a start.' She put a hand over the mouthpiece. 'Even I've heard of Helstrom and I've never used a lawyer in my life until now. Hello? Yes, my name is Mrs Farrington and I wanted to speak with Mr Helstrom, but I understand he's engaged with a client . . . yes, well I'm sure you can. Do you have a Mr Rolf Wallberg working with you? You do?' She swung round at Harry in triumph. 'She says he's in England on a sabbatical.'

'Yes,' Christina went on, 'I know he's in England; that's why I wanted to ask Mr Helstrom's advice. You see he's acting for me on a case over there at this moment. Would it be possible to make an appointment?' There was a pause. 'You can't? Yes, I see. But you will call me? I'm staying at the Emburg for the next day or two. Mrs Christina Farrington. Thank you.'

Harry raised his eyebrows. 'What was all that about at the end? I don't understand your lovely language.'

'I thought she might take more notice if she knew I was Swedish. She said Helstrom's very busy but he might see me for a quick consultation. She sounded rather surprised at the whole thing; but, Harry, he's genuine, he's a lawyer with the firm.' He looked at her. 'You're sure she said sabbatical?'

'Yes,' she assured him. 'Why?'

'Because he's supposed to be working with your solicitors, for God's sake! A sabbatical is a complete break from normal work; it doesn't mean joining a high-powered firm like Harvey & Stone.' Christina said something he couldn't understand. He cupped a hand to his ear. 'Sorry?'

She glared at him. 'I was swearing,' she said, 'in my lovely native language. Can't you be serious? I feel I'm walking through a fog, with you on one side saying he's something sinister, and Wallberg wanting me to trust him, and Richard gloating over a treasure taken from some poor murdered Jewish family . . .' She fell back into the chair and kicked off her shoes.

'You've got lovely feet,' he remarked. 'Very sexy. Now don't lose your temper, Christa, I'm trying to make you lighten up a bit. We're getting somewhere, and a hell of a lot faster than I expected. Let's put the whole thing on hold, shall we? We won't mention the noble Swede for the rest of the day. You put your sexy feet up and stop worrying and I'll leave you in peace, then I'll come back at around seven and take you out for a drink somewhere and dinner; nice and cheap because it's my treat. How would that suit?'

'It would suit just fine,' she said wearily, 'and we're not going to spend your money because I'm paying. You've come over here to help me and I insist.'

He went to the door, paused and grinned at her. 'Oh good, I hoped you say that. See you around seven.'

She closed her eyes, wanting him to leave, so she could try and sort out the chaos in her mind. Poulson had been tortured and killed two years ago – That woman's description had made her shudder – Tortured for information he didn't have, or maybe killed when at last he gave it . . . But why should this have any relevance to Richard's discovery? Because it was so rare and so valuable. If Rolf Wallberg knew it existed, then others must have known too and tried to find it. If they were right and James had stolen it, Rolf might have contacted him already. Humfrey Stone would know where to find him. She reached for the phone and dialled the office in London. Humfrey was unavailable but his secretary had the name and number of the hotel where Rolf was staying. Christina checked the time difference; six hours behind their time in Sweden, about twelve noon. He might be there, or at least he'd get a message.

There was no reply from his room. Christina left the Emburg's number and asked him to call, urgently, then she hung up. Telephoning had brought him vividly to life; the ice-pale eyes, the silver-blond hair, the force in him that repelled and invited at the same time. He had brought her to life and she hated herself for it.

Rolf went back to his hotel to pack. He'd booked himself out on the ten o'clock flight from Kennedy airport; he would sleep through the journey. The receptionist smiled at him. 'There's a gentleman waiting to see you, Mr Wallberg – he's in the bar. And there's a message for you; I have it right here.' She gave him the message about Christina's telephone call, and he looked at it briefly, then put it in his pocket. She was in Stockholm. Why, why after so long away from her homeland would she decide to go there now? Not to see family; the note said she was staying at a hotel. She had left a number to call back. The receptionist was a curious girl and she found this taciturn handsome man intriguing. 'Not bad news, I hope?' He looked as if it were. Might need a shoulder to cry on when she came off duty. She wouldn't have minded; she loved that white-blond hair . . . Rolf didn't look up.

'In the bar, you said? Through there?' Disappointed, she indicated the way.

'Next to the restaurant, on the left there.' Rolf strode away without saying thanks. Normally foreigners were so polite. She pulled a little face at his back view.

His caller was sitting at a table, with a glass of beer and a dish of pretzels, which he was eating. He looked up, saw Rolf and made a signal. Rolf came over but he didn't sit down. 'Come up to the room,' he said. The other took a quick swallow of beer and then followed Rolf to the elevator. They went up to the eighth floor in silence and walked into Rolf's room. Inside, Rolf simply held out his hand, and the man opened his jacket and took out an envelope.

'Everything is there?' Rolf demanded.

'You want the other stuff too – the Rolex, the jewellery? I can throw it away.'

'Better if I do,' was the answer. 'You get to keep the money and the Rolex, if you want it.'

The man shrugged. 'I can find a use for it. I checked the serial numbers, and they're not in sequence; it was just spare cash. The wallet and the cards – I've burned them.'

'Good,' Rolf said. 'Give me the jewellery.' James's three sets of cuff-links were handed over. Rolf put them in his inside breast pocket. He turned away and opened the envelope, drew out the contents and gazed at it in silence. The man watched him quietly.

'You've done a great service,' Rolf said slowly, 'I want you to know that. It was a risk, but it was worth it.'

The other smiled slightly. 'Risks are my business,' he said. 'I don't know what that is you've got there, but if you say it's worth it, then I'm happy.'

Rolf walked to the door and opened it for him. He held out his hand and grasped the man's firmly. 'I'll commend you,' he said, 'to the right people.'

He held it in his hands at last. It was still in its protective cover, and he touched it very gently. It was so ancient, so frail and yellowed, but the characters were strong and clear. He remembered Richard Farrington's ecstatic notes. 'Unbelievable condition, with very little loss of text!' Hundreds of years of living history, guarded down the centuries by Jewish families. It had survived wars, pogroms and persecutions, moving across Europe with the people who kept it in a sacred trust. That guardianship had ended in a night of cold-blooded mass murder in the North Sea.

Rolf Wallberg closed the cover over the delicate fragment of a people's past. Full circle, he thought calmly, and that stilled the tremble in his hands; he had paid the debt in full. He locked the envelope, resealed now, into his briefcase. The years of searching, of painstaking discovery of a crime and its consequences, had come to fulfilment in a New York hotel room, courtesy of an anonymous man with certain skills and secret affiliations, because he, Rolf Wallberg, had let nothing stand in the way of that fulfilment; neither scruples nor pity, honour nor the rule of law.

He took out the note about Christina's telephone call and her number from his pocket, crumpled it between his strong fingers and threw it accurately into the waste-basket; there was nothing to tell her that couldn't wait till he got back to England. He had felt alarm in the foyer down below when he knew she was in Stockholm, now he didn't care. Like all people with something to hide, he suspected that others must be deceivers, too. She would find out nothing that mattered. The only thing that was important lay in his briefcase on the first stage of its journey home.

He did put through a call to London, to the Lanesborough, where the woman was staying, waiting to hear from him; his contact with the glossy blond hair and the alligator instincts. After a pause he was connected to her room.

There were no civilized preliminaries, no enquiries about each other's well-being.

'Have you got it?'

'Yes, I have it with me. I'll be in London tomorrow.'

'I'll be waiting,' she said. 'We'll celebrate. Don't make any plans.' Then she hung up. He finished packing, ordered a steak sandwich from room service, and by eight-thirty he was in a cab on his way to the airport. James Farrington's cuff-links were in his pocket. He had forgotten about them.

6

'It's very kind of you to see us, Mr Helstrom.'

The solicitor smiled. 'Not at all. I would always make time to help a friend of Rolf's.'

Christina said quickly, 'Not a friend, a client. He's acting for me in a dispute over my husband's will.' There was a slight frown on the older man's face when she said that, but the professional smile remained.

'When I heard that, I assumed you must be a friend,' he said. 'Rolf asked for a year's leave of absence and, after the last three years, we felt he deserved a complete break from legal work.' They spoke in English out of courtesy to Harry.

'What sort of work was he doing? If we're allowed to know.'

Helstrom answered firmly, 'Certainly, we're very proud of him. We were engaged to trace Jewish property stolen by the Nazis and dispersed here in Sweden. Of course, we employed private detectives and Interpol co-operated fully, but it was

Rolf's assignment. It involved a lot of travelling, both here and in Germany, and a high degree of negotiating skill. He had a very high success rate.' Christina interposed then.

'He did say he'd been involved with compensating relatives of Jews murdered on their way to Sweden.'

Helstrom nodded. 'Then there's not much more I can tell you, but perhaps you can enlighten me.' He leaned towards her. 'I find it strange that Rolf should engage in practice without informing us.' He was waiting for an answer. 'I hope it doesn't mean he's decided to move to England.'

Christina stood up. 'I'm sure it doesn't. He misses Sweden; he's said so. I think he was attracted to my lawsuit because it's so different from anything he'd have to deal with at home. My husband left his property to our daughter and cut out his two sons, and one of them is trying to overturn the will.'

He looked surprised, even a little disapproving. 'No, we wouldn't have such a problem here or anywhere in Europe, Mrs Farrington. However, I hope you find a solution without going to court; family quarrels are best settled within the family. I'm sure Rolf will find the experience interesting, and, of course, he'll do his best for you, but you haven't told me why you've come to see me?'

Harry was on his feet too. 'We've lost track of him and my cousin needs to contact him urgently. We thought he might have come home for a quick visit.' His smile was broad and disingenuous. 'Gave me an excuse to see your beautiful country too. Thank you so much for your time. Christa?' He took her arm, guiding her towards the door. The lawyer gave him a look of quiet dislike; he had been outmanoeuvred.

In the street outside, Harry said, 'Why didn't you tell him Wallberg was working with Harvey & Stone?'

'Because it was obvious they knew nothing about it,' she answered. 'I didn't want to make trouble for him. Anyway we found out what we wanted to know: he told the truth.'

'Yes, but he lied to his firm. I wonder why?'

They crossed the street. Christina didn't answer. She'd protected Rolf instinctively and she wasn't sure she'd done the right thing. Why had he lied about taking a job in London?

'Maybe the old boy was right,' Harry mused. 'Maybe he does mean to settle in England and stay with Harvey & Stone . . . or set up his own practice. I'm just guessing, but it may be as simple as that.' He hailed a passing taxi-cab.

'I don't know,' she answered. 'I left a message for him to call from New York, and he hasn't called back. Harry, I'm going to phone James. I can't go up to Lindy and Papa without knowing what's happened.'

Harry considered for a moment. 'Why don't you let me do it? It's about time the brothers Grimm knew you had a member of the family on your side. He'll run with the news to cousin Alan.'

As the cab drew up at the hotel she turned to him. 'Alan will flip,' she said. 'I don't want him attacking you.'

He laughed. 'I do. I can't wait. Let's start with that stalwart James.'

'What's the matter with you, Rolf?' She had stripped off her clothes and stood provocatively in front of him. She reached out a hand to undress him, but he held it still. 'What's wrong?' she repeated.

'Nothing,' he said. 'I don't feel like sex; put your clothes on. I don't fuck to order, you should know that by now.'

'Well,' she pushed a long strand of blond hair over her bare shoulder, 'this is a first time. You have a problem suddenly?' There was anger in her eyes.

'If I do', he said, 'it's my problem, not yours. This is your way of celebrating, but it's not the way I feel.'

She began dressing briskly, without any attempt to arouse him. 'How the hell do you feel then?' She pulled the expensive dress on and fastened it behind her neck.

Rolf said, 'Drained, wiped out. It's been a long assignment, and I've had the euphoria; this is the let down. It happens; you should understand.'

She shrugged. 'I do. Trouble is, when I'm on a high I stay on it; I didn't guess you were so sensitive.' She came up and put her hands on his shoulders. Unexpectedly she was kind. 'Just so long as I haven't lost my charms,' she murmured.

'You haven't,' he said, 'be sure of that. I'm sorry. Next time . . . it'll be good.'

She turned away from him; she fastened a gold choker and slipped on a matching bracelet. 'There won't be a next time,' she said. 'You won't be seeing me again; not for a while anyway. Not till you come out.' She smiled at him. '*The Ice Man Cometh*. Wasn't that a play?'

He nodded, 'Eugene O'Neill. It was great theatre.'

'Only he didn't, this time.' She laughed. 'Let's go down and eat; if you haven't lost your appetite . . .'

She did the ordering in the restaurant and toasted him with champagne. 'You've done a great job. I'm criticized for not thanking people enough, so I'm making up for it now. We'll never forget what you've done. You may even have a street named after you.'

Rolf didn't answer. It was over; the dead would rest in peace. 'You'll be going home?' she asked him.

'No, not yet.'

'What's keeping you here?' She put the question lightly, but already she had guessed the answer.

'I want to see this Farrington case through,' he told her. He made it sound casual, but she wasn't deceived. 'Because of the woman? How can you help her now?'

'I don't know, but I've got to try. She trusted me.'

'Ah.' She sipped her champagne. 'You can't live without a cause? Take my advice; she's got good lawyers, let them fight for her. You go home.'

Rolf Wallberg looked at her. There was something in the pale eyes she recognized and had long since suppressed in herself.

'I would', he said, 'if I knew where home was.'

When he took the call James didn't recognize the voice or the name at first. 'Harry? Harry who?'

'Harry Spannier, your cousin. Remember me? I was the one Alan used to try and push around at children's parties.'

'Oh, yes, of course. How are you? Where are you? I thought you lived in South Africa.'

James had a vague recollection of a boy who'd responded to Alan's bullying by kicking him hard on the shins, but beyond that, he hadn't thought of him or heard of him for years.

'Not any more,' Harry answered. 'I'm home, in England. I'm taking on the agricultural business and thc farm. Actually I'm with Christa at the moment.' James stiffened.

'What are you doing with her?' There was an edge to his voice when Harry answered.

'Proving that not all the Farrington relations are utter shits. I hear Alan's taking her to court over the will.'

'Yes.' James was very guarded now. Harry Spannier . . . What the hell business was it of his . . . Wait till Alan found out he was taking sides . . . 'Yes, that's right. I'm not taking any part in it,' he added.

'But her lawyer's been to see you?'

That took James by surprise. Then he felt angry at the reminder. 'He certainly has,' he retorted, 'and you can tell her from me he behaved like a bloody thug. He threatened me, physically.'

'Good Lord,' Harry pretended to be shocked. 'Really? Offered a punch-up? That's not very legal. What have you done, James? Pinched something? Like an old manuscript? You were always pinching things, I remember . . .'

James shouted, 'You bastard! Alan'll sort you out!'

'Tell him I'm a big boy now,' Harry reminded him. 'I can do more than kick shins.'

He turned to Christina. 'He's hung up,' he said. 'But the noble Swede's been to see him and got pretty rough; threatened the miserable bugger. Didn't sound as if he was acting in the best traditions of Harvey & Stone . . . Maybe they do things differently in Sweden.' He was watching her closely. 'He took a risk, behaving like that. Did you know he was going to handle James that way?'

'No,' Christina answered, 'of course I didn't. But the manuscript?'

'I'd say he gave it back,' Harry said. 'So all we have to do is contact Wallberg, or wait for him to contact you.'

But there was no word from Rolf. He hadn't been in touch

with the London office, there was a recorded message on his answerphone in his flat, and the New York Hotel said he had checked out two days before . . . Silence. After another day of waiting, Harry suggested that they drive up to see her father and collect Belinda.

'Christina,' her father said gently, 'Christina, what's the matter? You can tell me. We never had secrets.'

She smiled up at him. They were alone; Belinda had gone into the village with Harry for supplies, and the stove was lit against a growing autumn chill. The simple room, with its plain functional furnishings, was the same as she remembered from holidays spent there so many years ago; nothing had changed. Life was easy, centring on sailing and fishing, long walks by the seashore, evenings spent talking, going to bed early, getting up with the dawn. Nothing had changed, except her. Even her father seemed immune from age.

He was the same kindly shrewd mentor of his children, convinced that simple honest philosophy of life provided all solutions.

'You haven't been yourself since you came up here,' he said. 'Is it this lawsuit?'

Christina sighed. 'Yes, of course it is.'

It was Harry who insisted that they stay with her father for a few days before flying back to England. 'Come on, stop worrying; there's nothing you can do. The noble Swede'll surface. The break'll do you good.' But it hadn't. She was restless, hoping for the old magic of the place to work, knowing it wasn't going to, that she had moved even further away from her past life than she imagined.

'Christina, why don't you stop all this?' her father asked. 'That house and the money aren't worth all the bitterness and fighting. What happiness will Belinda have in the end, even if you win? And you . . . what will your future be – living there among strangers. Without Richard you don't belong at RussMore.'

She looked at him. 'That's the trouble, I do. It's become part of me. It's Belinda's home and England is her country. I know you'd like me to give it up and come back to Sweden, but I can't.'

'Are you convincing yourself or me?' he said. 'There's something I've never asked you, I couldn't while your husband was alive. Were you truly happy? Really happy?'

'Yes,' she answered, 'I was very happy with him.'

'He was so much older,' the gentle voice persisted. While they talked, he had slipped an arm around her, just as if she were a little girl again. 'He was so different from anyone you'd ever known: sophisticated, rich, living in another world, and his children hated you. It can't have been easy; there must have been times when you had doubts . . . regrets?'

'Doubts, yes,' Christina admitted, 'about whether I was going to make up to him for all he'd suffered, all that misery . . . but he said I did. He said I was the only person in the world who'd made him happy when he thought his life was over – and I gave him Belinda. You only stayed with us once or twice, so you never really saw them together; it was lovely the way they related to each other. And I was never jealous, if that's what you're thinking, because he always put me first. As for Alan – it wasn't so much hating me as hating anyone who made his father happy; he was the one Alan hated. James only wanted to be loved, but Richard couldn't . . . Papa, not all families are like ours. Maybe we're just dull, maybe we don't feel things so intensely.'

'For that', he said, 'I'm thankful . . . I'd rather my children were happy and dull than like the Farringtons. Belinda has already learned to hate. She's talked to me about her half-brother . . . I was shocked. Is that how you want her to grow up?' The encircling arm had been withdrawn; Christina had hurt him.

She said quickly, 'Darling Papa, I'm so sorry . . . I didn't mean to criticize. I just felt you were being judgemental and that's not like you. God, how I wish it had been different! I'm having to fight, when all I want is to rebuild my life.' She looked at him and he recognized the stubbornness inherited from her mother. 'I won't run away. Richard relied on me to look after RussMore and Belinda, and I'm not going to opt out, so please try and understand, and don't let's talk about it. Please?'

'All right. I'm sorry too; I didn't mean to doubt your motives, I just needed to be sure you had thought it through. I like the cousin.' Better than the dead husband, he thought privately. 'It's good he's there to support you. Belinda likes him.'

'He encourages her,' Christina answered. 'He's as mischievous as she is, but he's no fool and he's a good friend.'

'More than a friend,' her father said. 'I think he wants more than friendship.'

She shook her head. 'No, you couldn't be more wrong. We are just that – friends. They'll be back soon, and Papa, I hate to cut our time short, but I must go to England. I'd like to leave tomorrow. Do you mind?'

He smiled at her. 'No, of course not. I shall miss you. Come again soon, Christa, and bring my granddaughter; I have Sven's children but Belinda is special. Give me a kiss. You'll always be my girl, you know that.'

As they embraced Christina's eyes filled with tears. They drove down to Stockholm the next morning and caught the midday flight to Heathrow. On the plane Harry went through the pantomime of holding Belinda's hand through the take-off and landing. 'Since your Mother won't . . .' and they both giggled at the joke. *He wants more than friendship.* Her father's words came to Christina and she dismissed them. Harry posed no threat; he teased and flirted without serious intent. When he looked at her, or touched her, there was no fierce fusion, no charge of sexuality. He wasn't Rolf Wallberg. 'Thank God,' she murmured to herself.

'Good morning, Mr Wallberg.' Rolf's secretary looked up with a smile as he came in. 'There are a number of messages for you; most are from Mrs Farrington. Shall I bring them in?'

'Please.' Rolf shed his overcoat. The autumn day was chilly; the skies overcast with rain-clouds. He hated the English climate. He longed for the crisp air of Scandinavia, the bright blue skies, even the blinding cold when it came was less depressing than this surly greyness. Christina would have been trying to reach him. He'd covered his tracks well, given himself time to think and make his final decision: he would stay until the case with Alan Farrington was won or lost.

He looked through the list of callers. She'd left four messages for him, asking him to make contact urgently; the latest was from RussMore. His secretary buzzed through.

'Mr Wallberg, Mr Humfrey would like to see you if you're free.'

'I'm on my way,' Rolf told her. Humfrey would ask about New York; he'd lie. Humfrey wouldn't question him too closely because he was Uncle Ruben's protégé.

Humfrey got up to greet him; he didn't like Rolf but he was always polite.

'How was your trip?'

He was expecting some kind of explanation, and Rolf gave it easily. 'Frustrating,' he said. 'Ruben Stone asked me to fly over and see a client who was on a business trip in New York. When I got there he was unavailable for two days. Americans don't give explanations . . . not to foreign lawyers anyway. I wasted time in the hotel till he was free, and then it was half an hour and goodbye Wallberg, nice to have met with you. But he did give the undertaking Ruben Stone wanted . . . I've had messages from Mrs Farrington; any developments since I've been away?'

Humfrey said, 'Farrington's counsel wants a meeting with Ken Hubert and us and the two principals. I suspect Farrington's behind this; it's not normal procedure.'

Kenneth Hubert was their chosen counsel, John Cunningham was Alan's choice; equally distinguished but with very different styles. Humfrey went on, 'Cunningham's a bully; he'll try to humiliate and harass Mrs Farrington.'

Rolf said quickly, 'Then she mustn't go.'

'Not unless Hubert advises it; he knows Cunningham well, I believe they're good friends outside court. He'll handle him if he tries to push her.' He paused and rubbed his nose. It was a habit that irritated Rolf; it was a sign that Humfrey was uneasy. 'I must say,' he went on, 'the tactics are not at all what we expected. I thought they'd drag their feet in the hope that she'd be forced to settle because of the costs, but quite the opposite, Farrington is pushing the pace. He wants an early date and a hearing as soon as there's room on the calendar. I can't understand it.'

'He must think he's certain to win,' Rolf suggested. 'Does Mrs Farrington know about this suggestion?'

Humfrey shook his head. 'I only got the papers this morning. I was going to write to her.'

Rolf said, 'She's asked to see me, so I can prepare her in advance of your letter. Shall I do that?'

'That's a good idea,' Humfrey said. 'She's come to rely on you, Rolf; much more than I expected. I really didn't think you were on any kind of wavelength to start with.'

'We weren't,' he answered, 'but things change. I've won her confidence; it wasn't easy.' He allowed himself a rare smile. 'Swedes are very obstinate, and determined.'

'So I've noticed,' Humfrey remarked. 'You'll be going to RussMore?'

Rolf hesitated. 'It might be better if I saw her in the office. I'll see what I can arrange.'

He went back to his office, closed the door and said he wouldn't take calls for the next half an hour. Alan Farrington was pressing ahead. He was very confident, but nothing that had come out so far justified that confidence. He sat there, concentrating, remembering something Christina had said early on, in reply to a question he hadn't asked.

'I'm not ready to answer such a question.'

Well, he decided, with the document gone, there was no money for a long campaign on her part. If there was something Alan Farrington had discovered that could affect the outcome, she must disclose it now. She came to his mind so vividly that he got up abruptly, disturbed by his feelings. Sex without emotion had been his creed. Now the sex was there, a desire so close to the surface that it surged in him at the thought of her, but emotion was there too; he couldn't separate them any more. He had paid one debt and been burdened with another. He had to win for her, and to achieve that he was prepared to be ruthless, to use any means that might help, whatever the cost.

Love, he thought fiercely, even if I loved her, I would hurt her to achieve the end; that had been his creed also, and he had lived by it.

Kenneth Hubert was at the top of his profession. He had taken silk at the early age of forty-two, and already declined the offer to become a judge. He loved the cut and thrust of the courtroom too much to give it up and settle for a place on the bench. He told his wife when she protested, 'I have no desire to sit in judgement, darling. I like the heat of the battle.'

'And the money,' she had retorted.

'And the money,' Kenneth agreed. 'So do you.'

They had been married young; she was also at the Bar, struggling with criminal law. She was a girl who was always rushing, her new wig slightly askew, her black gown flying; she was pretty, clever and dedicated, and he was enchanted by her. He was making money in a civil law chambers and she was on the breadline taking legal aid cases.

He married her, as she said afterwards, in spite of herself, and they had been happily married for twenty-one years and had two children. Molly Hubert continued to practise until the second baby came; Kenneth knew her too well to suggest she give up. When she reached that conclusion he pretended to be surprised. 'I can't do justice to my practice and to Tom,' she explained, 'so I've opted for Tom.'

'You can always go back,' he assured her. 'Keep in touch, don't get too rusty, and besides, I need you to help me.' He discussed everything with her. She had a naturally logical brain, whereas he had that slight twist that almost inclined to the criminal. That was what made him so brilliant, that deviant perspective that saw loopholes and weaknesses which others missed.

That evening at the beginning of September, they sat together in their opulent Lowndes Square penthouse, gin and tonics in their hands, and Kenneth outlined the Farrington v. Farrington action. Molly Hubert had skimmed through the brief and now it was time to discuss the details. 'It's all about greed, isn't it?' she remarked. 'The stepmother works on her dying husband

and grabs everything for her child; the son takes her to court and throws every kind of mud he can think of, and it's greed with him, too.'

'For once, darling,' he said, 'you're wrong. It's not greed, it's hate, and that's worse because it can't be bought off. I had a meeting with my client's solicitors; they gave a very clear picture of the stepson: a man who's obsessed with hatred for his father and who has transferred that hatred to his second wife and the innocent eleven-year-old daughter. He's making allegations of undue influence and alleging that the child is illegitimate. Apparently the Swedish lady led a rather colourful life before she married Mr Farrington – lots of free love; it was all the fashion a few years ago.'

'It's pretty much the fashion here too,' Molly interposed. 'All the young are in relationships, and none of our generation seem to stay married. I don't think that will count against the stepmother, and how can he prove the child isn't his father's? The father's dead, so there can't be any DNA. He can allege what he likes but he can't prove it.'

Hubert finished his drink. 'One more? Good, I'll join you.'

'I'll get it,' she said. 'You love being waited on; you're spoiled rotten in chambers and I spoil you when you come home.' The smile was as attractive after twenty years as when he first saw it.

'You know, when I get something like this, I realize just how lucky I am to have you and the boys. Very lucky. John Cunningham is acting for the plaintiff; he'll love this case, it's just what he revels in. I'm going to have to see the client and put some pretty straight questions to her; if she tries to hide anything, John'll skin her alive in the witness box. Farrington's solicitors have suggested a meeting between counsels and the two principals.'

Molly looked at him. 'They might be prepared to settle?'

'Not according to our solicitors; they say it's an attempt to intimidate. Farrington used that tactic in a one-to-one with his stepmother, apparently. He sounds a really nasty type.'

'It always amazes me', she remarked, 'that someone as nice as

John enjoys fighting for such awful clients. He's quite schizoid when he gets to court.'

Her husband grinned. 'He says the same about me, but someone has to defend the bad guys, darling, otherwise there's no justice. Didn't you have the odd villain as a client? And didn't you fight your hardest for them?'

'Yes I did,' she conceded, 'but it did help if I thought they *just* might be innocent . . . I remember one awful brute getting off a murder charge and he came up to thank me. I walked away, I couldn't bear to look at him; he was as guilty as hell.'

She sipped her drink. 'It wasn't only mother love that made me give up,' she admitted, 'some of the cases were beginning to get to me. But I'm sure you knew that, you old fox . . . you never said anything. Anyway, are you going to have this chummy meeting before you start tearing each other's guts out in court?'

He paused. 'Yes, I think I am. I'll see the Swedish lady in private first, then we'll have an idea of what John's going to throw at us. I want to see the stepson at first hand. How long before dinner?'

'Not long enough for another gin,' she said firmly. 'You go and open a nice bottle of wine while I get the food ready. It's your favourite, saltimbocca alla Romana.'

Kenneth got up and sighed happily.

'Clever, sexy and a brilliant cook . . . What did I do to deserve you?'

'God knows,' Molly said sweetly. 'I keep asking myself the same question.'

He laughed. 'We should have asked John round, he loves Italian food. I might have pumped him about his tactics.'

'Like hell,' she retorted. 'He's as foxy as you are; you're a good pair. Come on, darling, I like a glass of wine while I'm dishing up.'

They had an excellent dinner and settled down to watch their favourite programme on television, about a firm of high-powered American attorneys, all of whom were traumatized by alcohol, debts and inter-office love affairs. It made Kenneth

Hubert hysterical with laughter. The Farrington lawsuit was quite forgotten.

'Sit down, Christina, can I get you some coffee?'

His secretary had shown her in and was waiting by the door. 'No thanks,' Christina answered. He had suggested a meeting in his office; she was relieved but disconcerted. He had been brief, even curt over the telephone, avoiding any questions, and Christina stifled a treacherous feeling of hurt. He was coldly professional, as if nothing had ever passed between them.

'I'm very sorry,' he said, 'I've got bad news. I didn't want to tell you over the phone.'

'The manuscript? James didn't give it to you?'

'He couldn't. He was robbed in his flat, and it was in his wall safe; the thief took everything in it, along with cash and personal jewellery. It's true because I checked with the police. It's gone, Christa; probably destroyed. I am so sorry.'

He came round the desk towards her. The mask had slipped; he put a hand on her shoulder, and his pale eyes were gentle. 'I didn't know how to tell you, after I'd raised your hopes.' Abruptly he went back to his place behind the desk.

Christina said, 'It's not your fault. It didn't belong to me, so I wouldn't have taken money for it anyway. And please, don't blame yourself, you did everything possible. So what do I do now?'

'What we do now is get our case ready. Humfrey wants to see you. Your counsel and Alan's counsel want a meeting, with you and him and the solicitors present. I don't want you to agree.'

She said, 'Why not? If my side advise it, why shouldn't I?'

'Because of the questions you'll be asked, that's why. Christina, this whole thing will hinge on whether Belinda is Richard's child. Now I'm going to ask you, and you must answer me.'

She stood up. 'No,' she said, 'I won't. I can't.'

Suddenly he was beside her; he moved so quickly he caught her by the shoulders before she could back away.

'Why can't you?'

Tears filled up and overflowed; she put her hands to her face to hide.

'Why can't you tell me?' he persisted.

'Because I don't know. I've never known, all these years . . . I've watched her and seen her grow up like Richard. I've been sure she was his, but I *wanted* to believe it; I've no way of proving it . . . She's dark,' she went on, 'like Richard, but so was Jan. Jan was my lover; he left me just before I met Richard. We'd been sleeping together right up until he left the night before . . . then I made love with Richard. Later I missed my period. How could I know which one had made me pregnant?'

He looked down at her. 'Did you tell him before he married you?'

'Yes,' Christina answered. 'I loved him; he was so good to me, I couldn't have cheated him. I told him he couldn't marry me, as I could be having someone else's child.'

He pulled her close against him; for a moment she stiffened, trying to resist, but he was strong and she hadn't the will. He held her and she felt his hand move on her hair.

'I was sure,' he said quietly. 'I was sure you'd told him. You're not a woman who lies or cheats. What did he say?'

'He said he didn't mind,' Christina whispered. 'If it was my child, he'd love it as if it were his own. When Belinda was born he just looked at her and said, "She's a Farrington, my darling." That was all. It was never mentioned again.'

She felt his mouth against her forehead, then he lifted her face and kissed her on the lips. Richard, Richard, she thought in desperation, but then she lost herself and felt nothing but Wallberg's mouth and Wallberg's body. As if he knew her thoughts, he murmured as he held her, 'He's dead; you're alive. I'm going to help you.'

Then it was over. They stood apart, looking at each other. 'Oh God,' Christina said. 'Why did you do that? Why did I let you?'

He smiled. 'It doesn't matter why. What happens to us can wait; it must wait – you have to win this case first. Are you ready to tell your counsel what you've just told me? And Alan's counsel; he'll have questions too?'

'No,' Christina didn't hesitate. 'I don't care for myself; I've nothing to be ashamed of, but I won't bring Belinda into it. I shall deny everything. You're wrong about me Rolf, I can lie and cheat when it comes to my child.'

'Good,' he answered, 'that's what you must do: deny everything. And you'll win because the burden of proof is on Alan, and he can't prove anything. If Richard were alive he could demand a DNA test, but he's dead. Go to the meeting; you'll be safe.'

She said, 'Why did you do that? Why did you make me tell you?'

'To be sure you wouldn't tell anyone else,' he replied. 'Once a secret is out, it needn't be repeated. You're prepared; you won't be tripped up now.'

He took a handkerchief and wiped his lips with it. 'I'll take you to Humfrey.'

The meeting was held in Alan Farrington's solicitors' office in the Gray's Inn Road, and it lasted just under the hour. Christina left first, followed by Humfrey Stone and Rolf Wallberg, brushing past her stepson without a look. He addressed the two counsels and his own solicitor, scowling, hands stuck in his trouser pockets, aggression in every line of his body. The two lawyers, both tall men, emphasized his lack of height.

'Well, that was a bloody waste of time! She sat there, lying through her teeth, and you let her get away with it.'

He glared at John Cunningham. There was an awkward pause; his solicitor looked embarrassed. Cunningham looked down on his client with evident disdain.

'The object of the meeting, which, I must remind you, was at your suggestion, Mr Farrington, was to see if there were any grounds for an out of court settlement, not for me to bully your stepmother. She won't get away with anything in the witness box; if she's lying, as you say, I shall discredit her. If you aren't satisfied, then I suggest you find another QC to take the case. Good afternoon.' He nodded to the solicitor. His manner suggested sympathy at his choice of client. 'Bye, Ronnie, you'll let me know what Mr Farrington decides. Coming Kenneth?' He turned to Ken Hubert.

'I'll take a lift off you, John.' They left the room together. The solicitor was red-cheeked with anger. He wasn't intimidated by Alan; his firm was famous, prestigious and they could pick and choose whom they acted for.

'That was a very stupid exhibition, Mr Farrington!'

Alan stared; he wasn't used to being challenged.

'What the hell do you mean ... talking to me like that ... ?'

'I mean,' the older man said furiously, 'that you insulted one of the best men at the Bar, and the probability is he won't go on with the case! If you want to act as your own lawyer, then you're going the right way about it. Now let's get this clear, if I can persuade John Cunningham to stay with it, you will keep right out of everything until it comes to court. And when it does, you will say what you're told to say, and you'll keep your personal feelings to yourself. Is that clear?'

Alan had flushed a dark red; he felt explosive inside. The meeting, designed to frighten and expose Christina, had gone the other way; he could feel the atmosphere changing in her favour. His counsel's studied courtesy had infuriated him, another irritant was the foreign lawyer, who never took his eyes off Alan; the stare made him uncomfortable, it was a silent insult. He had a temper that he seldom bothered to control; he had used it as a weapon to cow opposition, to get what he wanted from people weaker or less aggressive than himself, but this was not the method or the man, and he was clever enough to realize it. He couldn't afford to lose the best legal advice that money could buy, and he surprised his solicitor by saying in a quiet voice, 'I'm sorry, I'm really sorry. I made a bloody fool of myself. Do what you can with Cunningham. I'll write to him if you like. It won't happen again.'

He looked at the older man and made an appeal for sympathy that surprised him even more.

'When I saw that woman sitting there, knowing how she turned my father against me and my brother, how she fooled him, because he was lonely after my mother's death, I lost control of myself. As I said, it won't happen again. She's hurt me and my children so much I can't handle being in the same room with her. I'll keep out of it from now on.'

The switch was unnerving. He seemed suddenly a vulnerable man, driven beyond caution by a terrible wrong. The solicitor actually came up and patted him on the back. He had sons near that age. God knew what parents could do to children, and vice versa. He'd had enough experience of the cruelty inflicted by families on each other.

'Don't worry, I'll sort it out. And if she has this effect on you, then keeping in the background is the only thing to do. Above all, Mr Farrington, you have to trust us to do our best for you. And believe me, John Cunningham is the best. Is your car outside?'

'Yes,' Alan said. He held out his hand. 'Thanks,' he said. 'I'll see myself out.' The grey Bentley was parked in the courtyard. He got in and switched on, but didn't drive away immediately; he called Fay on the car phone.

'Darling – how did it go?'

He didn't lie to her. 'I screwed it up,' he said.

'How? What happened?'

'I lost my cool with our counsel. So far as I could see he was pussyfooting round her, and I said so, then he as good as told me to fuck off and find someone else.'

'Oh, Alan . . . I should have come with you. Can't you put it right?'

'I've done my best. I grovelled to that old fart, Ronnie Hamilton, and I promised to keep out of the case. It'll be all right, I expect.' He sounded depressed.

Fay said briskly, 'Then don't worry about it, let them do the work. Why have a dog and bark yourself?'

He laughed. His spirits, often mercurial, lifted to a new confidence. What a girl. No reproaches, no nagging – wife in a million. 'How right you are, sweetheart. I'm on my way!'

Christina had paused outside the Gray's Inn office. Humfrey shook her hand.

'You carried that off very well, Mrs Farrington. I think both counsels were impressed, I know I was.' He looked at Rolf Wallberg for confirmation.

'It was good,' Rolf said, speaking to Christina. 'Calm and convincing.'

'I was so nervous,' she admitted.

'You didn't show it,' Humfrey insisted. 'Have you got a car? I have to go on to another meeting. Rolf could get you a taxi.'

'No,' she said quickly, 'my car's over there; I'm staying in London. Thank you for the moral support, Humfrey, it was a great help.' Then she turned to Rolf. 'And thank you,' she said, 'for all you've done.'

Humfrey said, 'We'll get on with the paperwork now; we'll need to take statements from you and from your husband's doctor and possibly members of your staff. Also, friends, relatives, anyone who can testify about his state of mind during his illness.' Seeing her confusion, he added, 'To refute the claim of undue influence. I'm sure that will be the easy part. Goodbye, Mrs Farrington.'

Then he was gone and she and Wallberg faced each other.

'When can I see you?' he asked. 'Tonight?'

'No,' she said. 'Rolf – I don't want this to happen.'

'I know, but it has happened and you can't stop it. You can't run away from me, Christa; you need me. If I promise not to touch you . . .'

'You promised that before,' she said, 'and you broke it; so did I. I don't want to have an affair with you; I'd hate myself. There were one or two men who tried while I was married, because of the age gap, I suppose. I never cheated on Richard.'

'I know that,' he answered. 'I'll make a deal with you: I'll be your lawyer and your friend till this case is over, after that, I won't promise anything. Does that satisfy you? Will you trust me?'

Christina started towards her car; Rolf walking with her. She opened the door, then she turned to him. 'Rolf, I don't know if I can trust myself; I don't know how to handle this . . .'

He touched her mouth with his fingertip. 'Don't try,' he said, 'leave it to me. Waiting never hurt anyone; it's said to be good for lovers. I'll come down to RussMore when I've prepared the papers, and I'll stay in the village. I want to kiss you, but I won't. Get in the car.' He slammed the door shut.

He didn't wait; he strode off towards the Strand and Christina drove away. Alone in the flat, she threw off her clothes and went under the shower, turning the water to full pressure as if she could wash herself clean of desire. That fingertip touch on her lips had been so light, so subtle, so arousing that it made her want to seize his hand and kiss the probing fingers one by one. Her image was blurred in the steamed-up mirror, a pale nude form hidden behind a mist. What kind of woman was she, to feel like this about a man she had initially disliked – wanton, repressed, a hypocrite who had convinced herself that she was happy and fulfilled? She dried herself fiercely, until her skin burned. What had he said while he held her? *He's dead; you're alive . . .* A simple fact, not an excuse. She hadn't gone into the grave with Richard, and trying to bury her feelings and needs had left her vulnerable to this strange man and his powerful sex drive. But with him it was more than desire, it wouldn't end with making love, however exciting, it would only begin. Perhaps that was what she feared. Suddenly, shrilly, so that she jumped in nervous alarm, the telephone rang.

'Hello? Christa?'

Harry! She'd forgotten about Harry.

'How'd the meeting go?'

She made an effort to sound calm. 'Well, I think.'

'Great, I'll pick you up about eight. You can tell me all about it then.'

He was taking her out to dinner; she had forgotten about that too.

John Cunningham slowed at the traffic-lights leading into the Strand. 'Drink at the club, Kenneth?'

'Good idea,' Ken Hubert responded. 'You certainly put that little prick in his place! Never heard such impertinence!'

'No skin off my nose if he wants someone else,' Cunningham explained, 'I've got more work than I can cope with. But I have a feeling he's not as uncomplicatedly nasty as he seems. I thought the lady put on a very polished performance.'

Hubert said, 'You didn't believe her?' Cunningham laughed.

'Not for a minute, and I don't believe you did either. She'll make a good impression in the witness box, but so long as I keep Farrington out of it, I think I can dent that. I don't know why I'm telling you my tactics, Ken. Here we are. Good old Garrick, best pink gins in London. Pity they let in women.'

Cunningham made a pretence of chauvinism. In fact he liked the company of women and never underestimated them as opponents at the Bar; he was especially fond of Molly Hubert. He had never married; he wasn't prepared for such a commitment and he took marriage seriously. There was no shortage of lady friends to take out in the evening, and go home with. They went to the bar and ordered their drinks: gin and tonic was Ken's preference, and Cunningham had his pink gin. Ken returned to the subject of Christina Farrington.

'You know, I'm surprised you thought she was lying,' he said. 'I actually found her very convincing.'

Which wasn't completely true, Hubert always kept doubts about a client in reserve, then they didn't catch him out.

Cunningham said, 'There's a stately home and a lot of land involved in this dispute. What woman wouldn't swear black was white to keep it for her daughter? According to the private investigator her stepson employed, she was quite generous with herself as a young girl and right up to the time she met Richard Farrington.'

'But there's never been a whisper about her since,' Hubert pointed out. 'Your charming client would have dug up something if she'd been "generous" after marriage. I rather like that description; it has a certain elegance. Do you really intend to take the case? I thought you were inviting him to engage someone else.'

'I don't think Ronnie will let him; he's a tough bird and I bet he stamped on Mr Farrington with hobnailed boots after we'd gone. Yes, I'll take it, so long as he does what he's told. In fact,' he smiled at his old friend and lifted his glass in salute, 'I shall enjoy doing battle with you Ken; it's always stimulating. Under that kindly courtroom manner you're a cold-hearted bastard, just like me. I wonder what judge we'll get?'

'God knows,' Hubert said. 'I only hope it's not Russell; he's impossible. Goes on and on, picking up on every tiny point. Stephenson would be all right.'

'Stephenson hates me,' his friend remarked, 'ever since I caught him out on that judgement and it made the newspapers. But he's fair and he's nobody's fool; he'll see through your pretty Swedish lady if she's what I think she is.'

Hubert looked at him. 'And that is?'

'An adventuress who saw an opportunity to grab a rich older man and set herself and her child up for life. Even if she played by the rules afterwards, it doesn't alter the case that if that girl is illegitimate, she can't inherit, and, according to Ronnie, her stepson insists he can prove it. I'm just warning you you're going to lose, that's all. One for the road?'

'No thanks, Molly's got friends coming for dinner, so I'd better get home. You could join us if you're free; she loves having you to dinner, says you make everyone laugh. Irritates me, rather.'

'How sweet of her,' Cunningham said, 'but I'm busy, wining and dining an old friend who's over from Spain. Gorgeous lady – American, widowed and very rich. In fact, I rather hope she'll take *me* out! Give my love to Molly.'

'I will,' Hubert promised. 'Enjoy yourself, John. But about that case . . . don't be too sure you'll win; I know I'm going to. Night!'

Harry had chosen a small French restaurant near Holland Park. It was simple, even basic, but the food was famous. Christina found herself thinking of Richard; he had always loved provincial French cooking and he would have appreciated this. He was so much on her mind that evening, as if somehow he knew she needed him.

Harry's first question had been about the missing manuscript. Christina had said, 'James took it, we were right about that. But he was held up at knifepoint and the mugger stole everything out of the safe in his flat, including the manuscript. So it's gone, Harry; it's probably been destroyed by now. No-one would know what it was, just scraps of old paper written in gibberish.'

And Harry had answered, 'You sound relieved, Christa. Are you?'

'Yes, it was never mine, or Richard's come to that. I couldn't have sold it and taken the money, not when I knew its history. So God or Fate, whatever, has solved that one.' She didn't mention Rolf Wallberg and to her surprise he didn't ask.

Harry ordered for her; he seemed determined to be light-hearted, as if he suspected that losing the chance of so much money to fight her lawsuit had really upset her and she wasn't admitting it. Her thoughts kept straying, from Richard to Wallberg, shying away from him in guilty panic, on to the prospect of taking Belinda to her new boarding-school.

Halfway through the evening, Harry said gently, 'By the way, I've just heard I won the lottery . . .'

Christina said vaguely, 'Sorry, what did you say?'

He sighed in mock exasperation. 'I started by asking how Belinda was, but you weren't listening, so I said I'd won the lottery; you didn't hear that either. Where have you been all evening, Christa? Not with me, that's for sure.'

'I'm so sorry, I didn't mean to be vague, Harry. It's been quite a traumatic day, and I *was* thinking about Belinda just then. She goes to St Mary's at the end of next week and I'm dreading it. I've never been separated from her before, and I'm so worried she'll miss me and be homesick after what's happened.'

'She'll be fine,' he assured her. 'Kids are much more resilient than we think. Poor old Mum was red-eyed for days after I'd gone to prep school . . . I never gave home a thought, I was so busy settling in. You're the one who's going to be miserable, and RussMore is a big old place to rattle around in. Where is St Mary's by the way? I'm not up on girls' schools.'

'It's on the Essex–Suffolk border, about two hours drive from home, and I can take her out on exeats and for a weekend. Richard said that all the Farrington girls went there.'

He said, 'I expect Mum did too. She dropped the Catholic bit when she married Pop; he wasn't that keen on it, so we were brought up as Anglicans, whatever that means now. Can't say I worry about it. I'll ask Mum . . . and I've had a great idea!'

She smiled. 'You're always having great ideas. What is it this time?'

'Drop Belinda off at school and then drive up and spend a few days with us in Norfolk. We'd all love it, and Mum would keep you so busy you wouldn't have time to miss her. Come on, don't go back to RussMore on your own; you'll only sit and fret about Belinda and worry about this bloody case. Say yes. Say you'll come.'

'I'd love to,' Christina admitted. 'That really is a great idea, if it's all right with Jane. I just hate the idea of driving back to RussMore and not having her with me. A few days' break would be wonderful. When I get home I've got so much work to do with the probate application; Rolf Wallberg wants to come down and take depositions from the Mannings and the doctor about Richard's mental state when he changed his will. They won't win with the undue influence claim, but they'll push hard on every issue. God, Harry, sometimes I can't believe it's all happening!'

'I'm not surprised,' he said. And then, almost as if he'd just thought of it, 'What was the noble Swede's explanation for disappearing like that? Or didn't you ask him?'

'No, once he told me the manuscript was gone it didn't seem to matter, and he was so upset about it, I had to convince him I didn't mind and it wasn't his fault. Harry, why do you call him that? The noble Swede?'

Harry grinned. 'To make him look stupid. It's quite a neat trick. There was this big hulk who was after my dear wife, so I started rubbishing him and she couldn't meet him without laughing in his face. I should have made fun of my good friend and partner . . . Never mind, if it hadn't been him, there would have been somebody else; she'd got bored, you see.'

'You don't have to rubbish Wallberg,' Christina suggested. 'You've never even met him.'

'No, but you've talked so much about him, Christa, saying you didn't like him, of course, and then saying it all over again. I was getting jealous.'

She laughed, 'Don't be silly. Jealous of what?'

'The noble Swede,' he retorted. 'This mysterious stranger from the frozen north . . . Don't you know I'm madly in love with you? I always make fun of my rivals.'

'You're impossible,' she said, 'but you do make me laugh and you've been sweet to take me out this evening.'

He pulled a face, 'You don't take me seriously, do you? You think I'm just acting the fool? Oh well, it's the story of my love life. My ex said she married me because I was so funny, then the jokes ran out. I'll get the bill. You look tired. And you're coming to stay; that's settled. No ringing up with excuses?'

'No excuses. I'm looking forward to it.'

He drove her to the flat, got out and walked up the steps with her.

'Good night, Harry,' she said gently.

'I'll wait till you're inside,' he insisted. 'Don't want some mugger leaping on you. Good night, Christa, see you in a week. I'll talk to you before, but there won't be any problem. Take care.'

It was the lightest brush on the cheek; affectionate, unthreatening. On an impulse, she kissed him back. The security lights went out as she opened the door, so she didn't see his face.

7

Ruben Stone put an arm round Wallberg's shoulders. 'You don't have to stay on, my boy; your time with us is up, you know. Shouldn't you go back and take up your own practice?'

'I told them a year,' Rolf answered. 'They're not expecting me. In fact . . .' he glanced at Ruben, 'I've been thinking about moving to England. Permanently.'

'Have you?' Ruben's tone didn't alter. 'That's quite a decision. Have you considered it carefully, or is this an impulse? You'd have to take English examinations. I can't offer you a place here, you know; there isn't room for a partner. You weren't expecting anything like that, I hope?'

'No. I shall set up my own office if I do stay here,' was the reply. 'What I would like is to see the Farrington case through to its end, I'm sure you won't object to that.'

'I can't, can I, after all you've done – all the work you've done for us,' Ruben said quietly. 'Which is what you're saying, isn't it?'

'It's what I'm asking,' Wallberg answered. 'I can't insist, of course, but I would like to stay.' The old man nodded. The avuncular manner didn't impress Rolf; there was a different status between them now.

'That's no problem,' Ruben answered. 'No problem at all. You'll learn a lot about our legal system, and it'll be very useful if you do decide to set up practice in England.' He sounded genuinely interested. 'You'd have a good Swedish clientele to start with; there are a number of Swedish-owned companies who could use one of their own lawyers . . . Any business I could put your way, I'd be only too delighted.' The friendly arm slipped away in dismissal. 'Now, let's get ready for war with Mr Farrington. This is one we have to win.'

He opened the door for Rolf. There was a moment when neither of them moved. Ruben looked into the wintry blue eyes and managed to hide his feelings. 'I'm glad I can be a help,' he said.

'I'm glad too. Thank you, Mr Stone.' Rolf went out and closed the door. When he had gone, Ruben Stone returned to his desk and sat down. An old proverb came to mind. '"He who sups with the devil . . ."' He murmured the ending out loud, '"needs a long spoon." How true. How very true.'

'Well,' Alan said roughly, 'if you will live in a bloody awful place like New York, what can you expect?'

James's call had upset him. Mugged at knifepoint in his own apartment. Instinctively he saw James as the younger brother. When they were children, Alan had defended him at school. It was all right for him to bully James, but no-one else, nobody outside the family.

'I'm all right,' James insisted. 'It was just unnerving. There've been some gruesome sex murders on men . . . torture and mutilation.' He didn't mention that the victims were gay. Alan was his father's son; he wouldn't have admitted something or believed it if he didn't want to. He continued quickly, 'Luckily I didn't challenge him and I didn't get hurt, but I'm going to move as soon as I find another place. Once you lose confidence in the security, you're never comfortable.'

'Look, why not come over,' Alan suggested. He was shocked by what he had heard; it only confirmed his dislike of America and Americans. 'You can stay with us if you like.'

James couldn't help it; he was moved by the sudden concern for him and the generous invitation. They were brothers, and Alan did really love him in his own way. James had never been able to resist him when he was kind.

'I wouldn't want to put Fay out,' he said. She wouldn't want him staying. 'But thanks, Alan, it's nice of you to offer. I might just take a trip over. I can book into a hotel; I'd like to see you. Any date set for the big day in court?'

'I hope we'll get a listing some time next week. I'd like you to be there, James. Whatever happens you won't lose your legacy, so don't worry about that. When I win, I'll give you Langley.'

When I win. James noted the certainty, the supreme confidence. Alan had always been like that, but this was something more, not just arrogance and bravado. His curiosity was like a nagging tooth. What did Alan know that made him so cast-iron sure of winning the case?

'Yes, I'd like to be there too. We're family; we should stand together on this. I tell you what, Alan, when you get the date, let me know and I'll arrange to take a vacation; I'm due to go to Connecticut, but I'll come home instead.'

Alan said briskly, 'If you had any sense you'd come home, period, but we'll talk about that. Soon as I hear I'll call you, and don't open the door to any strange men! See you.' Fay had come into the room while he was talking. 'That was James,' he explained. 'Some bloody mugger attacked him.'

'How awful,' she said. 'Was he hurt?'

'No, luckily he didn't try being a hero.'

'As if he would,' she retorted. If Alan was blind to his orientation, Fay was not. Suddenly she irritated him.

'Don't be such a cow,' he said sharply. 'He could have been killed. He's my brother, after all.'

Fay didn't back down. 'As if I didn't know,' she snapped.

'I've never liked him or trusted him and I'm not changing my mind because he gets mugged. You said he wasn't hurt, so what's the big deal?'

He knew her in this mood. She could be aggressive and combatant too and, in his way, he admired her for standing up to him. 'No big deal,' he countered. 'Just don't be a cow about it. I asked him to come over and stay.' He saw her pretty face harden angrily and he added, 'But he wouldn't; he knows you don't like him. But he's coming for the case.'

Fay shrugged; she sensed a retreat and she was satisfied. 'Well, that's all right then. Good. Are you going to get the car out or are we going to be late arguing about James?'

He scowled at her. 'I'm going to get the car out,' he said, and slammed the door hard as he went out. Fay inspected herself in the mirror in the hallway; her hair looked good, make-up fine, and her new sapphire ear-rings glittered when she turned her head. Alan was so generous; she shouldn't have riled him, but she hated that mimsy creep and she would never trust him to be loyal. *He's my brother*. How often she'd heard that said in explanation, as if blood relationship conferred some special immunity from ordinary judgement. Alan needed him, that was the trouble. She and the children had filled the emotional void in his life, but there was still a gap, and James was needed to fill it. She heard a long impatient blast on the horn and went to the front door.

He leaned across and opened the car door for her. He wasn't a man who held doors for women or carried their cases; she wasn't a woman who expected him to – she was quite independent. The car moved away and she said, 'I love my ear-rings. And I'll be nice to James, OK?' He nodded.

'OK.' He visibly relaxed; he hated quarrelling with her. 'It should be fun tonight,' he said. They were dining at Quaglino's with another couple; a rich successful couple in the despised Yuppie mode of the Eighties; their children were friends and went to the same smart school. She was bird-brained and giggled when Alan was rude to her, as if he was flirting; he rather liked her because she was a good foil to Fay. He liked the husband who had made even more money out of property management than Alan had out of fast food. They'd eat well, drink the best, and soon get down to talking business while their wives chattered about children and domestic trivia. He glanced at her; the ear-rings did look good. Blue was her colour and sapphires were her stones; he might think about getting her a brooch to go with the ear-rings for Christmas. And to celebrate winning the lawsuit . . .

'Mrs Manning,' Rolf Wallberg said, 'I'd like to start with you. And then if your husband has anything to add?'

The housekeeper settled her hands in her lap, and her husband nodded. It seemed rather odd that this lawyer was taking statements while Mrs Farrington was away. They'd loaded the school trunk into the car and said goodbye to Belinda, then two days later the lawyer had telephoned asking to come down and see them. Mrs Manning had referred him to the Spanniers where Christina was staying. Permission given, they waited with a mixture of excitement and curiosity. He wanted to take statements from them which could then be turned into affidavits for use in court.

'We've got to be careful, Joy,' her husband insisted. 'Don't say anything without thinking; these solicitors are crafty people.'

'But he's on her side,' his wife pointed out.

'Even so, I'd watch what you say,' he insisted.

'I'm going to. Hc won't get much out of me.'

The lawyer had booked into the local pub; the Mannings were relieved about that; they'd been uneasy about having a stranger staying while Mrs Farrington was away.

He interviewed them in their sitting-room, taking a quick stock of the comfortable furnishings. They were well set up and obviously well paid, and also suspicious that he might trap them into saying something that could affect their position. Rolf set out to win the woman's confidence; she was the most important of the two.

'Before I put a few questions to you,' he said, 'let me explain the situation. Mrs Farrington's stepson is alleging that she influenced his father to change his will when he was very ill and unable to judge what he was doing.'

Mrs Manning looked up sharply. 'That's nonsense! It wasn't like that at all!'

Rolf smiled. 'I'm sure it wasn't and that is really what I want you to say, but first let me ask a few general questions. How long have you worked for the Farringtons?'

'About twelve years. We came in the winter, didn't we George? 1983? Yes, that's right. I remember it was the winter because we thought it might be a cold old house like most of them are and we weren't too happy about that. I can't work if I'm not warm.'

'Presumably there was a housekeeper here before you?'

'Oh, yes. A Mrs Warren. Been here for years. She'd left when we were interviewed.'

'After Mr Farrington remarried?'

She was visibly relaxed now, on familiar ground. 'Quite soon after. The cleaning ladies told us she'd had things all her own way with the first Mrs Farrington, her being always ill and in and out of clinics. She didn't fancy a new woman running the place, so she started being difficult and Mr Farrington sacked her.'

'Mr Farrington, not Mrs Farrington?'

'Oh, no. He ran the staff. He did the interviewing when we came here. She was there too, but she was so young, and I remember saying to George, she looked quite out of her depth. She left everything to him.'

Rolf asked a question, more for his own curiosity than because it was relevant. 'And what was he like, Mrs Manning?' The answer proved to be very relevant.

'Quite a formidable gentleman. Knew exactly what he wanted. No beating about the bush there. Wages, conditions and what we were expected to do; it was all very fair and satisfactory and we took the job, but he was the employer, not that young girl. Of course, she learned her way round and took charge after she'd had Belinda; she'd got confidence by then. She was very nice to work for, very considerate and friendly, and she didn't change things much. "I want Mr Farrington to be happy," I remember her saying that. She didn't redecorate, like some second wives do, just for the sake of it, not for a year or two, and then she asked him about everything.'

'And would you describe them as happy? This doesn't compromise you in any way, Mrs Manning. Whatever you say won't be included in an affidavit if you don't want it to be.'

She didn't hesitate. 'Yes, Mr Wallberg. I'd say they were the happiest married couple we've ever worked for and we've been in domestic work all our lives. He absolutely doted on her, and on Belinda. He was a hard man, in some ways, especially with his sons, but she couldn't do wrong, Mrs Farrington couldn't.'

'It sounds ideal,' Rolf remarked. He could see the affidavit shaping up. He could also see Mrs Manning under cross-examination in the witness box if she had to be called.

'You said he was a hard man with his sons,' he said after a pause. 'In what way?'

She pulled a face. 'He didn't get on with them,' she answered. 'Alan was a lout, no other word for him. He left home soon after we came here, so I'm only repeating what I heard from the other staff, but neither of us liked him, did we?'

Her husband added, 'No, we didn't. He was twenty-two going on fourteen, by the way he behaved. The other boy wasn't bad – James.'

'I was sorry for him in a way,' his wife said. 'He never seemed to get it right with his father. He went off not long after Alan did.'

'This is a difficult question, but I'd appreciate it if you can give me an answer. How was Mrs Farrington with the stepsons? How did she react to them?'

'She didn't,' Mrs Manning said firmly. 'She tried at first, but Alan behaved like a thug to her from the start. She backed right off and left her husband to cope. They weren't here more than a few months anyway. I was glad to see them both go; the atmosphere in the house was so different after they went.'

Rolf said gently, 'And when he was ill? When he was dying? Did Mrs Farrington take control of things then?'

'She looked after him,' was the answer. 'He had nurses, but

she never left him, not even for a day; she was the one he wanted. But he was the boss, right up to the day he died. He sent for both of us and for Bob Thorn, the estate manager, and told us we had to take care of Mrs Farrington after he'd gone. Clear as a bell, he was, in his mind. He passed away two days afterwards.'

Rolf nodded and finished his notes. 'He left you a legacy, didn't he? Five thousand pounds?'

She stiffened. 'Yes. It was very generous of him, but that's not why I'm saying all this.'

'I know that,' he responded. 'In fact, it's a testimony to both of you. He doesn't sound the sort of man who'd leave money to anyone unless he felt they deserved it. Mr Manning, have you anything to add to what your wife has told me?'

'Not much. I worked mostly on maintenance in the house; I didn't have a lot to do with Mrs Farrington, more with him. But I go along with what Joy says: she never influenced him to do anything he didn't want to; she wasn't that sort anyway. It was those sons who were greedy. I remember that Alan saying to his brother one day, "When that bastard dies, I'm going to sell everything he liked. I'll change this place so nothing reminds me of him." I was shocked, I can tell you.' Rolf wrote something briefly, then closed the notebook.

'Thank you very much for your time, you've been very helpful. I'll work on these and get the affidavits typed up so you can read over them, and change anything if you want to. I'd like to see the estate manager. I'm going to be here for a few days, so if you'd ask him to contact me at The Crown?'

'I will,' George Manning offered, 'I'll see him this afternoon; there's some insulation on the roof over the garages that needs replacing. I'll tell him to ring you.'

Rolf left them then. Outside the air was wintry and cold, with the lowering grey skies that depressed him so much. He pulled the thick anorak closer and got into his car. The Mannings had given him exactly the kind of information he had hoped for. A good counsel like Ken Hubert would paint a very convincing picture of the young Swedish wife, thrust into an alien and powerful family, already deeply enmeshed in old hatreds. Richard Farrington was in clear focus now: Dominant, autocratic . . . a hard man, as the woman had described, but deeply in love with his wife, so much that his dying instructions to them had been to take care of her. Let Alan and his legal cohorts try and make undue influence out of that.

The Crown was originally an old coaching inn on the main road to London; it had been bypassed in the last century and become little more than a run-down pub for the local farm labourers. After the war it was bought by a big brewery and renovated; planning permission was not an issue then, and extra rooms and bathrooms were added. The accommodation was small, ten rooms in all, but it catered for the growing rural tourist trade, as English holiday-makers, restricted by currency laws, explored the hinterland and the great cathedral cities of their own country.

Rolf rather enjoyed the experience of staying there. His room was in the old part of the building; the low ceilings and heavy beams were a hazard to someone so tall, but the atmosphere intrigued him. The bed – mock-Tudor oak – was hard and uncomfortable, and there were no reading lights apart from a small bedside lamp with a loathsome pink shade, fringed with nylon. The bathroom was cramped and the hot water inadequate by European standards, and there was no shower. Even the discomforts were part of the experience. He asked for, and got, an anglepoise lamp, which he suspected came from the office. He was known to be Mrs Farrington's lawyer and so got special treatment.

He bathed in the narrow bath, soaping hurriedly in the tepid water, then he changed from the more formal trousers and jacket he'd worn during the day. He'd brought thick shirts and sweaters after being warned by Humfrey about English central heating in ancient English pubs, and casual slacks and a jacket, in case this was required in the tiny restaurant. It wasn't, so he pulled on a heavy polo-neck sweater and settled down to put the Manning's statement into the form of draft affidavits.

He had spent an hour and a half with the manager, Bob Thorn. He was a straightforward type of country man in his late thirties, educated and intelligent, and he insisted on showing Rolf around the estate. The size was a shock to him; it brought the bare statistic of acreage to life. He saw the farms, the woodland, the workshops and saw mills and the giant machines, all serviced on the estate in the maintenance sheds. The management was a life's work; the financial aspect as demanding and tight as any urban industry, with the added hazard of the weather. 'Always the bloody weather,' Bob Thorn had told him. 'You get a really wet summer and you can lose your harvest. Doesn't matter how much you mechanize and manage, you've got to put the weather into the calculation.'

When he went back to the manager's house for tea and to take the statement, he had won the man's trust. The response was much the same as the Mannings': Mrs Farrington was very nice, always friendly. No, she never interfered in the running of the estate. Her husband was the boss; very much so, he had added. The previous manager had been sacked eight years ago for raising the rents on two farms; he had mentioned it as an idea, but hadn't waited for Richard Farrington's given approval. Thorn liked Richard Farrington, but he knew not to take liberties.

'And I respected him for that,' he had said, while his wife poured Rolf more tea. It was a drink he hated, but he accepted with a smile.

'He knew his stuff, not like some of the jumped-up people who buy places like this as status symbols and leave everything to managing agents. He'd been to agricultural college and he was as much a farmer as any of the tenants round here. I never minded taking orders from him, but let me make it plain, Mr Wallberg, orders is what he gave.'

He had, he assured Rolf, been *compos mentis* right up to the day he died, going through everything with him, no matter how weak or doped up to ease the pain. He paused for a moment, then made an obvious decision. 'He told me, in absolute confidence, that he was passing RussMore on to Belinda. He wanted my assurance that I'd stay on and help Mrs Farrington.

He said, "I trust you, Bob. Nobody else knows. I want Belinda to grow up here and make it her home. Will you see them well on the road before you think of making a change?" And I said, "I can't see myself ever moving from here. I'll look after things and I'll help your wife to understand how it all works. You can rely on me." And I meant it. I'll give evidence if you think it would help.' It might, Rolf agreed. He would make an impressive witness.

It had been a very productive day. The next thing was to interview the family doctor. He had made an appointment to see him between surgery times. It was all going very well, he thought. He had a laptop computer and he put the transcripts down on disks; he could go over them again in the morning and edit some more of the non-essentials out. He felt in need of a drink and unusually tired; it must be the Lincolnshire air. He went down to the bar, where there was a wood fire burning, and he found a small table near to it. The size of old-fashioned English fireplaces fascinated him. He admired the brightly polished horse brasses, and regretted the dim lighting which made reading impossible.

He ordered vodka on the rocks; having once tried tepid English beer, he had never repeated the experience. There were a few people propped up by the bar: locals, drinking the pub brew; a couple of girls in very short skirts with their men friends and a middle-aged man in dense black with a startlingly white shirt and a black tie. He glanced over at Rolf and exchanged a few words with the woman serving drinks, then he turned and looked speculatively at the stranger by the fire, drinking alone. Rolf felt the scrutiny and looked up. Their glances met; the man nodded, and Rolf nodded back. He picked up his glass, full of dark ale, heavy as treacle, and moved across. 'Good evening,' he said.

'Good evening,' Rolf agreed. He didn't make it welcoming.

'Cold night outside.' He warmed his back by the fire. He wasn't going to move away. After a pause he said, 'Madge says you're working for Mrs Farrington.'

Madge, polishing glasses, was pretending not to listen.

'I am, that's right.' Rolf wasn't abrupt this time. His

instincts were sending messages – He's approached you for a reason. Maybe curiosity, maybe not – He knew how gossip flew through small communities. His business at RussMore with the Mannings and Bob Thorn that afternoon, even his appointment with the local doctor for the next day . . . the news would have reached the pub landlord by now, and Madge, the overfriendly barmaid, had even tried to pump Rolf himself for information. He decided to draw the man out. 'I'm her lawyer,' he said.

'Are you? Well, I expect you've got plenty of work to do sorting out that mess up there. Mind if I sit at the table? I've been on my feet all afternoon.'

Rolf said, 'Not at all. Doing what?' It was his turn to quiz.

The man looked at him in surprise. Then he smiled, understanding. 'Ah, you're a foreigner, aren't you sir?' The word lawyer produced the 'sir'. 'I've been burying an old lady over Winching way. Big funeral it was; she'd lived to a good age, near on eighty-eight, and there's a lot of her family round about. I'm on my way home, just stopped off for a quick drink. Haven't had time to get out of my business suit.' He gave a little chuckle. 'Puts people off if I come in here like this, though they all know me. I'm a builder too, you see. I do the funerals as well, but my work is mostly building. I did all the repairs up at RussMore that their lads on the estate couldn't do.' Rolf knew that his instincts had been right.

'Let me get you another glass. Beer?' The smile broadened.

'Real ale. Only half, please. I've to drive another fifteen miles home . . . Thanks very much.'

Rolf brought the small tankard back and set it down. 'You said there was a mess to sort out,' he remarked. 'I suppose you can't keep secrets in a village.' He was relaxed and friendly now. 'I'm Wallberg,' he said. 'Rolf Wallberg.'

'Mick Garrett,' was the response. 'Pleased to meet you. Well, as you say, you can't keep secrets, everyone gets to hear things. Not always the truth, mind, but you'd know if it was right or not. The word is that Mr Farrington's sons are taking Mrs Farrington to court.'

'One son is, that's right. The eldest.'

Garrett swallowed some of his ale. He pulled a face, but not because of the taste. 'Oh him, he would.' He took another swallow. 'Wants to take RussMore away from Mrs Farrington,' he said, 'that's what I heard.'

'That's about right,' Rolf agreed. 'You know him then?'

'Me? Oh no, I wouldn't say that . . . Saw him sometimes when I did work up at the place. He was a boy then; sullen little bugger, never talked to anyone, but then there were problems with the mother. I suppose that might account for it.' Truly Rolf thought, there are no secrets in a village.

'But you knew Mr Farrington then . . . if you worked for him?'

'Oh, yes. Mind, I got my orders from the estate manager. Very nice gentleman, but well . . . not that friendly. Bit of a squire.' He chuckled again. 'Those days are gone, even if your family's been in these parts before there *was* a village here. There's always been Farringtons at RussMore. He and that son of his never got on, everyone knew it. That's what surprised me.' He had nearly finished his ale.

Rolf said quietly, 'What surprised you?' There was a hesitation. He had reached the point, the reason for accosting the stranger who was working for the Farringtons on their legal case. He wasn't being dramatic, it was a natural reluctance to say what was on his mind; a doubt that he would be believed. Rolf repeated it, 'What surprised you, Mr Garrett?'

Garrett cleared his throat. 'Him coming to see his father in his coffin,' he said. 'I buried him, you see. My father buried his father, and so on; four generations, all buried by Garretts. Never went to fancy undertakers in Lincoln; always used us. It's a tradition.'

Rolf kept his tone of voice unchanged. 'Yes, I see. You say the son, Alan Farrington, came to see his father's body before the funeral?'

'That's right. Rang me up the night before, and asked if he could see his father. He was in Lincoln, staying at a hotel. Mr Farrington, the deceased, he was in our little chapel of rest, by the builders' yard. We keep a little place where they can lie over night.'

'And he saw the body?' Rolf asked. 'He actually came and saw his father's body?'

'Oh, yes, he did. I opened up the chapel for him myself. I didn't stay, of course; relatives like to be on their own, to say their goodbyes. I left him there. He didn't stay long, not more than a few minutes. He wasn't upset at all, not that I could see; very businesslike. "Thanks," that's all he said, and then he walked off to that big car of his and drove away. So far as I know he hadn't been down here for years. I said to my wife, Lily, not much grieving there, nor at the funeral either, not a tear. He just stood by the graveside scowling. Wouldn't stand anywhere near his stepmother and the little girl; didn't sit with them in the church either.'

Rolf said, 'Mr Garrett, why are you telling me this? It's not that unusual for a son to pay his respects to his dead father, even if they didn't get on well.'

'As you say, no, it isn't. But when he'd gone and I went to close up the coffin – it was quite late and no-one else was coming to view him – there was something I couldn't account for; in all my years in the business I've never seen anything like it. Horrible, it was, it's worried me ever since.'

Rolf leaned towards him. 'Tell me about it, Mr Garrett. Tell me what happened?'

'Don't worry about Belinda,' Jane Spannier said. 'She's such a confident child, she'll be fine; you're the one who's going to miss her.' She thought Christina looked peaky and miserable, not even Harry's clowning could cheer her up. Of course it was an emotional wrench; she'd become closer than ever to the child after Richard's death.

It was a good thing from Belinda's point of view that she'd gone away to school.

It wasn't surprising that Christina depended on her, after all, as she and Peter agreed, who else had the poor girl got to turn to? And that was when he had put into words what they had both been thinking. 'Harry thinks he's in love with her,' he said. 'I'm sure she doesn't realize it, but I don't want him to get hurt. Once is bad enough.'

'No, that mustn't happen,' Jane agreed. 'I think I might say something to her.' After she had been there for three days, Jane decided that the moment had arrived.

The men were out rough shooting, and they had spent the morning doing household chores and chatting about family matters: about Belinda's school; about the problem of their other son, who was coming over to dinner; and his resentment of Harry coming back to take over the business and run the farm.

'That's the trouble with children,' Jane remarked, 'you never stop worrying about them, no matter how old they are. I suppose I worry about Harry more than Tom, because Tom's happily married and got his family . . . he's set up now. But Harry's very impulsive, you know, and in spite of all the fooling about, he's vulnerable really.'

'I know,' Christina agreed. 'He's so kind; I don't know what I'd have done without him. You told me he was a wonderful friend.'

Jane took a breath. Tact was not one of her qualities, but she tried very hard this time. 'I think he's more than that . . .' she said. 'Peter thinks he's in love with you and I do too. So please, my dear, don't lead him on if there's nothing going to come of it.' Christina flushed.

'Jane, you're not serious?'

''Fraid so. You don't mind me saying it, do you Christa, but you're too wrapped up in your own problems to notice. Just be careful, will you?'

'Of course I will,' she promised. 'I'm quite shattered, Jane. I never imagined he felt anything like that for me. But my father said something too . . . oh God, what a stupid mess I've made!'

Jane was horrified to see her eyes fill with tears.

'I'm really fond of him, I'd never do anything to hurt him.'

'Course you wouldn't, and for Heaven's sake don't let on I've said anything, he'd kill me. And don't upset yourself over it . . . poor dear, don't do that. I feel awful now!'

She came over awkwardly and put an arm round Christina. Showing affection made her uncomfortable. 'I can hear them outside,' she said. 'Turn the taps off, and let's get the drinks out. Come on.' Her briskness made it easier. *Turn the taps off*. It was so typically Jane that it even made Christina smile. 'Don't worry,' she said, 'I'm fine. I'll get the ice.'

Moments later Harry and his father were in the kitchen and Harry was demanding to know if Christina liked pigeon, because he'd shot two. She didn't know; she'd never eaten any. He laughed; he looked happy and in higher spirits than usual.

'Well, you won't have to, because it's pheasant tonight. Couldn't give brother Tom a humble pigeon; he'd say we were being mean . . . I'll pour the gin, Pop. Can't have you getting pissed before lunch.'

After lunch Harry murmured to Christina, 'Stop fretting about Belinda; I bet she's in the thick of things by now, getting up to mischief. Come for a walk with me.' Caught by surprise, Christina fumbled for an excuse.

'Harry, I don't think so, I promised to help Jane . . .'

'Mum,' he said firmly and loudly. 'Mum, you're not to slave-drive Christa. She's not helping you, she's going out for a walk with me. See you at teatime!'

It was a very crisp day, but the sun shone and the flat Norfolk fields were criss-crossed by footpaths. He walked with a long stride, head slightly bent, hands jammed in his jacket pockets. 'We'll go up there,' he said, pointing to a gap in a hawthorn hedge. 'You can see for miles. That's what I love about this part of England; the Fens even more so. You feel you could go on walking till you stepped off the edge into the sea. You've been crying. What's the matter? Belinda?'

'No,' she answered. He was walking faster now, a few steps ahead of her on the narrow path.

'Didn't think it was. Not anything Mum said, I hope; she can be really club-footed sometimes. Doesn't mean it, but it doesn't stop her upsetting people.'

'Harry,' Christina said. 'Harry, yes, I was upset, but it was about you.' He stopped in mid-stride.

'Me? Christa, what about me?'

They were face to face on the path. 'Jane said . . . she said you were in love with me, and she doesn't want you to get hurt. Oh, dear God, she begged me not to tell you, but it just came out. You're not, are you?'

He tilted his head on one side, and looked at her with an expression that was slightly quizzical and also guarded. 'What would you say if I said no?'

'I'd be relieved,' she answered.

'And if I said yes? Just hypothetical questions, don't worry. Stop biting your lip; it'll get sore in this wind.'

'Harry,' she said unhappily, 'I'm afraid I've made a fool of myself . . . I shouldn't have said anything. Jane shouldn't have, either; it's just that she knows how hurt you were when your marriage broke up. She knows I'm not ready for anything like that with anyone.'

'I'm sure you're not,' he took her arm, as the pathway widened at the opening between the hedges. 'If I said no, I wasn't in love with you, wouldn't you be even a touch disappointed? Not that I've said it, mind. Wouldn't you?'

'No,' Christina answered. 'No, I wouldn't. I'm so fond of you, Harry, I couldn't be selfish or conceited enough to feel like that. I don't want you to be hurt either. She's not right, is she?' He pointed briefly, before plunging his hand back in the pocket.

'Look at that! Acres and acres, miles and miles of space, with that sunny sky. Doesn't it put things in perspective? My mother worrying about me; you worrying about something that's not your fault if it happens to be true, which it is.'

He stopped, his arm still linked with hers. He wasn't facing her; he looked ahead, squinting into the distance. 'I loved you the first night I ever saw you. Gloomy old RussMore seemed full of light the minute you appeared. Not just because you're a beautiful woman – I don't give a toss for beauty – My wife and her friends all looked golden and gorgeous; all you could think about was getting them into bed. I don't think about you like that; I like you. I want to go to bed with you, but it's not the most important thing. That's why', he still hadn't looked at her, 'we can go on being friends and see how things develop. Nothing may change; I don't know. Can you put the whole thing on hold? Forget what Mum said and I've said?'

Slowly Christina answered. 'I can't promise anything, Harry. I know how I feel now, that's all. I couldn't get involved with anyone.'

He had begun to move forward. 'Not even the noble Swede?'

'Most of all, not with him.' She'd said it before she could stop herself.

'But he's tried, hasn't he?'

'Yes,' she admitted and was suddenly relieved.

'He has.' Harry walked on. 'I thought so. Well I'll still be around when this bloody case is finished, one way or the other, and he'll be gone. Do you want to turn back? Are you cold?'

'No, let's go a bit further.'

'Changing the subject, let me fill you in about my brother. He has a nice cosy wife, two badly behaved children that drive Mum up the wall because they never go to bed before nine in the evening and we were all packed away by half-past six. He's a nice enough guy, and I'm fond of him; not a great sense of humour, but, unlike me, he never gave Mum and Pop a minute's trouble. He always did the expected thing. The unfairness is, they've always liked me better than him; I can't think why, but it's a fact. So I get to manage the farm and take over the business, which he'd thought would come his way when I emigrated. Not that he's been badly done by; Pop gave him nearly three thousand acres when he got married. They live very well; no pigeon for them! He'll be charmed by you; she'll be overawed – she's a bit of a snob, I'm afraid, but never mind – and they'll both be irritated by me! So I hope you're looking forward to a jolly evening.'

He laughed and Christina couldn't help laughing with him.

'I can't wait,' she said. 'I'll have to think of an excuse to go home . . .' A gust of wind swept across the open fields and she shivered. 'I think we might turn back,' she suggested, 'before we do end up dropping over the edge into the sea. So how near is the sea anyway?'

'Oh, God knows, miles over there somewhere. It just sounded a bit dramatic, I thought. Right then, back we go. You can make the tea and toast the crumpets while I murder my interfering mother.'

She stopped in alarm. 'Harry! Harry, you're not to say anything to Jane!'

He urged her forward. 'Bribe me,' he suggested.

'I won't tell your brother's wife you said she doesn't know how to bring up her children?' Christina offered.

He gave her arm a light squeeze. 'Bargain struck!'

'Bargain,' she agreed. He had a gift for making her spirits rise, she thought suddenly. Not even Richard had been able to dispel doubts and anxieties the way his cousin Harry did. When they came in, Jane looked up from her newspaper – she always saved it till the afternoon – and said briskly, 'You look perky Christa . . . had a good walk?'

'Very good, thanks,' she smiled back.

'Didn't let Harry walk your legs off? He tries with most people.' There was a question in her eyes. Christina answered it. 'He tried to, but I wouldn't let him. Don't worry.'

Jane put down her beloved *Telegraph* again. 'Oh, there was a message from your lawyer, Rolf Wallberg. He's coming down here tomorrow to see you. He said it was urgent.' Then she went back to her newspaper.

'Sit down Humfrey.' Ruben Stone knew by the pinched lines around his mouth that his nephew, Humfrey Stone, was worried. His unshakeable calm was part of his professional persona; it didn't change in front of family in the office.

'Now tell me, what's so urgent this morning?'

Humfrey looked at him. 'I had a call from Wallberg. I'm sorry to disrupt your meeting, Uncle, but this is really urgent. He's discovered something that could lose the Farrington case.' Ruben didn't even blink.

'Whatever it is, my dear boy, I'm sure it could have waited another hour or two. You must learn that there's no such thing as an emergency unless it's going to happen in the next five minutes. However, tell me about this disaster, whatever it is.'

He wasn't being unkind. He was devoted to Humfrey and to all his family, he merely wanted to teach the young man his own brand of oriental-style patience. It was going to be very difficult; Humfrey was volatile and emotional by temperament. He accepted the rebuke.

'I'm sorry,' he said. 'I was hasty, but it was such a bombshell.'

'So tell me,' Ruben repeated. It didn't take long.

Once Humfrey broke off to ask a question. 'Is it possible? Is Wallberg right?'

'Yes, there's no other explanation, except that Alan Farrington is insane and he's certainly not that. Wallberg is right.'

There was a silence when Humfrey ended his report.

'You know, Humfrey,' his uncle said after a pause, 'I didn't expect him to stay on; I didn't want him to stay. I thought he'd go back to Sweden. Now I suppose it's lucky he didn't.'

'I never understood why you took him on in the first place,' Humfrey ventured. 'I don't like him and I can see you didn't like him either. I don't know what it is about him . . .'

Ruben Stone said softly, 'I know. There's something in him that we recognize subconsciously and it makes us uneasy; he calls up echoes of the past. Why did I take him on? Because an old friend asked me, as a favour. In the end we may be grateful, but I'm not sure. In my heart I'd rather we lost the case and he'd gone back where he came from.' After a pause he said, 'Humfrey, put a call through to Simon Hart. We'd better double-check this. He's the expert; he'll have the answers. And now', with a slight irony, 'I shall go back to my meeting.'

Humfrey hurried out, too preoccupied to realize that his uncle had not answered his question.

Christina and Rolf Wallberg were alone. There had been an instant antagonism between him and Harry when he walked into the Spanniers' house; two males bristling on eye contact.

The impact was so obvious that Harry forgot to be flippant. Rolf hadn't wasted time.

'No thank you, Mrs Spannier, I won't have coffee. I have to get back to London after I've spoken to Mrs Farrington.'

The formality didn't deceive Jane; she saw the way he looked at Christina and his hostility to her son. She found him disconcerting, peremptory, almost rude. As if he sensed her criticism, he said seriously, 'Please excuse me; it's very kind of you to offer hospitality, but something very urgent and unexpected has come up and I must talk it over with my client.'

Christina said, 'What is it? What's happened? Jane, can we use the study?'

'Of course, and if you need me, or Harry, we'll be about. Peter will be back at lunchtime; we were hoping you would stay. In here.' She opened the door and closed it behind them. Harry hadn't moved.

'The noble Swede,' he said, almost to himself.

'Not at all what I expected.' His mother looked at him.

'What did you expect then?'

'A sort of smoothie, a Nordic sexpot. I'll have to give him a new name: Attila the Hun.'

The study was an untidy place. Jane's desk was piled with papers; magazines, sporting and agricultural, were heaped on the floor; and one of Peter's ancient English setters was sprawled, snoring, on the sofa. Rolf looked round, then he said quietly, 'You allow dogs on the furniture?' Then before she could answer he said, 'I'm sorry, I'm afraid I'm not very good with animals. Will you move that dog so we can sit down?'

'Sally, off! Get off the sofa.' Sally obeyed with a reproachful look and jumped up onto a chair instead.

'Rolf,' Christina begged. 'Rolf, what's happened at Russ-More?'

'Nothing, I got excellent statements from the Mannings and Thorn, and your doctor. It was all going so well, then this extraordinary thing happened; I spoke to the undertaker who buried Richard. He was in the pub and we had a drink together. Christa, did you know that Alan went to the chapel to see his father the night before the funeral?'

'He didn't! No, of course I'd no idea . . . It's the last thing he'd have done. He hated Richard.'

'Oh, yes,' Rolf agreed, 'he certainly did. This man, Garrett, the undertaker, told me that when he went to close up the coffin, he noticed something, something he described as horrible. There was a raw patch on the scalp, where someone had torn out a handful of hair.'

Christina's hands flew to her face. 'Oh my God. Oh God . . .'

He said gently, 'Don't let it upset you. Richard was dead.'

'It was desecration,' she exclaimed. 'He's mad, he must be, to do such a thing. Why would he do it?'

'No, not mad at all, far from mad. He knew what he was doing; he's got material for a DNA test, and he'd taken medical advice, because cutting the hair would not have been any use. Hair is dead, like nails. He tore it out because he needed skin attached to the roots.'

'I feel sick,' she whispered. 'Stop, please, I don't want to hear any more.'

He had noticed a tray of drinks. He got up and poured a measure of Peter Spannier's favourite after-dinner brandy. 'Here, drink this . . . no, you must. I'm sorry, but I had to tell you.' Slowly Christina sipped the brandy. She felt his arm around her shoulders; it was a gentle comforting embrace, and she didn't move away.

'All right,' she said. 'I'm all right now. What does it mean, Rolf?'

'It means that he can demand a DNA sample from Belinda,' he said. 'That's why he's been so confident, why he opted for a quick hearing in the High Court, instead of bleeding you financially. If the DNA doesn't match, then Belinda can't inherit under the terms of the trust. If it does, he's lost, of course. That is the choice you have to make.'

She put down the glass and turned to face him. 'I will never put Belinda through that. I will never chance her finding out that Richard wasn't her Father, *if* he wasn't. I told you, I don't know. Nothing in the world would be worth putting a doubt in the mind of an eleven-year-old child, even if the DNA matched. I will never expose her to anything like that, so there isn't any choice.'

She got up; she was still very white, but suddenly calm. 'What a vile revolting man,' she said slowly. 'I wish there was a God, so he could punish him. We have to work out how to settle. I'd better come to London.' He stood beside her.

'You may change your mind,' he suggested. 'Don't do anything in a hurry; think it through.'

'I have,' she answered. 'If she was your child, Rolf, would you subject her to that test?' He didn't hesitate.

'No,' he said, 'I wouldn't. You're right, I shan't try to persuade you . . . But don't initiate anything just yet. There's no date set for the court hearing. Let me look into the details, consult with Humfrey and Ruben Stone. That swine doesn't know we've found out what he did; he mustn't know. So you keep calm, stay on here and leave me to work something out. Please, Christa, let me take care of this.'

They were so close they were almost touching. She felt his arms go round her and she held on to him. The passion she feared didn't flare up; it was different this time – deeper and more disturbing. He said in a whisper, 'I love you, Christa. I've never said that to any woman in my life before. I love you, and I owe you. I'm not going to let this happen.'

When she told them what Alan had done, there was a shocked silence.

'He tore the hair out of his father's head . . .' Jane Spannier repeated. 'It's unbelievable. Oh, Christa, you poor girl . . .'

Harry moved towards her. Christina said quickly, 'Harry, I'm all right. It was a terrible shock, but I got over it. Please don't say a word of this to anyone. Rolf's going to consult with the other lawyers, and he's asked me not to say or do anything till they've discussed it. At least Alan doesn't know we've found out.'

Jane's rather square jaw jutted pugnaciously; she had

recovered herself. Two angry red blotches burned on her cheeks. 'You're not going to give in? You're going to fight him? Christa, you've got to fight him!'

Christina said firmly, 'No, think of Belinda.'

'But it's a lie,' Jane burst out, 'of course she's Richard's daughter.'

'I'm sure she is,' Christina answered, 'but no inheritance is worth what it would take to prove it.'

'He wouldn't dare to admit to such a filthy sacrilege,' Jane insisted. 'He'd be crucified . . . think what the press would make of it!'

'Think what a clever counsel like John Cunningham would do to Christa,' Harry spoke for the first time. 'She's right, Mum, she can't let the case go ahead.'

'I'm going back to RussMore,' Christina told them. 'I can't stay here. Please understand, won't you? I need to go home.'

'Of course,' Jane said readily. 'Of course you do. What a swine! What an utter shit!'

Peter came back early to say goodbye to her; she wouldn't wait till the afternoon. She wanted to get away from the kindly indignation of Jane and Peter, and the concern of Harry who had said he loved her, as that other man had done. She needed her own space, and she needed to go back to the house where she had been so happy, the home she had to leave to protect her child. She hardly noticed the drive; she felt numb, as if her feelings were suspended. Turning through the gates, the afternoon sun starting to sink in the sky above the rooftops, she seemed to see RussMore for the first time, all over again, as if the years had rolled back and she was driving there beside Richard, full of excitement. 'Oh, but it's so beautiful, darling, and so big.' He had squeezed her hand and smiled at her, so proud and happy that she liked what he loved best.

'It's your home, sweetheart. Houses have their own spirit. It'll love you as much as I do.'

And he was right. RussMore had welcomed her, and glowed with new life under the changes she made. She drove to the rear and parked the car, and Manning came out to bring her case inside.

'Mrs Spannier phoned to say you were coming, Madam,' he said. 'Nice to have you back.'

No, Christina told him, she didn't want tea, she was going for a walk round the gardens before the sun set. There was the rose garden she and Richard had planned, and the little eighteenth-century marble Cupid on his plinth in the centre, aiming an invisible arrow at the passer-by – he'd given her that for a birthday. They had sat there together on warm spring days when he was well enough. The rose beds were all underplanted with narcissi and grape hyacinth, making a bright show of colour; he had died before the roses came into bloom. On through the rose garden, up the steps between the tall clipped yews, through into the long herbaceous border walk, with the sheen of the lake at the end. *We have swans and ducks, geese too, at home.* Words spoken in a park in Stockholm by a stranger who married her before the month was out. The borders blazed with purple shades of Michaelmas daisies, and the rich reds and yellows of chrysanthemums. She had learned all the English flower names, joining Richard in his passion for planting and improving his garden. He was the expert on trees; he spoke of planting for the future, as his ancestors had done.

'You don't expect to see it, but your grandchildren will.'

To the right was the walled kitchen garden. It had been the swimming pool, built to please his first wife, and she had died in it, a miserable death by drowning, insensible from heroin and drink. As soon as Richard and she came home to England, he had had the place filled in, levelled and returned to its original use. Christina noticed that he never went there, not even to oversee the work. She didn't go there now, though it held no memories or ghosts for her. It was growing cold and the sky was flaming with the sunset, so she turned back to the house and went inside. The lights were switched on and the fire was alight in the red study. Christina went in and the nameless Tudor Farrington, who had died in childhood, gazed down at her, his plump little hand perched on his own skull. She did something untypical; she poured herself a drink and didn't drown it. She stood by the fire looking up at the picture; Richard had left it to her as a special legacy, and as she drank she realized that she was shaking with anger. She was filled with such a sense of fury and outrage that she suddenly wanted to smash the glass into the grate.

I'd set fire to the place before I let him have it. Richard's angry words came to mind as if he'd spoken them. Shocked by the thought that followed, Christina sat down. She swallowed her drink, as much to shut out the picture of his dead body being ravaged by his own son.

'I can't do it,' she said it out loud. 'I can't let him have RussMore; I won't let him have it.'

Capitulation was her first instinct – to shield Belinda. She couldn't risk her finding out that the father she adored was not her father, that she wasn't a Farrington, but the child of a man who left her mother after a brief affair. But if she *was* his daughter, if that could be proved before the case came to court . . . The telephone shrilled beside her and she grabbed it.

'Rolf?'

'No,' Harry's voice said, 'it's not Rolf. Are you all right?'

'No,' she answered, 'I think I'm drunk.'

'Won't do you any harm. You'd had a lover before you met Richard? That's what that bastard had over you, isn't it? Why didn't you tell me?'

'Because I didn't want to,' Christina said. 'Harry, I've made up my mind. I'm not giving in. Jane was right. I'm bloody not.'

Harry put his hand over the phone and said to his father, 'She's a bit pissed, poor sweet. Christa, good for you. Get some dinner down you and don't drink any more; you've no head for booze. I'm going to take a trip to London, then I'm coming down to hold your hand. And don't let me find Attila there.'

'Attila? What are you talking about?'

'Never mind. Talk to you tomorrow. God bless.'

Dear Harry. But Harry couldn't help; it was Rolf she needed now.

'Mrs Farrington,' Humfrey said, 'the Home Office would never give permission, that's why your stepson secured a sample before the burial. I wish I could suggest something else, but I can't.' Privately, he was a little shocked at her suggestion. He wondered who had put it into her mind. Briefly he glanced at Rolf Wallberg; it was the kind of ruthless expedient that he would think up. 'Exhumation is a very serious business,' he explained to Christina. 'You'd have to give a very strong reason, and a dispute which hadn't even come to court wouldn't be acceptable. I'm sorry.'

Rolf intervened. 'Supposing Mrs Farrington wanted her husband buried somewhere else. I've looked that up, permission is given in those circumstances.'

Humfrey said sharply, 'Yes, but not to open the coffin. If reburial is to take place, the original coffin is enclosed in a second container to protect the corpse from any kind of violation. The rules derive from the nineteenth-century crime of body-snatching. Graves were robbed and the corpses sold for medical dissection. It's a serious offence to desecrate a grave.'

'I would have thought it was more serious to traumatize a child,' Rolf said angrily, 'or rob her of her home and inheritance.'

Christina broke in, 'If that's impossible, what can we do, Humfrey? I've made up my mind, I'm not handing over RussMore.'

She had already made that plain before the meeting. Her vigour had surprised him; there was an angry resolve he hadn't seen before, and a sense of collusion between her and Wallberg. Now, despite earlier distance, they were working as a team.

'There must be something, some legal device,' Christina insisted. 'I mean it, I'll never give in to that unspeakable brute. When I think of what he did to my husband. I tell you, I'll set fire to RussMore before I let him put a hand on that house!'

Humfrey was used to clients losing control, but there was a fierceness about this woman in her new-found anger that alarmed him. She might actually carry out that threat; the idea made him shudder.

'Mrs Farrington,' he said soothingly, 'Mrs Farrington, let me talk to your counsel. Let me fix a meeting with Ken Hubert and see what he has to suggest. And try to be calm, please, I know what a terrible emotional shock this has been to you. In a way, it's a pity you had to hear the details.' He directed the rebuke at Wallberg.

'I'm glad Rolf told me,' Christina interrupted. 'I might have given in if I hadn't known exactly what he did. I had a right to know that my husband's body had been outraged. You're right, it was a terrible shock. I didn't think straight when I first heard; I was knocked back . . . All I could think of was Belinda learning she wasn't Richard's daughter. I've told you everything, just as I told Rolf.'

'Who hadn't mentioned it to us,' Humfrey noted.

'That's why I thought if I could get a DNA test done before the case, I'd have a clear choice. Now, I just know I'm not going to be beaten; I'm not giving way. Do please contact Mr Hubert and explain the situation. I can't believe there's nothing to be done.'

She stood up, ending the meeting on her own initiative. Yes, Humfrey decided, there had been a fundamental change.

At their first meeting when he came down to RussMore, after Richard Farrington had engaged them as his solicitors, he had found a charming, rather serene woman, unconsciously in the shadow of her older husband. A very secure and loving marriage had given her that calmness, that reliance on the dominant man to solve everything for her. What death and bitter family dissension had failed to do, that single act of barbarism committed by her stepson had achieved in one. She had found herself; she was in control for the first time. They shook hands. He tried once more.

'Try not to dwell on what happened,' he suggested. He wanted to say, and calm yourself, but he didn't like to; it wouldn't have been well received by this new woman.

'I'll call Hubert's chambers and set up a meeting as soon as possible. I'll be in touch.' Rolf opened the office door.

'I'll see Mrs Farrington out,' he announced. They went down together in the lift. 'You were good,' he said to her, 'very strong.

You have to push lawyers, or they will push you into taking the easy way out. I'm sorry my idea didn't work, but he knows the law. We'll think of something else. When can I see you?'

'I don't know,' Christina answered. 'Thank you for trying. You're right, we will think of something. Thank you for not trying to talk me into settling.' They walked out to the car park together.

'I'll only do that when I know there is really no way out, but I told you, I'm going to find one. You're more beautiful now, you know that? This thing has lit a fire in you, Christa; it was never lit before.'

'I've never hated before,' she said quietly. 'If I'm going to stop hating, I've got to defeat Alan.' She reached up and kissed him lightly on the lips. 'Then there'll be time for us,' she said in Swedish.

8

'It's not enough, Mr Farrington. You can't just produce this DNA report out of the blue and say it's tissue taken from your father.'

Alan stared at his solicitor. He had expected congratulations on his cleverness, instead, there was the old fart – as he dubbed him privately – Mr Ronald, God Almighty, Hamilton, looking down his anteater nose and throwing cold water over his announcement.

'What do you mean, it's not enough? I've given you my sample, it matches my father's. What more is there?'

'Proof that it is Richard Farrington's DNA,' was the answer. 'There's nothing here to say how it was obtained; there's no corroboration that confirms it. Your word isn't going to be enough, that's what I mean.'

He tried to be patient, reminding himself that not long ago he had felt sorry for this aggressive hectoring young man. He had to remind himself again that his personality was the result of parental harshness.

Alan said after a pause, 'You want to know how I got something viable to test, is that right?'

'Your stepmother's lawyers will certainly want an answer, and I need one before I enter it as evidence.'

Alan folded his arms; Hamilton recognized the defiant body language.

'I took some hair and skin tissue off my father's body. I thought I might have a fight on my hands, and that I'd need it if he'd tried to disinherit me. Will that do you?'

Ronnie Hamilton stared at him for a moment. 'You did what?'

'I went to the chapel of rest, or whatever they call it, and took the sample, and if you want a bloody witness, call the undertaker; he knew what I'd done. He wouldn't look me in the face at the bloody funeral. His name's Garrett; funeral specialist to the Farrington family. And I don't know what you're making such a big deal about; he was dead, he didn't feel anything.'

Ronnie Hamilton swallowed. He said, 'I've been in practice over thirty years and I've never come across anything like this. I really don't know what to say.'

'How about well done for quick thinking?' Alan demanded. 'For Christ's sake, if I'm right about that little brat, I've won the case for you! All you've got to do is ask for a sample, a blood sample is enough from a living person, that's all I had to give, and I'll lay you a thousand to one, Christina won't risk it. She'll back down.'

Hamilton buzzed his secretary. 'Pauline, could you bring me some coffee, please.' He didn't include Alan. He drew a heavy breath. 'My personal inclination is to refuse to act for you. I find this the most disgraceful act, perpetrated on a dead man – your own father.'

Alan's dark eyes had a reddish light in them. The rage was rising in him, threatening to get out of control. *His father*; that cold, unloving man, always so remote from him and so cruelly indifferent, even contemptuous, of his wife's misery. *A disgraceful act*. He stood up so abruptly that the chair rocked and nearly tipped over backwards.

'If I thought it would prove my right to RussMore, I'd have cut off his balls. If you don't want to continue acting for me, then I'll get someone else. There are plenty of people out there who'd be glad of the fees you're getting, and who are just as good as you. It'll be no skin off my nose.'

He pushed his way past the secretary who was coming in with the coffee. She had brought two cups. She said, 'He's got another twenty minutes left. Anything wrong, Mr Hamilton?'

'I just told him I didn't want to act for him. I don't know what the senior partners will say, but I'm not backing down. Thank you, Pauline. Pour it for me, will you? I could do with a good strong cup.'

Alan didn't go back to the office. After a storm of temper, depression usually set in. He had no appointments that couldn't be put off and, in his present mood, he didn't feel like seeing anyone. 'Count your blessings,' Fay reminded him when he fell into the trough. He had refused counselling with angry scorn, but Fay had taken advice instead, because she needed help in order to help him. Cool-headed and pragmatic, she had dispensed with the professional's services as soon as she had gained the necessary insight into her husband's problems – People like that tended to cling on, playing God to dependent clients. Fay cut off the visits, paid the bill and forgot about the incident, but she learned enough to discard the psychobabble and make use of the good advice.

She was out when he came home; she'd gone out to lunch and a fashion show with friends. The young nanny was nervous of Alan; sometimes he was friendly, other times short-tempered and sharp-tongued. It made her jumpy because you never knew what mood you would find him in.

He cut her explanations short. 'Where are the boys?'

'Timmy's out to tea with a friend, and Robert's upstairs. We were doing some nice drawing.'

'Bring him down to the sitting-room. Bring some toys and books . . . I'm no bloody good at drawing; had too much of it when I was a kid. "Draw a nice picture for Mummy . . ."' He mimicked a long-dead nanny, a starchy middle-aged version, quite different from the easy going twenty-two-year-old who looked after his sons. She fled upstairs.

Count your blessings. He could hear Fay saying it. 'Look at all you've got. Me, the boys, this lovely house, the cottage and our place in Antibes. We have everything we want. And look at the success you've made! You built the business up from one little sandwich shop. Alan, stop doing yourself down. We have a great time, a super life, lots of friends . . . stop looking back, for goodness sake!' At this point he usually interrupted.

'I know, I know; you've forgotten the fucking Bentley. I know I'm lucky; I know I am.' And wait for her to soothe him like a discomfited small boy. She was a tough bird, he reckoned, but not with him. She was the only woman who could mother him sometimes and get away with it.

She wasn't there, but he knew the antidote: his children. Timmy was out to tea; he smiled at the idea; Timmy was six and already he had a full social life. Robert was shy, less self-confident. Robert was very close to his heart, but Timmy was his eldest and his feelings for his first-born son were almost atavistic. Robert came in, carrying a story book and a box with a jigsaw puzzle. Alan held out his arms.

'Come on, come on Daddy's knee. There, now tell me, have you had a good day?' He never asked them if they had been good boys; childhood inhibitions again. He hadn't been good and the question used to turn into, Why haven't you been good today, Alan? Nanny tells me you did . . . on and on, the list of complaints becoming more serious as he grew older. The stern face of his father, angry, disapproving, with that poor shadow in the background, so often ill and absent, beaming silent sympathy towards him. Even now, thinking of his mother brought Alan close to tears. He gave his little son a hug. 'Let's play a game, Robby.'

'What game, Daddy? I was drawing a picture.'

'I know, never mind the picture. How would you like to live in a great big house in the country?'

The little boy said simply, 'That's not a game. I brought my jigsaw.'

'In a minute,' Alan said. 'We'll do the jigsaw in a minute. Think of a big house, very big, with lots of rooms and a lake, and birds swimming in it . . . You could have puppies and a pony. Wouldn't you like that, Robby?'

'Can I tell you something, Daddy?' Every other sentence began with that. 'I'd like two puppies; Timmy can have the pony. When can I see it? When can I see the big house?'

Alan pressed a kiss on his son's soft hair. 'Soon, darling,' he said. 'It was my house when I was a little boy and it'll be your house soon. Daddy's going to get it for you, and Timmy.'

When Fay came home she found him in a happy mood, the completed jigsaw on the floor and Robert shouting with laughter as his father insisted, 'Who's a pooey pig, then?' She marvelled that such a shrewd and clever businessman was still in the nursery when it came to humour. When the children had gone upstairs he told her what had happened at the solicitors.

'I'm not worried,' he said. 'There are plenty of smart lawyers who'll jump at the chance to take it on. I thought he'd have been over the moon, breaking out the champagne . . . Case bloody well won for them!'

'He's not a senior partner,' she pointed out. 'They won't lose you as a client. Someone else'll step in; let the next move come from them. Now, I'll get you a whiskey and tell you all about my day.' She smiled at him and flicked his cheek with her finger. 'I saw some lovely dresses. I'm afraid it's going to cost you!'

'So long as you look good, it'll be worth it. I don't mind paying for clothes so long as I get to take them off . . . how about going upstairs for a quickie?'

She laughed. 'Sounds good. I'll take the whiskey. If you want it, you'll have to come up to get it.'

He heaved himself up and watched her fill the glass and, as she passed, he aimed a sharp slap at her bottom. She said, 'Ouch,' and gave him an excited look over her shoulder. They had a marvellous sex life. Afterwards, lying relaxed together, Alan said, 'I had a great time with Robby today. He's a bright kid, and he loves jokes. We played Pooey Pigs and he creased himself . . .'

'I know,' Fay answered. 'I saw you. You're very good with the boys, you know. You're a wonderful father, and you're good with me too; what you did was lovely . . .'

'We'll be happy there,' he said. 'I was telling Robby about it.'

'Happy where?' She had been wondering if they had time to make love again before dinner.

'RussMore,' he said. 'And talking about spending money, you can write your own chit; I want you to refurbish from top to bottom. It'll be our house, and then Timmy's. That's my dream, Fay . . . to walk in there with you and the boys and say, "It's mine now, you rotten old bastard; you couldn't take it away from me."'

Fay knew how to deal with the morbidity, too. 'So long as you don't wait around for him to answer,' she retorted. 'Come on, darling, my dream is a nice cheese soufflé and it'll spoil if we don't get moving.' She would never admit, even to herself, that the last place in the world she wanted to live was that huge dreary old house.

John Cunningham closed the brief. He looked up at his junior. 'Frank,' he said, 'I thought nothing in human nature could surprise me, but I never imagined anything like this. I wonder if this blackguard has any idea of what he's going to look like to the world at large if I use this evidence?'

Frank Collins, unlike many junior barristers at the beck and call of a famous counsel in their chambers, actually regarded Cunningham as just below God. 'I don't suppose he cares,' he said. 'If he'd boast about doing it to Ronald Hamilton, he obviously doesn't see anything reprehensible. But you have to use it; it's a winner, isn't it?'

Cunningham tapped the blue brief cover with his index finger. It was a habit that grated on Collins, but then even the Almighty had mannerisms, like the use of archaic words like blackguard. Straight out of Oscar Wilde, he was, in some ways, and the cleverest and deadliest cross-examiner any witness would have to face.

'Only if he's right about Farrington's wife lying to him,' he said. 'If the child gives a DNA sample and it matches, our client has not only lost his case but he's destroyed himself. Again, I wonder if he realizes.' He sighed. 'I suppose, as his counsel, I shall have to point it out to him. Of course, the sensible thing is for Hamilton to get together with old Ruben Stone and persuade the woman to give the house up in return for some financial deal.'

Collins nodded, 'After all, that's what he wants, isn't it? The family house.'

'No,' Cunningham said slowly, 'there's more to it than that. We're dealing with a man who wants revenge. He wants to humiliate and expose his stepmother, because he can't hit back at his father in any other way; I don't think he'll be satisfied with less than that. Still, we have to earn a crust. The tabloids are going to pee themselves with excitement over this one. Ask the clerk to get me Ken Hubert on the telephone, will you? If I give him dinner, he may let something slip if the other side know anything about this. And then get me the Fry v. Porter file, will you, dear chap? At least that's an honest-to-God breach of contract.'

Ken Hubert smiled when he heard the friendly invitation. He called Molly and chuckled when he told her he'd accepted.

'We'll get a good dinner and some decent claret out of the old sod. He wants some information; it'll be fun not giving him any.'

Molly Hubert said gravely, 'You have no principles, darling, but then neither does John, and you'd try the same trick with him. Where are we dining?'

'Le Caprice,' was the answer.

'My God!' she exclaimed. 'He must want to find out something. I wonder what it is?'

'So do I,' he agreed. 'He's got something up his sleeve, or he thinks we've got something up ours.'

'And have we?'

He loved her sharp curiosity. 'Not that I know of, but I'll check with Uncle Ruben.'

Twenty minutes later he was saying angrily to Ruben Stone, 'Why the hell have you been sitting on this? Why wasn't I told immediately? This changes the whole outlook. I'm not pleased about this, not pleased at all.' The reply was emollient.

'We had to check the story first. I'd hardly come to you with some unsubstantiated gossip picked up in a pub over a few drinks now, would I, not till I'd checked it was true.'

'And it is,' Ken Hubert was not to be placated. 'You've checked and it's true.'

'The undertaker has given an affidavit. He's sworn that after Farrington left the chapel of rest, he noticed the scalp had been lacerated and a section of hair with skin attached had been ripped out. So the other side can demand a DNA test on the Farrington child.'

'Christ,' Hubert exploded. 'How low can you sink. The man's a psychopath! Look, John Cunningham's asked me to dine tonight; I'll bet it's because of this; he wants to know if we've discovered this, otherwise he'll spring it on us in court. We'd better set up a meeting early next week; I'm in court all day for the next three days. What's our client's reaction to the news? I suppose she'll want to settle, rather than involve the child in a mess like this . . .'

Ruben Stone said slowly, 'I'm afraid not. She was always persuadable, as I judged, given any reasonable proposals. She wasn't a fighter and she never struck any of us as greedy, but that's changed. When she heard what had been done to her husband's body, she dug her toes right in. She'll fight the case to the last. She even threatened to burn the place down if she lost, rather than let Farrington have it. I've never seen such a change in attitude. I really thought she meant to do it; I was quite alarmed.'

'I shouldn't be, that's just feminine hysteria. Quite understandable, but don't take it seriously.'

It was easy for Hubert to dismiss the threat, Ruben thought. He hadn't been there when Christina Farrington made it. Hysterical she wasn't, but burning with a very dangerous anger. 'I'll admit that bringing Wallberg into it hasn't helped; she won't deal with anyone else but him now. I suppose it was inevitable, being fellow Swedes, but he's encouraging her to be intransigent.'

'Well, you'll have to dispense with his services then, if we decide to try for a settlement,' Hubert dismissed that too. Easy for him to solve Ruben's problem from his lofty legal height; not so easy for Ruben.

'I'll set up a meeting,' Ruben said. And then, a little hesitantly, for Hubert could be temperamental with solicitors, 'Are you going to discuss this with John Cunningham?'

'Good God, no! Let him think he's got his ace up his sleeve. We'll have to find something to counter it, that's all. See you next week, and no more surprises, please?' He rang off. He couldn't wait to get home and tell Molly. There wasn't time to call her; he would have to work through without lunch to get home in time to pick her up and go on to Le Caprice.

'I'm Alan's first cousin,' Harry said pleasantly, 'once removed, I think. Our grandfathers were brothers.'

Fay said coolly, 'That's nice.' He had caught her by surprise. He'd just rung the front door bell and asked to see her.

She was furious with the witless Filipino, who'd let him in and brought him to the sitting-room, simply saying, 'There's a gentleman to see you, Madam.' Alan would have a word to say to him about letting strangers into the house.

She asked him to sit down and he accepted with a smile that wasn't quite as guileless as it seemed. He was very thin, dark and wiry and not very tall. There was a vague look of the Farringtons about him, she admitted. Probably because of the very black hair and deep brown eyes.

'I've been in South Africa', he explained, 'for the last fifteen years, so I never got to your wedding or to meet you.'

Fay wasn't aware that he'd been asked. It was a very small wedding, paid for by her parents, who were too proud to let Alan contribute. The only members of his family present were his toffee-nosed father and that patronizing cow, Christina. Even thinking about them made her simmer with resentment; they'd spoiled her happy day. Alan hadn't wanted to invite them, but she and her mother had insisted, especially her mother. 'Oh, you can't leave them out, it would be so awful, Alan dear . . . he's your father . . .' And he'd given in to please her.

There was something that riled her about this so-called cousin. There was just a hint of arrogance in the smile and the easy way he sat himself down, as if he had a right to intrude on her. 'I've been meaning to look up Alan', he said, 'since I got back. Then I heard about all the family troubles after my cousin Richard died.'

She said sharply, 'What's that got to do with it?'

'Well, I wasn't sure if it was true,' he parried.

'Well, it is. Alan was treated disgracefully and he's going to court. I hope that explains it to you.' She was openly hostile and he seemed quite unaware of it; he still smiled.

'Yes, so I understood. I used to go to parties at RussMore when I was a kid; I saw quite a lot of Alan and James. It always seemed to me that Alan could take care of himself; James was a bit of a creep.' He saw a gleam of agreement in the unfriendly stare. 'But then they did have a hard time, with a mother like that. Terribly druggy she was, even then.'

Fay said fiercely, 'They had a rotten upbringing. They were never given any love, especially Alan. We've got boys of our own, and believe me, we're not making the same mistake; Alan's a wonderful father.'

'I'm sure,' Harry agreed. 'I'm sure you're a wonderful mother too. I'm sure you're perfect parents.' Fay got up.

'What do you want? Why have you come here?'

'Well, I really came hoping to see Alan, but he seems to be out, so maybe you'll give him a message from me?'

'Maybe,' she snapped, 'it depends what it is. I have a feeling you're not on his side, Mr Spunnier . . .'

'Spannier,' he corrected. 'Harry Spannier. Remind him that when we were children and he tried to bully me, I used to kick the shit out of him; I'm sure he'll remember. If he goes on bullying a woman and a little girl, I'll come back and beat the holy beJesus out of him. Tell him that for me, will you? I'll see myself out.'

'You get out!' she screamed at him. 'Fucking well get out of my house!'

He was by the door when he turned and looked sadly at her. 'As God made them, He matched them. I can see you make a lovely couple.' She was still shouting obscenities as he closed the door.

'I love this walk,' Christina said to Rolf. 'It's so open and you can see for miles. I remember how shocked I was by the weather when I first came, but I got used to it and now I love that too. You get marvellous cloud formations, always changing because of the wind. It's a very old county, and there are villages here where nothing's changed for centuries. I suppose it's because Sweden's so much in love with the future that I found it fascinating . . . Belinda, don't take Sammy near the wood, she'll go hunting and we'll never get her back!' Turning to him, she explained, 'That's Richard's dog. He had the mother and grandmother. Sammy went down a rabbit hole and we couldn't find her for five days; he was heartbroken. I thought it extraordinary to mind so much about a dog . . . now I'm very fond of her too.'

He hadn't known what to say. He had never owned a pet as a child; his adoptive parents didn't keep domestic animals. He said, 'Isn't Sammy a man's name? Why do you call a bitch Sammy?'

'Because it's short for Samantha. All the terriers had names beginning with S. The mother was Susan.' He shook his head and said, 'I give up on the English and their dogs. Are you going to get Belinda a proper pony? I heard her asking about it at lunch.'

'No,' Christina said firmly. 'Not till next year.'

'Would you mind if I bought one for her? You choose it, of course. I don't know anything about horses either.' She had paused to stare at him.

'You? But, Rolf, you won't be here next year, will you?'

He had walked on, leading her with him. 'I may be, I like it here. I haven't decided yet, but I would love to give Belinda a present, if that's all right.'

'She'd love you for life if you did,' Christina admitted. 'If you're serious, it would be wonderful.'

She hadn't refused him; he had been hoping she wouldn't oppose the suggestion. He wanted to give the child a present. He had never given a child anything before, and he could imagine the excitement, the glow on her expressive face. It wasn't something he had experienced for himself when he was her age.

'Christa, can we turn back? I want to talk to you and to Belinda too.'

'Why her? What about?' Suddenly she looked wary. 'I won't have her worried about anything. I've told her everything's going to be all right.'

'That's what I'm going to tell her too, but I may say something different to you. She's running back now.'

Belinda caught her mother's hand. 'Sammy's behind those trees, Mum. Sam! Sam! Come here!' Christina said anxiously, 'Darling, you're freezing; your hand's like ice. I told you to put on a thick jersey.'

In spite of herself, Belinda shivered. 'Sorry, I forgot. It's very cold in the wind.' Rolf stripped off his jacket.

'Here,' he said. 'Wrap up in this.' He held it and she wriggled into it, pulling it round her. She smiled at him.

'It's lovely and warm,' she said. 'I love big jackets; all the girls in the sixth form wear them. Baggy and long like this . . . But Rolf, won't you be cold?'

He laughed. 'No, I *did* put on a thick jersey, so I don't need the coat. You look very smart in it.'

She blushed with pleasure. Christina murmured, 'I think she loves you enough *without* the pony . . .'

When they reached the house, she had started to unbutton his jacket. 'You keep it,' Rolf insisted. 'It suits you. Keep it till I come down again.' Delighted, she had rushed upstairs to inspect herself and hang it up.

In his mind he pictured them both again, gathered by the fire in the red study; Belinda sitting cross-legged on the floor, playing with the androgynously named Sammy. And he had begun by asking, 'Lindy, are you looking forward to Christmas?' She had smiled up at him. He thought how quickly she was growing up, not a pale beauty like her mother, but with a sweet gravity that made her pretty.

'Oh, yes. I'm longing for it. It's always such fun here at Christmas. There's a big party for everyone; all the children come and get presents and we play games . . . Will we do that this year, Mum, even without Daddy?' The bright eyes dimmed for a moment.

'Just the same,' her mother said. 'Just as if Daddy was with us, which he will be, darling, watching everything and wanting us to be happy.' Rolf saw a film of tears in her eyes too.

'Are you going to be in England at Christmas, Rolf? Or are you going home to your family in Sweden?' He had insisted that she stop calling him Mr Wallberg.

'I don't have a family,' he answered. 'I don't know what I'll do.'

'Then come here to us! Mum, wouldn't that be great, if Rolf came for Christmas?'

'Yes, of course it would.' Again there was no reserve.

He said gently, 'Thank you both for asking me. Can I think about it?' And then to the child again, 'Tell me, what is your favourite thing about this house. What do you love best? The gardens, the long walks . . . what?' She pulled a little face, half pleased and half embarrassed. He could see that she was thinking, What a funny question.

After a pause, while she considered, she said simply, 'All of it. It's my home and I love it, and Mum says Alan's not going to take it away from us. She's promised.' Rolf leaned a little towards her.

'And I promised too. A long time ago when you showed me the rose garden, I promised I wouldn't let it happen. I always keep my promises.'

Later, when she had gone to have supper and watch television, he turned to Christina.

'What are you going to tell her if Alan wins? How are you going to fight him if you won't let her give a blood sample? It's only six weeks before the case comes to court . . .'

'If we lose, I'll appeal. Ken Hubert says I can. If I lose that I'll go to the House of Lords.'

'Even if you get permission,' he said, 'you'll be ruined; you'll run out of money. I explained all that to you before.'

She said simply, 'I know you did. It doesn't matter, Rolf; I won't have Belinda involved and I won't give up RussMore. I'm going to the wire on this; I owe it to Richard.'

He'd taken hold of her and again she hadn't resisted. 'You owe something to yourself,' he insisted. 'You have a life to live. I love you, and I want to make a life with you; I could make you very happy and Belinda too. Don't destroy yourself for the sake of a house or a man who's dead. He loved you too; he wouldn't want that.'

'I want it,' she said. 'It's as much for me now as anyone. I can't say I love you, Rolf, because I don't know what I feel. Sex isn't love, I do know that.'

He held her close. 'How do you know what sex can mean? Come to bed and let me show you.'

'Mum,' Belinda asked, 'why did Rolf go so quickly? Didn't you ask him to stay?'

'He had business,' Christina answered. 'Lawyers work very hard, darling, even at weekends. He sent you his love.' She had been asleep when he left. She remembered that there was a thin linc of grey between the drawn curtains in her bedroom before she drifted into a deep exhausted sleep, his arm lying heavy across her.

'You like him, don't you? You didn't use to. Do you like him better than Harry?'

Christina looked into the innocent eyes of her child and said, 'I don't know, they're quite different.' Different. How to describe the man who had made love to her that night, except in that inadequate word. How to come to terms with what he had made her feel: self-discovery, a new dimension of physical pleasure, an abandonment that was almost a loss of self. But did she love him? That was the question she dared not ask herself because she would have to live with her sense of betrayal if the answer was no; betrayal of Richard before he was even a year dead, and betrayal of her own child, who believed that Christina's love belonged to her father.

'Belinda,' she said, 'I may like Rolf and Harry, but I only loved Daddy and I love you. So what shall we do today? Go into Lincoln and do some shopping?'

'Great,' she enthused. 'I'm rapt with the new Take That album. I've been saving up; I could buy it and take it back to school with me. My class are all rapt with them too.'

Rapt. Rapture. Was that a word to describe what Rolf had brought her to? . . . What he had experienced with her? It was inadequate too. He wasn't a man that fitted female fantasy, more a force of nature. She closed her mind on the memories and the questions. Surely guilt would come soon, but not yet. When it did, as surely it must, she might understand her own feelings more clearly. 'Hurry up then,' she said. 'We'll go to the record shop first.'

They spent a long happy afternoon in the cathedral city, and Belinda came home with the treasured album, two more records by another group and some clothes Christina couldn't resist buying her. She rushed upstairs to listen to her music. There were two messages on the answerphone.

His voice made her heart jump. 'Mrs Farrington, this is Rolf Wallberg. I'll be busy for the next few days, but I'll be in contact.' That was for Mrs Manning, who liked to play the messages back and then rewind the tape; it was irritating but harmless. Then he spoke in Swedish, 'I didn't wake you, you were sleeping deeply. I think you know the answer now. I love you. You showed that you love me.' That was all.

She switched the machine off. What had she shown him? Passion? Yes. A depth and intensity of passion she had never suspected she possessed, but tenderness, and the gentle joy of lying close when it was over, the loving words, even the laughter that can follow making love, there had been none of that, only an abyss of sleep that opened up and drew her down. Perhaps the explosion between them had drained all her energy, left no capacity for other feelings to emerge. Perhaps that would come later, like the guilt she didn't feel. The eye of the machine winked at her, its second message undelivered. She pressed the switch.

'Christa,' the voice said, 'just giving you a call. I'm in

London, staying over for a while. I'm at the Capital. Give me a *coup de telephone*, I'd really like to talk to you. Bye.' The tape stopped.

James. The French affectation filled her with irritation. How dare he call her after what he had done . . . She said contemptuously, 'Ring you? Don't hold your breath!' And then the idea came to her. She wouldn't have thought of it without that message, and once she did, it was so obvious she caught her breath in excitement. James. James was Richard's son; he would share the same DNA characteristics. If she could appeal to his conscience, perhaps touch his heart, he could answer the question that hung over her like the legendary sword of Damocles. But wait, she counselled herself, don't be impetuous; think the idea through very carefully. He's a complex unpredictable personality, deeply distorted; he might agree on an impulse and then reconsider; he might see what she asked for as a sign of desperation; or he just might believe the lie she was going to tell him. She thought, ironically, that her reputation for speaking the truth would be an advantage when she lied this time. Richard's condemnation of his son whispered in her mind: *Neutral at best, weak at worst. I could never look to him for support* . . . She had trusted him once, and he'd sneaked into the library and stolen his father's treasured document, but if she forgave him for that, even made him feel guilty by the lack of anger or blame . . . He had always been misjudged, condemned as a matter of course because of the duplicity of his nature; justly or unjustly, he knew he'd never been trusted. If she could show him she was different . . . It was a terrifying gamble to take, but she had no alternative but to go into court against Alan and fight him blindfolded, if she was going to shield her daughter. If she could get James to agree to her proposal, she would at least know whether she could win outright or embark on a bitter campaign of legal wrangling. She wouldn't ask Rolf's advice, or turn to Harry; she had to make the decision, and accept the consequences if it was the wrong one. She put the call through to the Capital Hotel and asked for James. When she rang off, she drew a deep breath. It was arranged; he was coming down to spend the night the day after tomorrow. Belinda would have gone back to school.

It was Fay's hostile attitude that made James get in touch with Christina. When he phoned the Chelsea house she'd told him Alan was away in Birmingham.

'Oh.' He had been put out. 'Oh, what a pity. When will he be back?'

'I've no idea. He's setting up a franchise for a new restaurant chain – curry houses. It's a big project and I don't know when he'll be home. I'll tell him you called.'

No welcome, no invitation to come round, after he'd sacrificed his vacation to come over and give moral support. He said spitefully, 'Curry houses? That's going down market, isn't it? I thought he was planning to float the shares on the open market. Go public and make a killing . . . what's he bothering with a lot of Pakistanis up in Birmingham for?' He had annoyed her and she snapped back; she had a very sharp tongue.

'I know you got hit on the head, but you can't be that stupid! If you want to know, ask *him*. Now I've got to go. Ring again, maybe he'll be here.' And she hung up. James was furious. She'd never have dared to talk to him like that in Alan's hearing. Jealous little cow. Common little cow, he fulminated. His father had been right about that anyway. 'Alan would pick that type of girl. It makes him feel superior.' It had been a cruel crushing judgement, but he relished it at that moment.

'You've lost weight, Christa. It suits you.'

'I haven't been trying,' she said. There was a strained silence then. He was watching her warily; he'd stolen the manuscript and was expecting her to say something. It couldn't be ignored if she was going to enlist his help. She put her cup down and straightened up in the chair.

'I always liked you James. I hoped that perhaps you liked me a bit too. Why did you steal from me?'

He sighed. 'Oh dear, I wondered what was behind the invitation. I've spent too many years in this house, in this room in particular, being accused of things. I don't think I'm going to be put on trial by you. If you're going to be unpleasant, I'll go back to London now.'

'I'm not,' she answered. 'I wouldn't have asked you here if that was my reason. I'll tell you something that may surprise you, I was hurt by what you did, really hurt; I'd begun to think you were a friend. I'm not angry, James, I promise.'

'You should be, it was worth a lot of money, so that nasty lawyer told me; millions, he said. I didn't believe that, of course, but I'm sure it was valuable or Father wouldn't have been so thrilled with it; he was positively gloating. Why aren't you furious, Christa? You're not a saint suddenly, are you?'

'No,' she said, 'I'm nothing like that. I don't know what Wallberg told you. It was a Jewish treasure, stolen by Germans, who murdered the family that owned it. I wouldn't touch blood money; I would have given it to charity if I couldn't trace any relatives. So you didn't rob me of anything, you just hurt me, that's all. It might help if at least you could give me a reason?'

He had been on his guard against antagonism, but there was no hostility, only a pained reproach that caught him unprepared. He said awkwardly, 'I'm sorry, I never thought of it like that. I was curious to start with, curious about this father of mine who'd always shut me out, never let me see him as he really was, as you saw him. I was bloody angry that night about being excluded, and I went to the library to look at something he'd never let me see, to find out what made him tick. And then, when I found it and read his notes, saw how excited he was, how much he valued the wretched thing, I got angry all over again. So I took it to spite him, to pay him back for keeping me at arm's length all my life, right up until he died; that's why I did it. Not to hurt you, I've never wanted to do that. I'm not Alan.'

Christina said quietly, 'I know you're not. Thanks for explaining, and it makes sense; I understand how you felt and I'm sorry too. Let's forget about it, shall we? And anyway, I've been thinking . . . or I've just thought of it, listening to what you said . . .' She hesitated.'James, is there anything personal of your father's you'd like? A memento of him? I'd really like you to choose something.'

He shook his head. 'Coals of fire, Christa? No, I know you don't mean it like that; you're very sweet to offer. I lost the cuff-links he gave me when I was twenty-one in that mugging; I'd like another pair of his, you choose them for me. I would like that very much. Thanks.' He looked at her and there was the sly appeal of the child still inside the grown man. 'If I'm forgiven, can I have another cup of tea?'

She poured it for him. 'I'm glad you're here, James. I mean that.' He was off guard. She'd done well; she was surprised by her own calculation, and glad that it was tinged with genuine pity. The offer was spontaneous, and that helped her go on with the deception she was planning.

They had dinner in the dining-room; Christina had wanted somewhere casual and intimate where she and Richard would eat, but he had vetoed the idea. The lay-out of the house didn't lend itself to modern living; he had added, 'unfortunately,' but she didn't believe he meant it. And Mrs Manning, who cooked for them when they weren't entertaining, wouldn't welcome Christina in her kitchen, so they either took their meals in the study, on a tray by the fire, or sat side by side in the panelled dining-room by candlelight.

'How I remember this room,' James remarked. 'Sunday lunches when we had to come down, looking tidy, as Father put it, and Alan always managed to have his shirt-tails hanging out or to be wearing his old jeans with holes in them. It was a nightmare and I used to dread it. You know they sat at opposite ends of the table? Not like when he married you. He must have hated Mummy, mustn't he? I tried to understand that because there were times when I hated her too: when she'd been at the booze or scored, that awful glassy look in her eyes and that silly smile. I could have hit her, Christa, isn't that a terrible admission?'

'No,' she answered. 'I don't think it is. I can't think of anything worse for a boy than growing up in a situation like that. It's amazing how well you've come through it. If only you could put it out of your mind, try not to think about it.'

He looked at her. 'That's why I went to the States; I thought I'd escape, get away from Father and Alan and all the feuding. It didn't work, of course, because you carry your baggage with you, but it helped. It's a pity I never got to know you, Christa, when I was living here, but Father didn't encourage it. He was jealous, I realize that now; he didn't want anyone taking your attention off him. And there was Belinda. God, talk about jealous . . . I was so jealous of her! How is she? I meant to ask.'

'She's at St Mary's and she's very happy. Children are much more resilient than we think. She'll always miss Richard, but she's coping well. I don't know how she'll take it when the case comes to court. There'll be so much publicity; I dread to think what the press will make of it all, and I'm really worried about the effect on her.'

Now, Christina decided. Now is the time to try. He's relaxed, nostalgic, the wine's gone to his head; you just might touch a genuine chord. 'James, I want to tell you something. I've been thinking about it a lot; I've even discussed it with my lawyers. Alan's main case is that Belinda's illegitimate, and he could be right.' She saw him stare at her. He put his wineglass down.

'You're serious?' She sounded very calm.

'Yes, I had an affair; it broke up only the day before I met your father. We slept together and I found I was pregnant. I did tell him, I want you to know that, but he wouldn't listen to me; he was certain Belinda was his. But, if she's not . . .' she let a pause develop. 'If she's not his daughter, then I would give RussMore to Alan.'

'My God,' he said and then repeated it, 'My God, do you mean that? Does Alan know?' She shook her head. 'No, James, there's only one way to find out. I've taken advice and it's quite simple – DNA. A blood test from you and one from her; if she's Richard's, it'll match with yours. James,' she leaned towards him, her eyes full of pleading. 'James, will you do it? It would save all the dreadful muck-raking and bitterness . . . If Alan's right, then he gets the house and the land and we'll make a home for ourselves somewhere else.'

He took up his glass again. For a moment he held it close

to the soft candlelight and the claret glowed a deep red. 'And if he's not, then his case collapses and you win? It's a gamble, isn't it?'

'Yes,' she admitted, 'it is, but it's worth taking. Will you help me?'

He put down the glass again; he hadn't touched the wine. She couldn't read his face.

'I don't know,' he said. 'I'll have to think about it. Sleep on it.'

He smiled at her; there was a secret look in his eyes, a look that filled her with despair. He had retreated out of reach. 'It would be a big responsibility,' he added. 'A bit like tossing a coin,' he said coolly. 'I never thought you were the type to toss coins with so much at stake. Perhaps you think the odds are pretty good?'

The change was startling. Christina recoiled from what seemed like hostility, in fact she was experiencing her stepson in an unaccustomed role; he was in control. His help was needed; he had power over her and she had given it to him.

'Is that why you asked me down here?'

'Yes, I don't deny that. I thought you were the only person who could put a stop to this whole nightmare before it gets out of control.'

'Maybe I am,' he agreed. 'How flattering; for the first time in my life I feel really important.' He laughed, but it wasn't a pleasant sound. 'I'll think about it, Christa. We can talk it over tomorrow, I don't want to rush into anything. Never make decisions after a good dinner and vintage claret. I can't remember who said that; maybe I've just thought of it myself, but it's good advice. Would you mind if I didn't have coffee? It keeps me awake.'

'I don't want coffee either,' she said. She had tossed the coin, and she knew without waiting for his decision the next day that she had lost the call.

'That lawyer, the Swede,' he said suddenly, 'he's a nasty piece of work. He threatened to beat the hell out of me, did you know that? Not very ethical, I felt; a violent type. I'm sure he would have done it too. I'd be careful if I were you, employing a man like that; he was almost more scary than the mugger. Can I still have a pair of Father's cuff-links? You won't go back on that if I don't give you a blood sample?'

She said sharply, 'Don't talk to me like that, James.'

'Only teasing,' he responded, 'I was really upset about losing mine. Three pairs in all; the others were very unusual, Tiffany's design, given to me by a good friend. One set with little rubies, and one with sapphires. They were lovers' knots, not that we are any more, but we keep in touch. He had great taste, my friend. Do you want to watch the late TV News? I wouldn't mind an early night if that's all right with you?'

'You go on upstairs,' Christina answered. 'I've a few things to do. Breakfast is at nine.'

'It always was,' he remarked, 'even in the school holidays; we were never allowed a late lie-in.' He bent and almost brushed her cheek; the gesture made her think of Judas. 'Good night, Christa, and don't look so worried. I told you, I'll think about it. After a good night's sleep, who knows?'

She shut the library door behind him. She felt drained, and there was an ominous tightness across her forehead that warned of a tension headache to come. *I'll think about it. After a good night's sleep, who knows?* That was teasing, too, he had made his decision; he had said it to keep her in suspense. It was no more than a petty cruelty he enjoyed inflicting, and yet she knew he didn't hate her. His personality was so distorted he was incapable of normal judgement. If the plan had worked and he'd agreed to give the blood sample, she'd have known whether she could defeat Alan, or have to settle into a long and ruinous legal battle, and she'd have known, for her own sake, whether Belinda was Richard's child. He'd refused, and the morning wouldn't bring a change of mind. Now the headache had begun, hammering behind her eyes.

It didn't matter, she insisted. Whatever the cost – and she'd mortgage everything Richard had left her – she wasn't going to give in to the son who'd violated his father's body. And then, unable to help herself, the disappointment and frustration overcame her and she started to cry. She was crying when the telephone rang and it was Rolf.

* * *

The flight to Geneva took about an hour and a half. Rolf didn't read and he refused coffee or snacks. He thought about Christina, about the conversation of the night before, hearing her weep in despair, and about making love to her. He recognized that emotions, long suppressed, had burst the barriers imposed. He had rejected love, along with friendship and intimacy of any kind; he had become a self-elected outcast. But no more; he wanted her so much he longed to absorb her, like a second self. He wanted to keep her, like some extraordinary treasure, forbidden to anyone else. Possessiveness so fierce it amazed him, vied with the urge to protect her, to make her happy by lavishing anything on her she wanted, without stint or regard for himself. Sexual passion he accepted, but this was more, this was love, for the first time in his life. That was why he was on his way to Geneva, to see his contact, the woman with a heart as empty as his had become full. She hadn't been pleased at the prospect, and had tried to put him off, but he hadn't listened. He was coming and he expected her to be there; he was giving the orders now. Outside, the freezing blue skies disappeared in a thick grey mist as the plane began its descent.

He took a cab to the plush Hotel Beau Rivage, paid the driver and went inside. She had a suite; whatever else she sacrificed, she didn't stint on her own luxuries. 'I like the best,' she'd said to him once. 'I pay for it, why shouldn't I have what I like?' He'd shrugged in acceptance. She owed him no explanations; he owed her none either, but she'd ask for them now. She came to meet him, immaculate in a mink-trimmed designer suit, her hair burnished like silk and drawn back into an elaborate knot. She always used the same scent, heavy and musky. Too often it had clung to his skin when they'd been together.

She brushed his cheek in a token kiss. 'What can I order for you? Coffee? Or a drink . . .? I'm going to have brandy and soda, I've got sick of champagne.'

'I'm sorry to hear that. It was your favourite.'

'Tastes change,' she smiled at him. 'Favourites start to bore after a while. Sit down, Rolf. Why have you come here? We've no reason to meet any more. I told you.'

'I know you did,' he answered. 'But *I* have a reason, even if you haven't.'

'So you said.' She sat, crossing those long legs, her fashionably short skirt riding up to her thighs. The brandy and soda was placed beside her, and she thanked the waiter with a brief nod. 'I have a nasty feeling that I'm not going to like your reason.'

Rolf betrayed nothing. 'And why should you think that? Why shouldn't it be our usual business?'

She sipped the brandy. 'Because I know there isn't any business, not for us, anyway. You'd better tell me, I'm going out and I haven't time to play games, not this sort of game.' She looked at him. Such hard eyes, he thought, not a gleam of feeling in them; he'd only seen them change when they glazed with lust. What are we made of, he thought suddenly; what's made her like she is and me like I am, or was.

'You're right, Irma. Last time we met you said I'd have a street named after me. I don't want a street, I want a favour instead.'

She had stayed silent, hardly moving, except to reach out at intervals and sip the brandy. At the end Rolf said quietly, 'They owe me, and I want this badly.'

She got up, uncoiling herself with feline grace. She looked at him. 'You fool,' she said, 'you've asked the impossible; you'll never be trusted again. Rolf, I'm not going to argue with you, I know you won't listen, but don't ask for this. Remember, we're not part of them; they use us, but that's all, and they don't name streets after people like us, but you knew that anyway.'

'Will you ask them? If they say no, I'll deal with it myself.'

She spoke sharply, 'They'll never let you . . . they won't risk it.'

'That's what I thought,' he answered. 'It's not such a big thing; it's been done many times before. I gave them back their past, remind them.'

She turned away from him, walked to the window, stared down at the view across Lake Geneva and then swung back to face him. 'You gave yourself something too: peace of mind. You wiped the slate clean, and I'm trying to do the same, only it's such a big slate . . . I haven't come to terms with who I am and what I am; maybe you have.'

He said, 'You shouldn't go on thinking like that. You've given your life to wiping out the past, in a way we all have. They must appreciate it.'

She smiled at him, but it was a bitter grimace. 'Would you? You think some art treasures are enough? Or some names and addresses? Are you suggesting they should be *grateful*?'

He wouldn't be drawn. 'Ask the question, that's all, just ask.'

'All right.' She stood before him and shook her smooth golden head. 'You really are a fool. If I persuade them, there'll be a price to pay, you realize that? It won't be cheap.' He got up. 'I realize. When will you let me know the answer?'

'It'll take some days, depending on who I contact and who they go to with the proposition. Where will you be?'

'In London.'

'Someone will get in touch with you there,' she said. 'Now you'd better go, Rolf, I'm going out and I don't like being late, so we'll say goodbye. I don't think we'll ever meet again.'

They didn't touch, not even to shake hands. She opened the door and stood aside. 'One thing,' she said. 'She's a lucky woman. I hope she's worth it.'

James had left after breakfast that morning. His mood of self-assertion had changed; he noticed how tired and drawn Christina looked, as if she hadn't slept, and felt genuinely sorry. He had tried to explain why he couldn't do what she had asked. 'I *did* think about it,' he insisted. 'I woke up very early because it was on my mind, and I really hoped I could see my way to saying yes . . . but I can't, Christa. I'm sorry.'

'You don't have to apologize,' she said. 'I knew last night you were going to say no. Let's not talk about it.' But he couldn't let it rest; he needed to excuse himself.

'I know you're disappointed, but I don't want you to hate me,' he said. 'I can't do anything that might hurt Alan. Don't you see, I can't. He's my brother.'

She looked at him. 'He needn't have known, I wouldn't have told him. James, you don't need to excuse yourself or go into long explanations. I'm only your stepmother and you said yourself you were always jealous of Belinda. It was stupid of me to ask. Let's forget about it.'

But he persisted. 'He'd find out,' he said. 'I'd probably end up telling him, I'd feel so guilty. I'm the only member of family he's got, and he's my only link with who I'm supposed to be. I can't relate to anything in my past, Christa, except him. He's been good to me in many ways; if I went to him for help, he'd give it. Fay hates the sight of me because she's jealous of this bond we have between us, but she can't break it, nothing can. Try to understand?'

Christina, hearing the self-pity, felt too tired to point out what a man with any principles or sense of adult responsibility would have done in his place. He wasn't an adult, or a full man, and he never would be. She thought, suddenly, that Richard Farrington had damaged his younger son beyond repair. She got up, closing the subject. 'You wanted a pair of your father's cuff-links,' she said. 'Go upstairs and choose something. I'd rather not go through his things this morning. Take whatever you like.'

She was in the hall, arranging a vase of dried flowers; they looked dusty and the colours had faded. On an impulse she gathered them up to throw out. He came up behind her.

'I chose these,' he said. 'I hope it's all right.' She glanced at the little red box and the oval gold cuff-links, engraved with the Farrington crest. 'They're the same as the ones he gave me for my birthday,' he said; 'the ones that were stolen.'

She recognized them. Richard wore them most days. 'Please take them,' she said. 'I'm going to throw out these flowers, they're dreary looking. I'll say goodbye then.'

'Goodbye, Christa.' He bent and brushed her cheek. 'I feel awful,' he added, wanting to be reassured.

'You needn't. Are you staying for the case?'

'Yes, Alan asked me to be there.'

'I'll see you in court then,' she said. 'Goodbye, James.' She went towards the door into the back quarters, with the flowers crunched up in her arms, leaving a trail of petals and leaves on the floor behind her.

In court, in three weeks. In the passageway she met Mrs Manning. 'Oh, let me take those,' she offered. 'Mr James gone then? He said he was leaving this morning.'

'Yes, he's gone. It was only a short visit. Throw these out please, Mrs Manning, I won't replace them. I'll wait till we put up the Christmas decorations. And I'd better look at the catering for the party; Belinda's so looking forward to it, I couldn't disappoint her.'

'Mr Farrington always enjoyed it too,' the housekeeper said. 'And don't you worry; we'll do everything just the same as we always did. You've got all this court business to cope with, so leave the catering to me.'

'Thanks,' Christina said, 'but it'll take my mind off it if I'm busy. It's so soon; three weeks . . .'

'Oh, it'll be all right,' Mrs Manning assured her. 'Your lawyer got some good affidavits from everyone down here; he was really pleased. And by the way, that jacket he lent Belinda last time he was here, it's still in her room. Shall I parcel it up to send on?'

'No,' Christina said. 'I'll be going to London to see the lawyers soon. I'll take it up with me. Leave it in my room, will you?'

'I did go through the pockets,' the housekeeper said, 'and I found some personal things; Belinda must have put them there. I recognized the crest. Lucky I found them – they were tucked away in the inside pocket. I'll leave them with the jacket then.'

The morning didn't drag as she had feared it might. She went through the food and present list, checked the invitations to be sent out and telephoned Jane Spannier to ask her if she and Peter and Harry would come over on Christmas Eve and spend Christmas Day with them. Jane said they were going to ask themselves anyway. Harry, she added, would be delighted.

'He wants to come and see you, Christa. He says you've put him off twice. It's not because of what I said, is it? I mean, don't take it too seriously, you can always be friends . . .'

'No, I've just been too busy,' Christina explained. Busy falling in love with Rolf? Turning to him in her despair, instead of Harry, and wanting his reassurance now, more than ever. She was going to London to see Humfrey Stone to ask his help in finding someone prepared to lend her money, and to see Rolf. She made the appointment for the next day. Rolf Wallberg was out of the office when she called; he'd gone to Geneva for the day, but should be back for the meeting. Christina took Sammy the terrier for a walk that afternoon. The rain held off, but it was very cold with a biting wind. She went upstairs to have a bath and change before dinner. That was when she found the jacket, neatly laid out on her bed, and beside it, on a square of white tissue-paper, three pairs of cuff-links.

Mrs Manning had said something about the family crest. Christina picked up one pair: lovers' knots, with tiny rubies in the centre. Red and yellow gold. Another in the same design, but with sapphires instead of rubies. Cuff-links, lovers' knots. What had James said . . . her fingers trembled and she dropped them. *Presents from a friend*. Yes, that was right. She repeated the exact words. *One had sapphires, the other had rubies. Lovers' knots*. She put both hands to her mouth, stifling something like a cry.

It was impossible; it couldn't be. They were hidden in Rolf's pocket . . . but the last pair gleamed on the white paper, four golden ovals, deeply engraved with the griffon crest of the Farrington family. They'd taken James out to dinner in London with some of his friends, for his twenty-first birthday; she remembered it quite clearly; his godparents had been there too. Richard had given him a pair of cuff-links; they were oval and gold, with the family crest engraved on both sides. She had gone to Collingwoods the jewellers to order them with him; Richard was wearing an identical pair, made by the same firm. James had chosen them that morning. She bent and picked them up, then turned them over; both sides bore the crest. The motto was one simple word, '*Fidel*' – Faithful.

It was on all the silver, and the family portraits. They were James's cuff-links and so were the lovers' knots. Rolf had gone to New York to get the manuscript back from James – she forced herself to think in sequence, to keep calm – but he was too late, James had been robbed and the manuscript taken out of the safe, *with cash and personal jewellery*. She could hear Rolf saying it, looking at her in sympathy. *It's probably been destroyed by now. I am so sorry.*

She felt such a sudden wave of nausea that she rushed to the bathroom, afraid she was going to vomit. She didn't, but her face stared back at her from the glass over the basin, haggard and stricken with shock. There never was a mugger; Rolf had waylaid her stepson. Hadn't James complained last night about how violent he was when they were face to face . . . Rolf had staged the robbery and stolen the manuscript himself, and taken the cuff-links to make it look authentic, then he'd forgotten about them. He had lied to her and cheated her because the ancient manuscript had been his objective all along. He had known it was in Richard's collection . . . How, how had he known that? Unless it was because the dealer Poulson had blurted it out under torture, and then been murdered to keep him quiet . . .

'Oh God,' she breathed in horror. 'Oh my God, what have I done . . .' She'd made love to him in that room, in the bed where she was sunk down in trembling shock. She had gloried in what they did, losing herself in a man who had used her for some dreadful private purpose, and committed the ultimate violation by seducing her with yet more lies. Only the night before she'd spoken to him in tears, and he'd been so comforting, so strong.

'You don't need anyone to help you. Forget about him. Trust me, my darling, I'm going to take care of you.' And she'd arranged a meeting in London with the solicitors, as much to see him as to talk about the case; to find strength in his arms, maybe to admit that she hadn't felt guilty because she was in love and hadn't realized it. But guilt overwhelmed her now, and such a rush of self-disgust and anger that she sprang up. He wasn't going to get away with it; there'd be no more charades between them, no more deceit. She threw the cuff-links into her bag, grabbed the jacket and started off downstairs. She met the housekeeper at the foot of the staircase.

'I was just coming up to ask if you were ready for dinner . . . Are you all right, Mrs Farrington? Are you ill? You look terrible . . .'

'I'm all right. I don't want anything to eat. I've had a change of plan, I'm sorry, I have to go to London. I'll be back around midnight. Don't wait up for me.' She saw Mrs Manning glance at the jacket slung over her arm. She said, 'I have to give this back to Mr Wallberg.'

She pushed past her and hurried out to her car. Then she remembered, the secretary had said he'd gone to Geneva for the day, but he'd be back for the meeting; she might go all the way for nothing if he hadn't returned. She got the number on her mobile as she drove towards the main road, and when he answered she could hardly trust herself to speak to him.

'I'm on my way to see you; I'll be there in two hours.' Then she cut off before he could answer. What was his motive? Money? He'd said the manuscript was priceless. What else could explain it, except some monstrous obsessive greed. Blood money, after the dreadful story of treachery and murder he had told her. He said he'd recovered other properties for Jewish relatives of the dead, but he had selected this manuscript for himself.

He was waiting, watching for her; she saw him outlined by the lighted window as she drove up. He came down the stairs and opened the front door of the apartments for her. He said quickly, 'Christa . . . Christa, what's happened, what's wrong . . .' She brushed past him.

'Not here. In your flat, Rolf. No, please don't touch me.'

He led the way up two flights. His door was open and she went inside. He closed the door and started to move towards her. 'My darling,' he said. She threw the jacket at him.

'You left this behind, and you left these in the pocket!' The cuff-links gleamed in her outstretched palm. He stood rigid, staring at what she held.

She said, 'These are James's. *You* robbed him; there never was a mugging. You stole the manuscript yourself, and you came into my life for that one reason. I don't know whether you helped to kill that poor dealer, Poulson, but that's how you knew where it was. What was the reason? Money? A million pounds?'

He had seemed frozen, but now he came to life. 'No!' he said. 'No, you're wrong. Money has nothing to do with it! I didn't mug James, someone else did that. I had no part in what happened to Poulson, I swear to you, but don't ask me to explain, I can't.' He stooped and picked up the jacket. 'But about us – would you listen to me? Please, Christa, just listen before you pass judgement.'

'I don't think there's anything you can say,' she answered. 'You lied to me, you stole from me, and you can't even tell my why.' He sat down still holding the jacket. He shook his head slightly.

'I forgot about the cuff-links.' He seemed to say it to himself rather than her. 'I completely forgot.' He looked up at her. 'Yes, I stole the manuscript. I've stolen many things, or got them by blackmail and threats. I'm not a nice man, Christa, but you always knew that; you sensed it, that's why you didn't like me. Your instincts were right, but you're wrong now. I'd never hurt you, never. I love you.'

'For God's sake,' she said bitterly, 'don't dignify what happened by talking about love. I'll never forgive myself for what I did!'

She saw a faint colour come into his face. 'It was love for me,' he said. 'Please believe that. I didn't want to love you, but it happened; I didn't want to grow fond of your daughter, but I couldn't help it. There's never been room in my life for loving anyone until I met you, then I started hoping there was, thinking I might have a life like other people, but now I've destroyed that. Even if I put you at risk by trying to explain, you'd never trust me, I can see it in your face. And anyway, I've been a fool.' He looked up at her. The pale-blue eyes were full of pain. It shocked her. 'I could never live your life. I could never involve you because, for people like me, there is no escape.'

Christina said, in spite of herself, 'Escape from what?'

'From the past,' he answered. 'What do you want me to do?'

She said simply, 'Get out of my life, and leave Belinda and me alone. Whatever you are and whatever you're mixed up in, we don't want any part of it.'

He didn't move; he crumpled the jacket between his hands and then flung it aside.

'I'm still going to help you,' he said.

'I don't want your help. I'm seeing Humfrey tomorrow, don't be there.' She walked to the door and let herself out. She felt calm, she insisted; it was done. She didn't even want to hear excuses or reasons. Thank God, she thought, he hadn't offered any. Something alien and frightening had touched her life; from her first sight of him in the library, she'd felt it and recoiled. Yet they'd shared something, a passion stronger than her instincts and his terrible isolation, and she'd seen real pain when he'd looked at her. As she drove out of London she began to weep, and realized that, in spite of everything, it was for him.

9

'I hope this doesn't inconvenience you, Mr Stone.'

'Not at all, not at all,' Ruben answered, 'but I am surprised. I thought you and Mrs Farrington worked very closely in the last few months?'

Rolf nodded. 'We did and I was fully committed to her. That's why I asked to stay on here and see the case through, but she has changed her mind.'

He was stony-faced as he explained. Recently Ruben had seen a more human side to the man, now he was his remote off-putting self again, and he was leaving, to Ruben's great relief, but if he had upset a client, Ruben wanted to know why.

'I imagine there was a disagreement between you,' he said. Surely Wallberg hadn't been indiscreet. He frowned. 'A professional disagreement, yes.' Quickly Rolf calmed his fears.

'She is a very headstrong lady,' he remarked. 'I didn't agree with her proposal to go on fighting if she lost the case, so she sacked me.' He gave a bleak smile. 'So, if it's all right with you, I'll clear up a few details of my other work here and be gone in about ten days? I haven't contacted my firm at home before speaking to you, but I'd like to let them know I'll be back in the office after Christmas.'

Ruben smiled. It was genuine because in ten days he'd be rid of the man. 'We'll be sorry to see you go, my boy. It's been a pleasure and your work here has been superb, quite outstanding. But does this mean you've given up the idea of coming to practise in London? You did mention that as a possibility.'

Rolf said, 'I made a few enquiries, but the financial prospects weren't good enough, and the wet weather helped me make up my mind. I would like to know how the meeting went the other day, with Mrs Farrington and Humfrey. Out of interest.'

'Not very well, I'm afraid, Humfrey had a difficult time with her. She is determined to resist any judgement in her stepson's favour, and she asked Humfrey to suggest a loan company where she could borrow at a high interest rate to finance an appeal. When he explained to her that she couldn't use the estate as collateral because it was not only in trust but subject to dispute, she offered her own assets in lieu. Everything Farrington left her, including a small picture that might prove to be very valuable: a family portrait of a Tudor child. She's asked somebody from Sotheby's to come and give an attribution.'

'I know it,' Rolf said slowly. 'And Humfrey couldn't persuade her not to mortgage herself like this?'

'No,' Ruben said. He shook his head in sadness at the woman's folly, and then, because he fundamentally disliked the man, he added, 'If she hadn't been told what her stepson did to his father's body she might have listened to reason, but now nothing will move her. If she doesn't win the case, she'll be penniless at the end of it all, but she doesn't seem to care.' He sighed. 'Ah well, we'll do our best for her, of course. I wish you a happy holiday, my dear Rolf, and don't forget to come and see us when you come over to London again. We'd be delighted to see you.'

'Thank you,' Rolf said. 'Thank you for accommodating me

here. You have been very helpful, very kind. I've enjoyed my time here very much.'

Ruben said, 'We must give you a farewell lunch before you leave. Some time next week?'

Rolf opened the office door and turned towards him. 'That won't be necessary, Mr Stone, you've done enough for me already. Thank you again.' The door closed after him. Ruben returned to his chair behind the handsome desk. Now he could throw away the long spoon, he'd supped with that particular devil for the last time.

Alan was in a buoyant mood. His brother was in London; they'd had lunch together – Fay seemed unenthusiastic about asking him, so they met during the week – and his new venture in Birmingham was going well. There had been opposition from the established business community and the interwoven family networks among the Pakistanis, but he was confident he'd bought enough of the smaller ones to set up his franchise and begin the new chain of Farrington's Curry Houses. There had been odd sounding telephone calls to his hotel, warning him to stay out of the business, but he hadn't taken them seriously. He was not a man to back down; opposition made him more determined. One of his Pakistani advisers, soon to take up the management of the franchise when it was up and running, mentioned aggressive Muslim elements among the community, but Alan brushed that aside. 'What are you worried about? A fucking fatwa against me? Forget it. Business is business and nobody understands the value of hard work and money better than you people.'

And then there was the opening of the case in the High Court. The counsels were ready, the barristers and solicitors straining at the leash, or so he liked to picture it; he loved a fight and this one was the climax to a lifelong battle. He and James – poor sod, always trying to please and getting kicked up the arse for it – it would be James's triumph too. He was convinced that he was going to win, doubt never crossed his mind, nor was it permitted to surface within his circle of friends. Fay held the same view. Christina had cheated a lascivious older man into accepting another man's child. There was only her word that she'd told him, nothing Richard Farrington had said or done during the marriage indicated that he'd known she was pregnant when he married her. Much as he disliked John Cunningham and resented his autocratic attitude, Alan longed to see the QC get his teeth into that piece of fiction; he'd rip her to bits. So honourable that she risked losing a rich husband and a lifetime of luxury in England? Remarkable! What moral rectitude! But not the same degree of moral sense when it came to having lovers . . . Alan had been given a brief outline of the proposed cross-examination, mostly to keep him from telephoning with unwanted advice. He had been almost sadistically excited by what he read, and that was just the outline. Christina was cunning and the Swedes were a shrewd people, but faced with John Cunningham and his relentless probing, she would destroy herself.

He couldn't wait for the show to get on the road. He went out and bought the very expensive sapphire and diamond brooch from Tiffany as a Christmas present for Fay. He didn't need to wait for the verdict as an excuse; he was on a winning streak, with his bold new business venture, and his struggle to defeat his father once and for all. In a moment of rare sentiment, after too much to drink, he shed a private tear for his dead mother. It would be her victory too.

Rolf's caller didn't suggest a meeting at The Lanesborough; plush bars were not his preferred choice. The Rubens Hotel in Buckingham Palace Road was a popular tourist venue; close to the palace and the changing of the guard, and the Queen's Gallery where there was a permanent exhibition of royal treasures. Inside there was a polyglot mixture of races: Japanese, Americans, Spaniards, a few Chinese, Scandinavians . . . He wouldn't be noticed and neither would Rolf Wallberg. They met, as arranged, at one o'clock, when the lounge bar was crowded and they had to share a table. Rolf found him because he was wearing a baseball cap with New Haven Yachting Club printed on the front. He'd kept a chair vacant. The other seats were occupied by a group of earnest Japanese, talking like a flock of magpies. He was younger than Rolf had expected. This casual-looking fellow with his cap turned back to front and his thick anorak slung over the chair, was younger than he was.

'Roy,' he said and smiled. It was only a widening of the lips, showing good even teeth, but the eyes were not smiling. Rolf nodded, but didn't say anything. 'You want something to eat? The burgers look good.'

'No, just coffee.'

He saw the waitress and hailed her. 'Hey . . . you take an order?' Typical brash tourist, American Hispanic or something like that, with swarthy skin and a black pony-tail hanging down his back. He ordered a beefburger with onions and two cups of coffee. The Japanese were shrilling even more and the girls were giggling.

'What's the answer?' Rolf demanded. The food had arrived and 'Roy' was smothering the inside of the burger with brown sauce. He took a bite, chewed it and swallowed.

'It's yes,' he said, 'but there are terms.' He swigged his coffee. He had uncouth manners which Rolf felt were part of the image.

'Tell me about them.'

He bit hugely into the burger, and rubbed a crumpled paper napkin across his mouth to catch a smear of sauce.

'You have to go,' he said.

Rolf answered, 'I'm going, next Monday; I'm booked.'

Roy shook his head; the pony-tail swung from side to side. With his mouth half full, he said, 'No, they mean *really* go, and no coming back. It's one way, you must understand that.' He'd dropped his voice and the crude eating habits with it. 'If they do what you want, you can't be left running around loose; you might be connected. So it's out and it's one way. You want to think about it? They don't want to push you, it's a big decision. I can call you tonight.' He finished his coffee.

'Have another cup,' Rolf suggested. Roy knew he was asking for time to consider.

'OK,' he agreed, 'but don't rush it. You going to drink yours?'

'No.'

Roy leaned across and moved the cup and saucer. 'Then I'll have it. It tastes like gasoline anyway.'

Rolf watched him slurping the tepid coffee. He wasn't seeing him; he wasn't hearing the Japanese, who were paying their bill and making a lot of noise getting their cameras and bags; he was seeing the rest of his life. He had to go; that was the price for what he had asked: a one-way ticket. Not such a big price to pay, after all, for making Christina happy, for keeping his promise to a child. A lifetime among strangers, never to see his home again, but he had never had a home, never belonged anywhere. He wouldn't have roots, but that was nothing new; his had been severed when he was born. She would be secure, able to live her life and bring up her daughter, to keep what was hers by right, given to her as a reward for the love and happiness she'd brought to that other lucky man. The same love and happiness he had imagined he might have, one day. Instead, he would have the sun. For the rest of his life.

Roy came into focus. 'If that's the deal', he said, 'then I go. No problem. When?' Roy slid a hand inside his jacket, pulling it round from the chair back, and passed the envelope to Rolf under the table.

'Tonight,' he said. 'You're booked on the nine o'clock flight – Direct. Your ticket and passport's inside. Be on that plane or nothing happens, all right?'

Rolf stood up. The envelope was in his pocket now. Unlike the cuff-links, which had ruined everything he had hoped for, he wouldn't forget the envelope. 'I'll keep my part,' he said in a low voice, 'so long as they keep theirs.'

Roy was on his feet, shrugging on the anorak, snapping his fingers rudely for the bill. 'They don't fail,' he said. 'You should know that.'

By they, Rolf guessed he meant *we*. He pushed his way through a new influx of students in search of some fast food, and went out into the cold crisp December day.

Friday evening and the weekenders were on their way out of London. Ruben Stone and his family didn't migrate from their big homes in North London; they all bought houses near each other and, though Ruben wasn't Orthodox, he liked to spend Saturday among his relatives and children. Humfrey was among them that weekend, staying with his wife and family at a cousin's house. There was a cheerful lunch in a local restaurant, where everyone talked at once and nobody told the children to be quiet. At one pause in the noisy exchanges, Humfrey said to his uncle, 'Wallberg's gone.' Ruben raised his eyebrows and his shoulders lifted in surprise. 'Gone? Already? He said ten days . . . Did he say why?' Humfrey shook his head.

'Not a word. He didn't come to the office, never said goodbye, just took off. There were enquiries from two clients and I tried to contact him, but he'd left his flat. Paid the rent in full and went. I can't say I'm sorry, but it did seem strange.'

'Well,' Ruben decided not to encourage speculation. 'Well, once Mrs Farrington wanted him off her case, there wasn't much for him to do. He'd asked for extra time to work with her, or he'd have been gone earlier. And neither of us liked him, so if he's gone, he's gone. How *is* the case shaping up, Humfrey?'

'No new developments. Ronald made a tentative suggestion that we might try for a settlement once more. He thinks his client, Farrington, is the pits and he said so to me. He won't deal with him direct, somebody else writes to him and takes his calls, but Ronald's the brains behind it all. I had to tell him we'd tried several times and failed.'

The case would come to the High Court on Monday of the next week. Christina had been sent a formal notice of the hearing and the time schedule; seats would be reserved for her and anyone she wished to bring with her. She had sent a message to Humfrey's secretary saying that her husband's cousin, Harry Spannier, would be coming to court. Humfrey took a careful forkful of the excellent food and, before he put it in his mouth, said, 'She's hell-bent on ruining herself. Nobody can stop her.' Then he began to eat. Ruben didn't answer; a grandson was claiming his attention across the table.

Kenneth and Molly Hubert were driving down to Hampshire;

it was a rare treat for him to have a day's shooting, but he had made a rule some years before to take a couple of days relaxing before the start of a big case. So he put last-minute work aside and set off with his wife to stand out in the freezing rain and miss some pheasants, as he explained. Making a fool of himself with the other guns would take his mind off Monday and the battle to come. He talked of winning just as confidently as before, but she knew he wasn't really confident. His friend and opponent, John Cunningham, had the DNA sample as his trump; whenever they met socially there was a smug look in his eye that infuriated Molly. She'd begun to dislike the obstinate Mrs Farrington, whose intransigence was going to end with Ken losing the case, instead of reaching a quiet settlement and coming away with his fees. Less fees than if he went through a long legal wrangle, but money didn't matter now, his reputation did. She wished she could have told Mrs Farrington what a silly pig-headed fool she was, and how sorry she'd be at the end of it all.

John Cunningham was staying in London. Unlike Ken, he worked up to the last minute before a big case, but not in the evenings. Evenings were reserved for going to the theatre and out to supper with some amusing lady, and the next day was spent playing bridge with devotees like himself. He described this as limbering up, fine-tuning the brain, like an athlete stretching his muscles before a race. He was smug, as Molly had detected. He was also excited because he loved the contest; he would seek out weaknesses and score off Ken Hubert as if they had been deadly enemies instead of friends.

All's fair in love and war, but nothing's fair in court. He wasn't shocked by what Alan Farrington had done; disgusted in an aesthetic sense, but not surprised. He had no expectations of people after so many years of discovering their capacity for brutality, deviousness and dishonesty when money was involved. He was prepared to tear Mrs Farrington's reputation to shreds when she was in the witness box; he didn't believe she was less basely motivated than her repulsive stepson. He had booked seats for a new Tom Stoppard play and was looking forward to the mental stimulus.

Christina was in London, and Harry Spannier was with her; they were both staying in her flat. She was in a mood she couldn't analyse: defiant, bitter, and, deep down, prepared to self-destruct if necessary; to destroy rather than surrender. She had pledged the painting, which had brought the Sotheby's expert to near hysteria with excitement, as it might well be a lost work by Hans Holbein. All she cared about was the seven figure sums he was mentioning if he proved to be right. Other household items were dismissed when she offered them; they were all personal bequests from Richard, but nobody was interested. The so-called Holbein was all they talked about, until she could have screamed, but there would be enough money to fight on, and that was all that mattered: not to lose to Alan. Sometimes she dreamed of setting fire to RussMore, and woke drenched in sweat from a terrifying nightmare in which Belinda was somehow trapped in the burning house.

She wasn't thinking clearly or rationally and she knew it. When she got back to RussMore, after confronting Rolf, there was a sense of shock and a deep pain that shamed her. Pain for the man she had seen lose hope in front of her that night; anger with him, but greater anger with herself for having been deceived, and yet not completely. He had loved her, for what it was worth; she knew that was true and it didn't help because it made her pity him. She had deliberately turned to Harry to help shut him out; Harry with his ridiculous jokes and his quixotic sense of honour. He was sharing the flat with her two nights before the case began, and slept in the spare bedroom without once suggesting he might move into hers. If he had, Christina would have let him, not because she wanted love, but because sex with him might be the antidote to sex with Rolf, but she didn't invite him and he didn't ask. They went to the cinema, to lunch, round an exhibition at the Tate Gallery, which she thought interesting, and which Harry rubbished so brilliantly that she found herself laughing. She knew that all he wanted was to take her mind off Monday, yet they couldn't stop talking about it. He didn't undermine her resolve; he was bullish and encouraging. Whatever his private forebodings about the outcome, he didn't express them.

'You'll fight that little bastard and you'll win! If you don't, I'll personally beat his head in . . .' He'd grin, but there was something not so funny about him when he said it.

Alan and Fay took their children down to the cottage in Sussex. Cottage was a misnomer; it was more of a luxury one-storey complex; modern in design, equipped with the latest electronic playthings, fronting on to its private beach and mooring for the yacht they sailed during the summer. They had left the nanny in London; they both enjoyed having the boys to themselves. Alan was in a buoyant mood, and Fay was in her element in the place, more so than in Chelsea. She cooked and looked after her husband and sons, wishing secretly that life could be more like this, less complicated and opulent. She refused to think ahead to what it would be like to live at RussMore, that was Alan's dream and she supported it. When he was happy, so was she; it was that simple really. She often thought that he was the only man in the world she could have loved without holding anything back; she felt he was flesh of her flesh, part of her being. She loved him more than her little sons, but, like her opinion of his feeble mother, she didn't tell him so. The boys loved being able to run outside, wrapped up against the cold wind off the sea, free from restriction and the hovering nanny. Country life was best for them, Fay agreed on that; another plus for RussMore. Neither she nor Alan wanted them growing up subject to the sex and drug culture of London. It was a joy to let them loose down there, without fear of some evil-minded stranger lurking, looking for victims. They were brave little boys, Timmy especially; he had his father's physical courage and liking for risks. Robert was more timid. It was one of the happiest weekends they had spent together, and on Monday they'd be in the High Court.

They left for London late on Sunday afternoon, Alan driving the Bentley, Fay muffled in a mink coat beside him and the children strapped into the back, with orders not to fight or wriggle out of their seat-belts. They took the coast road before turning up through Arundel; it was their usual route and there was little traffic. Alan reckoned on arriving at his front door in just over an hour and a half. He didn't check his rear-view mirror, so he didn't notice the motorcyclist who had been following since they'd driven away from the cottage. He switched the radio on, jumping stations till he found some pop music. They pulled up at some traffic-lights and the motor cyclist accelerated and drew up alongside them. For a moment Alan glanced to his right and saw the figure, muffled in black leather, hooded in a black visored helmet, pointing to his front tyre. It was an urgent gesture and Alan's electric window slid down. He didn't have time to ask a question; the motor cyclist raised his right hand and fired three bullets into his head at point-blank range. The lights changed from red to amber to green, and the rider slammed his foot on the accelerator and the motor cycle roared away and disappeared up the hill. Inside the car Fay was screaming; Alan had fallen forward over the wheel and blood was seeping from his shattered head.

Christina had slept quite deeply the night before, as if she had exhausted her capacity to worry. Now, while Harry was still asleep, she got up to make coffee and get ready for the ordeal ahead. She switched on the radio for the early morning news.

'I can't believe it,' Harry said.

They had turned on the TV news and the item came midway through, after a political confrontation in Northern Ireland and some discouraging unemployment figures. 'Fast food chain tycoon, Alan Farrington, was ambushed and shot dead in his car, in front of his wife and children, last night.' The details followed. The family were on their way back to their Chelsea home, when the killer fired point-blank through the car window as they were stopped at traffic-lights outside Arundel. The wife was under sedation, too traumatized to be interviewed by police, and the two little boys were being cared for by their grandparents. It was mentioned that he had received death threats over a proposed business venture in the Midlands. A court case disputing his father's will was due to begin in the High Court that morning. The police officer in charge of the investigation described it as a contract killing.

The newscaster changed to an item about a plan to build a bypass through Salisbury Plain, which was causing a lot of public protest.

Harry looked anxiously at Christina. When she woke him with the news she was sheet white. She was still so shaken that he said quickly, 'You look awful . . . Are you all right?'

'Yes. It was such a shock, I couldn't take it in. Harry – that poor girl and the children . . . Who'd do a dreadful thing like that?'

'They said he'd had death threats over a business scheme. You know Alan; he had a way of making enemies, but I suppose it means that the case won't go ahead.' He reached out and held her hand. 'I can't pretend I'm sorry he's dead.'

'I'm not either,' Christina said after a while. 'I'm not sorry, but I'm not glad. It's too horrible to know what I feel, except for Fay and those poor children. Is there anything we can do?' He shook his head.

'I don't think so. Best leave it for now, Christa. You'd better check with Humfrey, but I reckon the case will be adjourned and it'll be easier for you if we go home.'

'Easier? What do you mean?'

'The police called it a contract killing. I could be wrong, but I'm sure they'll want to interview you.'

She telephoned Belinda's school to warn them about what had happened and spoke briefly to Humfrey Stone. 'Terrible thing,' he kept saying. 'Terrible . . . in front of his family . . .'

En route for RussMore they bought the newspapers. Some emphasized the threats from business rivals, but as expected, the tabloids concentrated on the High Court dispute between him and his stepmother. There was a blurred photograph of Christina on the front page of the *Sun*. They reached RussMore at lunchtime and Mrs Manning came hurrying to meet them. She managed a show of sympathy, but it wasn't convincing. 'It's a horrible thing, Mrs Farrington. Dreadful. We're all very shocked. But I suppose you have to say it's an ill wind . . .'

And then when the luggage was brought in and Harry was fending off telephone calls from the press, she came upstairs to

Christina's bedroom with a sheaf of hothouse roses wrapped in cellophane. 'These came for you this morning,' she said. 'Wishing you luck with the case, I expect. Well, it won't happen now, will it? That's one good thing that's come out of it.' She waited while Christina unwrapped the flowers. 'I'll take them and put them in a vase for you,' she offered. 'The telephone's never stopped ringing all morning. Those awful press people. I just said I didn't know anything and rang off. Mr Spannier's coping with them now.'

There was a small envelope with the flowers, and Christina opened it. She saw Mrs Manning waiting and handed her the roses. 'Thank you, put them in the study for me.' The door was closed and she took out the card. A plain card, with a few words scrawled on it in a handwriting she didn't recognize. 'Be Happy. Both of you.' That was all. *Be Happy . . .* She sat down, the little card with its coded message of love and death clasped in her hands. In some hidden recess of her mind, she'd feared, as she listened to the news of Alan's death, that Rolf Wallberg was responsible, now she knew beyond doubt. She couldn't hide from the knowledge. *Be Happy. Both of you.* Alan had been killed the night before the court action that nobody believed she could win. Rolf's words were in her head, *I love you. I'm going to help you.*

She had closed the door and walked away from him; his face, strangely twisted in some private pain, swam before her closed eyes. 'I didn't want to love you, but it happened. I didn't want to grow fond of your daughter, but I couldn't help it.' And the words spoken when they first met at RussMore. 'I never break a promise to a child.'

Humfrey had told her he'd disappeared without warning, packed up and gone. Somehow he had arranged Alan Farrington's murder, and ordered the roses with the brief message, so that she would know he'd kept his promise. He'd saved RussMore for her and Belinda. There was a knock on the door, and Harry put his head round. 'Christa? Are you OK?' Harry, always so caring, so gentle in his concern for her. 'I'm just coming down,' she said and managed to smile at him.

'The police are here,' he said. 'They want to have a word with you.'

There were two of them, a detective inspector and a sergeant from CID; they'd driven down from London. They were polite and apologized for coming when she must be feeling shocked by the news. Even though, the inspector added, she was in dispute with her stepson. Christina had looked at him and said quietly, 'I wouldn't wish something like that on anyone, even if I hated them, which I did. I hated Alan, but I'm devastated for his wife and children.'

It wasn't the reply he had expected. 'That's very frank of you,' he remarked. 'Your legal case started today, didn't it?'

'Yes.' He took his time. His tone was pleasant, almost conversational.

'It won't go ahead now, I expect. That must be a relief to you, Mrs Farrington. Whoever killed him did you a favour too.'

'I'm not grateful,' she said. 'Inspector, why don't we save time? I didn't kill my stepson, I think that's obvious, and I didn't pay anyone else to kill him. I'm not going to be a hypocrite and pretend I'm sorry he's dead. If you want to know where I was yesterday, I was in my flat in London with my husband's cousin, Harry Spannier. He was coming to the High Court with me.'

The inspector answered, 'He's already told us that, Mrs Farrington. There's no suspicion attached to you, but we have to interview everyone who might have a motive, however unlikely. Our efforts are being concentrated in Birmingham. He had received death threats; certain restaurant proprietors didn't like competition from his curry house franchise. The Asian Community is very law abiding but even they have their criminal elements. The motor-cycle assassin is more of a Middle Eastern tool, but it's caught on in the drugs world for instance. It's possible that drugs were involved here too; Mr Farrington might have been getting into more than he reckoned. Well, thank you for your time. We'll be off now.'

Christina stood up and walked to the front door with them. On the top step the inspector turned to her. 'Nasty business,' he said. 'I hope we catch the man who did it, but I don't hold out much hope.'

Then he hurried down the steps to the police car, and they drove off. Harry had come out beside her. He slipped his hand through her arm. 'That was quick. I told them they were wasting their time. Come on darling, you're shivering; inside, out of the cold.'

She didn't notice what he had called her. In the hall she asked him, 'Do you think they'll catch the man?' He shook his head.

'Not a chance. He was a pro; probably out of the country by now. Contract murder is a very expensive business; the boys in Birmingham must have paid out a fortune. Hello, Mrs Manning. Those are nice roses.'

She passed by them into the study carrying a vase. 'I've done my best, but I'm not able to do arrangements like Mrs Farrington.' There was a fire blazing in the gate. The space above was empty; the Tudor child was still in London being examined by the excited experts. Mrs Manning put the vase on the table by the window. Christina took the white card out of her pocket and dropped it into the heart of the fire.

'Who sent those?' Harry asked. 'A secret admirer? I'm jealous.' She had her back to him when she answered.

'You needn't be. Just a friend, wishing me luck.'

'Well,' Harry said, 'you won't need it now; there won't be a case. My guess is Fay only went along to support Alan. So you're safe now, Christa; you and Belinda. I don't care if it sounds callous, but it couldn't have happened to a nastier man. Whoever killed Alan did you a favour.' For a moment she looked at the red roses, standing stiffly in a tall vase.

'Yes,' she said. 'I suppose they did.'

It was nearly a month before another police officer came. The hunt for Alan's murderer hadn't produced a suspect and public interest had long since died down. She had sent flowers and a letter to Fay, but Fay had ignored the letter and returned the flowers to the florist. The case was withdrawn from the High Court list. Christmas was only ten days away when a man from Scotland Yard's Special Branch drove down to see her. He looked round the hall, decorated with holly and ivy, and with the massive Christmas tree glittering in the oriel window. He was quite a young man, probably in his late thirties; he could have been a middle manager in some business.

'Lovely place you've got here,' he remarked. 'Christmas must be great in a house like this.'

Belinda and two friends came hurrying past them, giggling and clutching CDs. They were going through a pop music phase; Christina had given Belinda her present ahead of time. It was a complete record and CD player, state-of-the-art, she was assured by the salesman. It was upstairs in Belinda's room and out of earshot.

The policeman's name was Malcolm Dunn, and there was a faint Scots lilt when he spoke. 'It's very good of you to see me, especially at such a busy time,' he said, 'but I'm away after the holiday and didn't want to delay till I got back. Is there somewhere private we can talk, Mrs Farrington?'

In the red study they sat opposite each other. Mrs Manning, beady-eyed with curiosity, brought them a tray of sherry. The Tudor portrait, identified as school of Holbein, rather than a work by the great painter himself, watched them from above the fireplace. The experts had been deeply disappointed. Malcolm Dunn sipped his sherry.

Christina said, 'You said you wanted to ask me some questions, Mr Dunn. There's nothing more I can tell you about my stepson than I told the police at the time.'

'I haven't come down to talk about your stepson, Mrs Farrington. I'm here to make some enquiries about Rolf Wallberg.' He saw her stiffen. 'He acted as your lawyer I believe?'

'Yes,' Christina answered. 'He was attached to my solicitors, Harvey & Stone. My stepson was disputing his father's will. Would you please tell me what this is all about? Why do you want to ask me about Rolf Wallberg?'

'You spent a lot of time together,' he remarked, 'working on your legal affairs. He came down here quite frequently.'

He saw a flush of colour come into her face. He'd touched a nerve and he was satisfied.

'Yes, he did. So?'

'Don't misunderstand me,' his tone was conciliatory. 'I'm not questioning your relationship. He stayed here, and you also met in London; he must have talked about himself; it can't have been legal jargon all the time, surely?'

He could see how wary she was, how defensive. He decided to take a soft line; he didn't want her to hold anything back because he had antagonized her. He had a friendly smile and he used it then. 'Mrs Farrington, I don't want to be intrusive, but I have to ask these questions. Let me put it another way. Did you and he become friendly? Did he talk about himself?'

Christina hesitated. 'Not much. He was a very private person. I knew he was Swedish, like me, and he practised law in Stockholm.'

'And that was all he told you?'

Another hesitation, then she said, 'He did say he was adopted and brought up in Gothenburg; it sounded a miserable childhood. That's all I know.'

He sipped the sherry again. 'Well, that was the truth anyway,' he remarked. 'He was adopted by a couple and brought up in Gothenburg, but he is not Swedish. He's a German, Mrs Farrington.' She wasn't good at hiding her feelings. She stared at him.

'German?'

'Yes. Why don't I just paint the picture for you, then maybe you can come up with something that might help me?'

'If I can,' Christina said slowly. 'If I understood what this is all about.'

'Wallberg is his adopted name. Both his parents were German born, so-called refugees who got into Sweden at the end of the war. Your country was neutral, but it had a pro-German element; they made it easy for some very dubious characters to slip in and settle there, and Wallberg's natural father was one of them. His mother was only seventeen when he was born, unmarried – seduced by this much older friend of her family. It's a common story, happens all the time. When the boy was born, her family didn't want to know about him and the father didn't want to know either; they put him up for adoption and he ended up in Gothenburg with a childless couple – God-fearing Lutherans. If he told you it was miserable, I'll bet it was.' He paused. 'He was clever and studied hard. He left home as soon as he graduated; there wasn't much love between them, and he cut himself off as soon as he could – didn't even go to their funerals.'

'How do you know all this?' Christina demanded. 'Why would you investigate him like this?'

'Because it's my department's job,' he explained. 'We work very closely with Interpol. Terrorism is a worldwide problem and we rely on each other's services for this kind of information.'

Terrorism. He saw her hand clench on the arm of her chair; that had touched another nerve.

'Like a lot of adopted kids,' Dunn went on, 'even ones who've had loving parents and been happy, he wanted to find out about his real family. Being a clever man and trained in the law, he soon got the basic facts. Unfortunately that didn't satisfy him, so he started digging deeper. What he found, Mrs Farrington, had a disastrous effect on him; it changed his life.' He looked up at her shrewdly. 'His father was an SS officer, wanted for war crimes. He'd been based in Poland, working closely with the Gestapo, and had amassed a nice fortune from Jews hoping to save their lives by bribing him. He sent them to the death camps; he was responsible for hundreds of people going to Auschwitz. If he hadn't got out of Germany, he'd have been tried and hanged, but by the time Simon Wiesenthal's organization traced him to Sweden, it was too late. He was dead.' She had lost colour, but said nothing.

He went on, 'He'd managed to smuggle the loot into Sweden, because apparently he was living very comfortably until he died of cancer in the late Sixties. Wallberg was born in '58, so he'd have been about eleven at the time. He didn't try and trace his mother; what he discovered about his father was enough. Now a shock of that kind can affect people in different ways, either they brush it aside – "I wasn't born, it's nothing to do with me" – that sort of reaction, or defensive – "I don't believe it; it's lies put out by the Allies and the Jews." There's quite a few who took that line, and got on with their lives. But not Wallberg, he was different; it ate into him. I think a son of one of the biggest war criminals hanged at Nuremberg became a priest and tried to expiate the sins of his father like that, but Wallberg took another route. We only got on to him by chance. We were watching someone else – a woman; a very dangerous woman with the same background as his, only much worse. Her father had escaped to Chile via the SS underground organization that helped wanted Nazis with visas and forged passports. He'd married a rich Chilean girl, and this woman was their only child. Apparently,' he smiled in irony, 'she was her father's pet; he doted on her. She found out what he really was when the West German government tried to extradite him for war crimes. They didn't succeed because the Chileans protected him, but there was a lot of publicity. He'd been a general in the SS in charge of the death squads in Russia and Poland, and was responsible for the murder of a million Jews by mass shooting, burying alive, and finally the mobile gas chamber – that was his brainchild; it killed thousands in a day. When the truth came out his wife refused to believe it, but his daughter did; she left home and came to Europe. She was a wealthy woman and she used her money; she made contacts, and Wallberg was one of them; that's when we started watching him. I know this all sounds like past history now, but a group of Germans hunting down ex-Nazis was something new. The woman, Irma was the name she used, was involved in kidnappings and several murders. She'd made her own atonement by offering her services to Mossad, Israeli counter-intelligence, and Wallberg and others did the same. We couldn't pin anything on them, but we knew what they were about. When Wallberg came to England to work for a Jewish firm, he became our responsibility. He'd come here for something or someone, and you were the only person he drew close to. Has anything I've said made sense to you?'

Christina drew a deep breath. 'No,' she said.

He persisted. 'Nothing at all?'

'Nothing,' she repeated. 'In fact I find the whole story very hard to believe.'

'In a way', Dunn remarked, 'I feel sorry for him.' He had dismissed her denial. 'Guilt like that must be a nightmare. For him; for all of them. You know he's disappeared?'

'I heard he'd left,' she answered. 'Ruben Stone told me. I thought he'd gone back to Stockholm; his time in England was nearly over.'

'He's not in Stockholm,' Dunn said. 'We checked with his firm, and they don't know where he is. His flat's been cleared and the lease terminated; he's vanished. That's why I'm here.'

'Yes,' Christina said. 'Yes, I understand now.'

He shook his head a little; he sounded reproachful. 'I wonder if you do, Mrs Farrington? These people are driven by guilt to make amends, but the irony of it is, they're behaving true to their genes. Irma is more her father's daughter than she realizes. You can't wipe out blood by more blood. Wallberg hasn't been involved in actual violence so far as we know, but there'll come a time, there always does.'

He stood up. Christina didn't move. 'I've upset you,' he said, 'I'm sorry. But it's better you know the truth. If he gets in touch with you, will you let me know?'

'If I hear from him,' she said, 'but I don't expect to.'

He nodded. 'Probably not. My guess is he's pulled off something big for Mossad. I'd say he was in Israel; that's the deal they offer: a home and citizenship. Goodbye, Mrs Farrington. Don't get up please, I can find my own way out. And have a good Christmas.'

'Thank you.' She heard the door close. A log broke in half and one smouldering end fell into the grate. Christina watched it smoking till the little flicker of flame died out. Dunn's empty sherry glass was within reach; slowly she got up, put it on the tray. The housekeeper would come in to collect it, now that the visitor had gone.

The little red room was full of him, he seemed to materialize in front of her. She had the illusion of being held in his arms, trying to resist and wanting to surrender. The man who'd instinctively filled her with disquiet, had been fleshed out now by the soft-spoken policeman. Driven by guilt, without roots or ties; deliberately cut off from human love.

She shivered, the room felt cold, claustrophobic. Outside the wintry sun was bright in a cold blue sky. She needed to feel space around her.

She walked for a long time, crossing the hard ground of the parkland, still rimed with frost in places. The red roses had died long ago and been thrown away.

He would be a life-long exile, because he had broken his own rules and learned to love.

Snow clouds scudded up from behind the thick woodlands and a shower, already turning into sleet, blew up and stung her face. The sharp crystals melted with the tears already there, as she turned against the squall.

Ahead of her the house loomed up. That was his gift: RussMore – her home and her future. She hurried towards it.